MERGING WRIGHT

L.B. DUNBAR

WWW.LBDUNBAR.COM

MERGING WRIGHT
Copyright © 2022 Laura Dunbar
L.B. Dunbar Writes, Ltd.
https://www.lbdunbar.com/

Graphic Cover Design: Booked It Design

Editor: Melissa Shank

Editor: Evident Ink

Proofread: Gemma Brocato

Proofread: Karen Fischer

OTHER BOOKS BY L.B. DUNBAR

<u>Sterling Falls</u>

Sterling Heat

Sterling Brick

Sterling Streak

Sterling Clay

Sterling Fight

Sterling Touch

Sterling Stone

<u>Chicago Anchors</u>

Elevator Pitch

Catch the Kiss

Parentmoon

<u>Holiday Hotties (Christmas novellas)</u>

Scrooge-ish

Naughty-ish

Grouch-ish

<u>Road Trips & Romance</u>

Hauling Ashe

Merging Wright

Rhode Trip

<u>Lakeside Cottage</u>

Living at 40

Loving at 40

Learning at 40

Letting Go at 40

<u>Silver Foxes of Blue Ridge</u>

Silver Brewer

Silver Player

Silver Mayor

Silver Biker

<u>Sexy Silver Fox Collection</u>

After Care

Midlife Crisis

Restored Dreams

Second Chance

Wine&Dine

<u>Collision novellas</u>

Collide

Caught

The Sex Education of M.E.

<u>The Heart Collection</u>

Speak from the Heart

Read with your Heart

Look with your Heart

Fight from the Heart

View with your Heart

The Heart Remembers - a sequel

*To HGTV, Ben and Erin from Home Town,
and a small town named Wetumpka, Alabama.
Thank you for the inspiration.*

"Sometimes, if you stand on the bottom rail of a bridge and lean over to watch the river slipping slowly away beneath you, you will suddenly know everything there is to be known."

- A.A. Milne, *Winnie the Pooh*

1

Playlist: "Road Less Traveled" – Lauren Alaina

[Jane]

"Mr. Wright, you have a delivery," I announce through my boss's open office door. He hates it when I call him Mr. Wright. I hate how ridiculously handsome he is.

With artfully sculptured hair in a perfect palette of chrome and ink, the same combination lines his firm jaw. His mouth wears a permanent smirk that could either tease you into submission or cut you to the quick. Despite his typical attire of business suits with starched dress shirts and crisp ties, there's an occasional hint of color on the skin of his hidden arms. The same arms that often bulge underneath the stiffness of his professional clothing.

I hate how attracted I am to him.

"Have Rebecca sign for it." Mr. Wright—*Machlan* Wright—mentions his assistant without glancing at me.

He never looks directly at me, and I suppose it's for the best. If he did, my tongue might freeze under the glare of those earthy-brown eyes. Another part of me never ices over when he looks in my general direction, though. That area is all heat and pulsing thumps of unrequited desire for a man whom I equally loathe and lust.

"She's at lunch," I remind him.

Flicking out his arm, he bends his elbow just right to turn his wrist and sexily peers at his oversized silver watch like a practiced male model. He works excessively hard, and it isn't surprising he doesn't realize it's lunchtime for the rest of Chicago. "Just have it brought up."

Flexing my fingers before forming fists at my side, I take a deep breath and stiffen my shoulders. I'm one of the top account executives at Impact, a media marketing company, working my ass off under this man for eight years in hopes of becoming a full partner one day, and something like this is not my responsibility.

However, *no* seems to be something I can never say to my infuriating boss.

"Sure." I force a smile while chewing on the sarcasm. From the moment Machlan and his partner, Tucker Ashford, hired me, I set out to prove my worth. Marketing is not a stagnant field, especially with the boom of social media. For a woman with no life outside of her job, I've easily adapted to the industry changes over the past two decades. At the ripe age of forty-five, I've been in the business for a long time. I would have eventually retired from my previous employer if it hadn't been for an epically stupid blunder on my part that I swear will never happen again.

My pride and my heart cannot take another Ripley Edgar incident.

When I call down to reception on the ground floor of our Michigan Avenue building, the security man, Pete, informs me the item is too large for the elevator.

"Is it a freaking elephant?" I laugh into the phone. Pete and I have a good rapport. That tends to happen when you're the first one in the building or one of the last to leave at night.

"Nope, but close. Mr. Wright needs to come down to sign for it."

Curiosity has the best of me and knowing Mach—as the rest of the office calls him—won't take a break long enough to accept his own package, I ride down thirty-four floors to see what's too big for an elevator.

Mach, pronounced like the industrial truck with a hard *k*, fits the man who is a little smug and a lot tough.

"Hey, Pete." My heels click against the pristine white tiles in rhythm with a little wave I give him. The glass walls allow loads of sunshine into the lobby. I love this building. I love this city. Chicago is a heartbeat and a far cry from the small town where I was raised in southern Missouri.

"Hey, beautiful." The portly, older man smiles at me while tipping his head toward the revolving door. "His *Mach*-esty's item is out there."

I grin at the nickname I often use to describe my boss—along with His Royal Pain in my Hiney-ness, and sometimes just He-Who-Shall-Not-Be-Named, otherwise known as Volde-*Mach*.

Over the years, there have been all kinds of special deliveries for Mach. Bottles of alcohol with seductive messages. Once, a dozen balloons intended to be popped, revealed sexual suggestions inside. My favorite was the woman dressed like an elf who turned out to be a stripper. She already had carnal knowledge of Mach from a Christmas event he barely remembered attending.

I loathe how willingly women flock to him, including

myself, making me one of his many sheep. *Darn his charisma.* Then again, giving myself away to the shepherd is never going to happen again. I'd gone the route of lost-lamb-found once and been tossed aside by a man who really could have had a bigger staff.

I learned my lesson. Beware of the wolf in sheep's clothing. Keep my lust at bay.

My tumultuous attraction to Mach is more volatile than puppy love. I waver between deep displeasure with my boss's work ethic, which ironically matches mine, making me work too hard, too often without appreciation, and an overabundance of sexual attraction including fantasies of him taking me on his desk, showing me his gratitude for my tenacity. Most days, I want him to work me harder in ways that have nothing to do with client needs and market assessments.

Glancing through the immaculately clean glass of the street-facing windows, I crane my neck. People swiftly walk on the sidewalk, rushing to and from their destinations. A row of cars and trucks line the street closest to the building, momentarily parallel parking. Nothing looks out of the ordinary for a busy day in downtown Chicago.

"What am I missing, Pete?"

"That." Pete points.

Coming into focus better, my gaze lands on something one would rarely see on the bustling streets of a major metropolis.

"That?"

The item certainly is too large for an elevator. Not that it should be brought up to our offices. *That* belongs on the road and not traffic-packed pavement. *That* screams dirt, dust, and sweat; sunshine filtering through trees on back roads; and feet on a front dash with windows rolled down.

Mach's delivery is a sharp contrast to the man sitting behind a glass-surface desk in a corner office overlooking Lake Michigan. Between the black leather couch in his space and the crisp business suits he wears, not one speck of his persona coordinates with the item waiting for his signature atop a flatbed Ford on the avenue.

"That," Pete confirms with a large grin.

And I laugh.

2

―――――

Playlist: "That Ain't My Truck" – Rhett Akins

[Mach]

"**M**r. Wright, you need to get down here."

Jane's throaty tone with a hint of humor filters through my cell phone. I should chastise her for calling my cell like whatever is downstairs isn't business-related. Only a handful of people have this number. I keep a strict professional relationship with all my employees, especially Jane Fox. As our top account executive, she's a line I don't intend to cross, despite wanting to trace all her curves, zigzag over her planes, and unravel her lines before stringing them back together.

Jane is one of the few employees close to my age, and that alone keeps her off-limits as I have a penchant for the younger set. But my business partner Tucker and I also have a strict no-fraternizing-with-the-employees policy for ourselves. We already had more headaches than we needed with Tucker's late wife as our first client. Their relationship set the precedent.

Do not dip your wick where a flame might become an inferno.

Speaking of heat, Jane knows I hate it when she calls me Mr. Wright. There's something about her smoky, seductive voice using a formal title, like a schoolteacher about to scold me, and I'm buzzed on the anticipation of punishment. Like a dominatrix about to demand I spank her—not that I know about such things.

However, Jane and her voice inspire fantasies I keep under lock and key.

"What is it?" I demand.

Jane responds with a throaty chuckle. Her laugh is like a live wire straight to my dick, and I close my eyes, suppressing the sharp prickle of arousal rippling through me.

"You need to see this." Her voice rings incredulous with a hint of laughter.

Why can't she freaking tell me what it is? Or better yet, sign for the damn item and bring it up to the office?

"Jane, I give you permission to accept it. Collect the package and get back to work." The harshness in my tone is unnecessary as Jane possibly works the hardest of all of us. She comes in early. She stays late. She gives up weekends to complete projects, and she never complains. She grumbles. She grunts, but she doesn't openly whine. She doesn't think I notice, but I do. A woman like her is my equal in drive and determination. However, I like to play hard on occasion, and Jane clearly does not. The woman has no life.

"No can do." She laughs deeper. "This package needs proof of your acceptance."

Oh, for fuck's sake. "Fine. I'm coming down."

This is not what I need right now. I'm in the middle of figures on the Torres campaign. If the client wouldn't keep changing his mind. *Should we use blue or red? What about the curve of that line? Is it too much? Too angular?* I'm not part of the creative team—more a numbers and placement man—and the newest athletic influencer is going to be the end of me.

Pressing the down button for the elevator more than once won't bring the lift any faster, but I still jab my index finger into it twice.

What the hell is so special it needs my signature and personal acceptance for delivery?

Body coursing with sudden energy, my foot taps next, and I'm half tempted to take the stairs down thirty-four flights when the elevator doors open.

"Finally." I step inside and meet my reflection when the doors close. At forty-eight, I work hard to maintain a strong body and a sharp mind. I surround myself with creative, intu-itive people—both young and old—but I'm feeling my age lately. And I have no idea why. The years add up, but the figure is still only a number. In my head I'm still twenty-three with the added wisdom of experience. I love my scotch, an occasional cigar, and younger women to help remind me I can get my dick up. I once worried I'd need to take a little blue pill as I aged, but that doesn't seem to be an issue for me. My sex drive is like the rest of me—full steam ahead.

I'm arrogant. I get it. The trait might be one of the only things I inherited from a father I never knew. Pride runs in our shared genes. Too bad he was a dick, and his dick got him in trouble a few times . . . one of those times resulting in me.

Shaking off thoughts of a man I've never met, I exit the elevator on the ground floor. The early afternoon sunlight brightens the lobby, and Jane casually leans against the security desk. She's smiling at old Pete, who seems under her spell. Damn that voice . . . and her outfit.

Jane wears professional clothes like a high-fashion runway model. Today, she's in a hip-hugging, caramel-colored pencil skirt that hits right above her knees. The material looks soft, and more than once, I've wanted to run my hand over the fabric as it stretches over her curves and cups her ass. Dark brown heels accentuate the firmness of her legs, making them appear longer than they are. She's roughly eight inches shorter than me, but those killer heels scream don't fuck with me, not come fuck me, which would be my pleasure. Her shirt is an off-white color, and she has one-too-many buttons undone, hinting at a skin-colored bra underneath.

I try not to look directly at Jane. If I do, the fantasies of bending her over my desk, hitching up any skirt she wears, and driving into her, begging her for the smiles she gives everyone but me, take over. If Jane were a train, the crossroad gates are down, warning me to stay away from her.

"Pete," I snap as I approach the reception desk, causing the older man to straighten.

"Mr. Wright."

Jane slowly presses off the desk and turns to face me, meeting me square on with those brilliant blue eyes behind a sexy pair of yellow-rimmed eyeglasses. I look away. The accessory is a new addition to the torture of her daily office attire. Tight dresses. Form-fitting skirts. Blouses molding her breasts and always one button too low. Her walnut-colored hair contrasts with those eyes, and today she wears it in a loose twist at her nape, teasing me with the fine hairs that curl around the sides of her neck. Classy. Professional. Seductive.

But there's no time for those thoughts.

"And?" I bark, scanning the lobby for the mysterious package.

"It's out there." Jane points toward the floor-to-ceiling windows.

On the street is the rush of people at noon, a few parallel parked vehicles with their hazard lights on—presumably delivery drivers—and a flatbed truck with a classic pickup truck on it.

"I don't—" I double back to the pickup atop the larger vehicle.

The exterior is robin's egg blue with a dirty-white strip along the door panel and bed. A pair of fuzzy dice are distinguishable and hanging off the rearview mirror. The boxy, large cab is reminiscent of decades passed. The bench seat is light brown leather which I don't need to see to know it exists in the interior.

"What the—" My throat tightens.

"Mr. Wright?" Jane's voice filters through my ears but doesn't register clearly. The smoky sound distorts as I step forward, slowly, cautiously, taking in the 1976 Chevrolet C10 Cheyenne pickup truck. The vehicle is nearly as old as me.

Along with most everything else in my life, I'd left the thing I'd worked the hardest on as a teenager where it belonged—in the past.

Once I've stepped outside, I snap at the delivery driver waiting on the sidewalk with a tablet in his hand. "Is this some kind of joke? Get that thing out of here." I flick my wrist as if it will make the flatbed and all disappear.

The younger man looks up at me, eyes wide. "I'm waiting on the recipient to claim it."

"I'm the recipient, and I'm refusing delivery."

For a moment, the man looks flustered, uncertain even. What happens when one rejects the delivery of a classic truck that holds more history than the skyscraper at my back?

"Mach," Jane says behind me.

"No." I turn on her. I vibrate with memories I don't want retrieved suddenly stirring up like dust in a rarely visited attic. "This doesn't concern you. Go back inside."

Get back to fucking work, I want to scream at her, even though she doesn't deserve my wrath.

"Are you Machlan Wright?" the delivery guy questions, and I spin back to him.

"No," I state at the same time as Jane steps forward and responds in the affirmative.

"Sign here and here." He's holding out the tablet, but my arms won't work. My muscles refuse to lift my limbs.

Jane rounds me and reaches for the device, but the man retracts it.

"It has to be him." He nods at me.

What the hell is happening? The last time I saw this truck, it was not in its present condition. I close my eyes against memories of broken glass, deep dents, and screams in my head.

"I can't accept it here." My rough and raspy voice is unrecognizable. My heart races like tires on loose gravel. My palms sweat as if I can feel the bumpy grip of the steering wheel underneath my hand.

The delivery man double checks something on his screen before narrowing his eyes at the building behind me. "This is the address. End of the road for me."

"Just give me the tablet." Jane steps closer to him, and he flinches. There's that take-charge voice, the one about to put him in his place. She snatches the device from his hands and swipes what I imagine is her best impression of my signature across the bottom of the screen. Her acceptance in my name must appease Delivery Guy because he circles around the back of the flatbed, and the heavy scrape of chains rattles on the pavement.

"What are you doing?" I finally muster, crossing the sidewalk to him.

"Drop off." He pulls two ramps from beneath the flat portion of the larger truck, lowering them to the street.

"That thing doesn't even run," I state, giving away my recognition of the old pickup.

"Says in the paperwork it works just fine."

With the ramps at the correct angle, the younger man walks up one incline and enters the truck. With a sharp grind and a small *kerchunk*, the pickup comes to life, and I startle, surprised at the sudden rumbling purr. Another wash of memories cascades over me.

A pretty blonde in the front seat. Sweet laughter mixed with country music. Sunlight in brilliant green eyes.

No. I fight off the reminders from a lifetime ago.

"Mach," Jane's voice pops the balloon of the past. Her warm hand on my arm seeps through the shirt sleeves I keep lowered in the office, hiding all the ink. Hiding all the scars.

I stare at her, holding her eyes as if she might ground me in this moment. *Have I ever looked directly into her eyes?* I hate the sudden weakness I feel and pull away from her penetrating gaze, tugging my arm from under her hand.

With the classic truck in the street, the delivery man cuts the engine and exits the pickup. After rounding the front, he holds out the keys, and I snag them from him, fighting the tremor in my fingers.

"Thanks," I mutter without gratitude.

"Here." The young guy holds out an envelope. "I was told to give this to the owner."

When I don't reach for the slim package, Jane takes it from the man's hands. "Thank you. Do we owe you anything?"

My wallet is upstairs in my desk. A tip is in order, although advice is all I have for him.

Never trust a gift; there's always a stipulation attached to it.

"Nah." Delivery Guy smiles at Jane and receives one of her warm grins in response. He restores the ramps to their place then rushes around the large flatbed to the driver's side and fires up the beast's engine, leaving me standing on the city sidewalk wondering what I'm supposed to do with this behemoth paperweight from the past.

3

Playlist: "I'd Do Anything for Love (But I Won't Do That)" –
Meat Loaf

[Jane]

"What a fucking joke." Mach's bitter tone abrades my skin like rough sandpaper as we re-enter the building.

"Pete, find someone to move that thing into the parking garage," Mach snaps, tossing the keys at the unprepared security guard. My boss doesn't even wait for a response from the older man, stomping forward toward the elevator bank without a glance back at his delivery.

The ride up the elevator is silent.

I follow Mach toward his office, questioning the truck's safety on the busy street.

"Let's hope the police impound the thing. Or better yet, a semi barrels into it," Mach replies without glancing back at me.

He can be brash, but this is more than agitation. Something below the surface hints at history and hurt, and it's none of my business. Still, I follow him like the weak-kneed woman I am around him, worried about him when I should probably leave him alone.

"Let me know if you need anything," I offer outside his office, keeping my voice low once we arrive at his door.

"Could you come into my office a moment?" The directive is stated with all the stability of a professional asking a colleague to enter his space, but an undertone suggests unease. His emotions are anything other than calm. I've spent years working beside this man, observing him, smelling him— though that second part is neither here nor there in the moment—and I *know* him. His current reaction frightens me. This is not the Mach I know.

Even though he hadn't looked in my direction when he asked me to follow him, I nod and silently trail behind him into his corner office.

Once inside his office, Mach doesn't immediately break the tense silence, and I gaze out the window where the lake gleams off in the distance on a beautiful late August day. Summer is swiftly coming to a close, and my thoughts drift until Mach's sharp tone breaks the silence.

"What a fucking joke," Mach repeats.

I face him, and he tosses a letter onto his desk. His fingers squeeze his forehead, pressing against his skin as if forcing back a headache.

While I've admired Machlan Wright for years, I don't know much about his personal history other than those random deliveries and the countless number of younger women he's had on his arm at charity events or company-sponsored activities. I've always ignored the ache in my chest, telling myself it was for the best that he had those youthful pieces draped over him. Their presence was a reminder that Mach was not for me.

I would not date my boss. An office romance was not the path for me.

Sleeping with *Mach*-emy—another name I've called him to my sisters—would not be smart.

"Want to explain?" My voice remains low but tight. With my arms wrapped around my middle, I'm holding myself together. A strange sense of foreboding tickles my skin. While eruptions are not unusual from Mach, the tremble underneath his tone is. The tension around him is disturbing.

"My grandfather died."

"Mach." My arms fall to my sides. Everything in me wants to rush him and hug him. "I'm so sorry."

In my family, we were close with our granddad. Our grandfather was the only father figure us Fox siblings had, and he adored us each in his own way.

"Don't be." Bitterness and hurt fill Mach's knife-sharp voice.

I nod, although I don't know what I'm agreeing to. "Is that what the letter says?"

Mach shakes his head, gaze lowering toward the floor. He sits in his desk chair. His feet are spread, and his forearms come to rest on his thighs.

Assuming he'd like some private time to collect his thoughts, I swallow a lump in my throat, and say, "I'll leave you alone."

"No!" Mach's head snaps upward. Clearing his throat, he repeats himself, "No." He focuses on me as he had on the street. He's never looked at me like he did on that sidewalk. Like he's lost. Like he's confused. *Like he needs me.* That last thought is absurd. Mach is one of the strongest, most confident men I've ever known. I'd go so far as to call Mach egotistical and selfish, which I have called him on occasion.

"Jane, I'll be taking a few days off to attend the funeral and sort out this . . . this shit." He turns for the letter, lifts the paper, and then tosses the sheet back to the desk again as if it singes his fingers.

"I understand." He'll need me to cover for him as I've done in the past when he is out of the office. "If you could just bring me up to date on the Torres campaign and—"

"I'll need you to come with me." His eyes seek mine again, holding me pinned in place. The typically dark color is murky, almost as if pained to ask me—*no*, tell me.

"You . . . what?"

"I don't quite understand what's going on, but if I know anything about Fischer Wright, even from the grave, he has something up his sleeve that smells as fishy as his name. And I . . . I need a huge favor, Jane."

His eyes express the darkness of deep regret, and I'm not certain I like the look but hesitantly answer anyway. "Okay."

"I need you to pretend to be my wife."

4

Playlist: "Marry Me" – Thomas Rhett

[Mach]

Her mouth falls open and then clamps shut. I've just dropped the mother of all bombs on her.

Jane is a trusted employee. I'd go so far as to call her a friend in the way one considers a work colleague a friend. But despite my never-ending fantasies of spreading her wide on my desk, I do not have a romantic interest in her. Romance is a fallacy. Her drive—and that smoky voice—are sexy as hell but that's where the attraction stops.

Proposing she be my wife—I mean, asking her to *pretend* to be my wife—is a lot to consider. However, there's one thing Jane wants from me, and it's unfortunately not a romp on my desk. "I'll make you partner if you do this."

Her succulent mouth gapes. She rapidly blinks behind those yellow frames. Then, slowly her lips seal for another second before she speaks. "Are you bribing me?" Offense is deep in that raspy tone of hers.

"I didn't mean—"

"Stop talking." A raised palm and her sharp retort surprise me.

Something inside me that has no business thumping begins to thump. My blood warms back up after sliding into a deep freeze upon seeing my old truck outside and the note from my mother stating Fischer had passed away.

"Mr. Wright." Jane pauses. When she calls me the moniker in all her authoritative manner, my dick starts to rise. Now is not the time for a boner but her strong command, raised hand, and pointed glare have me wanting to bend her over the black leather couch in my office.

"I have worked here for eight years. I work hard, giving up weekends and vacations and family time—"

"Are you already married?" She doesn't wear a ring. I've never heard her mention someone special. She's speaking of family but what family? The thought is silly as her younger sister is the new love of my business partner, however, there is surprisingly little I do know about Jane.

She's been talking and her voice finally registers. ". . . and I will not have my desire for a partnership degraded to a condition of pretending to be your wife."

Did she just spit? I'm pretty certain venom left her lips at the unsavory idea of becoming *my wife*.

Pretending. Pretending to be my wife. "I didn't—"

"Furthermore, I cannot simply fake something." Her arms flail outward. "Acting in a sense, in a . . . a . . . situation I know nothing about."

"Meaning?" I cock an eyebrow.

"I've never been anyone's wife."

Tension slips off my shoulders. I'm strangely pleased she's never been married. "How hard can it be to pretend?"

She levels me with a glare that I swear could take down this building. Her schoolmarm posture of crossed arms and tilted head warns she wants to old-school spank me with a ruler. I might like the sting. The distraction would do me good right now.

I don't want to think about Fischer, or Ma, or that old truck.

"I'm not an actress."

"I didn't say you were." *But what else am I suggesting?*

Her arms fall to her sides again, widening the low opening of her blouse.

The hint of nude bra and the valley between those supple globes holds my attention. My thoughts turn reckless, as I imagine losing myself in her. I need a moment to suspend the disbelief that this is happening to me. Burying myself in her might do the trick.

Mach, come home. Bring a wife. My mother's swirling script flits back into my mind. She knows I'm not married, and there's hidden meaning in her request. Even headed six feet under, my grandfather is up to something.

"I cannot turn on and off my emotions," Jane continues.

"Who is talking about emotions?" My gaze catches those sapphire eyes behind her lenses, feeling the tug and yet fighting the pull. I could get lost in the depths of those sparkling gems.

Jane harrumphs and turns her head away from me, breaking the connection and freeing me from something foolish, like rushing across this office and pinning her to the wall. Taking her lips and burying my tongue inside her mouth. Submerging myself between her thighs for a few minutes in this struggle of grief and regret and pure hatred for a dead man.

A soft knock sounds on my office door, and despite not wanting an interruption, I speak out of habit. "Come in."

Amelia McCaryn enters. She's new and works more directly with Tucker on his accounts as he's recently started taking extensive time away from the physical office to work remotely in Michigan, where his girlfriend lives. "I'm sorry to interrupt, but I have a few questions about the Rolsten account, and—"

Glancing back at my top executive, our eyes catch, and a thought occurs. I tip up a challenging brow. I hate myself only a little before I do what I'm about to do, but the action might be the only way to get Jane on board with my request. "Amelia, I was wondering if you could do me a huge favor. I need someone to pre—"

"Fine. I'll do it," Jane interrupts with all the fire I've seen her exhibit on occasion when she's been asked to stay late or give up a weekend. *Has she really skipped vacations?* How did I not know this about her?

"Really?" I tamp down the relief in my throat. Playing dirty to get what I want isn't typically how I work. I'm beyond that type of behavior with an employee. But Jane is who I want for this mess.

I trust her.

It's only for a few days. What could possibly go wrong?

5

Playlist: "Take Back Home Girl" – Chris Lane

[Jane]

The following morning, I meet Mach at five a.m. with my bags. With no room to argue his proposal yesterday afternoon in the presence of Amelia, I was almost out the door of his office when he made his second unreasonable demand.

My heels clacking on the cement floor should give away my approach, but Mach doesn't look up at me. He stands hunched over the old pickup truck, chest rising and falling, aggressively. His spread arms brace him on the hood. His knuckles are bloody and raw. Sweat dampens the edge of his hair while his head tips forward.

"Mach," I whisper, worried about disturbing him. However, my voice echoes in the relative emptiness of the parking structure. Drawing closer, a fresh dent above the wheel well on the driver's side ruins the otherwise pristine condition of this classic vehicle. From the swelling on Mach's hand, two and two equals him going a few rounds with this inanimate object.

"You're bleeding." My voice remains low as I slow my steps, quieting as if nearing a wild animal.

The heave of his chest continues. He snaps his head in my direction, eyes unfocused. With a shaky hand, he swipes his fingers through his hair and shifts to face me. His gaze roams my body.

I'm wearing flared black pants with a nude-colored shirt, although I'd have preferred baggy jeans and my old Converse shoes for riding comfort. I haven't taken a road trip in ages and admit I'm a little excited at the prospect, despite the conditions surrounding it. My sister Mae recently went on the road trip of a lifetime, and while I was against her traveling across the country, the journey turned out to be the best thing to ever happen to her.

Mach is wearing dark jeans and a long-sleeved Henley, looking rather sexy in casual attire. Apparently, I missed the memo on today's dress code. His hair is raked through and through, mussing up the silver and ink combination. If I hadn't known better from the bleeding knuckles, I'd suspect him of taking a woman against the side of this truck. Her fingers running through his hair. His hands touching her everywhere—

"The trip should take eight hours. If we stop once for lunch and maybe twice for gas, it won't take more than nine total."

And good morning to you, too, Mr. Wright.

His timetable is efficient and no more than an average workday. However, everything about this arrangement feels like anything but a typical day at the office. I already hate the lie we'll need to tell Camilla Wright, his mother. I've spoken to her on occasion, answering Mach's phone to piss him off when I've seen her name appear on the screen, and forcing him to speak with her.

"I have a weak bladder. I might need to stop more often." I play his game of ignoring the *bleeding* elephant in the parking garage.

"Really?" He stares at me.

"You should know these things about your *wife*." I can't believe I'm standing here. Still upset that he tossed out the promise of partnership if I did this for him. I hate him a little more today.

"Well, we have eight hours to learn everything there is to know about each other."

Yes, because eight hours builds the everlasting love necessary to a committed marriage.

Why am I standing here again?

Mach nods at the carry-on suitcase I've tugged behind me. "Is that it?"

I didn't know what to pack, despite the itinerary memo he sent me yesterday afternoon in which he said only a few days would cover the major events. A funeral. A will reading. And getting back out of Dodge. Actually, the place we are headed is named Wrightwood, and I snorted at the similarity to his last name.

"Should you go wash off your hands? Or maybe have them looked at?" We'd need an urgent care as building management doesn't employ a medic. Hardly anyone else is on the property other than the overnight security guard who directed me to this spot in the parking structure. At the very least, Mach needs some ice.

Ignoring my concern, Mach steps forward, reaches for the handle of my suitcase, and tugs the baggage toward the truck. *I can haul my own luggage, thank you very much*, I almost say and then decide against it. The small act of chivalry surprises me for some reason. The action seems strangely husband-like. If we're going to *pretend* we are married, we may as well act like it.

I do a double take at the heavyweight pickup with its robin's egg blue color and dated white panel along the bed while Mach hitches my suitcases into the truck bed. "We're taking this?" Mach owns a convertible BMW, and I assumed we'd be driving the sporty car across state lines.

"Per instructions, yes." He grits his teeth as he speaks while fiddling with securing my suitcase. "Only I can't drive this thing." He cranes his neck to glance over his shoulder at the driver's seat. Once done with my case, he opens the driver's door and holds out the keys to me.

"If you don't mind. I have a few calls to make."

I should protest. I should tell him where he can shove those keys and remind him *I* have calls to make. I'm giving up days in the office for this farce. For him. And now to be a chauffeur for his ass, despite how fine his backside looks in his fitted jeans . . .

Why is saying no to him so blasted hard?

Snatching the keys from his hand, I edge around him and am relieved to find the pickup is an automatic instead of a manual drive. It's been decades since I've had to work a clutch, and in these heels, that quick-shift two-step needed to maneuver pedals would have been difficult but not impossible. Hiking myself into the driver's seat, I reach for the door, but Mach's hand remains on the frame.

"Thank you for doing this." The quiet, sincere tone in his rough voice unsettles me. While his eyes avoid mine, a shiver still ripples over my skin.

And something tells me the second he closes this door, my life will forever be changed.

6

Playlist: "Lake Shore Drive" – Aliotta Haynes Jeremiah
(from *Guardians of the Galaxy*)

[Mach]

"Care to tell me why you were beating up this beautiful old truck?" Jane begins as we pull onto the nearly-empty street in the early darkness of a new day.

"Nope." Out the window, the downtown area continues to sleep. Lights here and there speckle the windows of the buildings around us, hinting at other early risers like Jane and me. The skyscrapers stand for stability, prosperity, and the future. Returning to my small hometown, population less than the number of people employed in the building where we work, does not represent any of those things.

"Mr. Wright."

I groan, closing my eyes at the title. "You should probably call me Mach . . . as my wife."

"As your *pretend* wife . . . there are things I should know about you." Her hand smooths around the oversized steering wheel, and a memory hits me so hard I almost double over.

Tracy. Her delicate fingers caressing the old wheel. The heel of her hand casually guiding this beast.

My eyes close, and I turn my head away from Jane. There is no way I'm telling Jane the history of this truck. Or me. I open my lids again to aimlessly stare out the side window. Dawn is breaking in the sky. "You know enough."

Jane sighs. "We'll need to have our stories straight."

"What story?"

We speed out of the city and leave the cold comfort of steel towers behind us.

"The one where we explain how we met or how you proposed or why you married me." Her voice rises in irritation.

God, I love it when she starts to get worked up like she is. Her agitation pulls me from the haunting in my head, but her questions rattle me. "Who is going to need to know all that?"

"Your mother, for one."

I scoff. *Ma.* She'd be all too pleased to believe I've married Jane. Jane and her damn need to answer my phone on occasion when she notices Ma's name on the screen and then pass the device to me. She's spoken to my mother a few times, winning her over like she wins over everyone else. The idea of lying to Ma swells the ache in my chest, but the concept doesn't hurt enough to force me to change my plan.

She wouldn't explain anything over the phone when I called to find out how the old man died and what sending the truck to me was supposed to mean.

"You got the truck?" The soft Scottish lilt of my mother's voice sounded cheerful despite the passing of her father. Then again, if anyone should be pleased the crotchety miser is finally gone, she's the one. He'd made her life miserable . . . because of me.

While my mother doesn't know all the reasons I don't want this truck, she also knows enough of my history with the pickup, that I can't believe she is pushing me. Or that she'd sent it to me.

"I didn't send it. Da did." Da. Her father. He was dead. What game was he playing? What did he want from me? At forty-eight, I was too old for this shit. Still, everyone knows family can be as evil as enemies. I don't know how many times I overheard Fischer mutter, *Keep your friends close. Your enemies closer, and family the closest because they are the ones most likely to cut you the deepest.*

"We just stick to the truth. We met at work. We work together constantly. Everything grew from there."

Jane isn't wearing glasses this morning, and she squints on occasion as we drive down the streetlamp-lit highway heading south. Her nude-colored shirt hugs her upper body, accentuating her breasts and sticking to her smooth belly. The color hints at what she'd look like naked, minus the rosy tips of her nipples. *Or would they be a dusty brown?* Either color would have me hard if my thoughts weren't a jumble this morning.

Facing the cold steel structure of this truck, then kicking the tire and punching the side panel, was not how I intended to start the day. My knuckles ache as a reminder of what I've done. I should have at least washed off the blood, as Jane had suggested.

"How romantic," she mumbles.

"Romantic? What's romance have to do with anything?" I shift slightly to face her. "We're pretending to be married. Most marriages are an act. Romance is not a trait of the institution." Sitting inside this truck again, the words taste like ashes in my mouth.

Jane snorts.

"Name one happy couple *our age* you know?" I don't want her including young newlyweds who are blinded by the innocence of youth and the fearless hope of an endless future.

"My older brother Garrett and his new wife, Dolores." *Did I know she had a brother?* "And Tucker and Mae."

Tucker Ashford—affectionately called Ashe—is my business partner and best friend. He and Jane's sister are a newly-in-love couple, and the way they look at one another is almost sickening. The heat. The heart. I've never seen Ashe like he is with Mae, proving my point. When he was married, he was miserable.

"Look, it's only for a few days. We don't need to touch. We can say PDA bothers me." It's not far from the truth. Holding hands. Arms around one another. That stuff is for lovesick schmucks. "We keep it professional at the office. That will explain why we're practiced at not touching."

Jane's fingers curl around the steering wheel, gripping the leather harder, causing her knuckles to whiten. *What would her hands on me feel like?* Right now, she probably wants to claw my skin off.

My knuckles throb, and I should have taken her other advice to obtain some ice. Still, the pain is a good reminder of all I lost because of this damn beast we are riding in. All I'll never have.

My gaze lands on Jane's profile. Her dark hair is pulled into a twist, purposely intended to look messy but professional. Tendrils fall around her face, and those fine hairs curve around her neck. My fingers twitch to tug her hair free, letting those long locks loose. She chews at her lower lip, a sure sign she doesn't like what I've said about PDA, but not touching Jane is for the best. I don't trust myself.

And like I've explained to her, this trip is only for a few days. We have a funeral to attend, then the will reading, and a U-turn out of Wrightwood.

Growing up in a town named after my great-great-something certainly was interesting. You'd think with a name like Wright, knowing I was a descendant of the founding fathers of the place, I'd be treated like royalty. I wasn't. There's always a bad ruler or two among the lineage, and my grandfather, Fischer Wright, was mean and ornery.

You didn't get an A.

It was an A-minus.

Not good enough.

Nothing was good enough for him. Certainly not his daughter, my poor mother. Not his son either, her older brother. Yep, Fischer Wright lived with a lot of disappointments. He'd added me to the list long before I decided to leave.

"So, when is the first scheduled bathroom break?" Jane's smoky voice pulls me from my thoughts.

"Why? Do you need to use the facilities?" She can't possibly have to pee already. We're hardly out of the city limits.

"Just trying to get a timeline of the day."

"Just drive," I snap with undue agitation directed at her. We'll drive until we can't. Then we'll drive some more. We don't need to talk. I don't have much to say. I can't believe I asked Jane to do me this favor. I can't believe I bribed her with a partnership. Tucker is going to kill me for offering such a thing. I'm also a teeny bit disturbed that Jane accepted the offer, although she did fight me a little.

I'm well aware how hard she's worked over the years. She deserves the title of partner for all she does for the company; however, it's not something Tucker will agree to, and I dismiss my unease at the promise I've made her. I'll cross that bridge and her wrath once the time comes.

For now, I have miles to cover and memories to slay.

~

WE MAKE it just north of Indianapolis, roughly three hours south of Chicago, before we take our first stop. The location is good for topping off gas and a quick break. Again, I should consider some ice and some pain medication. Punching the truck was a stupid move. It didn't help ease the ache in my chest or the images in my head. I could have gone seven more rounds with this old steel thing, and the truck still would have won every damn time. That's the way of things.

"Coffee?" Jane rounds the front of the truck as I stand beside the gas pump.

"Yeah. Thanks." I reach into my pocket to pull out my wallet, but Jane is already walking away. She didn't even take my order. I like my coffee strong with a double shot of espresso.

Bad for the heart. Good for the pipes, Ma would say.

I haven't seen my mother since Christmas. She came to visit Tucker and me. Since the passing of Tucker's wife years ago, Ma has stepped up to play surrogate mother to a man who isn't her child. A man who should represent deep regret and bitterness in her life. Tucker doesn't hold anything against Ma, though, any more than she does him. I'll never understand that kind of forgiveness in people.

Jane quickly returns, looking sumptuously seductive as she sashays across the lot. Why does she have to look so good when I feel like shit? Irritation is ready to lash off my tongue in full force when she cuts me to the quick by holding out a to-go cup and saying: "Tall blond grandé, although that's not what they call it here."

I'm afraid to ask how the hell she knows my coffee order and afraid to ask what a tall blonde grandé at a roadside gas station might mean. Still, I take a sip, burning my tongue, and cursing. The sudden blisters match the raised welts on my knuckles, and the combination seems par for the day.

"I also got you some ice and ibuprofen." She holds out a baggie of ice cubes and a travel-sized bottle of pills.

The thoughtfulness pisses me off even more. I don't need Jane mothering me.

"Thanks," I grumble.

Re-entering the truck, I immediately grab my phone. The time is finally after eight, and I need to check in with Amelia, then Rebecca, and call Tucker. Jane reaches for the radio. This old thing doesn't have a surround sound system with HD capabilities. Narrowing my eyes, though, I note the radio isn't the original one. It looks similar but not quite the same.

Jane turns up the volume, and a deep bass comes from behind the seats.

"What the hell?" I shift despite the seat belt and then unbuckle completely to get a better view behind the bench where new speakers have been hidden. When my phone suddenly rings, the ringtone fills the speakers, drowning out the music. I glance around me as if I can visibly see the sound waves traveling inside the truck. "What the fuck?"

Jane laughs, and I still. "Sounds like this baby has had an upgrade." She gives the dash a loving caress. The action, along with the glee in her voice, contradicts her appearance. Her high heels. Her sleek clothing. Her personality. Jane is like my TAG Heuer watch, titanium and modern, not an antique wristwatch like this truck.

I don't even try to understand how my phone linked to the radio. Instead, I snap, "Turn that off."

"I need music to distract me while I drive, your royal—"

"Royal what?" I'm still wound up as I settle back into my seat, refastening the seat belt.

"Nothing," she mutters.

"No, just say it. I know you have all these little nicknames for me. Just say it to my face, Jane." I don't know why I'm egging her on. Perhaps I want her to bite back. I need to fight, but I also want the pushback she gives me.

Her lip chewing turns to aggressive bites, and I want to tug at that lower lip with my own teeth. Then, I want to press my mouth to hers, take the pain of those nips and suck at that sensitive skin.

Whoa!

I scrub a hand down my face, exhaling heavily in an attempt to calm down. *What am I thinking?* I do not want to kiss Jane. I cannot touch Jane. But something niggles inside me, hinting I might need that mouth. I could use her touch.

Yeah, that isn't going to happen, and I reach for the radio, turning the dial to mute the volume.

Then, I call Tucker. What I need is someone to talk some sense into me or at least distract me from thinking about foolish things like kissing my pretend wife for real.

7

——————

Playlist: "I Don't Know About You" – Chris Lane

[Jane]

Sometimes I cannot hate Mach more. Like when we stop for lunch. He wants to order something to go. I can't drive and eat a salad, and I tell him this. He doesn't want to listen, and I simply stalk away from him, seating myself at a table in the highway diner. We've been driving through Ohio toward Dayton, and the view has been flat. Cornfield after cornfield surrounded us, and I don't know how my sister was able to trek across the country from Chicago to Los Angeles. Then again, the cross-country scenery shifted, and she had an eager companion, although he was reluctant in the beginning.

The irony strikes me.

I am not happy to be traveling with Mach right now, and I'm certain he'd leave me on the side of the road if he'd be willing to drive this 1976 pickup. I don't understand what his apprehension is, but there's definitely a story behind the antique and him. A hundred times, I've wanted to ask his thoughts but dismissed questioning him. My riding companion has distracted himself with phone calls, his laptop, and staring out the side window.

He lost his grandfather. He's been given this truck. He's been asked to come home.

Those things in and of themselves feel overwhelming and I'm trying to be compassionate. When we lost our granddad, the hole in our family was deep and wide. After our father left our mother with four young children, she flailed. My older brother Garrett assumed the title of man of the house, but Granddad really owned it. As Mom was useless for years, wallowing in misery that our father abandoned her, I fell next in command.

Her hard lessons never left me. *A man will never stick with a willful woman.*

Eventually, Garrett had both feet out the door, ready to sprint once he left for college. Mae, Lindee, and I went off to our respective schools and didn't return to Missouri either. In a sense, my mother was left behind all over again. She's been alone most of her life, just like me. As much as I've not wanted to end up like her, I'm slipping into her shadow of loneliness.

"What can I get you, honey?" A kind-voiced server pulls a small pad of paper from her apron.

I remember my waitressing days when I was a teen. The summer job feels like a lifetime ago. "What do you recommend?"

"Burgers are always safe. The turkey club is one of my favorites. Real filling. And we have split pea soup today."

I gag a little. I hate split pea soup.

The curvy woman leans toward me and lowers her voice.

"I'd also recommend getting yourself one of him, but he's not on the menu." Her head tilts toward Mach as he stands near the pie case by the front door.

"Unfortunately, he's already with me."

The woman tips up a brow and then chuckles softly. "Well, hold onto him, honey. He looks like a keeper."

He's a tosser. I almost tell her, but something stops me as Mach leans his head forward, pointing at something in the case.

"I'll take the chef's salad." The waitress shakes her head. "And a diet cola." I can't go too wrong with raw vegetables. The soft drink will be my splurge item for the day.

When Mach approaches the table, he carries a small plate in each hand. He sets one before me.

I stare at the offering before glancing up at him. "What's this?"

"Apple pie. It was the last slice in the case."

"I . . ." I don't know what to say. Apple pie is my favorite, especially with the crumble on top like this one has. Heat this up and add a dollop of ice cream, and you have a dessert worthy of an orgasm. Pie is my go-to comfort food, but I have no idea how Mach would know this. He wouldn't know this, so I dismiss the gesture as luck and thank him for it.

Apparently, he ordered a burger, and I'm surprised to see him eat such a thing as his palate is eclectic. In the office, Mach orders food in daily—Thai, Vietnamese, sushi. And I'm ashamed to admit how often I've watched him eat as we've powered through group meetings to finalize campaigns, talk strategy, and develop projects.

His food interests are much like the women I've seen on his arm—diverse, youthful, and strikingly stunning.

"Let's talk strategy," Mach says after swallowing a bite of burger. "When we first discuss branding for a client, we take into account five facts we know about a person or their company or their product. If we learn five facts about each other before we get to Wrightwood, maybe that will help us pull off the pretend marriage thing."

The pretend marriage thing? I sit back in the booth, crossing my arms, and stare at my future fake husband. When I wanted to get our stories straight this morning, he scoffed at the thought. Now, he wants to talk about how we'll lie our way through the next couple of days.

The unsettling rumble in my stomach I got yesterday when he proposed his idea to me returns.

"I hate when my ideas are dismissed." That's one fact about me.

Mach's brows pinch. "O-kay. I was thinking something more personal."

"Like what's my favorite color?" *How the hell would that relate to anything?*

"Nooo." He rolls his eyes hinting there might be a playful man buried deep, deep, deep beneath the crisp suits and tough exterior. "More like interests or family stuff. Mae is your sister. How many other siblings do you have?"

I glare at him, astounded. Men are so ignorant. While I don't need him to know my family tree, he should recall my one brother and two sisters from the countless times I've mentioned them in eight years. Still, his ignorance is further proof that Mach doesn't know me, and I'm learning I don't really know him.

"Let's do it this way. Why don't we tell each other five facts we know about the other person? That way, we don't need to memorize something new." With all the sarcasm I can muster in my voice, I mockingly wink at him. "Easier to stick to the truth."

Mach lowers his burger to his plate and sits back as well. He turns his head to peer out the diner window for a moment before looking back at me.

"Okay." He tips his head at me. "You first."

"You first," I retort. *This should be interesting.* "This is your strategy meeting."

"Alright." His dark eyes narrow. "Fact. You chew your lip when you disagree with something I've said." He holds up a finger. "Like you're doing right now."

My teeth still but dig deeper into the lower swell of my lips. I'm aware of this bad habit, but I hadn't thought Mach noticed.

Lifting a second finger, he continues. "Your drink of choice is something called a Southside, which has a complicated recipe and not every bar has all the ingredients. Then you settle for a gin and tonic but only if it's Tanqueray. You like romance novels; the dirtier, the better." He wiggles a brow as he raises another finger and then his pinky. "You're good at seeing the whole picture while able to narrow down to a sliver." He hesitates before popping out his thumb. "And you've been hurt by someone. That hurt built an impenetrable wall around you."

My shoulders stiffen while hackles rise. The marketing industry is large, but the networking circle is compact. It's possible Mach knows my personal history—my past intimate relations—from one marketing firm owner to another. Although Ripley would never expose such a thing. He'd be uncovering truths about himself in any story he shares.

"I'll throw in another fact. I like the different glasses you wear." Mach's eyes meet mine.

I'm not wearing glasses today, not needing them as much for the long-distance viewing I'm doing as I drive. I'm also not certain how my eyewear is a hard fact versus his opinion. With his eyes on me, I suddenly feel uncomfortable, overheated, and slightly aroused. A sharp pulse beats between my thighs. My palms sweat. My nipples tingle. I'd like to say I don't have visions of him clearing this table and taking me on it, but that would be a lie. And we're already telling one too many of those for my comfort.

Instead, I lick my lips and then chew the lower one.

Mach's gaze drops to my mouth, and he frowns.

"My turn." My throat is dry. My voice cracks.

Mach purses his lips. The scruff on his chiseled jaw is heavier today, and the chrome and ink mixture only accentuates the puffiness of his lips.

"Fact. You can hold your eyes very still when you lie, while most people's eyes shift when they aren't telling the truth."

Mach does exactly what I've described, holding his gaze steady without a blink.

"You say you don't like sweets, but I've seen you rummage through Rebecca's desk for candy." I arch a brow, and Mach's mouth slowly curls. "You love classic 70s music, although you look like a country musician."

He tips a brow at that one.

"You're snarky and mean but can give a compliment when deserved."

He tilts his head, forehead furrowing. "You think I'm mean?"

"And . . ." I'm not certain how to explain the last fact. "You're a serial dater. You're probably open about what you want and what you don't, which suggests you value honesty but have intimacy issues. You move on quickly from one woman to another, so you don't hurt anyone's feelings."

"Do you think I'm a womanizer?" Holding those eyes perfectly still, his voice rises with disbelief. He almost sounds offended. Focusing on my eyes with that eerie stare, he says, "As my wife, you'll have to assume I'm faithful to you."

"As your *pretend* wife, there's no assumption. Keep it in your pants for the duration of the time we're in your small town. I hate cheaters. Real or fake."

Mach's gaze remains on me for an uncomfortable length of

time before he replies. "I would never cheat on you, Jane." The words fall like a gauntlet between us. "As for keeping it in my pants in my hometown, there's no fear of anything happening there. With anyone." His lids lower just the slightest, and the implication is clear.

He won't be with any woman, not even his wife.

8

Playlist: "Momma's House" – Dustin Lynch

[Mach]

As we continue our journey, Jane stirs in the driver's seat. She's been responsible for driving this entire trip, and I'm silently grateful. Sitting in this old thing seems like a cursed miracle. However, with all the repairs to this classic Chevy, including the updated radio, and the replaced leather on the seats, it hardly feels like the same truck. Even the fuzzy dice Jane refused to let me remove are new.

"You can't remove those," she'd argued. *"Fuzzy dice are for protection. Like a good luck talisman."*

"And you know this how?"

"My granddad told me. In World War II, pilots carried dice in their pockets for luck in battle. The tradition transferred to hanging fuzzy dice from rearview mirrors in cars."

I don't trust luck and we're certainly headed for battle, but the newer feel of this truck is helping keep my memories at bay.

As we near Chillicothe, Ohio, the scenery changes from flatland to rolling hills and off in the distance are the mountains we'll soon climb. When we cross the Ohio River, the natural barrier between Ohio and West Virginia, a sense of home hits me hard. Strange that I'm still calling this place home when I haven't been here in over twenty-five years.

So much happened so fast when I was young, hotheaded, and twenty-three, and the tailspin I was in back then took me away from Wrightwood like a cyclone out of control. Once transplanted, I never returned.

I can't say I know anyone who's ever brought a woman home for a funeral. Most guys who introduce a girl to the family do it under happier circumstances. Like a family reunion or an engagement party. An introduction is a rite of passage in a relationship, but Jane and I are not in a relationship. Still, it feels strange to be bringing her home to Ma.

Jane and I remain silent, and an anxious quiet settles around us. The radio is back on, but the volume is low. I haven't heard a single song the entire trip, but Jane has been tapping her fingers on the steering wheel or moving her lips, mutely singing along.

I need to prepare her for what she's about to encounter.

"I have a twin." Jane's head turns so sharply, she swerves the truck a little bit and I reach for the dash. "Whoa."

"Sorry." She rights the truck and returns her gaze to the road ahead, but her mouth falls open, ready to ask questions.

"I don't talk to him, but there's a possibility he'll be around." He lives in the old quarters behind the main house. The place Ma was banished with her twin baby boys when she came back to Wrightwood, young, pregnant and without a husband. If it weren't for her mother, Ma would have been homeless. We grew up close enough to that status, struggling for years before Myles charmed Fischer.

Myles was the favorite. Troublemaker. Instigator. Yet Fischer had doted on him.

"Just . . . ignore him. I will." Panic suddenly overcomes me. Jane shouldn't be anywhere near my brother.

My heart patters faster as the landscape becomes more familiar to me. A sign ahead reads "Wrightwood Rd. 1 mile." My chest clenches. The rhythm behind my ribs picks up steam. I don't need to point out the turnoff. Jane has had the map app on her phone guiding us.

We approach Wrightwood from the north on the road bearing the town's name and I'm thrown back in time. Everything looks the same and yet it doesn't. Nothing will ever be the same here again.

"Turn left at the rock."

Jane softly laughs until she sees a small boulder marking a path. In the distance, a large, two-story house sits on a hill. A house that overlooks the town's business district with a view of the river as well. Thankfully, we aren't crossing the rainbow-arched bridge over the Kanawha River, but the structure comes into sight soon enough as we climb the gravel incline. My focus returns to the house—white clapboard with a semi-wrap around porch. The place might look storybook to some. To me, it's a haunted mansion filled with disapproval, disappointment, and disillusions. How Ma can stand to live in the place now is beyond me.

Then again having a relationship with a father—positive or negative—is something I've never had. Raised by a single mother, ostracized by our grandfather for years, a father figure is an anomaly to me.

"It's beautiful," Jane whispers as she pulls beside the house and cuts the engine.

I stare out the window for a second, wondering what I've

gotten myself into. Worrying about what I've dragged Jane into. She's about to learn more than five facts about me and none of them will be pleasant. "I should have had you sign an NDA."

"What?" The eerie chill in her voice turns my head. She stares back at me, eyes full of surprise . . . and hurt.

"What happens here needs to stay here." And I'm not being snarky about some Vegas tryst.

"I would never . . ." She adamantly shakes her head, propping her arms over the steering wheel. Her position suggests I've offended her. Her shock tells me she doesn't deserve the offense. She's come with me—no questions asked. She drove the hours it took to get here. She's missing days of work for the shitshow ahead.

I'm such a bastard.

Her gaze remains focused out the windshield a second longer. Then her arms slip off the wheel, and she looks at the center of the steering wheel. Her expression shifts from puzzled to determined. She straightens. "Fine. I'll sign whatever you need."

I should thank her for being here. Express some kind of gratitude for the role she's about to play. Instead, I pop open my door and step into the yard where I had never planned to set my feet again.

Within seconds, Ma is out the front door and rushing down the porch stairs to me. "Mach." My name in her soft Scottish lilt tightens my chest. I'm close with my mother. I never faulted her for the mess of our lives. She did what she could to love us, care for us, protect us.

"Ma." I open my arms, bracing for the impact of her hug. She has a small frame, but a solid stature, and she hugs tight, like she can shield me from any storm despite her thin arms. I embrace her back while the soft crunch of gravel behind me suggests Jane is approaching. Releasing my mother, I wave at Jane. "Ma, you know Jane."

Ma turns to Jane. "You've picked the bonniest lass." Although our family is something like five generations from the original forefathers, Ma has a light Scottish accent, inherited from her mother who was born and raised in the homeland, as Fischer called it. Ma also adopted some Scottish affectations and sayings and uses them at her convenience.

I roll my eyes at Ma's comment while agreeing Jane is beautiful.

She steps up to Jane and brings her into a firm embrace, as if Jane was family, as if Jane is my wife. Ma holds a little longer than necessary and Jane peers up at me, brows furrowed as she pats Ma's back. Concern etches her pretty features.

"Ma, let her go."

"I'm afraid to." Ma chuckles before finally pulling back but keeping her hands attached to Jane's upper arms, like she really means it. She doesn't want to release Jane for some reason. "You must be tired from your trip. Are you hungry? I would have made haggis for ya' but it's banned in the U.S. Don't know what all the fuss is about. I made a good stew instead."

Jane looks up at me over my mother's head. She doesn't look like the stew type, but she surprises me.

"I haven't had a good stew in forever." She extricates her arms from Ma's grip but then hooks her arm through my mother's and leads her toward the house as if she's the owner and not the guest.

"Guess I'll get the bags." Sarcasm drips from my tongue.

"That's what husbands do," Ma calls over her shoulder, as if she'd know. And I almost shout back that I'm not a husband. Jane is not my wife. But Ma is already in on this farce. She's the one who told me to bring a wife with me, after all.

What I don't understand yet is *why* we're playing this ruse.

9

———

Playlist: "Kinfolks" – Sam Hunt

[Jane]

I adore Mach's mother. Having spoken to her on the phone and encountering her in our office once or twice, she's been pleasant and jovial, and so unlike her son. She's much shorter in stature than Mach's six-plus feet, but she's fierce in spirit. I'd place her no more than mid-sixties which means she had Mach when she was relatively young.

Mach and his twin.

Mach's statement that he doesn't talk to his brother explains only the teeniest bit why his brother has never been mentioned. I've heard rumblings that Mach and Tucker are actually brothers though I don't understand the logistics. I only know Tucker has a twenty-something son who beams when he looks at Mach and glares in disdain when he sees his father.

I've encountered the snooty Jude Ashford less than a handful of times, and it's a handful too many.

Camilla leads me into the house, which shows signs of age but is spotlessly clean. Hardwood floors with well-worn rugs highlight the front parlor on the right of the entrance. A dining room with ancient wallpaper and lit wall sconces brightens the left. A staircase before us looks unsafe as it's missing a banister and railing, and the walls could be misinterpreted as shiplap, but it's actually exposed wood slats.

Mach's mother continues to tug me forward, leading me to a kitchen off the dining room which has seen better days, not to mention the layout is cramped and curved in an L shape.

"Have a seat, lovey. Let me get you something to drink." She's doting on me like I'm the prodigal child, as opposed to her actual son, who sheepishly enters the kitchen a few minutes after us. His hands slip into his pockets, gaze taking in the room. Eventually, his head hangs as if he's embarrassed by this place.

"We won't be here long," he mutters only for me to hear.

"It's fine."

His mother rounds the L-bend in the room with small glass canning jars in hand, each containing a sliver of amber liquid. She places one before me, hands one to Mach, and keeps the third. Mach lifts his and takes a sniff.

"Ma," he groans as his nose scrunches.

"*Slàinte mhath.*" Camilla raises her glass.

"Good health." Mach lifts his own and tips it back.

As I lift my glass, the strong smoky oak scent of scotch gives me pause. Not wanting to insult Camilla, though, I tip back my glass and choke at the flame cascading down my throat. Mach is quick to come to my aid, offering a strong but awkward back slap. I wave him off. He said no touching. Even in his weak attempt to assist me from dying by fire ingestion, I don't want his hands on me.

Especially when I don't understand one bit why I'm here.

Camilla steps away from the table and returns with the stew in a cast-iron pot, setting it forcefully on the table. She disappears and returns once more with three bowls and spoons. "Sit," Camilla directs to me. Then turns to Mach. "Make yourself useful and get your *acushla* some water."

Mach narrows his eyes at his mother before reluctantly following her order.

"Og-u-what?" I whisper-choke, the liquid flame still burning my throat.

"*Acushla.*" Camilla winks at me when Mach disappears around the corner. "It's Gaelic, meaning darling. It literally means pulse. You are his heartbeat."

Oh my. My heart ridiculously flutters at the possibility and then my chest clenches at the truth. "Oh, I'm not—"

"I see it in his face." Camilla's fierce gaze holds mine as her fragile fist thumps once over her left breast. "He feels it in here."

Thankfully, Mach rounds the corner in time to save me from this unrealistic explanation. He gives me a look, questioning what his mother might be telling me.

I shake my head, dismissing both the romantic notion in Camilla's words and the reality that I've never been anyone's heartbeat.

Swallowing a new kind of burn in my throat, which has nothing to do with the heat of alcohol, I blink several times and focus on eating a stew dinner among people who are not my family.

～

"I don't know what Ma said to you, but she obviously upset you," Mach says to me before we climb the stairs to the upper level. After dinner and clean-up, I admitted to his mother that

I'd love a shower. I'm ready to end this day. We've been up since before dawn, and the day has passed with little conversation and tons of unanswered questions. My brain is habitually one step ahead of me working on the next move, the next project, the next agenda. Tonight, I'm too tired to care what the plan is.

Tomorrow. I'll consider the mistake I've made tomorrow.

"It was nothing." I don't want to tell him what his mother said about heartbeats. I'm not even certain I can explain why it bothered me. Maybe it's that I'd been in a long-term relationship in the past, and never once did I feel the depth of that man's heart when I'd given him all of mine.

I don't expect to be the beat within Mach's heart either.

Reaching for my suitcase at the base of the staircase, Mach practically slaps my hand away from the luggage and picks it up. I walk up the questionable staircase and find his mother in the upper hallway.

She waves at a room to her right. "I've put you in here."

"Where do you want me?" Mach asks, surprising me by his nearness behind me.

His mother scoffs. "Don't be daft. You sleep together."

Panic immediately sets in. Surely, Camilla knows Mach and I aren't actually married.

"Uh, Ma—"

"In," his mother states, with a determined look. She points once again toward the bedroom, adding a firm nod for emphasis.

Something in her eyes unnerves me, but I don't wish to argue with the hostess. Placing a hand on Mach's forearm, I speak to his mother. "I'm certain it's lovely."

Mach can sleep his ass on the floor. The position will serve him right for his cold behavior and grumpy attitude throughout the day.

I step past him and enter a room too pretty to describe. If I didn't know better, I'd call this room a honeymoon suite. The bed is made up with a white coverlet. A sheer canopy drapes the crème-toned wrought iron headboard. A dozen white roses, cut short and stuffed into a vase, stand on one nightstand while a glowing milk-glass lamp illuminates the other. The room is inviting and . . .romantic.

And panic returns.

A suitcase drops to the floor behind me, and I flinch. Slowly turning to face Mach's mother, I force a smile while sincerity fills my voice. "It's beautiful."

Pride shows in her returning grin and guilt settles deeper inside me. "Thank you, lovey. I decorated it myself." The curve of her lips brightens her face as she scans the room, wistfully taking in the space. "I have big dreams for this place."

Mach and I briefly lock gazes before I question, "Bathroom?"

"In there, dove." Camilla takes two steps and opens a door where a tiny bathroom sits inside what might have once been a closet. The tight space only allows for a sink on metal legs and a miniature clawfoot tub. There's no way Mach would be able to stretch his legs in the base, but something tells me Mach isn't a bubble bath kind of man.

I smile graciously at Camilla and reach for my suitcase.

"I'll give you kids time to settle in. Let me know if you need anything. Tomorrow will be a long day." Camilla pats her son's chest, tipping up on her toes to press a kiss to his cheek and then bids us goodnight.

As soon as she leaves the room, closing the door behind her, Mach hitches a thumb over his shoulder. "I've got some work—"

"I'm going to shower."

His Adam's apple bobs, and his gaze roams my body. Then, he spins on his heels, offering no further words.

I sigh in relief when he exits. Another scotch, like his mother served before dinner, might take the remaining edge off. Instead, the warm water of a shower soothes my mind along with the ache of my upper back and the cramp in my legs from sitting so long while driving. With my eyes closed, my thoughts flit through images of Mach. Just the casual slideshow I hold in my head of him until my lower lips throb and my fingers find their way between my thighs.

The moment feels deliciously wrong in my quote-unquote mother-in-law's home, but her son drives me mad, and the need to quell the throbbing between my thighs becomes too much. I imagine Mach on his knees, begging me to be his wife, begging me to let him please me. My fingers lazily stroke my clit at first until the fantasy shifts to me on my knees, my center balanced over Mach's face. His tongue laps at my slit. His grunts of attitude merge into moans of desire. My breath accelerates as my fingers move faster, and I bring myself to a quick release.

My head tips forward. My mouth opens in a mute scream.

The orgasm alleviates some of the tension within me.

And I need to relax because the next few days are going to be excessively long and disheartening, as second to cheaters, I hate liars. And now, I've become one.

10

———

Playlist: "You Are The Reason" – Calum Scott

[Jane]

In the middle of the night, something heavy falls onto the bed beside me, and I'd scream if I didn't instantly recognize Mach's scent—spicy, mountain, expensive. Being in a small town, the night is excessively black without overhead streetlamps. Inside the dark room, I can only make out the outline of Mach's broad form as he lies on his back. The heat coming off his body suggests he's no longer wearing a shirt. Reaching out for his arm, my hand hesitates before retracting.

Mach shifts, restlessly twisting his body until he faces me on his side.

"Jane," he whispers.

I hold my breath as my eyes adjust to the darkness. Can he see me? Does he know I'm looking at him?

Trembling, fumbling fingertips come to my forehead and

brush back my hair, scooping it around my ear. "You're so beautiful."

My mouth falls open but quickly shuts, noting the slur in his voice. That smoky scotch-scent slaps me in the face.

"Why must you tempt me?" he murmurs.

He has no idea what he's saying, and I have no idea what time it is, other than late.

His shaky fingers tickle the side of my neck and round down to my shoulder. His hand curls over it and then he traces the length of my collarbone. A single finger coasts lower, straight down my sternum.

My eyes close. This is not what I want. Nor does he.

When that finger reaches the swell of my breast, skirting along a hint of cleavage above the tank top I've worn to bed, I grip his wrist.

"Stop." The command is soft but earnest. Mach needs to stop before he does something he'll never remember, or worse, regret.

I gently push his arm away from me, holding his wrist down to the mattress for an extra second. When I'm confident he'll stay put, I release him.

He captures my forearm next, surprising me with quick reflexes, and settling my arm on the bed in a similar manner to how I held his. Pausing only a second, he then strokes over my wrist to cover my hand. His fingers slink between mine, spreading them until we are linked together.

"I'm drunk, *acushla*," he whispers.

My heartbeats halt.

After he exhales heavily, a quick snore follows. Our hands are bound together. For a man who said no public affection, I wonder if he knows privately that he's holding my hand.

He probably doesn't.

When I wake in the morning, his back is to me. I'm under the bedcovers while he's on top of them with a separate, throw quilt over his upper body. He'll never remember he touched me last night. Strangely, I'm touching him this morning, my hand pressed to his back as if holding him steady or perhaps keeping him at arm's length.

Quietly as I can, I slip from the bed. I'm wearing sleep shorts and a tank top as the weather is still warm here in the last days of August, but a chill fills the room. Rummaging through the closet, I find a WVU sweatshirt and slip it over my tank top. Without another glance at Mach, I exit the room.

In the kitchen, a man similar in build to Mach stands at the counter with his back to me. He's busy working at something and doesn't notice me. Deciding to silently retreat from the room, I hold my breath and take a step backward. Only, a creaky floorboard gives away my presence.

The man spins, and a mirror image of Mach faces me. His hair is a little browner than white and his scruff isn't as thick as Mach's, but there is no doubt who he might be. He clutches the counter behind him before slowly offering me a crooked grin that could rival Mach's if my boss smiled more. "Mornin' darlin'."

I return his infectious smile. "Good morning. You must be Myles."

The man's lips curl, seductive and tempting, but not threatening. No, the gleam in his eye says he's all flirt with no follow through. "I see Mach has spoken of me."

I hate to admit I only learned of him yesterday. Instead, I nod, my smile weakening. I'm a shit liar, and he reads the truth in my face.

His playful expression slowly falls, and he clears his throat. "Yeah, I'm Myles."

"I'm Jane. His . . . wife." The word feels foreign on my tongue, and I choke.

"Mach is married again?" His brows arch. His hands tighten on the counter.

Again? The final word punches me in the gut. When had Mach ever been married before? Chewing on my lower lip, a sudden lump clogs my throat, so I croak, "Yes."

"When did this happen?" His forehead pinches with curiosity.

"Don't talk to her." The gruff masculine voice behind me makes me jump.

"Jesus," I murmur, clapping a hand to my chest and spinning to face Mach. My mouth falls open. Before me is a man I've never seen before. The almost blinding white T-shirt exposes colorfully decorated solid arms. Light gray sweatpants hang low on his hips. The sudden drool at my lips is a slow trickle compared to the waterfall between my thighs. Mach is bright and beautiful, and the stark T-shirt accentuates the myriad of designs on his arms. With his arms crossed and his feet parted, his body language, however, screams thunderstorm ahead.

"Mach," Myles says.

Mach approaches me, fixing his eyes on my face. "You're wearing my sweatshirt."

I glance down at the soft, worn material covering my body. Clearly, he's offended by my wearing the precious item. Before I can defend myself, he speaks again.

"You should dress." His gaze doesn't leave mine, and the hard edge of his cheeks and set jaw warn me not to argue with him. *Well, looks like someone got up on the wrong side of the bed.*

And I hate taking directions, especially when he's looking at me like he is. Fire yet ice. A line might be drawn that I'm not supposed to cross, but I won't play his game, especially after the whammy I've just learned.

He had a wife.

"Tea first." Forcing my voice to be cheerful and pleasant, I stare him down.

Mach steps even closer, crowding my space. Despite nipples

peaking and the mouthwatering appearance of him and that ink, I don't move. He leans closer to me, bringing his face within an inch of mine. The mint on his breath kisses my lips. I anticipate him actually kissing me, or at least pissing around me, as his aggression is nothing more than an alpha male exerting possession. Which he doesn't have, because I'm not his wife.

We stand nose to nose a second. My mouth salivating. *Will he kiss me?*

Our eyes lock. His are bloodshot and fierce. His nostrils flare once. Then, he pulls back, causing me to flinch at the sudden retreat. He moves around me, and rounds the L-corner of the kitchen, disappearing from sight. Cabinet doors slam and a faucet runs. The microwave churns. I don't mention that you can't make a decent cup of tea in a microwave.

Myles watches his brother, opening his mouth to speak and then clamping it shut as Mach stomps around like there isn't another person in the room.

Maybe I'm the one seeing a ghost. Myles might as well be one because he's invisible to Mach until the loud *thwack* of something falling to the ground makes both Myles and I flinch. Mach walks toward me, not even acknowledging that he kicked something over.

"Here." He holds out a mug. My eyes dart over his shoulder where Myles takes a hobbling step forward before bending down to retrieve what fell. When he stands upright, he leans on a cane.

"What the hell?" I mutter, attempting to catch Mach's eyes. When he refuses to look at me, I step left, allowing him to walk around me. I'm not leaving this room after that petty display.

"Are you alright?" I ask Myles, who stares at Mach's back.

Mach steps into my line of vision. "Jane, dressed."

"See the caveman act doesn't work any better with this one." Myles chuckles, bitterness lacing the knowing laugh.

My brows pinch as I peer back at Mach. His fingers curl into a fist. The hand holding the tea mug tightens. The liquid trembles within the ceramic, threatening to overflow.

Suddenly, the tension in the room becomes clear to me. Two brothers. One woman.

Struggling with a mountain of emotion, I take the mug from Mach's hand before he spills it and forcefully set it on the table beside me. Without a word, I spin away from him and head for our room.

Acushla? What a joke. Another woman was his heartbeat. Another wife . . . who I'd never known existed. The omission hurts. The reality of it is like a knife to my chest. He loved another woman enough to marry her. And I'm being ridiculous.

Taking the stairs two at a time, my heart hammers. The faster I can get through these next few days, the better. Because I need to get my head out of the clouds about holding hands in the dark and whispered compliments from the man who isn't actually my husband.

11

Playlist: "Spirit in the Sky" – Norman Greenbaum
(from *Guardians of the Galaxy*)

[Mach]

F uck!
Everything in me fights the urge to turn on my brother and rip into him. He had no right to tell Jane what he did within minutes of meeting her. He has no right to speak to her or even breathe her air. He hurt her. Her suddenly sad blue eyes gave away her pain, and I hate him with every fiber of my being. What the fuck is he doing in Ma's kitchen?

As quickly as the question arises, I recall he lives in the house out back. Ma lets him have free range here. She forgave him. I never will.

With fists clenched and jaw tight, I swipe Jane's mug from the table, and follow her. Once inside our bedroom, Jane is rummaging through her suitcase. My gaze falls to the back of her toned legs, long and sleek beneath short shorts. Her ass is perfection in the tiny amount of material. Her feet are bare. She's more beautiful this morning than I've ever seen her.

And she was wearing my old WVU sweatshirt. I nearly had a heart attack seeing her in that shirt. The material now lays crumpled on the bed, as if she ripped it off and tossed it aside.

Fuck! "Jane."

"Don't," she snaps, pulling things from her bag.

"Look, Myles and I . . . It's complicated."

"Complicated?" She spins to face me. "Maybe we should have played the five facts game your way because this is something I certainly should have known."

"This?" I choke despite knowing her meaning.

"You were married!" Her voice rises before she clears her throat in an attempt to lower the volume. "You were married, and you didn't think to mention it. And your brother? When you said you didn't talk to him, I thought . . . this is more than what I thought. He was invisible to you."

"He is invisible."

"He's injured."

Her concern for Myles claws at my chest. "Do not feel sorry for him."

Jane glares at me with scorching blue eyes. "I feel sorry for you. That might be worse."

She moves toward the bathroom, but I step before her, forcing my chest to bump into hers. With a sharp inhale of surprise, I catch a whiff of her. All fucking day yesterday, trapped in that truck, her scent surrounded me. Summer rain and freshness. The scent of her haunted my dreams, suggesting she was close, giving me strange comfort as we slept in that small bed. "Jane . . . it's—"

"It's simple, actually." She scowls. "You tell me the truth because the only thing equal to a cheater is a liar."

"I didn't lie." I didn't. I just didn't tell her this one additional fact about me. "It was a long time ago."

"And what happened to her?" Jane's eyes search my face as if answers are written on my skin.

My throat tightens. My mouth goes dry. "She—"

"You know what? Never mind." Jane's eyes widen. "Keep your secrets, Mach. I know enough, right?" She tosses my words from yesterday at me like a wet towel.

"Jane." How do I explain Tracy? Does Jane really need to know this piece of my past? Does my previous marriage matter? Jane and I are only faking our relationship.

"It's all pretend, anyway." She speaks as if she has read my thoughts. Then she stomps around me, disappearing into the small bathroom and leaving me to wonder why she's so upset.

Giving Jane space, I leave the room but eventually return to find it empty. My head is a mess, and I shower in preparation for Fischer's funeral.

The night before, I'd headed to town with Ma's homemade scotch in hand as memory after memory flooded my thoughts. Weaving down the hill, I stumbled as I drank trying without much success to ignore the bridge over the river. That damn bridge, shaped like a rainbow of hope, and yet the thief of dreams. I stopped short of Bridge Alley, the main street that curves through Wrightwood's business district, looping back to the bridge thoroughfare named Wrightwood Road. *Wrightwood*. A name that should be full of pride for us Wrights. A name I'd come to despise.

I had a love-hate relationship with this town when I was a child.

Ma was revered here, both for her kind spirit and the courage it took to return and face her demons. The devil lived in her home. Eventually, Ma grew bolder with her da. She moved into the big house when we were teenagers, allowing Myles and me to remain in the smaller structure out back. The evil truth is the cabin was once a servant's quarters. Ma was banished there upon her return to Wrightwood, young and pregnant without a husband.

Myles and I grew up under scrutiny. Bastard boys. *Who was their father?* Our biggest nemesis was our own grandfather. Over time, Fischer warmed to Myles. The bitterness of Fischer's rejection was something I couldn't let go of, though. And I couldn't wait to separate myself from this town.

Then I'd met Tracy.

Pushing away thoughts of her, my mind wanders to Jane.

At one point, I woke last night to find us holding hands in the tight bed. Surprised, I released her fingers and rolled away from her to give us distance. From that point on, I struggled to sleep as everything in me wanted to turn back and tug her entire body against mine, molding her against my frame.

But I'd already taken enough advantage of her just by bringing her here, forcing her into this farce, and asking her to be my wife.

Then again, she isn't my wife. She's here for the coveted partnership.

And why do I wish she was here for other reasons, like simply ... for me?

THE FUNERAL PASSES as funerals do, with words of sympathy. I'm not certain many of the condolences are heartfelt. Fischer was a miserable old man, exerting his power over a town named after his forefathers. He owns all the buildings on Bridge Alley as well as most of the property around the town's center. Most people might have moved away if it weren't for my mother. She was the kind buffer between a miserly man and a struggling community. Somewhere between the unwanted memories of growing up here and the glances of empathy for more than just Fischer's passing, I begin counting the minutes until I can drag Jane away from this godawful place.

She wears a form-fitting black dress today. One panel of fabric crosses over the other and strings tie at her hip to keep the material in place. A deep vee hints at the valley between her breasts, appropriate but still sexy as fuck. Something about that spot—where one breast almost kisses the other—draws my eye often. Not to mention, I fantasize about tugging the knot at her hip, opening that dress and revealing what she wears underneath. My fantasy includes something thin and black and damp with need for me.

We pass the dreary day circling one another. I introduce her as my wife, and she listens to peoples' stories about Myles and me like we were the best of kids and not the town's outcasts for a large portion of our lives. Jane tends to Ma often, who remains strong and with a smile on her face.

We still haven't discussed why her directive was to bring a wife with me.

And I hold my breath for tomorrow, predicting the truth will suffocate me when it's finally revealed.

12

Playlist: "What's Your Country Song" – Thomas Rhett

[Mach]

"To my daughter, I leave the main house, the property connected to said house that includes seven acres of land and woods," Landon Hobbs reads my grandfather's intentions as he sits behind a large desk in his office the morning after the funeral. For an old guy, he's surprisingly fit and still has most of his hair, even though now it is blindingly white. His age falls between my uncle Frank and Ma, and like Ma, he has lived here his entire life. He was actually a good friend to my uncle Frank when they were kids, but Frank didn't remain in Wrightwood. He married, moved a few towns over, and runs a real estate agency. Strangely, his wife Becca isn't present today, although she'd been at the funeral yesterday.

"To my son, I leave my 1965 MG." The empty silence that follows the single item causes Frank to shift and my mother to gape at her brother, shock written on her face. The classic convertible was a restoration project which Fischer prided himself on rebuilding throughout Frank's younger years. When Frank was old enough to drive, he and a friend took the car out for a ride without Fischer's permission and crashed the thing. From stories we'd been told over the years, Fischer rebuilt the car a second time piece-by-painstaking piece, promising that each material expense plus the laborious time taken by Fischer would be deducted from Frank's inheritance. Apparently, Fischer hadn't been joking.

"That's it?" Frank snaps.

Landon looks up at his old friend, chagrin in his expression. "That's all."

Frank curses under his breath, and Ma shakes her head with disappointment in a man who disappointed her in more ways than one throughout her life. She shouldn't be surprised her father left her older brother so little.

"To my grandson Myles. I continue to gift the Small House, the official name given to the smaller structure on the property of the aforementioned address, allowing for his comfort until such time he is no longer comfortable in said space. At which time, the building will revert to Camilla Wright."

Myles scoffs at the details. "Still considering me a cripple even from the grave."

The comment surprises me. Myles and Fischer were close. Closer than ever when I finally ditched this place.

"And finally, to my grandson Machlan, I leave the town of Wrightwood."

"What?" My outburst is echoed by several other voices.

Landon glances at me over his reading glasses then shifts his gaze to my mother before continuing. "The buildings, which include twelve business-zoned properties, along with several municipal lots, and a strip of riverside land used for both recreational and professional purposes, which in short includes the entirety of the Bridge Alley area, are all bequeathed to Machlan Wright."

"What the hell am I supposed to do with the town?" I straighten in the uncomfortable wooden-back chair I've been sitting in. Jane sits quietly beside me.

Landon eyes me once more. "With a contingency."

"Of course." I huff.

"The deed to said property will be shared in joint ownership with his wife with the understanding they are to rebuild Wrightwood together."

"Rebuild?" Uncle Frank interjects.

"My wife," I blurt.

Landon eyes his old friend but continues. "The endeavor should take no more than one year, at which time a sum of one million dollars will be bestowed upon Machlan as his rightful inheritance."

I stare at Landon, uncertain I've heard him correctly. *The town of Wrightwood. Shared jointly with my wife. One million dollars.* Fischer knew about Tracy. He *knew* I was no longer married. How could he do this to me?

"Why the hell would Da want to rebuild this town?" Uncle Frank mumbles.

Ma narrows her eyes at her brother.

"This is all contingent on me having a wife, correct?" I strain for clarification.

Landon's eyes shift to Jane. He lowers his glasses, peering at Ma a moment before returning his attention to me.

"I'm going to spell this out in more simplistic terms. You and your wife"—Landon glances at Jane—"are to rebuild this town within one year. Upon which time, you will then receive one million dollars. Another million has been set aside for the sole purpose of restoring Wrightwood to what it once was, at your discretion for expenditures which must be made on the properties mentioned."

"This is bullshit," Uncle Frank argues, and I have to agree with him. "Da knew I had plans for this town."

"And if I don't have a wife?"

Landon glances at Ma once more. *Why does he keep doing that?* He turns back to me. "Your grandfather was clear. No wife means no money. And no project. Thus, the land will be turned over to the state of West Virginia."

Frank gasps. "The state?"

Landon pauses before continuing. "I'm going to be blunt. Refusing this directive puts all the businesses in the downtown area at risk of losing their livelihood and disrupting the economics of this community. Without industry of some type, the owners and their families will be forced to move elsewhere. Wrightwood will have no appeal. We'll essentially turn into a ghost town."

"What do I care?" I snap.

"Mach." Jane rests her hand on my forearm, reminding me of her presence in the room.

I scan her profile. Why would she care? She isn't my wife. We aren't actually married and, like Frank said, this is bullshit. If my uncle had plans for the town, why didn't he inherit it?

"There are rumors a foreign energy company is interested in the land. To use the river for electricity," Ma adds.

"And?" I bark again, wondering why this is an issue.

"Mach, these are peoples' lives we're talking about," Ma says, visible pain filling her eyes as she clutches her hands at her chest, trying to explain this fucked up situation. "People you grew up with. People I adore."

She might adore the town, but this town had made my life hell.

"What does this project involve?" Jane asks.

Her calm tenor turns my head in her direction. *She can't be serious.*

"Fischer's wish was to rejuvenate the town in hopes to

rebuild the community and possibly encourage tourism," Landon explains, tugging his reading glasses from his face.

"Tourism?" Uncle Frank and I say in unison.

Then I take my surprise one step further. "Who would willingly visit this place?"

"Mach." Jane tightens her hold on my arm.

No, this is bullshit. I don't want this town. I don't even want to be *in* this town. I don't want to rebuild it. And for whatever sick reason, Fischer wrapped up a wife in his fucking departing gift.

"I'm not even married."

The silence following my exclamation feels almost as heavy as learning Frank only inherited a classic car.

Jane shares a glance with Ma, communicating something as only women can. Slowly, her hand slides down my arm, and her fingers dip into my palm before spearing between my own, combining our hands.

Unsolicited, my fingers respond, holding onto hers.

"Mach is correct. We aren't married yet. We knew of Mr. Wright's ailments, and we were hoping to come down here when he was feeling better. We wanted to surprise the family with an engagement. We planned to be married here. Unfortunately, Mr. Wright's untimely death preceded our arrival and happened before we could properly marry."

"Ailments?" Uncle Frank scoffs. "He was terminally ill."

I didn't know this, or if I did, I'd pushed it out of my head. And just what is Jane doing?

Landon eases back in his seat. "But you do intend to marry?"

"How is that an option?" Frank stammers. "The will states him and his wife. Not marrying some woman after the fact. That means the land is up for grabs and I'll be issuing an injunction. Da knew I wanted this town."

Ma's gaze darts to Landon and holds. As for the *some woman* comment from Frank, my fingers tighten on Jane's. "You'll watch what you say about my fiancée," I state, surprising myself.

"Your fiancée?" Frank chides. "You need a wife. And you work with her. An office side piece does not make a wife."

"Spoken like a man who had an affair with his assistant," Myles mutters.

I'd laugh if I wasn't ignoring Myles's presence in the room. Why isn't he inheriting the town? He's the one who stayed here.

I'm also fuming at my uncle. Shifting in my seat, I lean toward him but Jane's hold on my hand tightens. Pointing at his face, I snap, "Show some respect."

Landon clears his throat. "There's a final condition. If the project can be completed in time for this year's Kringle Fest, Myles Wright will inherit two million dollars."

"What?" Myles and I say in unison, reminding me of when we were kids and we spoke at the same time, with the same thought, as twins can.

"Kringle Fest?" I bark. The festival of lights and night of celebration happens in town the weekend before the Christmas holiday.

"That's only four months away," Myles adds.

"And two million dollars if you get the town rebuilt by then," Landon says.

Myles shakes his head, pressing his thumb and forefinger to his forehead.

"What a fucking bastard," I mumble. How this man tied up Myles's inheritance with mine is just unconscionable. Not to mention, it's so typical of Fischer. Myles always got more.

Jane clears her throat and squeezes my hand. "So if we don't marry, the town goes to the state because Mach isn't fulfilling the terms of the will."

Frank scoffs for some reason and looks out the window in Landon's office.

"Correct," Landon states. "And the terms of one year are solid. Fischer was clear in his instructions. If you divorce, separate, or fall short in any manner, the town defaults to state property."

"And if we finish earlier, Myles benefits," Jane adds for clarification.

"Correct." Landon nods.

"But falling short makes the property up for grabs for someone else to purchase?" Frank questions, sitting forward with renewed interest.

"Making it the state's property to then do with it what it wants. Honestly, I don't think most states are interested in rebuilding existing small towns. We're thirty minutes from the state capital. From a state perspective, their efforts and funds would be better served elsewhere. They'd let us be swallowed up as a suburb of Charleston despite the thirty-minute commute."

"Or sell the land to the highest bidder and turn us into a power plant." Ma scowls at Frank.

"But if we were to marry immediately, the town is saved provided we complete the rebuild in a year?" Jane asks.

"Three-hundred and sixty-five days from the reading of the will." Landon points at the papers before him on his desk for emphasis.

"Or one-hundred and twenty, give or take a day," Ma explains for Myles's benefit.

Jane stares at Landon. "Which means we must marry . . ."

"Today," the lawyer adds.

"They can't do that." Frank glares at Landon.

"There's nothing that says they can't. As long as they are married before the will is read . . ." Landon stares down his old friend. From the corner of my eye, I catch Ma ducking her head to hide a mischievous smile.

"But the reading was before a wedding." Frank's voice rises, and he glances around the room for support.

"Not if I can get a justice of the peace in here." Landon exaggerates looking at his watch before leaning forward and typing something on his open laptop. "My calendar says I'm reading this will at four p.m. this afternoon."

"But you didn't." Frank clenches his teeth while gripping his thighs.

"My watch says we aren't anywhere near four o'clock," Myles adds, not bothering to glance at his wrist.

Frank eyes Myles's arm. "You aren't wearing a watch."

"Funny, my watch says we have six hours until four, which is good because I have a wedding to attend before the reading." A giggle fills Ma's voice as she holds Landon's gaze again.

"Then I guess you'll need to get the justice of the peace in here," Jane murmurs beside me, and I turn to her, still clutching her hand like I'm a drowning man.

Frank grunts as he shoots from his chair, pointing at Landon. "This is bullshit."

And it hits me while I tug at my tie, needing some air . . . I'm marrying Jane, for real.

13

______

Playlist: "Red" – Taylor Swift

[Jane]

"**W**hy would you do this?" Mach turns on me the moment his uncle leaves the room and Landon excuses himself to make a phone call, presumably to the justice of the peace. I'm also assuming he'll be calling in a couple favors at the town hall to obtain a marriage license on short notice.

Glancing down at our fingers still locked together, I shrug. "I don't know. I just don't want your town to go to waste."

"This isn't *my* town. Let some power company have it."

"Machlan Jonathon Wright, I will not let this town be turned into a power plant," Camilla states defensively, her voice full of disappointment while she's still pressing her hands together as if in prayer.

"Ma, I didn't mean—"

"Yes, you did, and you've sulked long enough. Marry the girl. Rebuild our town. Save my home." She pats her chest. "I have plans for that house."

That's the second time Camilla has alluded to plans, and I'm curious what she's thinking. If she says grandchildren, I'll renege on my offer to officially marry Mach. At forty-five, that ship is a wreck at the bottom of the ocean with my heart buried in a treasure chest. I always wanted children. I always hoped I'd be a mother, but little heartbeats do not happen when you aren't someone else's pulse.

"If you don't want to marry me, I understand." What I don't understand is the sadness in my own voice. Ours won't be a real marriage. We aren't doing this because we've fallen in love. We're here to save a town and the lives of others. We're here to restore their faith in the community.

And for some reason, a thrill ripples through me at the thought.

"Why didn't this fall on Myles?" Mach turns to his mother, overlooking his brother who sits two chairs away from him.

"Da had his reasons."

"And what could those be?" Mach shifts in his seat, still holding my hand, but aiming his irritation at his mother.

His mother shakes her head. Either she doesn't know or isn't willing to tell him.

Mach finally releases my hand and abruptly stands. "I need some air." His biting tone is directed at his mother, but his overall anger permeates the room. He hastily exits the office, and when the door slams shut, I jolt in my seat.

I meet his mother's gaze.

"I knew I liked you." Her Scottish lilt softens but accentuates. "You're one to hold onto."

Yesterday, she hugged me like she didn't want to let me go. *I'm afraid to let go.*

The sentiment was strange in the moment, and I dismissed

it in the haze of exhaustion, but the statement creeps back with more meaning today. Camilla knew the terms of this will, and she knows something about that energy plant.

"Why didn't you just tell him?" I ask her.

"He would never have come here willingly." Whatever the relationship was with his grandfather and this town, Camilla is right. Mach wouldn't have returned, especially if he knew these conditions. In being here, maybe the hope was that submerging him in his history would open his heart. He's a brash man, but his present disgust and dislike are more than I've ever witnessed.

Where is his compassion? I don't want to believe he really means the town can perish.

Mach formed a scholarship for Rebecca's daughter when Rebecca's husband suddenly passed away. He paid the out-of-pocket medical expenses of another employee at Impact when he was diagnosed with cancer. He contributed to many of Rochelle Ashe's side causes for single mothers, despite hating Rochelle. This disconnect in empathy for others is not like him.

"What if he doesn't return?" I whisper to his mother with genuine concern about Mach's sudden disappearance.

Camilla slowly smiles, tapping her fist over her left breast again. "His *acushla* will call him home. He'll come around."

Her confidence in her son's connection to me astounds me. Her belief in my power over him, the strength of my heart over his, is beyond comprehension.

I, however, am not so certain Mach won't take that old truck and leave me behind.

WHEN MACH HASN'T RETURNED by lunchtime, Landon orders in sandwiches for Camilla, Myles, and me. I listen as Camilla and Landon discuss the town, telling me more about the various businesses while sharing smiles with one another. Landon doesn't wear a wedding ring which means nothing in this day and age where some men don't. Then again, he's roughly Camilla's age, and I sense a romantic history between them.

Unrequited love seems to be a theme around here, although no one mentions love regarding Mach and me.

Myles is decidedly quiet, offering sympathetic smiles and an occasional joke to keep the tension low. "I'd marry you myself if those were the terms of the will."

While identical to Mach in many ways, he's good-looking in his own right. He isn't as firm around the middle as Mach and there isn't an edge in his expression like his brother's. Myles is more playful while protective. Still, he has a commanding presence. In the twenty-four hours I've known Myles, it'd be an honor to be his wife if I were attracted to him, but I'm not. That sounds strange considering how much he looks like Mach, but they aren't the same person, and my loyalty lies with my absentee fiancé.

By twelve-thirty, Landon has secured a marriage license and the services of a justice of the peace. Camilla suggests I return to the house to freshen up. I not only don't have a white dress; I don't have any dress to be married in. I brought a black wrap dress for the funeral yesterday and I'm wearing a somber navy suit for the will reading. Real wedding or not, I'm not getting married in either outfit. I never imagined walking down the aisle in anything other than a white dress. Then again, I never thought I'd get married at my age, and I definitely never pictured marrying Mach.

"I don't have anything to wear," I tell Camilla. She sizes me up. We aren't exactly the same stature with her petite frame and older curves. I'm more upright and angular, taller than her by inches.

"Bliss is the name of a boutique in town. It might not be your style, but the place is one of the properties you'll soon own. It wouldn't hurt to take a look inside. You might be surprised. Just be back by three," Camilla suggests.

Mach has been notified of the time, but he hasn't responded to anyone's texts. He left the truck behind. Then again, I have the keys as he refuses to drive the thing. Using the navigation on my phone, I seek the dress shop.

Bliss is located on Bridge Alley, the main street through the small town of Wrightwood. From the outside, the place lacks appeal, and the merchant sign is atrocious for a specialty shop. Inside the uniqueness of dresses, including a selection of bridal gowns, is a delightful surprise. The layout, however, isn't doing the store justice for the lovely items it carries. If I didn't have another goal today, ways to improve this place would be spinning in my head.

The dress I always envisioned myself wearing isn't something others might expect. I wanted something princess-like with layers of feathers on the skirt and a tight, strapless bodice in contrast. Unfortunately, I don't think this place will have one of those hanging on the rack. That kind of dress needs to remain in my head for a real wedding, if there ever is going to be one for me. Shrugging off the doubts for my future, I tell the salesclerk what I want. "I need a wedding dress for today. For me."

The woman is roughly my age and, thankfully, doesn't give my request a second thought. She eyes me up and down instead. "How do you feel about something non-traditional?"

I have no idea what that means, and she continues before I can ask. "I have a unique dress that's been waiting for the perfect woman to wear it. And I think you're the perfect woman."

With a sales pitch like that, I can see why Bliss is in business. Tanza introduces herself as the owner. She steps into the back of her store and returns with something that has a basic halter bodice and a slim-fit skirt on a full-length gown. The style is classy and classic, and certainly my taste.

"Let me help you into it," Tanza suggests, and I sheepishly follow her to a curtained off section serving as a fitting room.

"Your taller stature is perfect for this piece." She fluffs out the straight material of the skirt to expose deep slits up each side and cigar pants underneath. Slipping into the dress, I spread my legs apart and note how the pants hug my legs like a second skin underneath the skirt. The bodice is form-fitting with a ballerina back of crisscrossing ribbons that tie at the waist. Thin straps cut close to my neck and hold the bodice in place. I can't wear a bra, but cup inserts support my breasts.

"He's going to lose his mind for you in this dress," Tanza whispers behind me.

I stare at my reflection in the mirror. Am I really doing this? Am I really marrying Machlan Wright? Do I want him to lose his mind over me?

I'd prefer if he lost his heart to me.

14

Playlist: "Hooked On A Feeling" – Blue Swede
(from *Guardians of the Galaxy*)

[Mach]

"Where the hell is she?" I glance at my watch for the seventh time in as many minutes. Jane is late, which is so unlike her.

"She'll be here," Landon states from his seat inside the justice of the peace's office. Having friends in high places—or as a Friday night poker buddy—helps get things done quickly in a small town.

I fiddle with the cuff of the shirt I wear beneath my three-piece suit. The same suit I wore to Fischer's funeral. The attire feels prophetic.

"Aw, look how anxious he is as a blushing bridegroom," Myles jests behind me, and I turn on him, although I've sworn to never speak to him again.

"What are you doing here?" I tighten my fists as irritation courses through my blood. This is not how I envisioned getting married. Hell, I never pictured getting married ever again.

"This is where I stood during your first wedding." Myles's eyes match the anger in mine as he stares back at me.

The reminder is like a thousand tacks jabbed into my skin. "Yeah, well, some best man you turned out to be." I turn my back on him.

"Mach, we should talk about what happened." My twin's voice softens.

I don't want to talk to him. Glaring at Landon, I ask, "Why is he here?" The question is inconsequential compared to all the other ones I have. Why didn't Myles inherit this shitshow? Why can't he take a wife and have the town? Why is my inheritance linked with his?

Landon brushes off my question with a shrug. "You need a witness."

"And you can't be that?" My agitation has no boundaries today and Landon is on my list of offenders. My grandfather's attorney. My uncle's old friend. My mother's . . . whatever he is. I didn't miss the lasting looks between Landon and Ma. Just what are they up to? And how do they benefit from this marriage trap?

Landon Hobbs has circled our lives for as long as I can remember. When Ma worked to sweep up hair in the beauty salon, Landon was next door in the barber shop. Yep, the renowned attorney is also the town barber and head of the city council. How's that for a small town? Eventually, Ma learned to cut hair and became an esthetician, offering a full skin and hair care package. She rose up from the ashes, one head of hair at a time, eventually taking over for Trixie of Trixie's Trims.

"I'm here for moral support and to commit perjury by swearing I read a will hours after I originally did so we can get you legally wed and started on your marriage."

"You mean, the project." My inheritance *project*, which includes restoring an entire fucking town. I don't know the first thing about running a town, or rebuilding one, nor do I want this headache. But it seems my top account executive has done what she always does and charmed this little group into escalating this farce to a new level.

And now I'm getting married.

As apprehensive as I am about marrying Jane, I'm more afraid she won't walk through the justice of the peace's door in the next few minutes.

My palms sweat. I spread my fingers then clench them back into fists. I tug at the sleeve of my shirt at the cuff of my suit. I can't believe I'm getting married again, something I swore I'd never do. One and done for me. The wreck at the end of my first marriage was a lesson learned. Trust is a fallacy. Commitment means nothing. Romance truly is dead.

However, nothing is similar to the first time. Strangely, I do trust Jane. She's living through this hell with me. And despite the little twist of fate, in which we will no longer pretend to be husband and wife but actually be joined legally as a couple, she's committed to this project for some reason. As for romance, that's a non-issue with Jane. There's nothing romantic about our situation.

The door opens, and I feel like I can breathe for the first time in hours.

Jane stands there in a dress the color of champagne bubbles. The slim cut hugs her body, highlighting her subtle curves and emphasizing her breasts. Her dark hair is up in that messy-knot twist which allows the short hairs near her neck to curl softly by her elegant throat. The slender column is further emphasized by thin straps near her collarbone. My mouth waters to take a sip of her skin right there. Then nip at the juncture of her neck and shoulder and tear the delicate ribbons free.

I've always considered Jane a beautiful woman but seeing her in that dress, with her head held high and a soft smile on her lips, steals that first breath. My heart patters faster. My dick rises to the occasion. But it's the strange relief that settles under my skin that has me puzzled. My reaction is so much more than I expected.

Ma precedes Jane across the room, and then Jane comes forward carrying a small bouquet of white roses similar to the ones on the nightstand in our bedroom at the house.

Shit. I should have bought her flowers. With limited time and the sudden rush to wed, I'm lucky I found wedding bands.

Jane stops before me, and my mouth is suddenly dry. She's stunning and when she lifts her lids, shyly peering at me, my heart skips a beat.

What is happening to me?

The justice of the peace speaks. "Machlan, please take Jane's hands."

Lifting my hands, palms upright, I'm practically holding my breath as Jane hands her flowers to Ma before reaching for my hands with shaky fingers. Once we touch, the strange relief of seeing her settles into a blanket of comfort. On reflex, I gently squeeze her fingers.

The vows begin. My vision blurs.

Jane's sapphire eyes are turned toward the man reading how we will be joined to love, honor, and cherish one another. Her hands feel small clutched in mine, and without thought, I rub my thumb over her knuckles, unable to stop touching her, confirming her presence. She's really doing this for me. We're really standing here doing this together.

My throat tightens, knowing I shouldn't do this with her, but also knowing there's no one else I want to help me tackle this mess.

Eventually, Jane looks at me, and the officiant asks me if I take Jane to be my wife.

"I do." Eyes still, I hold her gaze. Can she read how grateful I am? Can she see how confused I am as well? When she agrees to be mine, my chest churns with something I haven't felt in a long time. The soft curl of her mouth after her commitment to me turns that stirring inside me into a whirlwind of desire.

When the officiant asks for the rings, Jane's eyes widen as I present her with a silver band. Her voice trembles and her fingers shake when she places a matching ring on my finger, symbolizing our attachment, our commitment, and the idea of never-ending love. Her focus remains on the band of silver gracing her ring finger while the justice of the peace finishes the ceremony.

"By the power vested in me—"

"Not so fast," Ma interjects, causing Jane to flinch and tighten her hold on my hands like she might slip away other-wise. Or maybe I'm holding hers more firmly, afraid to let her go, afraid she'll walk away.

Ma approaches and holds out a long strip of white linen. "In the Scottish tradition, you must bind your hands."

This ritual wasn't performed in my first wedding, so I don't understand why Ma is pushing it now. But when I glance up at Jane, noticing the grin on her face as Ma joins our right hands together and begins to wrap them, I keep quiet.

"Let this cord unite you as one, binding you today and through your tomorrows. May you work beside one another, guide one another, support and love each other. Remember the hand that holds yours today. The heartbeats that belong to only you for always."

Ma places one hand over and one hand under the joining of Jane's and mine. While I'm not certain her words are legal or binding in any manner, something overcomes me as Ma slips her hands away and Jane and I remain tethered together.

"Now, can I pronounce them husband and wife?" the offi-ciant teases.

Ma laughs while dismissingly waving at him. "Pronounce away, Harold."

"You are now husband and wife. May nothing break the bond that has joined you today. You may kiss the bride."

How I'd forgotten this part, I don't know, but Jane's gaze leaps from our bound hands to my eyes. The sapphire gleam in them sparks brighter than any gemstone. I should have bought her an engagement ring. One the color of those dark blue eyes, surrounded by diamonds.

Then I remind myself this isn't real. It's legal but not love.

Reaching for her cheek, I lean forward, pressing my cheek to hers. Rubbing the bristle of my scruff against the softness of her face, another ripple of desire rips through my body.

"Jane," I whisper near her ear. Afraid to kiss her. Afraid to not.

"This is the only wedding kiss I'll ever have, Mr. Wright. Make it a good one."

The challenge in her voice causes me to chuckle and I pull back, dragging out my retreat as our jaws touch before my nose rubs against hers.

"Whatever you say, Mrs. Wright." My mouth lands on hers.

The kiss is nothing I ever expected and more than I ever imagined. Jane is fire and flame, and my body instantly burns. Our mouths move as one like I've fantasized about our bodies. Lips meld. Tongues seek. She's the crispness of a sunny autumn day. The taste of change in the air. The flavor of spice, spirit, and something new. My free hand slips into her hair, fingers digging into the loose, messy knot at the nape of her neck.

Her fingertips scrape my bristly facial hairs.

Our heads shift. The kiss deepens. Gripping her hand bound to mine, I tug her closer to me, not feeling like we are close enough. We step into one another, bodies pressing together, clicking like puzzle pieces. I want to bury myself inside her.

A sharp throat clearing echoes around us.

Breaking apart, Jane and I are breathless. With chests heaving, we stare at one another. The air around us crackles. If we were alone, I'd have her against the wall in seconds, grinding into her, relieving the ache deep inside me for her.

Another short cough resounds.

Unwillingly, I release her hair, but our right hands are still wrapped together.

Her fingers hesitantly slip from my face before her hand lands on my chest.

My heart hammers. What did Ma call Jane?

Acushla. Heartbeat. Pulse.

That can't be true. My reaction to Jane is simply a result of that kiss. A powerful kiss that leaves my mouth thirsty for more and my body in need of the kind of quenching which only Jane can provide.

An excited clap further dissolves the buzz around us, and Jane and I face my mother, her attorney, and my twin. A little dazed and clearly confused, we are congratulated and awkwardly hugged and ushered out of the courthouse.

"I'm so happy for you." Ma pulls me into another embrace. "Enjoy your night."

I have no idea what Ma means but, as I'm still attached to Jane, I follow her because she's being directed by Landon into a waiting car. When the door closes behind me, locking my wife and I in a bubble that instantly fills with sexual tension, I turn to her. She faces me, questions in her eyes along with desire that matches mine.

"Jane." My voice is rough, edgy with need. "One more kiss?"

With her gaze locked on my lips, she chews on her own. "Only in the car?"

My mouth on hers is my answer.

15

Playlist: "Craving You" – Thomas Rhett, ft. Maren Morris

[Jane]

We kiss for an eternity and a millisecond. This kiss is a glorious fall day with hints of autumn spice, leaves dancing in a breeze, and flickering candle-light. And the longest kiss of my life is over too soon.

A soft cough along with a quiet, "We're here," breaks us apart.

Mach's mouth is red, and I'm certain mine matches his. Draped over him as he leans back on the large backseat, he'd tugged me closer to him, dragging me partially over his firm chest. My nipples are sharp peaks, desperate for release from the tightness of my dress which only feels tighter from the ache in my breasts. My panties are damp. My entire body rages with a deep desire to have Mach inside me.

However, we agreed to only one more kiss.

Reality crashes into me as I peer around Mach to glance out the side window. "Where are we?"

Mach cranes his neck to look over his shoulder. He softly chuckles. "A hotel."

The multistoried building tells me we are definitely not in Wrightwood. *A hotel?* Suddenly, nerves return. I can't spend the night in a hotel with Mach. I can't spend another five minutes with him. I'm so fiercely aroused a simple breeze might cause me to spontaneously combust.

Mach watches me retreat. Our eyes lock as my body slowly drags over his. My nipples are so tender, the sudden movement causes my breasts to ache more. The heaviness in them confirms what I already know. I want Mach.

"We're in Charleston," he clarifies, although I didn't ask. "It appears we've been set up for our wedding night."

Oh God. It's bad enough we've shared a bed two nights in a row at his mother's house. While he was drunk the first night, he was quiet the second. Last night, he sent me to bed long before he collapsed beside me similarly to the night before. There was no telling me I was beautiful or tempting him, but at some point, our hands joined again. I woke with my fingers entwined with his.

Mach's gaze moves to my mouth. Without thinking, I touch my lips, fingertips coasting over the well-kissed skin. The corner of Mach's mouth curls. "I like seeing my kiss on you."

My eyes widen, fingertips halting their caress. "How can you see a kiss on someone?"

"Your lipstick is smeared. Your mouth is swollen. I did that to you." With a fingertip, he traces my puffy lower lip while his tongue glides over his own lips. His voice drops when he says, "I can still taste you."

My entire body shivers. Oh God, I want him to taste me. I want him to take my lips, suck on my skin, and taste other places on my body. He's less than a foot away from me and I can still feel his lips against mine, like a phantom kiss—an accessory I'll wear forever.

Mach reaches for the linen binding still connecting our hands, and slowly unwraps the material. The agonizing time he takes feels like an undressing. The sliver of underwear I'm wearing is soaked. My clit pulses. The arousal between my thighs is almost unbearable.

Eventually, Mach crumples up the fabric and tucks it into his pocket like coveted panties. He reaches for the door handle and scoots out of the car, gently dragging me along.

When I stand beside him on the sidewalk, we both stare up at the hotel for a minute. Mach turns to me. "I forgot to tell you how beautiful you look, Mrs. Wright." His eyes roam my body, a slow appreciative perusal, but also like a second undressing. I'm coming out of my skin. My pussy has never throbbed so fiercely, so desperately.

Nearly giddy from arousal, I simper under Mach's charm. "Thank you, Mr. Wright. You're rather stunning yourself."

With my hand still in his, he loops my arm through his and leads me forward. The gesture reminds me of hundreds of times I've seen Mach escorting women to events, and a tightening occurs in my lower belly. *This isn't real.* While legally married, we are not a couple. We aren't in love. We aren't enraptured with one another. This is an arrangement between us. A sort of partnership.

The thought refreshes my goal. I want to be a partner at Impact. My life is in Chicago, working hard days and long nights to brand others' products and influence buyers.

What is my *brand, though? Who am I?* I dismiss the questions. Now isn't the time for self-reflection.

Mach checks us in and then steers us toward a restaurant instead of the room. "I'm starving."

My stomach rumbles in response.

Mach chuckles. "Sounds like you need food, too."

I hardly ate the sandwich Landon bought me earlier and skipped morning tea for the second day in a row. Was it only this morning we'd sat in Landon's office? I am hungry, and maybe eating something will settle my growing anxiety. Once seated in a private alcove near a window, Mach orders a bottle of champagne and immediately orders us each a steak I'm certain costs eighty dollars.

"You said something earlier that struck me." Mach looks at me once the waiter steps away from the table. "You mentioned how you'd only have one wedding kiss. Had you ever considered being married before?"

That hunger in my belly turns to sour turnips at the question. I take a breath to collect my answer. "I always dreamed of a fairytale wedding with a large princess dress," I begin, remembering the feather dress I thought I'd wear. "But the opportunity never arose. I work too much." I try to make light of the fact that my job is my life and a proposal never happened despite years with Ripley. However, I don't want to think about another man tonight. "But let's not share our sad stories."

The seductive curve of Mach's mouth punctuates his agreement. "Alright. Let's not. How about you tell me one fact I don't know about you? Maybe something no one else does." Mach wiggles his brow like I'm about to reveal some deep, dark secret. Other than my years of crush-lust on him, I don't have much hidden.

I tap a finger to my lower lip, the one still tender and swollen. The motion is intended to mean I'm pondering, but the touch of my own mouth distracts me. Mach traced my lip earlier like he could erase that incredible kiss. However, I want more kisses from him. I want this man charming and sweet. I want us to be real, which is a foolish thought and a secret I'll keep.

"I love to dance," I admit.

Mach's brows lift. "Dance? Like what kind of dance?"

"Just dance. I always thought I'd be a ballerina when I was a child, but I was too tall and not very graceful. Now, I crank the music at home and dance around my condo when the mood strikes."

"I need to see this," Mach teases.

He'll never see me shaking my groove thing around my apartment, though. Like a plié turned to a plop, it hits me again this is all pretend.

I clear my throat. "What about you? Something no one knows."

Mach searches my face for an uncomfortably long time before lowering his gaze to my neck. "I've lusted after you from the moment we hired you."

"You . . . what?" *He has?*

"But I knew I could never act on it. Tucker and I have a strict no-fraternizing-with-employees policy for ourselves. We don't want to complicate things at the office."

I nod, knowing all too well how complicated an office romance can get and how devastating it can be when one doesn't work out. "Makes sense." But where does this leave us? We're officially married now, and we work together.

"We have a year to finalize this mission, Jane. And I should send you back to the office to take over for me. I can't go back there yet until I learn more about this mess we're in."

Mess? Right, this marriage to save a town.

"But I also need you here, Mrs. Wright."

The teasing moniker hardly diminishes the ache in my chest. I'm not *really* Mrs. Wright. I'm his wife in name only.

"It's probably best if we don't tell people at the office about us and we stay here for a while longer. I'll talk to Tucker."

What he's saying makes sense, but I'm not happy with the secrecy. Then again, what would we announce? What would be our story? No one in the office would believe we fell in love and spontaneously married.

"I haven't told Mae. I haven't told anyone in my family."

His brows lift while his eyes shutter for a brief second. "They don't know you're married?"

"We've only been married a hot minute. It's not like I had time between finding a dress and actually attending my own wedding." The day's events roll through my head like flipping through photographs. Will reading. Dress shopping. Quick wedding. I ignore the fact Mach didn't actually propose to me, or I don't have an engagement ring. I touch the new ring on my finger, working the plain band up to my knuckle then back down.

This isn't real.

"You need to tell your family." The command comes out a bit sharp for a man calling our marriage *this mess.*

Thankfully, our champagne arrives, and the waiter opens the bottle. He pours us each a glass. Mach lifts his. "To my bride."

For some reason, the toast hurts my heart. I'm not his.

"To the groom." My words are more precise. He isn't mine.

We drink and Mach returns to our previous discussion. "So, we'll stay in Wrightwood a little longer."

"A year?" The details of the will return to my thoughts. A year sounds daunting and considering I have only a weekend's worth of clothing, I'll need to make some arrangements with Mae. Which is another reason to tell my family about my situation. But I also have clients and projects scheduled with Impact. Staying here a year is a disruption to my entire life.

As if a marriage of convenience to my boss isn't.

"Let's take it month by month," Mach interrupts my thoughts as if reading them. "If we need to fly back to the office, we can do that. Maybe I can find a construction firm or contractor to take over the project and all we need to do is check in on the details."

I nod although I don't like this plan. And accepting this is my wedding night, these aren't the topics I thought I'd ever be discussing. Our conversation feels like a working dinner at the office, not a marriage celebration.

When our steaks arrive, we meander through small talk, which I hate, while we eat. Mach learns—*again*—that I have one older brother and two younger sisters. "I was raised by a single mother because our father left when I was roughly seven."

Mach stalls in lifting his fork. "I was raised by a single mother." This I've known for years. "What happened to your father?"

"He didn't want to be one anymore, so he left and never looked back."

"Jesus." Mach lowers his fork.

"What about you?" I ask, curious.

"He was never in the picture. He died before I could meet him."

"Were you young?"

"I was twenty-three when I learned who he was. I was too late to tell him how much I despised him."

Ouch. Although I sympathize a little with the sentiment.

"So your grandfather was your father figure?" I question.

Mach huffs. "Yeah, he wasn't exactly father of the year or grandfather of the century. He didn't openly embrace my mother when she returned home. Granny threatened Fischer, though, and that's how we ended up in the Small House."

Looking out the back of Camilla's home, I've seen the structure where Myles now lives. Without stepping foot inside, it's evident the space is no more than a decent sized, studio apartment. Camilla raising two growing boys in that tight space must have been quite a feat.

"Fischer didn't speak to Ma for years. He ignored us as well, until one day Myles snuck into the main house and ingested some of our grandfather's pipe tobacco. A near-death experience opens your heart a little, I guess, and Myles became a favorite. He was constantly causing trouble, but Fischer turned a blind eye. But me? I could never do anything right and was punished accordingly."

I hate to consider what that might have meant for him as a boy.

"By the time I was a teen, I was too big for the belt. Fischer found other ways to make me suffer."

I'd ask what he means but this discussion has turned depressing, and again, not quite wedding feast conversation. "I'm sorry that happened to you. My granddad was a good man. He was our role model after my dad disappeared. He treated Garrett like he was gold as the only boy, but he was still fair and loving toward us girls." Granddad paid for each of us to go to college, so we didn't have to take out student loans. He'd been a man to save all his pennies for a dream he didn't live to have come true. He wanted to own land and move away from the factory where he'd worked his entire life. Thinking of him gave me immediate resolve to help Wrightwood. I'd hate to see a small community disappear because some big power plant wants to take over the land and use the river. My granddad would have hated that idea. I suspect Mach's grandfather felt the same way despite any other impressions Mach has of him.

"How is it your family owns an entire town?"

Mach sighs. "It's a long story, but the short of it is, the Wrights settled here when the Scots crossed to America. Seen that show *Outlander*? It's something like that."

I snicker. "Have you seen *Outlander*?"

Mach shrugs, and I laugh harder.

"Anyway, my great-great something settled here and built up a small town around the woods. Wright's woods. Wright-wood. They lumbered or raised sheep, or something." Mach dismisses this part of his history. "They loved the rolling hills here, reminding them of the homeland. Most towns develop on a river as a water source plus transportation. Makes sense. The land remained in the family while the businesses changed over time into what they are today. The family owns the buildings, and the shopkeepers pay rent."

"So, if your grandfather wanted to sell off the buildings . . ."

"There are entitlement laws or something similar that restrict the land from being sold outright. I imagine that's why Fischer left the property to the state."

"But he doesn't want the state to have it," I remind Mach. "He wants his town."

"He's dead," Mach snaps, a little too sharply for my liking. "And for some reason, he's given the damn place to me."

"Which you're going to restore." I tip a brow at him. "Because that's why you married me."

Mach pauses on his last bite of steak, staring across the table at me. "Right. And you married me for a partnership." He slows his jaw as he chews his final piece. His reminder stings.

This is a business arrangement.

"*I* married *you* so you can save the town."

"We . . ." Mach waves between us with his fork. "Need to do it together."

"I'm up for the challenge." I mean what I've said. *Tomorrow.* Tomorrow I'll dive into saving Wrightwood. Tonight, I'm still wrapping my head around sitting opposite Machlan Wright as his wife.

16

Playlist: "Run" – Matt Nathanson ft. Sugarland

[Mach]

When dinner ends, we haven't finished our bottle of champagne, but I'm done with this table in a relatively public place. Ma must have organized this portion of the evening. We're headed to the honeymoon suite next.

Inside the room, which hosts a king-sized bed covered in white rose petals, Jane and I stand beside a small table where a new bottle of champagne rests. After popping the cork, I pour us each a glass.

Holding up the flute, I'm ready to toast my bride again when Jane stops me.

"Aren't we supposed to do something special like entwine our arms and take a drink?" She laughs at her explanation, and

I'm reminded of the handfasting Ma did. I'm also reminded the linen is in my pocket.

"Okay." I hold up my arm and allow Jane to wrap hers around mine, but I'm distracted by the thin straps over Jane's collarbone that accentuate her slender neck. Not to mention, the back of her dress reveals her spine down to her waist, and I hadn't seen that portion until our ceremony ended. The pant-skirt combination has had me hard since Jane entered the justice of the peace's office. My dick reached unprecedented hardness during our make-out session on the car ride here.

We're finally alone, and I have a proposition for her. "How do you feel about wrecking that dress?"

Our arms are still linked when Jane glances down at the masterpiece hugging her body. "I only plan to wear it once." Her eyes lift to meet mine. I like her answer.

"To us," I whisper and tip my glass toward my lips.

Only when Jane lifts hers toward her own, I link the base of my flute with hers, forcing it to shift and spill champagne over her open mouth and down her chin.

"What the hell?" Jane mutters, irritation thickening her voice as dribbles of champagne drop onto the silk of her dress. It's wrecked alright, and I plan to ruin it more.

"What a mess," I teasingly chastise. "Let me help you." Leaning forward, I kiss her mouth, licking her lips to remove the spilled bubbly. Next, I suck her chin, tracing the trail of sticky champagne.

"Mr. Wright." My name isn't more than a breathy whisper. All agitation has dispersed. And that title in her smoky, quiet voice is an electric current straight to my cock.

"Jane." My voice teases her name as I pull back from her lips. Wrapping my hand around her back, I tug the ribbons tied at the base of her spine. "It's our wedding night. For one night, let's continue to pretend."

Her brows pinch, hesitation etched between them. "For one night?"

Only in the car? Earlier, her voice was laced with the same puzzled tone.

"Let me do what I want to you," I whisper my demand in her ear before sipping kisses down the side of her throat.

Her body shivers, and her flesh pebbles. "What will you do?"

"Anything you want. Everything I want. You can stop me at any time. We can use a safe word if you wish."

Jane pulls back, her eyes locking on mine as her hand comes to my chest. "Safe word? How about stop?"

I've heard her say *stop* before, although I can't recall when or where. "I'll stop whenever you ask, but I'll also give you more when you beg."

She eyes me another minute. "The dress might be ruined, but don't rip it."

I tip my head, curious why I shouldn't shred the outfit. If she's only going to wear it once, what does it matter? Will she destroy the thing after our arrangement is over? The idea of being over with her, though, sours my stomach. To restore the sweetness, I lift my champagne glass and hold the lip at Jane's mouth. "Drink."

"You're going to spill it on me again, aren't you?"

"Would you like that?"

The blue spark in her eyes answers me. I dribble more liquid than I did the first time and chase the drops, licking along her chin and along the column of her throat before lowering to kiss the stains on her dress.

"Turn around." I've already loosened the slim ribbons at her lower back, and make quick work of unthreading them, exposing her entire back to me. Pressing a hand between her shoulder blades, I bend her forward, so she leans over the small table. Lifting my champagne glass, I trickle more down her spine, then press my lips to her flesh, lapping up the river racing over her skin.

"I want to coat every inch of you in this bubbly, Jane, and celebrate your body."

"Oh God," she whimpers.

Christening her with more champagne, I suck at the stream along her vertebrae. Then I lift for her nape and nip her there.

Her knees buckle.

After setting the champagne back on the table, I skim both hands around her body and slip them inside her dress to cup her breasts. The tight swells fill my hands. Her nipples are sharp and erect.

"Jane, do you have any idea what you do to me?" I'm so hard my head spins. "I need you out of this dress."

Her head shakes as I release her breasts. I massage up her spine and hook my fingers into the delicate straps near her throat. The material easily cascades down her arms.

With her back still to me, I reach for her breasts, now bare and exposed to the coolness of the room, and cup the lush mounds. The perfect swells fit my palms. I tug Jane upward, so she stands against my front, and I glance over her shoulder.

Soft-pink-colored nipples confirmed.

"God, you're stunning." I exhale against her cheek, fixated on the place where thin straps held her dress over her shoulder near her neck. I nip her there again.

Jane moans, throaty and deep.

Keeping her upright by palming her breasts, I knead them, massage their perfection, and tweak those pert nipples.

"Tell me you want me inside you." My voice strains at her ear.

"I want you inside me." Her tone is a whispered plea as she tips her head back, resting it on my shoulder.

I pepper her with kisses, breathing in her summer rain scent.

Her arm reaches back and loops around my head, and then she twists, facing me and crashing her mouth over mine.

The second our mouths meet, it's our first kiss and that car ride all over again. Her hips rock forward. Mine respond. I need to be closer to her.

Ripping my mouth away from hers, I glance at her breasts. "Beautiful." Then, I take one in my mouth, sucking hard, tugging at the roundness, biting the aroused nub. Jane squeaks as I nip her, and I move to the other breast.

Dipping my hand under the skirt panel, I cup between her thighs where I find the silky pants wet and warm at her pussy. I release her breast and stand. "You're soaked."

"For you." Her eyes are hooded, but she isn't drunk on champagne. She's high on my touch.

I plan to take her to a new level.

Jane unzips the skirt's hidden zipper. As the bottom of her dress lowers to the floor, the unveiling reveals the thinnest strip of fabric serving as her panties.

"Jane," I choke. The material is drenched and slipping between her lower lips. "Take that off as well. Leave the shoes on."

Strappy sandals delicately wrap once over her toes and again at her ankle. With her in nothing other than those glittering shoes, I drop to my knees and spread her legs, forcing her to balance against the table behind her. I want to drink from her and use the flat of my tongue to swipe her folds.

With the first lick, Jane cries out. One of her hands reaches for my head, threading her fingers through my hair. She rocks forward as I suck at her clit before sinking my tongue into her. Jane is a crisp fall blend, rich and robust, and I never want to stop sipping her.

"Mach," she whimpers, rocking faster. She mentioned

dancing earlier, and I want her to move over me, but first, I want her to explode on my tongue. I add fingers to this slow, sensuous tango, slipping into her warm, wet heat. *Fuck*. She's a mess of arousal and I need more of her.

I pull away.

"No." Jane grips my hair. Her lids are lowered. Her mouth agape. "Mach, I need this."

"Don't worry, Mrs. Wright. I'm going to take care of you." I lead her to the bed, guide her to sit and reach for my glass of champagne again.

Jane's legs spread on their own. "Mach," she croons. A deep ache fills her voice.

While tipping her back on the bed, I fill my mouth with champagne. Then I lower between her thighs and release the sparkling liquid.

"Mach," she screams as wetness seeps over her, dripping between her thighs.

Eagerly, I lick and lap at her, placing two fingers inside her heat and loving the mess. She's sticky and sweet, and quenching a thirst I didn't know existed inside me.

Her feet lift to the edge of the bed, heels digging in. My name comes on a hallowed cry once more before her body submits.

I want to witness her falling apart, but I also don't want to break the spell she's under. As she trembles against my tongue, I suck and slurp and savor every shiver until she stills.

Quickly, I stand and stare down at her sated body. "Beautiful." Her head tips to the side. Her lids are half-mast. Her breasts lift and lower.

Tugging at my own clothes, I nearly rip my vest. I remove my shirt over my head and shuck off my pants, kicking off my shoes before removing my socks.

On bent elbows, Jane perches upright and watches me strip.

"*Mach*-nificent," she purrs, taking in the bright ink covering my arms and under my collarbone. "You're beautiful, Mr. Wright."

Jesus. The compliment spurs me on. I lean forward and drag a finger along that sweet valley between her breasts. "I like this spot on you."

Reaching for the champagne, I pour droplets along the path my finger drew, then lower to coat my tongue in the bubbly again. Filling my mouth once more, I rain over her breast and lick her clean. Then repeat the blessing on her other swell.

With her nipples hard as diamonds, I reach under her arms and press her up the bed, climbing over her as she moves. Her legs spread, and I settle between them, my dick dancing against the mess we've made of her. Gripping myself, I drag my heavy cock along her slick slit, teasing her clit and torturing me.

"We're married, Jane, which means we don't need protection unless you want it."

"It's . . . I haven't been with anyone in a long time."

"Define long?"

"A few years."

How has this incredibly sensual woman gone that long without sex? "I'm clean. I had a check-up six months ago and haven't been with anyone since before that."

A heavy pause falls between us, the awkwardness of the necessary conversation stealing the moment.

"What about getting pregnant?" She's in her forties, but it could still happen.

Jane just shakes her head on the pillow and shifts her eyes away from me.

"Hey." I grip her jaw, forcing her attention back to me. "We can talk about that later, okay?"

She nods and I lean down to kiss her, taking my time while my cock is screaming for more. Slowly, the intimacy returns, and I grip myself once again, guiding my needy cock through her sleek heat.

"That feels so good," she strains. Her head tips back. Her arousal builds again.

"I know what will feel better." Bare. Raw. Real. I slip into her, and my eyes shut, blocking out anything that could steal my attention away from this incredible moment where Jane and I connect. I haven't been without coverage in forever. The flame of Jane, the wetness, the completion, is too much. I easily slide in and glide back out, repeating the motion over and over. I'm coated in her essence, and I steal a glance, watching as I disappear into her, making us one.

Fuck. What is happening to me? I like this too much.

Jane's eyes are closed. Her head back.

"Look at me." I want to see those sapphire gems light up as I take her over the edge.

Her lids snap open, and she holds my gaze as my hips rock. Back and forth, I move. The tension builds. My lower back tightens. My balls seize, but I want another release from Jane while she's looking at me.

Slipping my hand between us, I rub my thumb on her sensitive nub.

"What . . . oh my . . . that's . . ."

I love that she's losing her mind over me. I love how close I feel to her, how close I am to spilling inside her.

"Jane," I warn. "I'm getting close."

Her leg hitches over my hip, sliding up my ass and wrapping over my lower back. The position opens her up more.

"Fuck." I grind. Hips thrusting. Cock surging. I slip to my knees and clench Jane's hips, tugging her lower body up my thighs. I'm deeper, moving faster and return my thumb to that bundle of nerves. "Claim me, baby."

I want her fucking dripping over me.

Jane locks her legs around my back and stills, tipping her

hips upward the slightest bit, and I feel her come undone. She clenches. She clutches. She wrings me out, and I go off inside her, releasing a fountain of pent-up desire. No fantasy compares to this moment, this release, this need to fill her up and do it again.

Only for tonight?

One night will never be enough.

17

Playlist: "Heaven" – Kane Brown

[Jane]

After rich food, sweet champagne, and two orgasms that rock my world, I'm exhausted. The events of the day catch up with me, and I fight the emotions threatening to overwhelm me. Threatening to remind me this isn't real.

I'm also sticky in ways I've never imagined.

"You okay?" Mach asks as I sit upright a little too fast. His hand comes to my lower back and swipes up my spine.

"Just . . . need a minute to clean up." I don't look back at him, fearing one look will bring on tears. I don't know why I'm suddenly reacting as I am, sensitive and scared. I'm not typically emotional, but my body quakes, a sure sign of a breakdown coming. I slip off the bed and enter the bathroom. With the shower heating, I look at myself in the mirror. Evidence of

Mach's kisses swell my lips. My nipples are still peaked and tight. One breast bears a purple mark from Mach's suction.

With the bathroom steaming, I don't bother removing the hairband or pins holding my hair in place but step into the shower. Facing the spray, I allow the warm water to wash the sudden tears down the drain.

"Hey," Mach says behind me.

I jump. I didn't hear him enter the bathroom. The shower doesn't have a door but a glass panel wall with an opening at the end.

His inked arms circle me, and his mouth comes to my neck. "What's this?" The tenderness in his voice is disarming.

"Today's just been a lot, I guess." I swipe my cheeks, keeping my face to the spray as I brush back the tears and hope they'll simply disappear in the moisture of the shower.

"Only for one night." His quiet voice rumbles against my skin. "Let it all go tonight, okay?"

Tomorrow. I nod.

Mach kisses the side of my neck. Another kiss presses below my ear. His hand cups my chin, and he turns me until our mouths meet. He kisses me, slow and sweet.

This kiss feels like how a husband might savor his new bride, but I quickly dismiss the thought.

Our lips come together and pull apart, seek each other, and separate once more. Over and over, he softly peppers my mouth with tender kisses until he leans away and reaches for my hair.

"Let me help you." His fingers weave through the knot, gently searching for the pins. Then he removes the band. My hair tumbles downward, and Mach spins me, so the shower spray hits my back. Standing before me, he finger-combs my hair, spreading it under the warm water. Next, he reaches for the hotel shampoo and lathers up my locks, massaging my scalp before rubbing at my nape.

"Washing someone's hair is one of the most romantic gestures ever," I whisper.

"Romantic?" Mach states in mock mortification. Slowly, he smiles. "I'll remember that the next time the shampoo girl at QuickCuts washes mine."

I choke on a laugh. "You don't use QuickCuts." Leveling a glare at him, I fight the spur of jealousy that another woman touches his hair wherever he does get a haircut.

"I don't have a shampoo girl, either." Mach watches me as he continues to massage my head. "I go to an old-fashioned barber shop."

I smile weakly and we fall silent a second as he rubs my scalp.

"We never had cake."

The out-of-nowhere comment makes me laugh. "I'm not really a cake woman. I prefer pie."

Mach stills his fingers, then slowly removes them from my hair and tips my head back to rinse the suds under the spray. "Five facts. I already know this one about you. Apple crumble with ice cream is your favorite."

The idea that he knows my favorite pie surprises me. Maybe it wasn't just luck the other day in the diner when he picked up the last piece for me.

"How do you know that?" I whisper-strain.

"I pay attention to details." His eyes lock on mine for an intense second before he clears his throat.

"I'm kind of a pie man myself," he adds. While one hand works my hair to rinse it, the other coasts down my middle, along the valley between my breasts that he'd confessed he liked. Straight between my thighs he slides to emphasize his preference for pie.

"Mach," I moan. "Again?"

His fingers stroke lightly over my folds, tickling me, winding me up.

"It seems my body is saying yes." My wrist is encircled, and Mach draws my arm forward until my fingers brush against the firmness of him. I wrap my hand around his hard shaft. "I normally need more time to recover."

We aren't young, and I've heard it can take a man a little longer to perform a second time as he ages. Thus, the invention of little blue pills. But as I take my time to stroke Mach's heavy dick, he grows within my palm until he's long, hard, and ready once more.

His fingers intensify in the pressure, giving me the pleasuring friction I need.

"If I only get one night, I'll need you more than once." Mach kisses my shoulder and then my neck.

I purr in agreement as we lazily stroke one another until my breath starts to hitch. Mach removes his fingers, and I squeeze him extra hard, wanting his touch back.

"Turn around, baby," he commands.

I release him, spinning toward the wall.

Mach reaches around me, quickly returning his fingers to my clit while bending me forward. "Tell me you want me inside you again."

"I want you inside—"

He surges into me, taking my breath. I pitch forward, but he tugs me back to him. With my hands braced on the tile, I leverage myself to match the rhythm he sets of rushing into me on repeat. He's suddenly wild, and the rapid slap of us connecting meshes with the pattering of the shower. His fingers work my clit as fast as he slips in and out of me.

"Mach," I choke as the tension builds quickly, and I recognize him reaching the end.

"Gotta come, baby," he groans behind me.

I rock back, dragging him to the hilt inside me. "Yes."

"Not without you."

The comment startles me, and I concentrate harder to get

where I need to go. He pinches my clit, and I scream as that does the trick to send another bubbling release. As I pulse around Mach's heaviness inside me, he pumps inward—once, twice, a third time—and then stills. The strain in his grunt echoes off the tile around us. One hand holds my hip, keeping me in place. The other cups me, where he enters me, fingers spread to accommodate his entrance. The position feels intimate and different, as if he's holding himself within me.

His forehead comes to the back of my head. "Fuck, you're better than champagne."

Feeling drunk on my husband, I laugh.

WHEN WE CLIMB INTO BED, Mach pulls the covers over our naked bodies and tugs me into his chest. His body molds to mine as my back absorbs the heat of him from the shower.

"We didn't dance," Mach sleepily mutters against my nape. For a man who doesn't believe in romance, he's certainly a stickler for wedding rituals.

Then again, he's done this before. I'm not the first Mrs. Wright. I'm the good-enough-for-right-now wife. With such heavy thoughts, I close my eyes, pushing away the negativity.

Tomorrow, I will accept the truth. Tonight, I'm going to bask in the man at my back. My hand rests on his forearm braced against my breast and I absorb the heat of his skin while noticing the unevenness of it. Small bumps and jagged ridges blend within the ink on his arms. In the darkness of the room, I'm not able to inspect the colorful design or the subtle dips of puckered ridges over his arm.

Did something happen to him? Are these scars?

My thoughts drift. Tomorrow, I'll ask.

I HAVE no idea what time it is when I eventually wake. Mach has twisted away from me, but his ankle hooks over mine. I roll to face him.

Laying on his back, the sheet falls to his waist, and I admire the view in the dim light of the room. We never closed the room darkening shades. The city lights of Charleston reflect through the glass and highlight Mach's features. His strong forehead. His solid nose. The scruff on his jaw.

Again, I trace a finger down the bumps on his arm hidden by ink. Mach doesn't stir.

My gaze wanders to the swirl of hairs on his chest and the dark trail leading below the sheet. Gently, I pull back the covering and admire the view. Mach's dick is a piece of art. Long, thick, and powerful when hard. My channel clenches. My lower lips flex. Being with him has been an experience.

Lazily, I stroke over his hip, and his leg flinches. I still my motions, glancing up at his face. He remains asleep, and I don't intend to wake him, but I want to explore this masterpiece. *Mach*-apiece. I'll add the new nickname to my list, along with a snapshot of all that he is.

Only one night.

"Jane," Mach groans without opening his eyes. He's hardening. Taking a risk, I stroke my fingertips up his length. His leg twitches, and I bite my lip to suppress a chuckle. Shifting, I slip lower on the bed. As if Mach knows where I'm headed, he spreads his legs, allowing me to climb between them and take him in my mouth. My tongue twirls around the head before lapping once across the seeping slit. Opening wide, I take him to the back of my throat.

Mach curses. His hips jolt, forcing him deeper, and I choke.

"Sorry," Mach mutters, petting my hair while his other arm covers his eyes. His fingers comb through my long hair as I return to sucking him, savoring the thickness. Then I release Mach with a pop.

"Hey," Mach grumbles as I scoot forward and reach for the flute of champagne on the nightstand. The bubbles are gone, and the drink is flat.

"You wouldn't?" The challenge in Mach's tone only encourages me.

"All's fair with champagne and cocks."

Mach groggily laughs.

I wet my mouth before lowering to his thick shaft. Liquid streams from my lips. I lick along his length, chasing the dribbles until I fill my mouth with the solidness of him.

"Jesus," Mach grunts while my tongue teases and my cheeks hollow. Suddenly, he sits upright and tugs me off him. "Need to be inside you."

"I wasn't finished," I grumble.

His mouth covers mine in a kiss that's hard and deep. His tongue plunges forward as he falls back, bringing me with him. My breasts collide with his firm chest. His hands clap on the back of my thighs, spreading my legs so I straddle him. His mouth doesn't leave mine as the thick wedge of him rests against the heat of me.

Abruptly, I release his mouth and sit upward, fingertips pressing into his chest. Mach moves me by my hips, so I coast down the length of him, my folds encasing him.

"Feels so good," I purr. We rock back and forth a few more times before I tip up on my knees and adjust him. Placing the crown at my entrance, I lower, taking my time to draw him into me.

Mach closes his eyes and hisses as I envelop him until he's fully inside me. I move only my hips, clenching and clutching. His gaze returns to me, latching onto my eyes before lifting his head to watch me move over him.

"You're perfection," he mutters, his voice straining. His palm lands low on my belly until his thumb stretches toward my clit. He rubs delicious circles where I need him as I undulate over him. Reaching for my breasts, I draw a fingertip around the swells then pinch my nipples in tandem.

"Fuck," Mach moans.

My entire body relaxes as I let loose and move. My hips roll back and forth. I drag my hands up my chest and lift my hair. Closing my eyes, I'm lost in the moment, feeling complete.

"So fucking stunning." Without looking at him, I know he's watching me.

My mouth hangs open. I move faster. "Mach . . . I . . ."

Whatever's happening to me, it's going to be big. The flutters in my lower belly. The curl of my toes. My hips move of their own accord, and suddenly I'm soaring. I'm coming so hard, I fall forward, squeezing and gripping on his dick deep within me. My fingertips scrape through the hairs on his chest. I come undone like I never have before. This is my fourth orgasm in less than seven hours, and nothing has ever felt like this one.

I'm shattered, and then Mach flips us. My legs are tugged upward, knees near my shoulders. Mach holds my shins as he pummels into me, muttering things I can't comprehend. I don't think I've stopped coming, or maybe a second one trailed the first. My head rolls on the pillow until Mach grunts, "Fuck."

Then he stills his body while his dick goes off inside me. Every jolt, every jut, every jet satisfying me.

He collapses, and I take his weight as he mumbles into my neck. "I always knew being with you would be fire, but I never expected it to be so explosive."

I chuckle, and Mach twitches inside me. We both freeze, and then we laugh again.

He's *Mach*-ilicious.

18

Playlist: "I'm Not In Love" – 10cc
(from *Guardians of the Galaxy*)

[Mach]

Reality hits hard when my phone alarm goes off in the morning. The driver told me he'd return at nine to bring Jane and me back to Wrightwood. We don't have anything to wear other than her ruined wedding dress and my three-piece suit. Before we leave, I ask Jane if she wants to shower, but she declines.

"Maybe when we get back to the house, and I can put on something clean."

In the meantime, she'll smell like us—champagne and sex. Needing a minute to regroup, I excuse myself. Last night was insane. Sex with Jane was so much more than I imagined. The chemistry between us was what I'd always fantasized. The emotional connection was what I hadn't expected.

When I found Jane quietly crying in the shower, something broke inside me. This strong woman always holds it together. In the eight years I've known her, I've never once seen her break down. But yesterday was a lot. The will. The wedding. Our night together.

Only one night.

As I stand in the shower this morning, all the reasons why Jane and I cannot be more flood me.

Tracy. Myles. The town. The partnership.

What Jane and I have is a business arrangement. Sure, it's gone a little too far and I've made an empty promise, but we can get back on track. The sooner we figure out the issues with the town, the sooner I can get away from Myles and the memories of Tracy. Then, I can deal with Jane.

One year. For three-hundred and sixty-five days, Jane needs to remain my wife. She won't need a partnership as she'll inherit one million dollars. I don't want the money. She can have it all. I'll consider it a settlement for sticking out this farce.

Only last night didn't feel fake to me.

And it's all the more reason to keep Jane where she belongs —at arm's length from me. I can't love someone like her. I can't ever love anyone again. I loved Tracy. *She* was my person, my heart, and she's gone. Tracy took my heart with her.

The reminder puts me in a sour mood. When I find Jane sitting in her soiled wedding dress on the edge of the bed, that mood turns to burning acid.

How could I do this to her? With her?

"We should probably get going." My pants are wrinkled. My shirt hangs open. I sit on the edge of the bed myself, keeping a wide distance from Jane as I snag my socks and shoes.

Our one night is over. I'm treating her like all the other women I've dated over the years, but this is for the best.

Fact, Jane said to me. *You're a serial dater.* Intimacy issues.

She wasn't wrong. I hate liars and cheats as much as she

seems to, and I am always upfront with a date, thus no repeats. One and done because I can't risk becoming invested in anyone again. I know my heart. I'm a possessive fuck. I love hard, which means it's better not to love at all.

"Once we get back to town, maybe we should divide and conquer, walk through Bridge Alley and speak with the business owners." I have no idea why I'm mentioning the project or what I'd even say to the local townsfolk, but I need to distract myself and dissolve the awkward tension between Jane and me. She's eerily quiet. Everything in me wants to tug her back on the bed, enter her again and again, and call in sick . . . for a week.

But I won't.

Work is what we both need. Then we can get out of this mess.

I stand once my socks and shoes are in place. Stepping around Jane, I slip on my vest and hold out my jacket for her.

She gazes up at me from her seated position on the bed. "Why are you like this?" Her voice is sad and soft.

I don't have a single answer for her. The reasons are vast.

Jane slowly stands before me, staring me down despite the desperation in her eyes. "Why am I afraid the second we walk out that door, everything will change?"

"We need to save a town so we can go back to who we are."

"Who are we?" Jane's voice is too quiet.

I only stare back at her, afraid to admit all the feelings rumbling inside me—who I want her to be and what I know she shouldn't mean to me.

Jane steps forward. Her hand comes to my chest.

My heart actually hurts under her touch.

Acushla. The term is wrong. Jane cannot be my pulse.

"Kiss me," Jane demands.

A heavy pause falls between us, and I recall her challenge at our wedding. I loved her challenge. *This is the only wedding kiss I'll ever have, Mr. Wright. Make it a good one.*

In a year, Jane will be free to marry again. She could have another wedding kiss, a nicer ceremony, and a better man.

"Jane," I whisper, eyes avoiding hers, but she grips my chin with strength I don't expect.

"Convince me this was nothing."

At first, I can't. The second Jane steps closer and wraps her arms around my neck, I'm giving in for one more minute. One more thrust of my tongue and lap over her lips. One more taste of that sweet mouth that had sucked my dick with champagne in her throat. One more—

Then I still. My mouth holds firm. I remove my hands from her hips and clench them into fists.

Jane freezes against me. She pulls back, hands slowly slipping from my shoulders. "Calling you Volde-*Mach* doesn't do you justice. It's an insult to the leader of the death eaters."

Her slur couldn't be more accurate. I hate myself at the moment.

If only Fischer hadn't been such a dick and put that bullshit clause about a wife in his will, we wouldn't be in this position.

And if only I'd been able to steal from Death, my past would be different.

19

Playlist: "Blue Ain't Your Color" – Keith Urban

[Jane]

"**Y**ou're married!" my younger sister Mae shrieks into the phone two mornings after my wedding.

So much for Mach's demand *I* tell my family.

Since our truly awful parting kiss and the severe ripping of my heart, I've hardly seen my new husband. We returned to Wrightwood in silence. I couldn't look at him despite the soft cry of my name once we arrived at his family home. Looking back always means you're looking in the wrong direction, my youngest sister Lindee once told me. Upon entering Camilla's house, we found the place full of family and well-wishers for a wedding brunch.

"Shit," Mach had muttered behind me. That was certainly one word for our uncomfortable entrance in day-old wedding clothes. Thankfully, I was able to beg off a few minutes to shower and change, leaving Mach to tackle those gathered.

In the shower, I was torn between wanting to wash away how used my body felt and wishing to keep every mark, every kiss intact for an eternity. The scalding water did its damage, though, ridding my skin of Mach's touch and slightly warming the hard freeze within my veins.

I like seeing my kiss on you. Jesus, he was such a good liar. Had he held his eyes still when he spoke those words to me? I couldn't remember. I was in such a kiss-drunk haze I didn't know any better than to follow him wherever he might have led me.

Stupid shepherd. Stupider sheep.

Because where he led me was a night of unbelievable bliss and unhealable heartbreak the following morning.

"So, Tucker told you," I respond to Mae. My voice is lackluster with the waning enthusiasm of both my body and my spirit.

"He did." Mae laughs through the phone. "But now I want to hear your side of the story."

"There's not much to tell." How could I explain myself? Did I say I was doing Mach a favor? Did I tell her it was all an act? Did I mention that this would make me partner? The idea made me feel like I'd sold myself to the devil, and in many ways I had. Volde-*Mach*. I needed a new term for him. He was worse than innocent Harry Potter's nemesis. He was worse than Darth Vader, Darth Maul, and any other Darth out there. In my opinion, Mach defined the dark side.

I hated how much he had hurt me.

To my dismay and surprise, Mach made it to our bed last night. After our wedding brunch, a few men convinced him to join them for drinks at a place in town called Trophy's.

He didn't get a proper bachelor party, Myles had mocked. Did

Myles have any inkling to the bachelor-ness of his brother? Sleeping around, breaking hearts was all in a night's work for Super-*Mach*, the anti-hero.

At some uncertain hour, Mach had fallen next to me on the old spring mattress. He'd turned toward me, but I'd refused to look over my shoulder at him. The moment reminded me of nights with Ripley near the end of our relationship. An end I hadn't seen coming.

Again, stupidest lamb in the flock.

For an intelligent woman and smart businessperson, I'm dumb about love. And sex. I was spot on in my five facts about Mach. He valued honesty. He lacked intimacy. He was upfront about what he wanted, and he didn't want me.

Only one night. I'd gotten the memo loud and clear the following morning.

The interesting thing about Mach coming to our bed last night though, was by this morning, his ankle was wrapped over mine like it had been when we fell asleep on our wedding night. In fact, both his ankles held my leg hostage, curling around mine like a manacle. I should have kicked his feet free of touching mine, but instead, I'd taken a foolish moment to absorb his heat, enjoy skin to skin, before slipping out of bed.

"It's so irresponsible of you." Mae's chuckle snaps me back to the moment. "I mean, maybe irresponsible is the wrong word. Just spontaneous. I'm so proud of you."

Pride is the last emotion I have at the moment.

"Why wasn't Tucker at the funeral?" I already know why he couldn't attend our wedding. Six hours to initiate a plan and implement it isn't enough time to hop a flight to West Virginia.

"Mach was adamant he needed Tucker at the office. We're in Chicago now."

My sister owns a flower shop and garden center in a small town in northern Michigan. Mae's Flowers is her joy next to her two grown boys. Since Mae and Tucker have declared their love for each other, Tucker spends a large portion of his time working remotely from my sister's home. With Mach's absence, it makes sense Tucker should be in the office.

"What did Tucker tell you about Mach and me?"

Mae sighs. "He mentioned Mach was excited to be married to you. Tucker is surprised but just as thrilled as I am." My sister pauses. "I didn't know you two had hooked up."

Oh, we'd hooked up alright. *Hook, line, and sink me in that river.* The words are perfect for a country love song.

"Yeah, it was kind of a last-minute thing." I didn't know what direction to take this conversation. I didn't know how much information I could, or should, share. While neither Mach nor I saw our current status coming, we still need to present a united front. At least in front of our clients, which happen to be the entire town of Wrightwood.

The idea sparks some energy, reminding me our arrangement is business. I can do this. I can get through our situation if I focus. If I had to stand by and watch Ripley do what he did to me, I can handle this heartbreak as well. Then again, the current ache in my chest feels so much worse. The cheerleading act isn't exactly working but, if I give myself this pep talk every day, the lie might eventually sink in.

We are saving a town. That is the plan.

The idea adds a little more *umph* to my self-motivation speech. This could be good for me. I love a challenge.

And you'll be partner after this year. The statement isn't as inspiring as it should be. For eight years, a partnership has been my personal end-goal. A lot of things can happen in a year, and a year out of the office is a long time. But as Mach said, we can take things month-by-month. For now, I need a minute-by-minute distraction because working side-by-side with Mach for three-hundred and sixty-five days is going to be hell. Like devastating to my soul because I now know what he feels like inside me and how he can kiss and the romantic way he is without realizing he's being romantic.

"Mae, I hear Mach calling me for breakfast. Can I call you back a little later?" The lies are adding up and I hold my breath, surprised at how easily they roll off my tongue.

Like the one where I convince myself I don't want Mach.

"No more Volde-*Mach*, huh? I'm so happy for you," Mae gushes through the phone. She is the romantic among us Fox sisters, wanting the fairy tale of husband and home. She got it alright, but along with her marriage came years of misery. Her kids and her business are her greatest achievements, she'd told me once. Her happily-ever-after came after her divorce.

Maybe mine will too.

One year.

"Yeah. Happy," I mutter.

"Jane?" Mae pauses.

I don't want her to worry about me. I'm the worrier in the family. I'm the responsible one. As she pointed out, spontaneity isn't synonymous with Jane. I organize. I strategize. I schedule.

And right now, I need a plan.

"Talk later, okay, Mae?"

Mae sighs. "Sure. Talk later."

～

I DON'T BOTHER SEEKING Mach. I look for Camilla instead.

"I need a place to use as an office."

"Anything you need, dove." She beams a smile at me that could paint the sky in rainbows. I shouldn't forgive her for her part in this farce we are playing, but I can't help liking her. With her hands clasped before her, she stares at me with eyes that match her son's, only hers are filled with hope. "My father had an office here."

Her voice drops a little at the mention of her dad. Their

father-daughter relationship isn't something that's been discussed. Other than Mach opening up to me on our wedding night, that's all the information I have about Fischer and Camilla. My granddad came to the rescue of his daughter when her deadbeat husband left her with four children. Obviously, the situation between Camilla and Fischer was different. He'd ostracized his daughter. He hadn't supported her family. And in the end, Fischer Wright hadn't left her—or her brother—this town. *Good ole Granpa gifted things to Mach.* Leaving something so vital to the community to the family's black sheep didn't make sense.

"I'm so sorry again about the loss of your father. Were you close?" Mach has hinted they were outcasts, but the people I'd met during the funeral were more than sympathetic with Camilla. There's no way an entire town could pretend the empathy expressed during the funeral service or the luncheon that followed. Most well-wishers were good-naturedly laughing with Camilla and making plans to see her at book club, knitting night, and a wine tasting festival.

"My father and I had a strained relationship." Camilla hesitantly smiles. "But I forgave him. Living a life without forgiveness makes for a difficult path."

I nod. "Myles and Mach appear to have a strained relationship as well." Was I fishing for information? Absolutely. I needed some answers for what I was dealing with between the brothers.

"Ah. Another example of a bumpy road." Camilla's smile falters.

I'd love to ask for details, but this is something Mach should be the one telling me. It's his story. I reach for her arm and squeeze. "Another time." I don't need all the answers in one day.

Camilla's shoulders sink in relief. "I use the office for my things, but I'm happy to give it up to you. Or we can share it."

The hesitancy in her voice does not convince me sharing her space is her preference.

"How about the dining room table? I don't want to continue to impose." Considering the imposition Mach and I could be for a year, I add, "Mach and I should probably find a place of our own."

Camilla's frown turns upside down, and she's back to beaming a full wattage rainbow of hope at me. "A place? Here? I know the perfect house."

Oh boy. "Well, you can share that information with your son. In the meantime, I'm going to set up a few things in the dining room. Then I'm going to take a walk into town."

Divide and conquer, Mach suggested.

"Mach said the meeting went well last night," Camilla adds.

"What meeting?" I pause after taking a step away from her.

"He went to a planning meeting. City council president. Director of the business district. The mayor."

I frown. "I thought he had a bachelor party."

Camilla's eyes widen. "Bachelor party? What does he need a bachelor party for? He's been partying his entire life. Plus, he's not a bachelor anymore." Camilla pats my arm like I'm the virginal bride no longer with a precious seal intact.

"He didn't mention the meeting," I mutter. We haven't exactly spoken.

Camilla dreamily smiles, glancing in the direction of the dining room. "The two of you at my dining room table will feel like old times."

"Old times?" An unsettling brick slowly sinks to my belly before Camilla even explains.

"Yes, when Myles, Mach, and Tra—" She quietly gasps, and her fingertips cover her lips. "When the boys were young and had friends over to study. Now, you're just bigger kids with more important work to complete."

If my heart wasn't so busy hammering, I'd ask about the

person whose name she cut off, but somehow, I know it without needing an answer.

Mach's wife sat at that table with him. She wasn't just his first wife but a teenage sweetheart. The realization is one more splinter of my heart when I didn't think it could be shattered any further.

20

———————

Playlist: "Yours" – Russell Dickerson

[Mach]

Jane wouldn't look at me, but worse, she wouldn't speak. Her behavior should have felt like a typical day at the office. She could run hot and cold, and I enjoyed that aspect of her temperament. Her silence now was more than I could bear, though.

That damn morning after. I should have kissed her back, proving to her our wedding night meant something to me. However, I didn't respond to her *because* our night meant too much. The way I feel about Jane I haven't felt since Tracy, and it's . . . frustrating.

"Is that Jane?" Landon asks as I sit in the barber's chair.

"Where?" I turn my head toward the window of The Barber Shop. A simple name for a simple place in the heart of Wrightwood.

"Whoa," Landon cries out. He stands with the beard trimmer in hand, arms up. "Warn a man."

Despite trimmers at my throat, I didn't give a second thought to what Landon was doing when I swiveled to catch a glimpse of my wife.

"Where did you see Jane?" Sunshine streams through the window causing a clear view of the street, but I don't see her.

"Walking on the other side of the street."

Shit.

"I take it wedded bliss is going well," Landon teases, resting a hand on my shoulder to settle me in place before returning to the heavy scruff on my face. I should have had a trim and a haircut before my wedding day. I should have handled a lot of things differently forty-eight hours ago.

"How did I get into this mess?" I mutter, casting my gaze to my boots.

Landon clicks the trimmer on again. "What mess? Marriage?" He tips my head back to clip along my jaw. "You can't tell me being married to that woman is a hardship."

Glad to see that even in his late sixties, Landon still recognizes a good-looking woman. Unfortunately, I don't want him noticing how hot *my wife* is.

I want to be the only one aware of that ass and how it feels under my hands. Or those breasts and how they fill my palms. Or her mouth that kissed me like I was everything to her.

Deflecting a discussion about Jane's physical assets, I snort. "She's strong-willed."

"Huh. Sounds like another woman I know." Landon meets my gaze in the reflection of the mirror. He arches a brow for emphasis.

I know exactly who he means. "How do you and Ma fit in this farce?"

"Farce?" Landon crooks a smile. "I was simply your grandfather's attorney. And let me assure you that document is solid."

"So you knew the details in the will. But isn't there some attorney-client confidentiality that slipped your mind when you told Ma about me needing a wife?"

"I don't know what you're talking about." Landon's smile curls into an all-knowing grin.

"Then tell me this. Why did he do it?"

Landon stops trimming and looks at me through the reflective glass. "Only that old man knows his reasons. But if I had to guess, I think he thought it was time for you to come home. Time to make amends with your brother. And time for your heart to move on."

My forehead furrows. "Are you serious? Fischer never forgave anyone. The only hatchet Fischer would like to bury was one in my father's back. And I'm not certain dear ole Granpa had a heart."

"Son, every heart loves differently. I don't believe old Fischer didn't have a heart. He just didn't always recognize the beat of it."

Good God, Landon sounds like Ma and her fucking *acushla* thing.

"What's going on with you and my mother?" I tip up my chin, risking Landon nicking me.

He stills, lowering his gaze. "Your mother and I are old friends."

"Uh-huh. And?"

Landon pats my shoulder, glancing back up at me in the mirror. "And nothing more to tell."

"Something else slip your memory, old man?" I tease.

"Not a thing about your mother ever left my memory."

That's what I thought. But does Landon have a crush on Ma now? As long as I've known him, he was married to Cecelia, a teacher at the elementary school. Their children were younger than Myles and me, so we didn't run in the same crowd. As bastard boys, we wouldn't have been welcome in their social sphere anyway. Cecilia died a few years ago.

Landon finishes trimming my facial hair in silence, and my mind drifts to memories I've tried to forget. Being home has pushed everything to the forefront of my brain. Tracy Evans being the center of most recollections. My high school sweetheart wasn't in the same stratosphere as Myles and me either. She was sweet and good and kind but wanted a walk on the wild side with the town bad boys. This did not please her daddy, the local sheriff.

But the heart wants what it wants, and when it can't have it, that pesky organ becomes more determined to have the forbidden.

We snuck around, keeping our relationship a secret. Then she followed me to WVU. Everything came out when I asked her to marry me, and she accepted. Life fell apart when I wanted to leave this town in my rearview mirror. And Tracy didn't.

"So, what's the plan?" Landon interrupts my thoughts, and I'm grateful for the distraction.

"The sooner we can assess everyone's needs, the faster we can get this project done." We have ten locations in town, plus the local restaurant, the old bait and tackle shop, and a park.

"And get back out of here." His West Virginian mountain accent drops deeper as he stands before me, assessing his work on my face.

"Exactly."

Landon shakes his head and leans against the counter behind him. "Still running."

"Nothing left to run from. I don't live here anymore." And anyone important to me once upon a time is gone. Ma might remain, but she's different. I don't include Myles on my list.

Landon purses his lips, crossing his arms, and glares at me. "You're running from your new wife, I suspect."

I tug on the cape over me, forcing the snaps to pop and the material to uncover me. "You don't know what you're talking about."

"Didn't miss the radio silence between the two of you at your wedding brunch." Landon rubs his forefinger and thumb along his jaw like he's some mystic who knows all my secrets.

"We'd been ambushed again," I remind him as I stand.

"Machlan, let me give you a bit of advice from an old man who's made plenty of mistakes. Don't fuck this up."

"Jesus, Landon." I laugh bitterly. I'd mock him for swearing if I didn't read in his eyes the depth of his warning. "Don't worry about your precious town, Landon. We'll figure it out."

"I was talking about your marriage."

My jaw clenches. "I'll take it into consideration."

Landon watches me as if knowing I'm not open to advice from him or anyone else in this godforsaken place. He slowly shakes his head again. "Gonna do what you wanna do." Disapproval coats his tone, but he isn't wrong in his assessment.

"I always do." I smirk.

"That's what always got you in trouble." He laughs and presses off the counter.

I'd tell Landon he doesn't know what he's talking about, but I'm certain his steel-trap memory remembers all the issues I caused in this town. The fights. The bad attitude. The girl.

"So, whatcha think?" Landon tips his head, implying the cut and trim. I'm already standing, itching to get out of his shop and be free of his advice, but I check myself out in the mirror. My face is familiar to me but behind those eyes peering back is a man I no longer recognize. A man full of regret and bitterness. Resentment and distrust. And in matters of the heart, a hole exists in my chest.

And in one night, that hole started to slowly fill in.

21

———

Playlist: "If I Didn't Love You" – Jason Aldean & Carrie Underwood

[Jane]

The first place I visit in town is called On The Curve, a counter-service coffee shop that reminds me of bygone days. High-top stools line the long counter that runs the length of the exposed grills and coffee machine, curving at the end, providing for a few more seats. It isn't called On The Curve because of this curled counter space, though. The location is literally on a curved portion of Bridge Alley, the main street running through the small business district.

I don't drink coffee, but I am desperate for tea. Camilla told me this place makes the best scones, although I don't typically eat sweet things for breakfast. The place is busy, and the man and woman behind the counter work in sync like a married couple in a kitchen. I quickly learn they *are* married.

"I'm Kirk. This is Stella." The tall, lean, late-thirtyish man sports a man-bun while the woman working beside him has long brunette hair with multiple braids here and there. They both look bohemian and rustic, but kind and good natured.

After introducing myself, I tell them, "Camilla Wright told me you have the best scones."

"She should have said I have the best buns." Kirk wiggles his brows at his wife, and I laugh.

"We make them just for her." Stella's comment is a testament to how people feel about Mach's mother in this community. "Tea?"

"I'd love some, especially if you have English black tea. The darker, the better." Most breakfast places offer Earl Grey, which is okay but not my first choice.

Stella winks at me. "We keep that in the house for our favorite lady as well." As Stella steps away from me, I notice a little girl sitting at the end of the counter, coloring on a sheet of paper. The dark-haired child looks up at me, and I smile. She gives me a weak smile in return and focuses back on her coloring. No adult sits near her, and I assume she belongs to Stella and Kirk.

"You have a beautiful daughter," I say when Stella returns with my tea.

Stella grins, pours hot water over the dark tea bag in a mug, and leans forward. "That's Willow. She belongs to Theo Clarke. He's her great uncle."

The little girl looks up at the sound of her name, and Stella winks at her. Willow smiles larger and returns to her silent coloring.

"How old is she?" My brows pinch as I watch the girl.

"She just turned five. She's in kindergarten but told her uncle she had a stomachache. I take her in after school. We're only open here until two."

Looking back at Stella, I ask, "Do you have children?" I

wrap my hands around the warm mug, allowing the heat to warm my suddenly cold fingers.

"We have two boys, five and eight. I used to be a teacher, so I tutor here when school lets out. Kirk coaches a middle school basketball team."

Gazing back at the child, I can't seem to take my eyes off her, and she looks up at me. I wiggle my fingers at her. Willow's second sheepish smile at me is a little bigger this time.

"Theo works days laying brick." Stella pauses before lowering her voice. "She's so sweet, but the older a child gets, the harder it is to be adopted."

I turn back to Stella, tightening my hold on my mug. "Adopted? What about her uncle?"

"He's too busy to take on a little girl, but he was the next of kin, and the state asked him to keep her for a bit while some caseworker takes her sweet-ass time placing Willow with a foster family. It's awkward for him being an older, single man and never having had a family of his own. The community steps up, though. It takes a village, right?"

Leaning on the counter toward Stella, I lower my voice, so Willow won't hear me. "What happened to her parents? Am I allowed to ask that?"

Stella feebly smiles. "Boating accident." She nods toward the window. "That river is temperamental water, and some places are safer than others. About a decade ago, there was a canoeing accident with three local high school boys. One died immediately. One found later. One missing. The community was rocked to the core. And you know about Camilla's daughter-in-law."

"I—" I didn't know about her. However, I don't feel right asking a stranger for details. Instead, I offer my own commiserating smile to mark a loss I know nothing about.

To shake my thoughts of histories I haven't learned, I continue my stroll down Bridge Alley. A wooden telephone pole that looked like a giant, naked stalk poking through the sidewalk stood about halfway down the street. An abundance of electrical wires hung from the pole. Both were an immediate distraction and eyesore. In addition, the exterior of the buildings along this strip are bland, dated, and worn. The atmosphere is melancholy and I curse a man I've never met. Fischer Wright. How did he let his own town get so rundown?

Then again, it doesn't matter. Mach and I are here to restore this place, and while the task seems daunting, my excitement grows with every step I take.

Next to On The Curve is Needles & Thread, a combination tattoo parlor and yarn shop. It's a rather eclectic concept, and I'm not certain it's legal to have two businesses in one location, so I add that quandary to my list of things to investigate. Continuing my walk, I make a mental note of the locations on this side of the street. An empty store. An artisan shop selling jewelry and crafts from local artisans. And Bliss, which is my first official project.

After Tanza's help the other day, I have a few ideas I want to run by her as I plan to renovate here first.

"Hey. Congratulations on your wedding," Tanza greets me upon my entry. "How was the big day?"

Enchanting. Disheartening. Which adjective works best? How do I explain the event was nothing like I imagined, and the wedding night was more than I dreamed?

"It was . . . good." More lies. More ease rolling off my tongue.

"I heard there are some changes coming to town." Tanza straightens a display of bracelets on the front counter. The glass display case is reminiscent of something from a 1970s jewelry store and doesn't fit the theme of Tanza's store or the elegance of her products.

"That's one reason I'm here. Tanza, tell me five facts about you and your place."

And so begins my research to help rebuild Wrightwood.

~

THAT NIGHT, I'm awakened by the face of a man who looks like Mach but also does not.

"Hey." I struggle upright on the couch in Camilla's front room. "What time is it?"

"Time for sugar plum fairies to be in bed." Myles gives me a warm smile as he tips his head toward the window. The glass is dark, and the deep black sky tells me nothing more than it is nighttime and possibly late.

I scrub my eyes with the heels of my hands, certain I'm smearing my mascara. "I fell asleep."

Myles chuckles. "Already working hard." After learning Mach's history with the dining room table and his late wife, the front living room felt like a better option for a workspace. Myles is perched on the low table before the sofa where my laptop sits open, and papers are scattered around it. A notebook has slipped to the floor. A crochet blanket covers my lap, so someone spread the covering over my body while I slept.

"We have a lot to tackle," I remind Myles. The faster we complete this restoration project the faster the benefit falls to him.

"You'll figure it out. Ma's been singing your praises for years with secondhand stories from Mach. I have faith in you, Jane Fox."

I awkwardly laugh. Maybe his confidence could rub off on me a little. Project management is my forte, but I'm already overwhelmed. This isn't one new client but a dozen all at once.

"It's Jane Wright, now." A deep but low voice fills the room. "And what the hell is going on here?"

Tipping to the left, I peer around Myles where Mach stands inside the front room entrance. His arms hang at his sides with fingers clenched in fists. His jaw tics as he glares at the back of his brother's head.

"Just checking on our girl," Myles says, winking at me without twisting to face his brother.

"The fuck you are," Mach growls.

Here's the thing; I don't feel a single threat from Myles. Despite his similar looks to his twin, I also don't feel that magnetic attraction I can't seem to tamp down when it comes to Mach. Even though it's been days of nothing more than simple words about our project, looking at Mach sets my heart racing and my clit clenching in memory of champagne kisses.

Calling me *our girl* is Myles's way of razzing his brother, riling him up. However, I don't want to be caught in the middle of their feud, old or new. Tugging the blanket higher against my chest, although not a stitch of me is revealed, I narrow my eyes at Myles.

"She's not yours. Go home," Mach adds.

"I am home." Myles slowly twists his upper body toward his brother. "It's you who has forgotten what this place is."

"Trust me, there's a lot I want to forget. And the sooner we get out of here, the faster I'll put this place behind me again."

Myles turns back to me, his eyes hurt but softening. "Never gonna be able to outrun your past." Is he speaking to his brother or talking about himself? He rises off the low table. With a hobbled first step, he quickly aligns his balance and uses his cane to assist him exiting the room through a second entrance leading toward the back of the house.

Once Myles leaves, I turn back to Mach.

He takes a large step forward. "Do not let him get to you."

His directness has me sitting straighter. What is it with these brothers? "Maybe you shouldn't let him get to you." I point between him and the door where his brother disappeared.

I've had my fair share of squabbles and disagreements with my siblings, but I can't understand the distance Mach has placed between him and his twin. My brother might not be close with us sisters, but we still love one another and reach out to each other. My sisters and I might have different personalities and lifestyles, but we still respect one another.

Mach shakes his head. "It's late. Come to bed."

He's kidding me, right? The comment is so husbandly, but he's been nothing like a husband toward me. The hour is late, and I have no idea where he's been. Then again, we had our night. Now, it's business as usual.

"I'll be up in a bit," I lie. The sofa is comfy enough, and I can't spend another night next to Mach. I can't wake to him holding my hand or wrapping his feet over mine.

"Jane, you need sleep."

I need my husband. As fast as that first retort develops, a second thought arrives, telling me how ridiculous the comment would sound if said aloud.

I reach for the notebook on the floor and babble. "I spoke to a few of the businesses today."

"Jane—"

Flipping through the pages, I aimlessly search for notes, not able to read a word of what I've written. "And I'd like to start with Bliss. The store needs a social media presence, a new logo, and an overhaul in physical layout."

"Tomorrow, Jane."

I pause on a page full of writing and a small sketch, but I can't focus. I just ramble. "Tanza was so kind to me, and I think I can make a big impact by starting with her place."

Mach's shoulders lower, as does his head. His mouth quirks, but the curl of his lips isn't a smile. "Tomorrow, baby."

The endearment sends a rush up my middle, like the

bubbles softly popping in the champagne he poured over my body. I recall his mouth on my nipples, which currently peak within my thin T-shirt. The sharp nubs protrude against the cotton material. Whispers of Mach's praise dances against my skin. *I like seeing my kiss on you.*

I want to smack him right now . . . or maybe myself.

His eyes, lasered in on my breasts, answers the question of whether he can see how turned on I am by his nearness. Heat slowly crawls from my neck to my cheeks. My lips tingle with the reminder of his mouth on mine. I lick my lower lip, swallowing hard, refreshing the taste of Mach and bubbles lapping against my tongue. His gaze shifts and holds on my mouth.

"In a little bit," I say again. If I go anywhere near him right now, it's a toss-up between reacting like a cyclone of desire or a tornado of destruction. He winds me so tight I could spring either way.

"Jane, bed." His deep voice softens but still commands. Defeat rests on his shoulders, though. He knows I'll keep fighting him.

"Good night, Mr. Wright."

With a huff, he leaves me alone. All the oxygen in the room follows him. I cover my face with both hands, fight against tears, and return to the notebook on my lap. Unfortunately, all I can do is focus on one word.

Bliss.

Maybe someone else will have a happily-ever-after from Tanza's shop.

22

———————

Playlist: "Hold Back the River" – James Bay

[Jane]

After a few days of circling one another, Camilla demands Mach and I get out of the house for an evening. Between accounts at Impact and developing a strategy for Wrightwood, we've been going nonstop, and the only conversations we have revolve around our projects.

"Take a break," his mother encourages as we stand in her kitchen. "Go to Trophy's for a while."

Trophy's is located in what was once a convenience store. Two decades later, the place is one of the most popular locations in the area as it sits on prime real estate—overlooking the river. The bridge is highlighted in the backdrop. At some point, an extensive back porch was added to the structure, supported by heavy beams that give the impression of a balcony over the flowing water. The place is one of the businesses we are obligated to renovate, and I haven't been there yet.

"I think I'll stay in. Maybe take a bath," I say to Camilla.

"No bath," Camilla admonishes. "I'm hosting my knitting group tonight, and we need to gossip."

"Ma," Mach groans from behind me.

"I'd love to sit in," I counter. Who doesn't love a night of yarn and gossip? Will they serve wine?

"Do you even know how to knit?" Camilla asks me.

The skill eludes me. It isn't from a lack of patience as I cross-stitched as a child but knitting never interested me.

Camilla observes me as I purse my lips and shift my eyes to the side. "That's what I thought." She softly laughs. "Plus, we're going to be talking about you, so you need to go."

"Ma," Mach groans again and I turn to see him swipe a hand down his face.

"Who better to dispel the gossip than the source," I joke.

"We don't want our gossip dispelled. We want to gab," Camilla teases. She lifts her hand and motions like an alligator chomping. *Yack. Yack. Yack.* The message is clear—get out.

"I'll go change," I mutter. Mach and I made arrangements with Tucker and Mae to send us each a box of clothing. My sister sent me only casual wear, which is no surprise from her. Jeans. T-shirts. Flannel shirts. The attire is something Mae wears to her garden center, but I wanted to present a professional front to Wrightwood. Unfortunately, unless I wanted to invest in an entirely new wardrobe, business casual is my new look.

Wearing jeans, ankle boots, and a cotton blazer over a T-shirt, I walk beside Mach down the hill to town.

Our marriage is only a week old. I have fifty-one more weeks to endure. The idea of perseverance versus passion in a marriage is daunting. I'd wanted to get married someday to someone, but my current situation was never what I had in mind. And while I didn't date anyone after Ripley shredded my heart, my strange attraction to Mach reminded me I could still have feelings. *Stupid feelings.* Even walking down the hill, everything in me screams to hold Mach's hand. I want his assurance we can do this. We can pull off this farce as a team. As partners.

"We should consider getting our own place," I blurt. We need separation from his mother and space from each other. After Myles found me on the couch and Mach acted like something was going on when it wasn't, I fell back on the cushions and returned to sleep. But I don't want to sleep on a couch for fifty-one more weeks. And I can't *come to bed* as my husband requested, only to wind up holding hands or hooking ankles.

"We aren't getting our own place." Mach's tone is sharp, snide even.

"Let me rephrase then. I need to get a place." I continue walking but Mach has stopped short. Spinning to face him, I cross my arms preparing for battle.

"You are not moving out." An edge I've never heard fills his voice. "You are not leaving me."

"I'm not leaving." I swipe a hand through my hair which is long and loose tonight. "But I need some space." A two-bedroom rental would be plenty big enough for a year.

"We're married. How would it look for you to live separately from me?" Mach's eyes narrow.

"How would it look?" I choke, incredulous. It will look like the truth. We're married in name only.

"We need to present a united front. If we want to rebuild the town, we need to think about morale. We"—He waves between us—"are in this together."

"But we aren't together." I stare at Mach as his eyes widen. An entire conversation happens from the depths of those dark eyes. A conversation that is one sided and unspoken. Speaking of morale, though, this employee's spirit is dying inside.

"You aren't getting a separate place." Mach steps closer to me, scooping a section of my hair behind my ear. His fingers curl around the fine hairs near my neck. His voice softens. "We'll get things settled and then be out of here in a few more weeks."

Then why did we have Mae and Tucker ship us clothing? And how will someone else handle all that needs to be completed? And what if I don't want to leave Wrightwood? This project is unlike anything we've ever done. Rebranding a town might be more in our wheelhouse than renovating one, but the potential to rebuild, restore, rejuvenate the entire community has something refreshing bubbling inside me. I'm energized in a way I haven't been in a long time. A way I hadn't noticed meant something was missing in me before. With partnership as my only goal at Impact, I'm growing stagnant in my job.

And I'm not certain I want that partnership anymore.

"Don't give up on me yet, Jane." Mach turns his head to the side, eyes focused on the dimming light of the evening. His thumb continues to stroke the column of my throat. The gentle plea settles my racing heart, making me believe he needs me.

Baa! Stupid sheep.

Entering Trophy's, Mach is immediately accosted by a sharp squeal and female arms wrapping around his neck. The woman jiggles up and down against him like a vibrating toy.

"I'm so excited to see you," she squeaks at his ear before gripping his shoulders, stepping back, and looking him in the face.

"Charlese Frasier?" Mach's eyes widen as he stares at the woman. His expression turns to ash like he's seeing a ghost.

"I'm so sorry about Fischer. I wasn't able to attend the funeral, but I've heard about your inheritance." She whistles. "What a dick, that old man."

Mach's gaze seeks mine over Charlese's head. Do we have

the same thought? *What do people know about his inheritance?* Do the townsfolk know that marriage was a stipulation in helping them? Regardless, Mach is married but the way Charlese strokes Mach's arms, refusing to release him, fills my belly with a sickening sensation. The title of wife means nothing to him other than a means to an end. He's married. He rebuilds a town. He inherits money.

"I'm so sorry," Charlese says again. Her tone softens, and her voice cracks. The intensity in her second round of sympathy is a shift from Fischer's death to an apology for something else.

Mach returns his attention to Charlese before tipping his head in my direction. "Charlese, this is my wife, Jane."

"Your—" Charlese twists while still gripping one of Mach's arms. A wide smile beams at me, and then she's tugging me into a tight embrace, jostling up and down against me.

My, she's enthusiastic.

"I'm so freaking excited for you." She pulls away from me and faces Mach. "You have a wife." She glances back at me. "You are his wife."

Yes, it seems we've established Mach has a wife. What I don't understand is her enthusiasm or the pinched note in her voice as if she's convincing herself she's pleased. Maybe she's confirming the notion. Maybe she's surprised because she knows a truth I don't.

Most people in this town do.

Reminders of Ripley play out. How I thought I was everything to him, while everyone else knew the truth. He had someone else on the side.

I chew my lower lip and Mach watches me.

"Beau, do you remember Mach Wright? This is his wife, Jane." Charlese is tugging Mach toward the bar, where a broad-shouldered man with a scowl on his face stands behind the counter. He tips his chin in greeting to Mach and glances at another man sitting on a stool.

Myles is here.

"I'm not Charlese Frasier anymore. It's Charlese Mitchell now. Beau is my husband, and we own Trophy's."

While this explanation happens, another set of arms wraps around Mach's middle from behind him. Mach stiffens as the woman says something to him. Cautiously, he peers over his shoulder, and a pretty blonde steps around him. Her eyes are green like moss on trees but bright and focused on him. Love blooms across her face.

"I can't believe *you're* back." Mach's voice strains in response to whatever she said to him first. My insides boil as I watch another woman hold onto him, another female with history, another secret I don't know about him.

"I'm sorry about Fischer." Her condolence is genuine, but I detect the same sincerity of deeper-meaning sympathy in her tone.

"Yeah, well . . ." Mach hasn't removed his eyes from her face. She hasn't been introduced to me yet, and I'm counting the seconds until he remembers me.

His Adam's apple softly bobs before he says, "I didn't know you were living here."

"Came back a few years ago. Divorce. Three kids. Pathetic story." She cringes while still offering him a too-friendly smile and a dismissive wave. Is she suggesting she's available?

Taking my jealous bull by the horns, I step forward and hold out a hand. "I'm Jane. Mach's wife."

Her head swivels from me to Mach and back before she shakes my hand. She doesn't offer a name and turns back to Mach.

"You're married again? I'm so happy for you." She pauses, offering me a tight smile. My own grin pinches. "Too bad Myles never moved on."

Her words are said low, but Myles is near, and I'm certain he heard her. When Mach doesn't introduce the woman to me, I step forward and wedge myself between Myles and the stool occupied beside him. I need a drink.

"Do you know how to make a Southside?"

Beau Mitchell looks at me like I've just spoken a foreign language to him.

"How about gin and tonic? Do you have Tanqueray?"

Without a word, Beau reaches behind him and pulls forward a bottle that is not the distinct green bottle of my favorite gin.

"How about a glass of white wine?"

Beau snorts and turns for the wine fridge while Myles chuckles beside me. "Hitting the hard stuff?"

"I'd do shots if I thought I could get away with it," I admit, glancing over my shoulder. Two more women are near Mach, building a harem around him. One presses up to whisper something in his ear, and he smiles back at her, offering her that charming grin of his. I twist back to the bar, waiting on my drink.

"She's her sister," Myles offers.

My gut knows the answer, but I ask anyway. "Whose sister?"

"Ainsley Evans. Ainsley Boyd now. She's Tracy's younger sister."

I hate that I didn't know Mach's late wife's name. I hate that I didn't even know he had a wife before me, and I hate even more that I still don't know her story.

I peek at Mach again. Ainsley's hand is still wrapped around his upper arm, and he sneaks another glance at her. A different woman has an arm wrapped around Mach's back, but he's oblivious to her touch, holding his gaze on his first wife's sister. Is he seeing a ghost or the prettiest face he's ever seen? His expression is frozen in that smug smile he uses to ensnare the ladies.

Sheep beware of the wolf in disguise. He'll drown you in champagne and leave you thirsty for more.

When my white wine is placed before me, I turn to Beau. "On second thought, how about a shot of whiskey."

23

———————

Playlist: "Chasing After You" – Ryan Hurd, Maren Morris

[Mach]

When Ma suggested Jane and I go out, I didn't like the idea. When Jane suggested she take a bath, I really didn't like that idea, either. Imagining Jane wet in our room's small tub instantly had me hard, especially as I've experienced her body fully saturated under a shower spray. Too many nights have passed without us talking, without us touching. The separation is driving me mad. And as Jane has been avoiding our bed, falling asleep on the couch instead, the wedge between us grows worse.

I want my wife in bed with me every night.

"Do you even know how to knit?" Ma had asked her. I have no idea if Jane knits. *A husband should know these things about his wife.* For all the things I know about Jane, the list of things I want to learn seems endless.

Does she always make that little gasp before she comes? Will she kiss me again like she never wants to let me go? Will she eventually mold her entire body to mine at night, not just hold my hand or hook ankles?

As we walked to Trophy's, I nearly had a heart attack when Jane suggested we needed a house separate from Ma's. My initial intention was not to remain in Wrightwood for more than a month. However, as each day passes and we wade through zoning, construction needs, and taxes surrounding the business district, I don't know how I can hand this project over to another person. I've never done anything half-ass in my life, and I don't intend to do it now, despite my dislike for this mission.

As for Jane's suggestion she move out—*fuck that*. The separation at night has been rough enough. She isn't going to be living separately from me, not even in a different bedroom from me.

Jane and I need to talk, and Trophy's wasn't what I had in mind. However, I thought maybe a casual dinner and a drink or two might loosen us up. I wasn't prepared for all that happened as soon as we walked through the door.

First, Charlese Frasier, now Mitchell, is a little older and a lot rounder, yet her jovial smile and bright eyes are still exactly the same. She was Tracy's best girlfriend, and her second apology said it all. All these years later, she was still sorry about Tracy. As she stood before me, stroking her hands over scars hidden under ink and my long-sleeved T-shirt, my body stiffened. Charlese knew the troubles Tracy and I faced during our younger years. She also knew the issues we had once we finally married.

Jane was watching me with Charlese. Her tell-tale sign of disapproval—chewing her lip—sent a strange ripple through my chest. Was she jealous of Charlese? She shouldn't be. Charlese is married, as am I. As are *we*—Jane and me—and I wouldn't look at another woman as long as Jane is my wife.

Then, there was Tracy's younger sister, Ainsley Evans, now Boyd. Struck dumb by an expression that matched her older sister despite aging, I stared at a mirror image of my first wife like I was looking at a photograph from the past. Ainsley has blonde hair and bright green eyes, and for a moment, I imagined she looks now how her sister would have looked. *Pretty, sweet, small-town.*

Ainsley chattered away about her kids and re-introduced me to people I didn't remember, all offering hugs, handshakes, and pats on the back, kisses to the cheek and soft sympathy in my ear. My head was swimming in memories of how small towns can be close-knit. People share a history, marry one another, and this could have been me. It was me for a bit, but I had plans bigger than this town.

The thought has me looking up, seeking my wife, and noticing the barstool where my brother sat is now vacant. The space beside him where Jane stood is also empty.

Fuck.

As Charlese rushes past me with a tray of drinks, I stop her. "Have you seen Jane?"

"Lost your wife already?" she teases good-naturedly. Her head tips toward the entrance. "I think I saw her leave a little while ago with Myles."

That is not what I want to hear. "Are you serious?"

Clouds fill her eyes, bringing us both back to the same memory. A point in the past I don't want to recall.

"I'm out of here," I say to no one and everyone. Extracting my arm from Ainsley's, I excuse myself, but not before receiving another sympathetic look from Charlese that has nothing to do with Fischer's passing.

～

FORTUNATELY, it doesn't take me long to find my brother . . . and my wife. The firelight glowing from behind the main house gives away their location. As I stalk up the hill and round the house, I pause when I find them sitting on opposite sides of a fire pit, updated with raised brick compared to the old barrel bottom we used to use.

"So, they were high school sweethearts," Jane clarifies.

What the fuck? If she has questions, she should ask me. Then again, I should have told her this story. My head hangs with disappointment in myself while fear rolls around in my gut. She shouldn't be hearing anything from my brother. His version will be skewed.

Everything in me says I need to interrupt, I need to interject, but I'm curious how Myles will twist this tale.

"She was the love of his life, and he was hers." Myles pauses, taking a pull from a beer bottle. His interpretation surprises me. "He never thought he was good enough for her. We had a reputation for being trouble, although Mach got in twice as much as I did. Typical bad boy, good girl. They kept their relationship a secret at first." Myles scoffs. "As much as you can keep a secret when it's young love in a small town."

Jane focuses on the fire. *What must she be thinking?*

"Mach went off to college. He was determined to make something of himself. Be better than this place." Myles keeps his eyes on the dancing flames.

"I know the feeling," Jane admits.

My brother's concentration doesn't waver from the fire. "I never thought there was anything wrong with Wrightwood, though. Tracy didn't either."

The fights Tracy and I had come back to me. She didn't want to leave. I didn't want to stay.

"Mach pushed for them to go. Tracy finally gave in."

That is not what happened, and I hold my breath, wondering what lies Myles will spew next.

"Then there was the accident . . . and well, you know the rest." He grips the beer bottle in his hand, staring at the neck of it.

Jane sits up, placing her hands on her thighs and stiffening her shoulders. She exhales. "Actually, I don't know anything."

Myles leans forward in his chair, and I tuck back in the darkness, keeping my position hidden by the corner of the house.

"Mach should tell you the rest of the story, then," Myles states.

Taking this as my cue to reveal myself, I step forward. "Yeah, he should be the one telling *his* wife this story." I glare at my twin. We were once best of friends. Then we turned eighteen and slowly became the worst of enemies. Twins are supposed to have an uncanny connection, unconditional love, and a constant vibe between them. Looking at Myles, I feel nothing.

His mouth opens while he stares back at me, but after a second or two, he clamps it shut. He drops his gaze to the firepit and nods once. "I think I'll call it a night."

Good fucking idea. I don't give him a second glance even as he slightly struggles to lift his body from the outdoor chair. I step forward and drag another chair closer to Jane before taking a seat.

Jane keeps her focus on the flames, gently crackling in the dark night. The air is cooler than when we left the house. Time seems to have passed in a blink. It's late.

Watching her face glowing in the firelight, I note her features. Her dark hair has a fiery glow from the flames, high-lighting the hidden depth to the color. Her blue eyes glitter in the dancing light. Her nose has the slightest lift at the end, and her lips are lush and a deep purple tonight. My wife is so beautiful.

"Why did you leave the bar?" I ask as soon as Myles is gone. More importantly, why did she leave with my brother?

"You were busy." Her terse response surprises me. Then she levels me with a sharp glare. "You promised to keep it in your pants."

"I . . . what?" My brusque question echoes in the quiet of the night, and I clutch the armrest as I shift to face her.

"It's the one thing I asked in this farce. Don't disrespect me." Her eyes hold mine, narrowing like miniature daggers aimed for the heart.

"Jane, I'm not disrespecting you." *Where is this coming from?* "Do you think I'd cheat on you?"

"I don't know what to think." Jane exhales and lowers her head, taking her eyes away from me and hiding her face behind a curtain of her hair. Her hunched shoulders suggest I've hurt her somehow.

A heavy pause falls between us as I flip back over the past hours. Woman after woman—ancient acquaintances, unfamiliar faces—hugging me, kissing my cheek, holding my arm. Stark realization burns inside my chest like the tangy scent of charring wood and autumn air. Although my behavior earlier was innocent, I'd really hurt her.

"I'll never be unfaithful, Jane. I made a vow to you." My fingers grip the armrest tighter. Everything in me wants to reach for her, tug her to my lap, and kiss her senseless. Only a fool would cheat on Jane, and any man who had the notion to stray from her doesn't deserve her. I don't deserve her, but I'm faithful to her. I take my vows seriously, even if this isn't love.

"Somehow, I doubt those vows mean anything to you." Her cold words are a sharp slap to my pride.

My skin prickles with the accusation. "I was a good husband." *Am* a good husband.

Am I a good husband?

I scoff. I've been shit to Jane, and we both know it. I want to argue this is all pretend. We aren't real. We're fulfilling an obligation. But the moment her fingers laid on my palms before the justice of the peace, everything changed.

"How would I know?" Jane quietly interjects. "I'm learning about your first marriage from others."

"I told you not to talk to Myles." My brother has filled her head with I don't know what, just like he did with Tracy.

"You can't tell me what to do," Jane states, her voice eerily calm.

"One of five facts . . . I can. You're my wife."

Her head snaps up, and those bright eyes are scorching flames. "A position that means nothing to you."

We glare at one another, chests heaving like two bulls preparing to charge. I'll wrestle her to the ground, spread her thighs, and impale her with one hard horn if that would convince her she's the only one I want to be with.

"What about you?" I raise my chin. "How do I know you'll be faithful to me? I'm asking you to stay away from Myles, but you refuse."

Her mouth gapes. She shifts her upper body to face me head on. "How dare you?"

I've seen Jane full of venom over the years—mostly aimed at me—and she's ready to strike. She's aiming for the heart.

And because two can play that game, I strike first. "Yeah, well, I know all about your tryst with Ripley Edgar."

Jane's shoulders fall while her breath hitches, like the wind was knocked out of her. Jesus, did I really do that to her?

"A tryst?" Her head flinches back before she purses her lips and lowers her eyes. "Is that what he said?" Her quiet questioning tone suggests I might not have all the facts. Ripley is an asshole, actually, and I should know better than to believe tales from him.

"Jane, I—"

"Well, if that's what you think." She holds her head higher, standing abruptly as her voice grows stronger. "I guess you don't know me. Or anything about what happened between Ripley and me."

"What did happen?" Ripley bragged for years about his office sidepiece. Then suddenly, he was marrying Kaye Hamilton, some influential society woman. When I joked with him about the office girl, he'd said she'd quit. Then he'd told me she'd give good desk head if I ever wanted to test her out. That's when I learned he meant Jane. She worked for me. I wanted to punch him in the middle of The Athletic Club. Instead, I doubled down on my no-fraternizing policy and kept Jane at arm's length for eight fucking long years.

When Jane doesn't answer me, I ask another question. "Did you love him?" Everything in me hates that I'm asking. Even more so, I hate how she might answer.

She looks in the direction of the house. "Would it matter?"

"It wouldn't." Ripley is in her past. I have my own history with love. Still, I don't like that she gave her heart to such an unworthy human being. Jane deserves so much better. She deserves more than me and the position we are in.

"Good night, Mr. Wright." All the barbs in her tone are gone. Also gone is the playful woman challenging me to kiss her on our wedding day.

"Jane—"

She rounds the chair, arms wrapped around her middle, and rushes away from me.

I should chase her. I should let her be. I'm so torn before deciding that her putting distance between us is for the best. Because I'm struggling to keep mine from her, and one of us needs to be strong before hearts are broken again.

24

———————

Playlist: "O-o-h Child" – The Five Stairsteps
(from *Guardians of the Galaxy*)

[Jane]

By the following afternoon, I've traveled the opposite side of Bridge Alley, finding a vacant bank building full of promise. Next to it is another vacant location and then Camilla's shop, Trixie's Trims. Beside her shop is The Barber Shop. Not a very original name, but I've learned that Landon Hobbs owns the place, passed down from his father and grandfather. At one time, Landon's dad had been the mayor, and he found cutting hair was one of the best ways to learn what made the town tick or left people ticked off. The former mayor also developed ideas from suggestions made by the ole boys' club. Landon keeps up the tradition as both a local attorney and part of the city council.

The final space on the block is a store on an angle,

mirroring the strange structure of On The Curve across the street. A small sign on the closed door reads: Adventure Dex. The business isn't open, but I peer through the window, noticing a disarray of kayaks and paddleboards balancing against each other, plus camping equipment haphazardly piled by one wall and half-full clothing racks of outerwear. The place could use a facelift like most of the other businesses in town.

Crossing the street, I head toward the sound of rushing water, where a giant deck rests on a plot of land overlooking the Kanawha River. The weather-worn wood planks are covered in light moss and damaged in spots. A gazebo might have once stood in this place. A broken bench lines one angle of the octagonal layout. A little person sits on another bench facing the water, kicking her thin legs.

Cautiously, I approach her. "Willow?" She swipes at her long, brown hair, disheveled and covering her face. "I don't know if you remember me, but I was in On The Curve the other day. My name is Jane."

Not another adult or child is present as I glance around us. "Are you here by yourself?"

She nods.

Concern tightens my shoulders. "Does your uncle know you're here?"

"He's sleeping." Willow shrugs, her legs continuing to swing.

The days are blurring together, but being a Sunday, he must have the day off. And Willow probably shouldn't be sitting here alone. I risk stepping closer to her and take a seat on the opposite end of the bench. "How did you get here?"

Shrugging again, she answers. "I walked."

Oh dear. This has abduction risk written all over it.

"Do you come here often?" Glancing upward, I hear the river rippling below. This location could offer a pleasant view if only a massive, dead tree trunk wasn't splicing the picture-perfect image in half.

"I like to watch the water." Willow stares at the burbling rapids. Is she thinking of her parents?

"It's pretty here." Or it could be. The worn deck boards need to be replaced and the broken bench repaired. The area around the structure could use a cleanup and new shrubbery, flowers even. Mach comes into my periphery, and I shift on the bench where I'm seated.

"I was looking for you." His gruff voice should startle me but it's the tenderness that throws me off balance.

I offer him a nod and turn back to Willow. "Willow, this is my . . . this is Mr. Wright. He's Camilla's son. Do you know Camilla Wright?"

"She gives me candy when I visit Trixie's." Willow's sweet smile grows. "You look like Mr. Myles."

"Mr. Myles is his brother," I explain, peeking over at Mach before turning back to the child. "You can call him Mr. Mach if you'd like."

"Like a Big Mac?" She giggles.

I laugh at the twinkling sound she makes while sneaking another glance at my husband, who lowers his head but slowly grins.

"Just like a Big Mac." The name is fitting.

A breeze blows. The river flows like an irritated lullaby below the raised bluff, but it's peaceful here. A few yards from the deck is a building, scorched and blackened on one side, as if charred by a fire. In the distance behind the scarred structure is the roofline of Trophy's, and then the bridge that crosses the rushing water and gives the shopping district its name.

"There used to be a gazebo here," Mach explains, and Willow and I both look over at him. He walks to the middle of the octagon, slips his hands in his pockets, and stares out at the river. "The big house owned all this land, and the gazebo was part of the private property. Eventually, the area was given over for public use." Mach looks at me. "But as we know, it's still privately owned."

This area is part of the riverfront property to be improved in our rejuvenation plan.

"The building over there"—Mach nods at the burned structure—"was a bait and tackle shop. Ma told me, in recent years, you could smoke fish there, which is how the building burned. Poor exhaust system, probably. That place was nothing more than a shack and needs to be torn down."

"Did you fish in the river when you were young?" There is so much I don't know about Mach's childhood, so much that might explain why he is the man he is.

"All the time." He squints at the water, keeping his gaze forward as the river flows toward the bridge. His silence tells me he's done talking about the subject.

Turning to Willow, I have an idea. "Willow, what would you like to see done here? What could we do to make this deck better? This area better?"

"Fix the wood. I got a sliver here once."

Mach softly chuckles. "Me too."

I glance up to find him watching Willow and me.

"A swing would be nice. A slide, too." Willow's enthusiasm grows.

"A playground?" Suddenly, I see it as I gaze around the deck. One of the best features of this area is the river, and people need to be encouraged to come down here and use the public space. There should be a park with an area for children —something water-themed, replicating the bridge and Wright-wood's nature. "That's a great idea, Willow."

I envision tables and outdoor games—giant checkers and chess pieces, oversized building blocks, and cornholes, or as we call them in the Midwest, bags. Maybe even a bocce court.

"Willow, how would you like to be on the park planning

committee? You can be an unofficial supervisor." Because that's what we need. We need to start somewhere, and we need someone to start designing and building. Time is ticking.

Willow excitedly kicks her legs as she sits beside me, and I risk another glance at Mach. His lips are curled in a crooked grin, and my heart aches. I miss him. Despite everything happening, I miss the hate-to-love him sensation I had whenever I worked beside him. I miss the flow of us working collectively on a project and the demands of his work ethic to get things done—fast, efficient, effective. *We're* missing that balance we've developed over eight years. Not a work-life balance, but the scale of us as a business team.

His mother hasn't failed to notice our sleeping-together-but-existing-separately relationship, although I've been avoiding sleeping with him as well. It would be embarrassing if she didn't know the truth of our marriage of convenience. However, the only people this marriage has been convenient for is the Wright family and the town of Wrightwood. I might bear the name, but I'm neither a Wright nor a member of this community.

Turning back to Willow, I wonder if she feels the same. Or maybe quite the opposite. All she has is this town. *It takes a village*, Stella said, mentioning the old proverb.

"Willow, honey. Can I walk you to On The Curve? Let's get some hot chocolate, and then maybe Stella can give you a ride home." The suggestion comes because I don't know where Willow lives, nor do I think she should get in the truck with me, a stranger to her. I also don't think she should sit here staring at the river that took her parents when *at least* a village is willing to love her.

She has more than me in that manner.

I'm an outsider here. There's a ghost shadowing me. I'm no more than Claire in *Outlander*, slipping through a time warp. I've entered into Wrightwood's lives, not the other way around.

When Willow stands, I follow and ask Mach if he'd like to join us.

His mouth falls open but then shuts. He shakes his head. "I'll let you ladies have your fun," he says, confirming what I already know. I'll never be part of him or this place.

"Hey." A light brush across my forehead has me waking up once again on the couch. I'm hugging a notebook to my chest.

Mach finishes stroking along my hairline and pushing my hair behind an ear before pulling his hand away.

I'm wearing glasses, and I quickly sit up while righting them. "Hey. Hi. So, I wanted to tell you some ideas I have for the park and a thought about the old bank building. I think the town needs—"

"We should talk." His deep tenor drops. He's sitting on the coffee table in a similar manner to Myles the other night. His arms rest on his thighs while his fingers dangle between his spread legs and he glances down at them. I fight the pull to look between those legs, knowing what is behind the zipper of his jeans. I'd been dreaming when he woke me.

We were getting married again. I was in that princess dress with feathers. Mach wore a vest and pants in champagne colors. His shirt sleeves were rolled to his elbows, and the brightness of his tats was on display as we stood inside a gazebo by the river. Our hands were being wrapped together when the breeze tickled my forehead.

Unfortunately, it was only Mach's fingertips.

"We are talking." I open my mouth to continue with my ideas, but Mach interrupts me again.

"Not about the town. About us." He glances upward, his brows pinching in frustration. Or is it consternation? He's puzzled and upset.

I lower the notebook from my chest to rest on my lap,

concentrating on the cover while I smooth my hands over it. Taking a deep breath, melancholy ripples up my spine. "There is no us, Mach."

A heavy pause falls between us, but I can't take the silence. Still avoiding looking at him, I say, "I have an idea about the bait and tackle space—"

"Jane."

"Mr. Wright." I swallow around the title, fighting against the urgency in his voice. We simply need to return to business. Get back on track as we were before. Before we became Mr. *and* Mrs. Wright. A heavy lump forms in my throat while I trace a finger over my notebook. Like a lovesick teenager, I'm drawing a heart.

"Dammit. You won't even look at me," he snaps.

The force of his tone brings my head upright. It's too painful to look at him, knowing what we've done. How he touched me. How he kissed me. And how very real the fakeness of our marriage is. Quickly, I avert my gaze.

"You spoke of disrespect the other night, so quit disrespecting me by sleeping on this fucking couch every night." Mach's tone turns sharper, and he scrubs a hand down his face.

Disrespecting him? How is sleeping on this couch a sign of disrespect? "Where should I be?" Distractedly, I continue to draw on the notebook cover.

"In our bed."

My head snaps upright. I dig my teeth into my lower lip as my eyes latch onto his.

"And now you're doing that thing where you bite your lip when you disagree with me."

I sigh. We don't publicly display affection, but Mach introduces me as his wife, placing a hand on my lower back when he does. He stands close to me when we speak to people in the community. However, the other night we were quite the opposite, and I don't think we're fooling anyone into thinking we're a happy couple in love.

"We don't need to practice in here what we do out there. When it's only us, we don't need to prove anything to one another. You don't owe me anything other than a partnership when our truce is over."

"Truce." His voice is too quiet as he purses his lips and turns his head, staring off toward the front hallway. "Is the partnership all that's important to you?"

No. "I've worked hard to prove who I am despite what you might have heard from Ripley." Hard work is all the more reason not to accept a partnership under the conditions of a carrot dangled on a string before me. Over and over again, I've proven my worth and this charade isn't the way I want a title like partner.

Mach turns back to me. "Jane, I didn't mean what I said."

My eyes widen. "Now, you're doing that thing. Where you hold your eyes still . . ." *While you lie to me.*

"I haven't lied to you." His voice rises while his forehead furrows.

I huff. "Omission is a lie of sorts." We glare at one another and suddenly, we're discussing two different topics. Only we aren't discussing anything. He hasn't told me about his past, and I'm over this present conversation. I stand, tossing the notebook to the cushions.

With his spread legs engulfing the narrow space between the couch and table, Mach doesn't move, so my knees knock into his. For half a second, I think he'll grab my hips and force me back to the sofa. He'll tell me about this mysterious first wife and what she meant to him. Maybe he'll even press me against the cushions, kiss me hard, and tell me how important I am to him.

Then I laugh at myself.

He proved our night meant nothing the morning after our

wedding. He hasn't intimately touched me in days, confirming his position.

All we have is an arrangement.

I don't know why I keep hoping things will change. Too tired to argue with him, I simply tip my chin when he doesn't offer any response to me standing before him. "I'm going to bed."

Our bedroom is the last place I want to be, but it might be the safest place in the house. My husband definitely won't touch me in there.

25

———

Playlist: "Hey Brother" - Avicii

[Mach]

Jane isn't a door-slammer. The soft click of our bedroom door is almost worse. She's so angry, so distant, and I don't blame her.

This is all on me.

I scrub both hands over my face. Despite the trim from Landon the other day, I could already use another one. Or maybe I need someone to talk to.

"Love is hard." Ma's voice travels into the front room. She leans against the edge of the wide entrance, holding a mug. Eyeing me over the rim, she sips.

Saying I'm sorry feels harder.

Earlier, I'd followed Jane to the old gazebo when I noticed her walking in that direction. Hoping we could talk, I wanted to apologize. For my behavior at the bar. For my accusations about Ripley. I'd misunderstood the situation and I wasn't giving Jane the credit she deserved. The respect she deserves. She wants a partnership at Impact, and I need to come clean with the truth.

However, when I saw her with that child—Willow—my steps faltered.

Jane had been tender toward the little girl. Her actions reminded me there is so much I don't know about Jane. On our wedding night, I'd foolishly entered her several times without protection. I didn't know if Jane wanted children. Despite her age, she could still get pregnant. If anything, I was worried about the risk to her. Still, my thoughts dappled with images of Jane and a small swell on her belly.

Knowing kids were never in the cards for me, I popped the picture.

But I wanted the practice involved in making babies. I want to have sex with my wife, and I was fucking everything up.

I tip my chin at Ma, needing something strong to calm my racing heart. "Got something hot in there?"

She sheepishly smiles. "I might have something just for you." She tilts her head toward the hallway. "Follow me."

When I enter the kitchen, Ma is already seated with three fingers of scotch in a glass jar set opposite her on the table. I miss crystal tumblers, but the old canning jar reminds me of days working beside Ma to make pickles and preserve tomatoes. We made homemade applesauce and stored pears. Ma took care of us when her own family lived across the yard and wouldn't lift a finger. She's the strongest person I know.

Ma leans back in her chair, staring at me across the table while I take my first, fast sip, allowing the alcohol to scorch my throat.

"Denying things in your life isn't worth the pain," Ma

begins. My mouth opens to contradict her, but she raises a hand to stop me. "I want to tell you a story."

This is how she began the explanation behind my birth twenty-something years ago. The moral of her truth-telling story then was how my heart will go on.

"When I first returned to Wrightwood, alone and scared and basically homeless, I stayed at the Hobbs's. Landon was your uncle's friend, but he was also dear to me." She warmly smiles. "Before I went to Charleston, Landon used to tease that I was a shooting star."

Ma laughs and arches a brow. "More like an asteroid bound for a collision with Earth." Her voice softens when she adds, "Reminds me a little bit of you."

I shake my head, wondering where Ma is going with this tale.

"While I was pregnant with you and Myles, Landon asked me to marry him."

"What?" I meet my mother's gaze across the table.

"He was twenty at the time and set to finish college soon. He said we could marry, and he'd raise my children. He'd save face for me, as we called it then. He'd give me a home, a name, and be a father to my boys. But I didn't love him then. I was foolishly still hung up on the man who stole my heart and a few other things from me."

"Ma." I don't need to hear how my father took her virginity.

Her eyes sparkle with mischief, and I assume that's how she got in trouble in the first place. "I denied what was right in front of me. He was more than a name or stability. He was offering to love me, as I deserved to be loved, but I didn't see it that way then." Her voice turns more serious. "I declined his offer, giving him a list of reasons, including how I didn't want to ruin his life. Certainly, the town would outcast him as they'd done to me. They'd know he wasn't the father, even though he suggested we lie." She shrugs. "I couldn't do that to him."

"Even after my rejection, though, he checked in on me. He sent gifts. He came to see me. He tried to soothe Da. His friendship might have been the thing to open people's eyes and hearts to me. The giant scarlet A on my chest became smaller and smaller." Ma draws an X over her heart. She had committed adultery. She'd been with a married man, unbeknownst to her, until after their affair. "Then Landon met someone else, and I saw the light."

Ma sighs. "I was too late. For the second time, I couldn't steal his life from him. His heartbeats belonged to someone new."

"Ma." My chest aches. My mother has been alone most of her life and I selfishly don't want to hear this tale of unrequited love. My heart can't take it. The best woman I know, the one most deserving of love, never had it as she should have.

"Cecilia was a beautiful woman. Kind, generous, intelligent. She loved Landon with everything she had, as he deserved. And he loved her." Ma's voice saddens. "I accepted he and I were not meant to be."

Ma studies my face. "But you. Your *acushla* rests upstairs. Do not deny her. Do not deny yourself what's right in front of you, my beautiful boy."

"Ma." I shake my head, choking on humorless laughter. "Tracy was my heart. Stop calling Jane my *acushla*." As soon as I say the words, I regret them. Not only is it not true—my heart doesn't only beat but hammers, gallops, races at full speed when Jane is near me because she frustrates the hell out of me —it also isn't fair because I do feel something for Jane. I feel . . . alive with her.

"You're wrong, Mach. Tracy was the heartbeat of your youth. That quick racing, never stopping, always moving kind of beat that is young love." Ma shimmies her shoulders, her voice rising with the explanation. Then she sighs and settles back in her seat. "But Jane? She will be your everlasting heart-beat. The steady ticker with a wiser tempo that slows down time, takes in a moment, and breathes in the concept of forever. That's the heartbeat you need now, son."

Ma stares at me.

Her message takes its time to burn through me, much like the scotch I reach for and drink until the glass is empty. The scald of alcohol fills my belly while the heat of Ma's words enflames my heart. She isn't completely wrong.

Jane makes my heart beat.

I don't respond to Ma, though. She isn't expecting me to say anything.

"I also think it's time to forgive Myles."

"Ma," I groan, hanging my head while I clutch the glass jar.

"You can live with regrets. People do it all the time. Lord knows I have. And you can let those regrets eat at you for the rest of your life, festering and feeding. But what a sad, lonely life you'll lead, without love, without your brother." Her emphasis falls on the last words. *Your brother.* I could argue she's always defending Myles but that wouldn't be true. She defended me most of our younger lives. She stood by me when Tracy became mine, and I still wanted to leave Wrightwood.

The heart knows what it wants, Ma had said. *Its rhythm is fool-ishness. Its melody love.*

"I have Tucker." I'm not tossing more of her mistakes in her face, but Tucker is the brother I gained when I lost Myles. My connection with Tucker is twisted in the bizarreness of fate and the brazen actions of a man too full of himself.

"And aren't you fortunate that relationship turned out to be what it is? But you have another brother who needs you too. And you might need him."

I huff. "What I need is a construction foreman." My thoughts leap to Jane and her constant flow of ideas and stream of suggestions. She's tackling this town like a giant marketing campaign, and in many ways, her thought process works. We're here to rebuild, which means rebranding. But we need an actual builder.

Ma pulls a business card from her pocket and slides it across the table to me.

Reading the name, I bitterly chuckle, disbelieving the words written there.

Wright Construction Company, Myles Wright, Owner & Contractor.

Myles has just as much at stake as I do in rebuilding this town. He has double to gain if we pull the renovation off in a timely manner. So why hasn't he offered his services? Why isn't he stepping up? I answer my own questions. Myles and I don't get along. I don't want his help anyway.

"He's waiting for you to ask," Ma speaks as if reading my thoughts.

Jane has taken on the role of project manager, which means if we use Myles's construction company they'd be working closely together. That also means I wouldn't be able to return to Chicago anytime soon because I don't want Myles anywhere near Jane. And I already know Jane isn't interested in leaving. She's embracing our time here like a passion project.

"Fuck," I mutter.

Suddenly, Fischer's intentions become a little clearer. He wanted to place a woman between my brother and me again.

"Did you know about this?" Standing opposite Jane in the dining room of Ma's house the next morning, I toss Myles's business card on the table and slip my hands into my pockets.

"I didn't suggest him because I didn't want to upset you." Jane holds my gaze, waiting out my reaction.

She's mostly correct. The suggestion of using Myles would have upset me. Only, I don't know if I'm more upset that she knew about his business and didn't mention him. Or Ma suggested him. Or Fischer had a plan I'm slowly piecing together.

Then again, I appreciate Jane admitting she didn't want to upset me. She's taking my feelings into consideration, something that shouldn't happen in business. We have a job to complete. Emotion shouldn't play into the process.

City plans, building blueprints, and rough sketches from our creative team at Impact are spread over the table. We've asked Impact for some ideas with minimal interruption to our current clients. Tucker has been very understanding.

"But we need help, Mach." Jane's voice softens. "We both know that in a small town connecting with tradespeople, really knowing them, is half the battle in getting things done in a timely manner."

And the clock is ticking. If I want us out of here, the sooner we get things done, the better for all of us.

"You've never told me about your small town." I'm hit once more with all I don't know about Jane. Where is she from? Why did she leave? What was she doing with that fuckwad Ripley?

Jane lowers herself to a dining chair while I remain standing. Her hair is pulled back in a ponytail today. Her shirt is one of my old flannels paired with skinny jeans. She looks different. Still stunning. Still professional but different. Something about her . . . glows.

"I grew up in River City, Missouri, a town not too different from this one. The river was the focus but so was a factory. My granddad worked in that factory his entire life. When my father left, Granddad took on more responsibility, working overtime. He was suddenly helping my mother raise four kids. He provided for us when he should have been done with raising and supporting children."

Jane reaches for her ponytail, curling the hair around her fist then dragging her hand down the length. I want my fist there. I want her story more.

"I know this might not make sense to you, but this project means something to me. My hometown was rundown like this one, but it had so much potential. Granddad gave his life to a factory, and he'd never want a power plant to take over a town. I don't want an energy plant to take this one." Jane swallows, as if quelling the sudden emotion claiming her voice.

"Why didn't you stay in River City?" Maybe the answer is obvious—a factory was its focal point.

Jane bites her lip. "Granddad wanted bigger things for my siblings and me. He sent us to college so we could have more, be more. Garrett went to California. He has the Midas touch. I didn't need to be rich, I just wanted to be successful, and Granddad saw I'd fall into a rut if I stayed in River City. I'd already taken on so much responsibility, sort of second in command to my mother. She struggled with my father's absence." Jane glances away, hinting there's more to her mother's side of the story, but I only want Jane's. "You've met Mae, who is more of a free spirit. And then there is Lindee, who is a bit of a drifter. We're best friends but clash on occasion as our personalities are so similar."

"You mean you are both bossy," I teasingly mock the take-charge woman I know.

"Determined." She grins but it quickly fades. "I'm a survivor. Someone had to be in charge, and it was often me. Worry and fear were ingrained in me."

"Worry?" Fear? I've never seen a trace of either. She's one of the strongest women I know next to Ma. Her tears on our wedding night were a total surprise.

"The next meal. The next paycheck. We weren't destitute, but my mother was open about our financial constraints. There was an underlying threat, a fear, that we'd lose our home, have to move away, and . . . I don't know . . . fend for ourselves, maybe. I never wanted to be that concerned about food and shelter again. Of course, I had unspoken faith that Granddad wouldn't let anything happen to us."

It was strange to hear some of my youthful concerns echoed by Jane. The difference in our stories might be my mother worked hard but never complained. She went from sweeping clippings to washing hair to fashioning updos and owning the place. Camilla Wright was a survivor. We didn't want, but we knew we had less. Fischer made certain we knew we were less than others. Jane's granddad sounds like a dream.

"What did you want most as a kid?"

Without a blink, Jane answers. "I wanted to be taken care of."

Like a sucker punch to the sternum, the comment hits hard. I'm not taking care of Jane. She doesn't need my money. She doesn't lack food or shelter, but I'm not providing her the reassurance that she can rely on me. I'm here for her. Hell, she's been here *for me*. She fucking married me.

Why did she do it?

The partnership whispers through my head.

"Look, we need Myles." Jane's quick topic shift has me blinking. I don't want to hear these words, but the truth settles like a slow dripping faucet. *Plunk. Plunk. Plunk.* I don't want to deal with Myles, but I might not have a choice.

Shaking my head skeptically, while tightening my grip on the chair before me, my shoulders fall in concession. I don't like it. I don't want it. But with a heavy sigh, I cave. "Fine."

"Really?" Her voice cracks, but there's something more in the sound. Not only is she surprised, she's . . . happy.

My head pops up, registering her enthusiasm to work with Myles. *Dammit.* "You're going to be here for more than a month."

By mentioning the timeframe, I'm hoping Jane will want to leave.

But her lip knowingly curls. The glow in her face starts to brighten even more. "I'm in. I want to stay." Excitement fills her voice.

"I can't leave you here alone, though." There is no fucking way I will leave my wife with my twin brother.

Jane's shoulders fall. Her enthusiasm visibly dissipates. Her hands are underneath the table and I'm guessing her leg jiggles. A fact I've noticed about Jane is her leg would bounce with anxiety or eagerness as we waited out a client's decision. There are so many details I've catalogued about her over the years. How many times have I wanted to reach over to stop the jostling motion and then keep my hand on her thigh, skimming her leg, leading between them?

My hold on the chair tightens. "I'll have to stay with you."

Jane's face returns to that brightness. She's nearly beaming, but the lip chewing begins.

"You'll stay with me." *Is there a question in Jane's voice?*

"Things are going to get messy. We might have to do some of the construction work ourselves." While Myles owns the construction company, he's more a contractor than a worker. We can speed things up if we join the montage of volunteers and workers we need.

Jane's rickety wooden chair creaks, and I have my answer about her bouncing leg. She's excited about this project. She's hungry for it. I've seen her like this in the past. A type of electricity vibrates off her.

"Do you even know how to use tools?" My voice drops, an innuendo beneath the asking. She certainly knew how to work *my* tool on our wedding night, and I need another crack at her. I need another glance at the blueprint of her body, to memorize the sounds she makes as she builds to an orgasm. I want to restore the connection we had that night.

"I know my way around a paintbrush, and I'm good at demolition and cleanup." Jane pauses. "I can hammer if you need me, too."

Sweet Jesus. Yes, let's hammer and nail and every other construction term that's sexual.

"What about you?" Jane tips up her chin, challenging my abilities.

"I rebuilt that truck." I nod toward the dining room window where the Chevy remains parked outside.

Her mouth falls open. "What?"

"I'd been wanting a truck, and Fischer taunted me with giving me one. If I got an A in Chemistry. If I did this. If I did that. I jumped through every hoop of his for a year. That thing arrived from the heap. *You never mentioned it needed to run*, he mocked. I fixed it up with every dollar earned mowing lawns, working fields, and doing odd jobs. My only tools were me and a mechanic's book." And Myles on occasion, but I leave that part out.

Jane stares at me, and I recall how I was as a kid. "I liked to take things apart and put them back together." And sometimes I'd watch Fischer rebuild that classic MG his son destroyed. Only Myles was allowed near that precious car, but it didn't mean I didn't inspect it for how parts fit.

"That's impressive." Jane's hands lift above the table and clasp underneath her chin. "So, you agree Myles can be our general contractor? You'll work with him?"

My mouth falls open, but Jane continues. "You'll stay with me?"

Did her voice drop? I exhale, turning my head a second, willing away the possibility of hope that she wants me to be here because she wants to be with me. "I'll stay."

Jane lets out a little squeak, surprising us both at the sound. The expression on her face is a combination of excitement and determination. Her gem-colored eyes sparkle while her cheeks flush a rosy-shade that makes her look like a blooming flower. I'm nearly blinded by her smile.

It kicks me in the chest.

Because Jane is finally giving me one of those smiles she grants to everyone else.

Only, this one is extra special because it's aimed at me.

26

Playlist: "Come and Get Your Love" – Redbone
(from *Guardians of the Galaxy*)

[Jane]

Nothing could have shocked me more than Mach's agreement to hire Myles. While the difficulty of the decision was written in his expression, he wasn't blind to reason. We needed Myles. Whatever their issues were, Myles had a vested interest in this inheritance scheme as well as Mach. And while I wanted to use Myles's company, the decision had to come from Mach.

What also surprised me was how much I wanted to work on this project.

For Willow who stared out at the river with sad eyes and a heavy heart at only five years old. And Stella and Kirk who serve this community with their fresh scones, amazing tea, and excellent breakfasts before catering to children by tutoring some and coaching others. For Tanza, a single mother raising a teenage daughter, who believes in happily-ever-after like I do despite being alone and once jaded by love.

These people give me hope.

For the first time in a long time, I'm truly excited by our newest client—Wrightwood.

I want to get my hands involved. Tearing down a wall might be the energy release I need because every time I look at Mach, I want to jump him. I want to kiss him, remind him of our night together, and prove it meant more to both of us.

My leg had jiggled under the table as we spoke. My breath held, waiting on his decision. The concept of rebranding and rebuilding an entire town had me bubbling with enthusiasm I hadn't known was missing in my life until this project arose.

Is this a chance opportunity? Or a once-in-a-lifetime experience?

For half a second, I thought Mach was going to send me back to Chicago. I thought he might decide to hand everything to Myles.

"I'll stay."

If I wasn't ready to catapult myself over the table to hug him, I might have missed how he was holding his eyes still. With resolve but sincerity, he wasn't lying, though. I squealed a little, surprising even myself with my squeaky excitement. In response, Mach gave me what might have been the best smile he's ever given me—white teeth pinned to his bottom lip and a little color on his high cheekbones. That smile was a gift. So was his decision.

We were staying.

～

Within a day of Mach's decision, our town rejuvenation begins. First thing on the agenda is the removal of the excessive overhead electrical wires and the no-longer-needed telephone pole. The electric company rerouted the power a few years back, and the pole in town wasn't necessary. Eventually, we'll be painting the exterior of each storefront and hanging new merchant signs, giving the street a fresh look with an old-world feel. The designs for the future area remind me of walking through quaint, small towns in England, Ireland, and Scotland.

From my vantage point at the end of Bridge Alley, a man in a lift basket is hoisted above roof level to dismantle the power lines. A crew of workers hover below him. While this project begins, we have a deck-builder restoring boards and staining the ancient gazebo base. Volunteers will soon work on cleaning up the park area, trimming trees and clearing brush. I have a meeting later this morning with Tanza to finalize plans for Bliss before demolition and renovation starts in her store. And Mach and I have an appointment with Camilla. Although she declined the renovations, Trixie's Trims is getting a makeover.

At the opposite end of the street, someone comes into my periphery as I watch the power line worker rise into the air.

Then I do a double-take.

Walking toward me is a man I hardly recognize and yet wouldn't miss in a crowd. With bright inked arms highlighted by a white, short-sleeved T-shirt, he also wears faded jeans, construction boots, a baseball cap, and aviator sunglasses as he struts toward me. Despite not seeing his eyes, I know his tunnel vision is on me, and my breath hitches and holds. His demeanor reminds me of Chris Pratt in *Guardians of the Galaxy* walking through a cavern listening to music. While Mach is minus the Walkman and dance moves, he has two times the swagger. Like "Come and Get Your Love" suggests, Mach is fine. *If only he were mine.*

He comes straight for me. Stunned by his appearance, his strut, his attention, I'm transfixed and don't move. When his fingers coast my jaw and delve into my hair, and then his mouth crashes over mine, I do nothing other than respond.

His lips are warm and possessive, leading mine to follow his as he sips at me. Once, twice, three times, he sucks on my mouth before releasing my lips but not his hold on my head, fingers still tangled in my hair which was collected into a ponytail. "Good morning, Mrs. Wright."

"Mr. Wright," I croak, uncertain where that kiss came from or what has him in a mood today. Stepping to the side, he remains close enough I catch a whiff of his spicy, woodsy scent. He removes his hands from my hair, slipping his fingers lower to cup my nape. With his warm touch on my neck, he shifts again to face the construction crew, and I have a sudden explanation for this performance.

"Gonna piss a circle around me next?" I stare at his profile.

"Need me to whip out my dick and prove you're mine?" He slowly turns his head back to me.

His suggestion has me tongue-tied for a moment. I gulp. "Nope. I'm good. You can keep it in your pants."

Mach lifts his aviators, latching his gaze on mine. "Only place it's going to be, except when my wife wants it."

Jeezus. My face heats fifty degrees.

"What's on the agenda today?" he asks rather cheerfully, turning his attention to the work down the street. Too dazed to comment, my own focus returns to the utility crew preparing to remove the unsightly pole in the middle of the sidewalk.

Briefly, I wonder if a wire came loose, one still live and full of energy, because the electricity coursing through my body gives me another sense of hope I shouldn't be feeling.

My husband called me his.

27

Playlist: "Starting Over" – Chris Stapleton

[Mach]

Entering Trixie's Trims is like stepping back in time. Not much has changed in the old beauty parlor. The swivel chairs are still a dated mauve color, while the wallpaper is paintbrush streaks of mint green, turquoise, and more mauve.

Hello, the 80s called.

When I found out who my father was, my intention was to force him to pay Ma every dime of back child support even if Myles and I were no longer children. However, Ma didn't want me to seek out dear old dad. Her wish was granted as he'd died before I could confront him.

Ma refused to take money from me over the years, although I had plenty, and wanted to share some with her.

"I don't need this place fixed up. Save the money for

another project," Ma argues as I take a seat in the chair beside her current client. Sitting here reminds me of being a teen and visiting Ma after school or before a job.

"Camilla, the project includes renovating *all* Bridge Alley spaces," Jane explains. "Plus, we're doing The Barber Shop next door."

This argument does not convince Ma as she stands over the head of someone, working at teasing her hair for volume. "Everyone knows this place is up for sale."

"Apparently, not everyone." I stare at Ma with her new-to-me information. "Since when?"

"Since Da passed."

Ma is a piece of work, putting her business on the market almost as fast as her dad died. My head tilts. She's been dropping hints about the big house. *What is she thinking?* She can't sell the place. The land is entailed to her, as the will explained in greater detail. If no family was alive to claim the property, it would revert to the state, like Fischer mentioned.

Surprisingly, Uncle Frank has been quiet about his meager inheritance. If he crashed that MG again to say screw it to his old man no one would be shocked. Then again, the car is worth a pretty penny.

"What are your plans for the big house?" I ask as Ma swivels her customer in order to continue working on her hair.

Jane stands near the front counter, only a few feet behind Ma.

My mother's eyes sparkle as she glances at me. "We'll talk later." When I was a child, this was her way of schooling me in front of others without scolding me. Later was never good.

Next on our list of business visits is The Barber Shop, which is nearly as dated as Ma's place. Upon opening the front door, a wall separates an old office from two barber chairs off to the left. Landon stands inside his shop area, glancing around at his collection of scissors, trimmers, and combs.

"My father loved this place," Landon says after we greet him. "He would have been excited to see the town revived." As the late mayor, Landon's father might have been in constant conflict with Fischer. Politics and business make strange bedfellows, and I didn't want to ever be in a position where the two had an affair.

History lives in this barber shop. This location is the center of town, not to mention a mecca for the men who live and work here. Landon needs his place updated with a nod to what has stood the test of time in this community. Not to mention, the place could use some *man*-upping. It isn't masculine in here.

"Myles has already been in here to discuss demolition. He can't get a crew in here until next week," Landon informs us.

"Then Mach and I will start."

Jane volunteering us has me staring back at her. She hasn't mentioned our kiss this morning other than to tease me about pissing around her. If that's what it takes to mark her as mine and make a statement to those schmucks drooling over my wife when they should have been working, that's what I'll do. Jane belongs to me. And I'm not certain she understands how attractive she is. Her damn smile nearly brought me to my knees the other day.

"We need to clear this place out. Do you have somewhere to store your collection?" Jane speaks as she examines yellowed articles framed on the wall and the once-silver pieces in a display case. "Mach and I can demo."

She peeks around the wall separating the barber area from the old office. "I'm assuming this wall goes." Jane pats the plaster like she's a master carpenter. She has a radiance about her today. Not only is she taking charge as I've witnessed her do with clients, but she's vested in this project. And she looks a little too excited to demo this place.

"Can't wait to get a jackhammer in your hand?" I tease. Would she like a tool that vibrates?

"No one mentioned a jackhammer. But a hammer and a crowbar could work wonders." Jane smiles, looking directly at me, and I lose my train of thought.

"We'll be back tomorrow, Landon," she says to him.

Like a dutiful husband, I merely nod at Landon and follow my wife. I swear I hear him chuckling at me as we leave.

JANE and I agreed that Impact and our accounts with the firm cannot be jeopardized, so while Tucker is taking the lead and Amelia is pulling extra weight, Jane and I still spend our mornings working for Impact. Afternoons are for Wrightwood. Today was reversed, and I have a conference call this afternoon, so Jane and I part ways.

She has a meeting with the owner of Bliss and then plans to head to the park area to help where she can.

Later, she goes out to dinner with a group of volunteers. People are slowly coming onboard to help revive the town. I don't want to be a miser about Jane's time, but she and I really need to talk. Our kiss this morning was only the beginning. I have things to tell her, and then I want to propose something for us.

Later that night, I find Jane sprawled across our bed, fully dressed, feet still inside new boots she bought for stomping around town. She's facedown, ankles hanging off the edge of the mattress. Her position has me imagining all kinds of things with that ass, accentuated by skinny jeans.

"Jane." I sit on the edge of the bed, pressing a hand on her back. After jostling her only a little bit, she shifts her head, but her eyes remain closed.

"*Mach*-nificent," she mutters.

I grin. I've heard her use my name in a variety of forms,

from her Volde-*Mach* remark to calling me this nickname on our wedding night.

Is she dreaming about that night?

I tip to my side on the bed, perching on an elbow while keeping my other hand on her lower back. "Jane, baby, wake up."

I don't really want to disturb her, but she should shower, or at least change out of her clothes. When she doesn't budge, I rise, and start unlacing her boots. With a snug fit, the first tug jostles her body, and Jane flips to her back. Her foot remains awkwardly in my hand.

"What are you doing?" Her smoky, groggy voice is like a live wire to my dick.

"You fell asleep. I was taking off your boots for you."

"Oh, you don't—"

I drop the first one and pick up her other foot for the second boot.

"Oh God. My feet probably smell, and you really shouldn't—"

I tug her sock, unconcerned with a little foot odor. "You always smell like summer rain."

Jane stares at me as I massage the pad of her foot. "Oh God," she groans, and I want to hear that sound again and again, only I want to touch her other parts to make her hum and purr.

"I was wondering if we could renegotiate the terms of our arrangement."

Jane's eyes flutter closed as I dig the pad of my thumb into the arch of her foot, pressing upward to the ball. Her leg jolts. "That tickles."

I smile to myself and move my other hand to her ankle, stroking along the narrow portion of her leg.

"Jane. Our arrangement." I want more with her.

Her eyes focus on my face. "What did you have in mind?"

"No one in Chicago knows we're married. Here in Wright-wood, people are learning you are my wife. We should put that into practice. I'd like to reconsider our only-for-the-wedding-night agreement."

Jane's head turns away for a second, and I'm reminded how I kissed her the morning after. Or rather, didn't kiss her in response to her plea.

Kiss me. Prove this didn't mean anything. Did she really believe that night meant nothing to me?

She rolls her head and locks eyes with mine. "You want me to be a secret."

I keep my focus on massaging her ankle. "Not a secret. Not here." What's the harm in playing up the act? We are married. Kissing can be on the table. Sex on the dessert menu. Holding hands can even be an appetizer.

"I swore I'd never be anyone's secret again."

My hands halt at Jane's comment and I look up at her face. "What do you mean?"

"You know about Ripley." Her voice cracks. Her gaze locked on me.

"Actually, I don't know anything. I'm sorry I mentioned him the other night. I only have his side of the story."

Jane huffs and gazes at the ceiling, attempting to pull her leg from my grasp.

I squeeze her calf to get her attention. "Tell me what really happened."

"We were together for seven years." Her voice drifts upward since she refuses to look at me.

My fingers pause their massage. *What the fuck?*

"I worked for his father first but was moved to work under Ripley."

Ripley Edgar Sr. started Edgar Media, and his son took over when the dad retired.

"Ripley didn't want the office to know about us. As long as

we remained professional by day, I had his attention at night. Mostly." Jane's eyes shift to watch me massage up her leg to her knee. Her leg flinches when I hit another sensitive spot. *Note to self, she's ticklish on the backs of her knees.* I lower her left leg to reach for the right, wrapping my fingers around the arch of her foot.

"We didn't go out in public, and I didn't question it. For years, we worked side-by-side and escaped to his office after hours or took weekends away. Business trips. Once even a vacation I wasn't allowed to mention." Jane's voice drops, mocking the words, "*Could draw suspicion.*"

"Then . . ." She takes a deep breath. "Then I found out I was pregnant."

Holy fuck. My hands still again. Everything in me rebels. Not my Jane. Not with Ripley. I remain holding her foot while she stares up at the ceiling once more.

"Ripley was upset about the pregnancy. He wanted me to . . ." Jane closes her eyes, shaking her head. "I was thirty-seven. It might have been my only chance to have a child. I wasn't willing to do it."

Her eyes open, and she exhales heavily, like a warning of what happened next. "I lost the baby." Her voice is small, and she shrugs, but I don't believe the dismissive action. "It wasn't meant to happen."

I drop the foot that I hold and climb up the bed over her. Balancing on all fours, I cage her in, needing to protect her, wanting to comfort her.

Her hand lands on my chest. "Don't," she whispers. "Please. Don't."

I don't know what she's stopping me from or what I even intended to do, but my arms vibrate with the desire to hold her.

"Within days of the miscarriage, he announced his engagement to Kaye Hamilton. They'd been together for five years. He always told me she was a family friend. They were each other's stand-in as he couldn't take me to events or activities outside of something strictly work-related. Even then, at office parties, we kept our distance. He didn't want the other employees to know he was fraternizing with one of his staff. Dallying with me, as he eventually called our relationship."

I stare down at her. Every part of me wants to touch her, bring her to my chest and keep her against me. "What a fucking prick."

Jane purses her lips. "He is."

I collapse to my side, allowing no space between us, accepting that this is as close as she'll let me for now. My chest presses against her bicep, and my arm falls over her midsection. I hold up my head as I perch on my elbow. "So, he broke it off with you?"

Jane shakes her head. "He announced his engagement at a company dinner. That was my memo we were over."

"Shit." What a motherfucking dick.

"I quit the next day. He didn't bother to chase me or even inquire into my leaving."

That's how Jane came to Impact. She admitted during the interview she was ready for a professional change. She wanted to work for a better company, and we were her first choice. We hired her on the spot. She had incredible experience and a glowing recommendation from Ripley. Then he said what he said a few months later at The Athletic Club. I completely misunderstood their relationship.

"I'm so sorry, Jane." Leaning forward, I can't help the kiss I press to her temple, lingering against her skin.

She exhales. "If I stay down here and you return to Chicago, no one will know the difference in our status. Then we can divorce when the project ends. That's less than four months if we press for Kringle Fest."

I pull back and prop up on my hand to stare down at her. With an arm over her belly, I shift to spread my fingers over her stomach. "Jane, that wasn't what I meant at all when I suggested we renegotiate this arrangement."

"What did you mean then?" She looks up at me with the most innocent eyes, filled with hesitation. *Fear*, she'd said to me. She'd constantly feared as a child.

How could I tell her what I wanted? How could I ask her for sex after the shitshow that happened to her? Instead, I ask a different question. "Do you think you might be pregnant after our wedding night?" The timing was almost a month ago. Surely, she'd know now or know soon if she was.

Jane abruptly sits up.

Removing my hand from her waist, I follow her movement, bracing my arm behind her back to support me. The desire to stay close to her continues. She doesn't look at me over her shoulder. Instead, she directs her words toward the bathroom door.

"I can't get pregnant, Mach. So, there's no cause for concern."

"I wasn't—"

Jane scoots toward the end of the bed, but I shift with her, catching her around the waist.

"Wait. I wasn't concerned. Just . . . curious." I lower my face, lips landing on her covered shoulder. A sudden case of nausea roils in my belly. I recall another woman's disappointment when she wasn't pregnant. I never knew how she felt when she finally was.

"What do you mean you can't get pregnant?" Jane is in her mid-forties, which seems a little young for menopause.

She simply shakes her head in response to my question. "Don't worry, Mr. Wright. I can keep a secret. Our marriage is in name only."

That isn't what I want, either. I don't want her to be a secret. And I don't want marriage in name only. Now doesn't feel like the time to tell her these things, especially after the bomb she just dropped. I groan at her misunderstanding. "Jane."

She slips from my grasp and shuts herself in the bathroom. If we didn't live with my mother, I would make a scene of hammering on that door and demanding she open for me, insisting we talk.

Maybe we should rethink living with Ma.

But doesn't that keep Jane a secret as well?

I fall back on the bed. *Fuck*. I'm no better than Ripley Edgar.

28

———

Playlist: "I Want You Back" – The Jackson 5
(from *Guardians of the Galaxy*)

[Mach]

After what Jane told me, I couldn't *not* touch her. She finishes her shower and climbs into our bed where she assumes her typical position, on her side with her back to me. But I wasn't having it. I scooted up behind her and molded my body to hers, wrapping my arm over her waist and tucking my knees behind hers.

"Mach, you don't have to do this." Her voice is quiet in the darkness of our room.

"Just let me hold you, Jane." My arm tightens around her.

Her head shakes on the pillow. "I'm okay."

I hear the words, but I don't believe them. If I were looking at Jane, she might be chewing her lip in disagreement with herself.

Reaching for the side of her face, I blindly brush back her hair and scoop it around her ear. I clump the thickness together and push it to the side to get my face into her nape. Returning my arm over her waist, I tug her tighter to my chest.

"Mach—"

"Jane. Shut up."

She chuckles, her body vibrating against mine. "Still the boss."

"Call me Mr. Wright," I tease into her skin which smells once again like summer rain.

"Mr. Wright." The title is breathless, and I feel her exhale.

"Get some sleep, Mrs. Wright."

Jane stiffens, but when I kiss her nape, her body relaxes. I press another kiss to her shoulder and then stop myself. If I sip more of her skin, I'll want more of her, and tonight Jane needs my comfort more than my cock.

Tonight, I need her to just be . . . with me.

PARTS of our bodies touch each morning when I wake, as if somehow, we reached for one another during the night. Typically, Jane wakes first, and I linger, relishing the hook of her ankle over mine or the heat of her hand in mine.

It's no surprise, Jane is absent from the bed in the morning.

When I find Ma in the kitchen, she tells me Jane is at the park again. "She looked determined." Ma chuckles.

"Determined?" I grip the back of the chair, vibrating with a need to greet my wife with a proper good morning.

"Like she could tear down a house single-handedly. Your *acushla* has gumption," Ma teases.

My heartbeat. Inside my chest, there's a thump at the thought of Jane. I wanted to ask her to up our charade with sex.

But is this a charade? Is this only sex? We *are* married. And I want to know more about my wife.

Jane told me her history with Ripley, and I want to tear him to shreds for breaking her heart. How could he not support her through the difficulty of a miscarriage, and then marry someone else? He didn't deserve Jane's love.

I'm certain I don't either.

Then again, I wasn't about to suggest everlasting love to my wife. I was going to propose we have sex together.

I scrub at my forehead. I'm such a dick.

"Ma, I need to find Jane." I can't keep the urgency from my voice. "The park you said?"

Ma nods.

I rush down the hill to On The Curve for a double shot of espresso in a black coffee and purchase Jane the black tea she likes with two spoons of sugar. *A husband should know what his wife drinks at breakfast.* I need a new approach with Jane. The idea of wooing my wife feels foreign, mainly because I don't pursue women.

For years, I let women come to me. A pickup line I didn't mind falling for. A suggestion I didn't mind accommodating. Being with random women was mind-numbing. Then, I became more selective, more upfront with women in my circle. They knew what I had to offer. A date for an event . . . and sex. One night. There was no promise, no *let's do this again*, no rings. God, no, never a ring.

The thought has me swallowing a lump of regret in my throat. I should have bought Jane an engagement ring. I didn't even offer her a proper proposal. The will was read, and a wedding happened.

Way to be a schmuck, Machlan.

My self-chastising comes to a halt as I near the park where I hear voices and then a chainsaw but don't see Jane.

The octagon decking is being restored. Tables will be added

soon, and outdoor games provided. The general lot is being cleaned of dead brush, and new landscaping will happen before fall fully hits. Instead of adding play equipment, it was decided to hang a tire swing and two wooden plank swings from tall trees near the edge of the park property. A perfect view of the river and the bridge is obstructed by a dead tree, and it's on the chopping block today.

Two people are standing on the bluff, which dips downward rather sharply. The tree trunk destined for demise shakes. The chainsaw starts up again as I reach the cliff and I stop short. Jane stands beside the swollen dead trunk while Myles works the chainsaw, cutting into the base. The angle seems backward to me as Myles is cutting in the direction of the slope instead of the river.

He stops sawing and lifts his safety goggles. "Okay, Jane. Give it a kick." He laughs after his loud instruction.

My heart halts.

Jane gives the tree a swift kick with the flat of her construction boot.

The tree trunk quivers, but nothing else happens.

"Again," Myles yells, his voice carrying up the incline.

Jane strikes the dead wood once more.

A sharp crack resonates upward, and for a second, I think *that's it*. The tree is going over.

Jane kicks one more time. The tree topples toward the river.

And Jane loses her footing, sliding down the remainder of the slope and slipping into the water.

At this portion of the river, the first few inches of water from the shore are shallow, but then the bottom drops off drastically. The speed of the water varies depending on rainfall and wind. The middle is unforgiving.

Time stands still as I process my wife's slide into the river.

She isn't popping up.

I drop my coffee and her tea and race to the water.

29

Playlist: "If I Die Young" – The Band Perry

[Jane]

My first thought upon hitting the water is—*fuck, it's cold.*

My second—*I am in the river.*

The shore drops off quickly, and the water moves fast. I can't seem to swim.

Instead, I catch the bald trunk preceding me into the water. Stripped of all branches and leaves, the dead wood rolls like a lumber log. *This isn't good.* The tree heads toward the bridge's underpass.

I'd closed my mouth as I went under, but my nose and ears are clogged. Sounds are muffled. The only noise is the roar of the water around me.

Could a fish be beneath me?

Do fish eat humans?

Will a fish mistake me for a giant plant?

My heart races with fear of being eaten versus the danger of being dragged down the river.

With a thud, the giant log stalls on the bridge footing. The trunk is in the way of me grabbing onto the bridge base. I can't fight the current to go around the tree. I can't risk swimming to another bridge support. Instead, I struggle to hold onto the large trunk, threatening to roll me under.

Maybe I can get on it, like a canoe.

With an arm draped over the tree, I attempt to wrap my leg over the slippery hump. I lose my grip and plunge beneath the surface. My ears fill again. My leg is stuck. *This is really not good.*

I lift my head, gasping for air. My boot laces have caught on peeling bark. With my ankle practically above my head, I can't reach my foot. I twist and go under once more. River water fills my throat. Every scream for help is met with another rush of water.

I can't breathe.

You can drown in two inches of water, if you panic.

I don't want to die by . . .

Rushing river.

Deep water.

Fish eating me.

My head slams into something, and everything goes dark.

TIME PASSES in a montage of flashes.

My name.

Chest burning.

Throat aching.

Muddled sirens.

My name again.

Body lifted.

Peace in nothingness.

SOMETHING BEEPS NEARBY.

Opening my eyes, drop-ceiling tiles are overhead.

Wherever I am is dark.

I can't seem to will my body to move, so I close my eyes again.

My name is spoken.

Mach-ilicious, whispers through my mind.

WHEN I WAKE NEXT, my body is sore. The back of one hand is stiff and pinching where an IV needle pierces my skin. Gingerly, I roll my head on a pillow, registering I'm in the hospital.

Mach sits in a chair beside the bed. His head rests on the edge. One of his hands is on my forearm. He looks peaceful with his lids closed and his mouth slightly agape. His salt and pepper facial hair is a little fuller than normal. The flannel shirt he wears hugs his arms. He looks good casual or classy. I'm jealous how easily he pulls it off.

I risk moving my arm, reaching for his hair. My memory is fuzzy. How long have I been out of it?

Mach's head springs upward at my touch. "Hey." His voice is full of sleep and strain, and he scrubs a hand over his face before looking directly at me. "You're awake."

"How long have I been sleeping?"

Mach huffs. "Sleeping? You were out cold, baby. Do you remember what happened?"

The tree. The river. My boot.

"I was stuck." My forehead furrows, and something pinches

my skin. I move my hand with the IV despite the tight pull of my flesh. Reaching for my head, I discover a square bandage near my hairline.

"You hit your head. A couple stitches up there. You'll still look beautiful." Mach's voice rasps with the compliment.

"What happened?" My forehead furrows again and I flinch at the tug of flesh.

"The second I saw you slip, I was down that riverbank." Mach sits upright and shifts so his hand slides underneath mine on the bed. "I couldn't get to you fast enough."

"You went in the river after me?"

Mach and I lock eyes before he frowns. "You're my wife, Jane."

"So what?" I huff a laugh.

He didn't need to risk his life for my stupidity. I slipped. I got stuck on a tree trying to climb it while it bobbed in a moving river.

His hand tightens around mine, and he shakes his head slowly, lowering his gaze to our fingers. When he peers back up at me again, those dark eyes are a storm cloud of emotion. Instead of speaking, he lifts my hand and cups it with his other one before pressing his lips to my knuckles. His lids lower.

"I couldn't lose you, baby," he mutters to my fingers.

A tear escapes the corner of my eye. I hadn't felt it form.

"Mach," I whisper before closing my eyes. I don't want him to see me cry, which is ridiculous as shutting my lids won't keep him from seeing the tears. My hand is dropped. The chair's metal feet scrape across the tile floor. The mattress depresses, and a warm hand cups the side of my face. I try to shake my head, willing away his touch. When Mach's lips come to my forehead to the side of the bandage, another tear seeps free.

"You're okay, baby. I wouldn't have let anything happen to you, especially not that damn river."

I nod, but the tears continue to leak. I want to curl into

myself, push away from him, but Mach holds my face and lingers on my forehead. And more damn liquid trickles from my eyes, flowing down to my ear.

Mach saved me. He came after me. I don't want to read into his actions. He clearly reacted to a life-or-death situation. He jumped in after me so I wouldn't drown. There isn't more to his response. His reaction was only instinct.

I wouldn't let anything happen to you.

More tears fall as relief and hope clash inside me.

"I'm tired," I whisper, although I'm certain I've been sleeping for long enough.

Mach gently presses his forehead to mine. "Rest, baby. I'll be right here. I'm not going anywhere." As he releases me, I can't look at him, so I only nod with my eyes closed. Then I shift to my side with a sharp wince before drifting into fitful dreams.

As I'm surprisingly not suffering a concussion but sore ribs and a cut on my head, I'm released after twenty-three hours of observation. Mach is incensed, but the hospital needs the bed, and I don't want to be here any longer.

Our ride home is silent. To my amazement, Mach is driving his truck. I have so many questions about why he hasn't driven it and what made him drive it now, but my head hurts too much for deep conversations.

When we arrive at the big house, Camilla flutters around me, asking how I am, if I'm hungry, do I need anything. She's a buzzing bee of attention and anxiety.

"Ma, let her be," Mach directs, holding my elbow like I'm an invalid.

I can walk. I'm just weak.

"Whatever you need, dove. You just ask." Camilla is sweet,

and my own mother should probably know I nearly drowned, but I don't have the energy to call her and explain everything. I can hardly comprehend all that's happened myself. Fortunately, Mae never called our mother to out my secret marriage.

"You need rest," Mach says behind me.

I want to argue that what I need is to work. I've lost a day or two with the river debacle, but I can also admit I'm not myself yet. Staring at a computer screen or trying to decipher a business plan hurts my head just thinking of either.

"Okay." I head for the stairs.

Mach follows me. His attention would be everything to me if I thought it came from his heart and not someplace else—like obligation. If I had died, his inheritance would have been jeopardized. He needs a wife as stipulated by the will. We still have months to live through this arrangement. Death has no place in our predicament.

Still dressed, I crawl onto the bed.

"Change, baby," Mach softly commands. "Or I'll undress you myself."

Even with stitches in my head and an ache in my chest, his words set my blood rushing. I want to draw him to me, hold him tight, and thank him with my body for saving me. Having sex with him would only confuse matters, though.

The other night, he mentioned renegotiating the terms of our arrangement. I had no idea what he wanted to suggest as our conversation fell off-topic with my big reveal. I don't know why I told him about Ripley and me. Or why I mentioned the baby. No one had known, not even my sisters. I had been hoping to get to three months before I'd announced my pregnancy. Twelve weeks felt like a safety net. I'd miscarried at seven and a half.

The memory adds to my exhaustion.

"I can do it myself," I mutter, sitting upright and wincing at the pain around my mid-section. Thankfully, I hadn't broken any ribs.

"Let me help you." Mach rushes forward as if to catch me. As if I'll tumble off the edge of the bed.

"Why?" The word comes out harsher than it should, so I try again. "Why?" My voice cracks on my second attempt. *Why is he being so nice to me, so attentive, so sweet?*

"I just . . ." Mach swipes a hand over his hair, and his eyes hold on mine. "I want to help." That uncanny ability he has to hold his eyes still would typically upset me. But I don't have the will to fight him. His lies fill me with sorrow instead. I don't want help because of some misplaced sense of duty.

"I can do it." I stand on shaky legs while Mach watches me cross the floor to the dresser containing some of my clothing. We each have a box in the corners of the room, emphasizing the temporariness of our situation.

Only eleven more months. Less than four, if we rush.

I fumble in the drawer for comfy leggings and a loose shirt. My hand wades through the things my sister sent me until I brush against something silky smooth.

"What's this?" Mach questions from behind me, glancing down at the dresser drawer over my shoulder.

"My sister thought she was being funny by sending me lingerie." The black one-piece with thick straps has a deep cut between the breast panels. The negligee is more lace than silk, revealing and risqué, and still has the price tag attached because I've never worn it.

Mach reaches around me and pulls the sexy lingerie from the drawer, but I'm quick to grab the thin material and force it back underneath other clothing.

"You've been keeping a secret from me, Mrs. Wright." His voice deepens, and his breath whispers across my neck. I hate how the pulse lower in me rachets up a beat, drumming faster, pumping harder. Even weakened, I want him. I want to feel alive, compared to this off-balanced sensation I have around him. I want to feel like I did on our wedding night. I want him to ravish me.

Screw my heart that doesn't like the idea.

I need to be close to someone, be physical and free, and that someone is my husband standing too close to me.

"I'll just be . . ." I point at the bathroom with more conservative clothing in hand. When I turn, Mach is still too close. Our eyes lock, and his lips tempt. He caught me off guard when he kissed me on the street the other day, but the kiss previous to that—the one where he made it clear I didn't mean anything to him—made its mark.

I twist away from Mach, catching my breath and shutting my eyes for a second before taking shaky steps to the bathroom. My faltering has nothing to do with the condition of my body and everything to do with the man behind me.

30

Playlist: "Best I Ever Had" – Gary Allen

[Jane]

I wake during the night to find Mach staring at me. He's seated beside the bed in a wooden high-back chair that is more decorative than functional. The frame creaks under his weight, and the cane seating crackles. His elbows are braced on his thighs while his fingers steeple before his lips.

"Hey," I whisper groggily. Our room is dark minus dim moonlight streaming through the window. "What are you doing?"

He looks like he's deep in thought, almost praying. Some might consider it creepy that he's watching me, but the darkness in his eyes offers protection more than fear.

"Did I wake you?" His voice is rough, distant even.

"No." Attempting to sit upright, I wince at the stiffness in my midsection. "What time is it?"

"Late." Mach doesn't bother glancing at his expensive watch. He shifts on the seat again, reaching out to cautiously press me back to the bed. His eyes focus on my body. "You need to sleep. Lay back down."

Not making it very far in my effort to sit up, I gingerly lower back to the bed.

"What's on your mind, Mr. Wright?" My question is as quiet as the night around us.

"I was married." His voice deepens, rough and strained. "I was young." His tone lifts with reflection. "Tracy was the love of my life." Mach drops his steepled fingers and dangles his hands between his thighs. His head lowers, eyes aimed toward the floor.

The truth that she was the love of his life stings.

"We were so different. She was such a good girl, and she was Myles's friend first. I didn't notice her much. Too busy making trouble, never considering she might be interested in someone like me. Bastard child. Troublemaker. Always angry. Eager to move on." Mach exhales. "Then my senior year happened."

His head rocks slowly side-to-side. "It started as a dare at a party. She kissed me. We started sneaking around. Her dad wouldn't have approved. I didn't want Myles to know." Mach glances at me. "We're twins. We share almost as much as we don't, and I didn't want to share whatever Tracy and I were doing with him. I wanted something that was just for me. She was his friend but my lover. We were only having fun. I was eighteen. She was a year younger than us."

Mach pauses, swiping a hand through his hair, before continuing. "We did the long-distance thing my freshman year of college, and then she joined me at WVU. We no longer needed to sneak around. When I was a junior, she found out she was pregnant." He hangs his head again. "She lost the baby."

My mouth falls open, but I hold back my gasp. I know her pain. I see his in the drawn, sorrowful expression on his face.

"I told her I'd have married her baby or not, and so we did. I was twenty-one. She was twenty. And I still had dreams of leaving this place. I did everything I could to be top of my class, earning a scholarship to graduate school. Kellogg Business School at Northwestern University, outside of Chicago." Pride fills his voice. "I'd assumed she'd want to go all the places with me. I was wrong."

Mach glances up at me. "She didn't want to leave Wright-wood. Her family was here, she argued. Her friends. Myles."

I chew my lip, watching Mach's expression shift again. Harden a little bit.

"He hadn't gone to college. He wanted to build. I wanted to own. He was comfortable here. I couldn't wait to leave. He convinced her to stay." Mach's voice turns edgy, tight and dark.

"When I graduated undergrad, I wanted her to come with me to Chicago. I didn't trust the distance. Nine hours was too far away. And Myles was here."

Did Mach not trust his brother? Did he not trust his wife?

"There was a graduation party for me. Charlese hosted it. I'd been drinking. Tracy wanted to leave." Mach's voice comes faster. "She took my truck. Myles went with her."

"Her best friend." Mach spits the words and continues his mockery. "He understood her."

I stare at Mach as he's momentarily lost in a memory he doesn't share with me. With a deep sigh, he carries on.

"Charlese lived on the other side of the bridge. I had this sick sensation about Tracy leaving with Myles. We'd had a huge argument earlier in the day. She'd told me she didn't want to leave. She wasn't going to transfer in her senior year of college. She said I was selfish. I wasn't listening to her. I didn't hear her needs. I didn't love her like she loved me."

He takes a deep breath. "Myles understood. He loved her. She was leaving me for him."

Mach scrubs both hands over his face as if wiping away the recall. He sits up straighter. "There was an accident. Something in the road and Tracy swerved. She crashed into a pylon on the opposite side of the road, on the edge of the bridge, and slid down the embankment." Mach exhales. "That truck is a classic. It didn't have airbags or safety features like modern vehicles. Myles had been pinned by the crushed door on the passenger side. The truck was half-submerged in the water on the driver's side."

He closes his eyes as if re-seeing that night. "By the time I arrived, Myles was screaming for me to save her. He couldn't reach her, wedged against the door. Tracy was out cold. Her head bent into the steering wheel," he chokes on a strangled sob and swipes at his face.

"Mach," I whisper, surmising the rest. His wife had slammed her head into the steering wheel, snapping her neck.

"When I heard the sirens, I just knew . . ." He swallows hard. "Shoved my arms right through the driver side glass. I still don't know how I had the strength. I struggled to remove her. Paramedics told me later my efforts hadn't mattered."

"Mach, I'm so sorry." At some point in his story, I raised a hand and covered my mouth. The image in my head was horrific. The truck sinking. Tracy's head bent forward. Myles beside her, pinned and watching helplessly as his friend—and Mach's wife—died.

"I later learned she was pregnant." Mach doesn't look at me. "Myles told me."

Dear God, does he think his wife was pregnant by his brother? I don't want to think it. I don't want to believe it. And I don't ask. The possibility is too much, and Mach's story is already heartbreaking.

He remains silent for a long time, eyes blinking as he stares at the floorboards.

I let his thoughts settle before I reach for him. "Why aren't you in bed?"

I need to touch him, hold him. He doesn't need my sympathy. He had it, but he didn't need to hear another apology. There were no words to express the pain I felt on his behalf.

"I didn't want to disturb you. I can't seem to lay in bed beside you without touching you, and I don't want to hurt you."

The reminder of my aches conjures images of me sliding into the river. I can't imagine what Mach must have thought, must have felt, as I traveled downstream.

"I'm okay." I wiggle my outstretched hand at him. "Come to bed, Mr. Wright."

"I didn't want to lose you, too," he whispers, like a weak breeze flickering a candle flame. My heart melts, like wax dripping down a pillar.

Waggling my fingers once again, I stretch for him. "I'm okay, Mach. Come to bed."

IN THE MORNING, Mach is wrapped around me, and while it aches to lie on my side, I don't move. Our legs are entwined; one of his over mine, and one of mine over his, with our ankles hooking us together. His warm hand coasts down my arm from shoulder to wrist. Then, he slips to my waist, outlining my midsection, before skimming over my hip. He massages the top of my outer thigh, and my back arches. Something long and hard presses into my backside.

With my eyes still closed, I relish the feel of his thickness pushing at the seam between my lower cheeks. I've had that *Mach*-nificence inside me, filling me, making me whole in a way I've never felt before. I want that sensation again.

Mach's hand slides upward, retracing my hip before slipping forward and landing on my lower belly. He gently presses his hand flat, and I arch my body again, tapping against him, wedging the firm length of him against my backside.

"Mrs. Wright," he purrs against my nape. His breath is hot. The title scorching.

I'm his wife. And I want my husband.

Mach tips his pelvis, rocking forward. His hand on my lower belly drags over my hip again and lands on my backside. Fingers dig into the globe of my ass. "Ever have anyone here?"

The question should be inappropriate. Instead, it's decadent and dreamy, and fantasies fill my morning thoughts. *Take me.* Take me everywhere.

I shake my head against the pillow. One of my hands remains under the stuffed case, and I clench on the fill. I want him inside me. I want us connected.

After his revelation last night, the desire to comfort Mach is strong. My willpower is waning. This might all be an arrangement, but I want to reassure him I'm his—if he wants me— I'm his.

"Mach." My body grows desperate. My legs rustle against his. My pussy clenches. I crave him.

"Fuck." The expletive tickles the back of my neck, and then he's off me. He shifts so quickly it's like ripping off the blankets on a cold morning. I shiver as I fall to my back. Mach sits on the edge of the bed, his muscular back to me. His hands grip the mattress like he wants to tear it off the bed frame.

What happened? I stretch my arm, reaching for him but stop short of touching him. Is he thinking of her? Did he imagine I was his late wife? Did he not know it was me . . . the new Mrs. Wright?

"Mach?"

He stands. With his back still to me, my gaze falls to the brilliant colors up and down each of his arms. The ink covers scars. I'd felt the rises and dips of his skin the night of our wedding. Drunk on *Mach*-lust and champagne kisses, I hadn't asked questions later as I'd planned. I simply drank him in that night and ignored answers that might have burst the bubble of our erotic evening.

"I don't want to hurt you," Mach states, shifting through clothes draped over a box. He wears snug boxer briefs, and I don't have to see his front to know what the heavy shaft behind cotton looks like. I already know what it feels like as well, and I want him again.

"Then don't," I whisper. On the inside, I scream, *Stop breaking my heart.*

Mach stills and glances at me over his shoulder. A deep crease forms between his brows. Once again, we're having separate conversations. He means physically, in my condition, he doesn't want to harm me. I mean emotionally, in our position, he's killing me. We're married, but in name only, and I'd been wrong to interpret this morning's cuddle as anything other than what it was—a mistake.

Perhaps even mistaken identity.

I'm the wrong wife on his mind.

31

Playlist: "Without A Fight" – Brad Paisley ft. Demi Lovato

[Mach]

Jane was out of commission for days by doctor's orders, but that did not stop her from working. The first recovery day, she was in our room, laptop open and plans spread across the bed. Two days later, she was in the front room on the couch again.

"What are you doing out of bed?" I snap, frustrated by three mornings of waking wrapped around my wife, fighting the pull to outline her body and cover every inch of her skin with kisses.

I don't want to hurt Jane, as I told her. She needs to recover. Then, we can talk.

"I need to work." Jane waves at the notebook and pens, the papers, and her open laptop.

She's a machine, but she's also a woman I want to explore. The curve of her hip. The press of her ass against my dick. The sharp, short intake of her breath when I touch her. I need more of her. I want my wife.

"You need to rest, baby," I groan because the sooner she gets better, the sooner I can touch her like I want.

"Jane, lovey, you have a visitor." Ma's cheery voice has me spinning to face little Willow standing beside my mother, holding her hand. Theo Clarke stands hesitantly behind Ma.

"Hi, Willow." Jane waves, offering the child a huge smile. The brightness reminds me of the grin she gave me when I accepted Myles as our contractor and said we would stay the duration of this renovation project. By Christmas. That was the new end goal.

I step toward Theo, offering a hand. His voice is quiet as he explains their visit. "I wanted her to know some people survive that river."

I nod, understanding his intention. He needs Willow to know Jane is safe.

Jane motions for Willow to come to her, and she clears a spot on the couch beside her. Willow steps close to Jane, and Jane rubs a hand up the little one's thin back. Willow's brown hair nearly matches Jane's. She has blue eyes as well, and for a moment, I envision the child Jane might have had with Ripley Edgar. My stomach clenches. I hate the idea of her having his kid, and despite Jane's broken heart, I'm happy she didn't have one with him. He didn't deserve a baby any more than he deserved Jane.

"How is the park coming along?" Jane asks Willow, using an authoritative tone like Willow is the chief inspector or project manager. "Is the work passing inspection?"

"They fixed the boards and painted the wood. There's a giant Connect-Four game." Willow's little voice fills with excitement.

"You need to promise me a game." Jane swipes a hand over

Willow's hair, brushing it back from her sweet face. "What else is down there?"

Willow explains the other additions, including the new swings hung from trees. "And the dead tree is gone." She refers to the tree trunk that Jane had kicked into the river. Willow's small fingers reach for the buttons on Jane's shirt, which happens to be another one of my old flannels from high school. Jane looks good in my faded clothing, younger, fresher. Not that she isn't stunning on the daily, but the casual attire works for her as well.

"Did you hear how I pushed that old thing into the water?" Jane asks.

"You fell into the river," Willow corrects, pointedly looking at the bandage on Jane's head. With shaky fingers, she traces around the square patch of gauze and hospital tape.

Jane stills. I have no doubt we think the same thing—Willow's parents died in that river. Tracy died in that water as well. I shudder to think what could have happened to Jane.

"I did fall in the river." Jane lifts her voice, sitting up straighter. "But I'm okay now." She bops Willow on her nose.

"My Mommy fell into the river, but she didn't come back out."

Sweet Jesus.

Jane doesn't falter. "Well, in my case, Big Mach saved me." Jane glances at me, offering a grateful smile while questioning me with those blue eyes. Did she really think I'd let her go? She is my wife. *I love—* I stop the words I can't possibly feel for Jane. Feelings I won't ever risk again. That river took my heart.

My acushla, Ma calls Jane. She cannot be my heartbeat when I don't have one to beat.

"Does it hurt?" Willow's tiny voice pulls my attention back to her and Jane.

Jane reaches for the bandage. "Oh, it smarts a little bit but nothing a few stitches can't heal." She sucks in a breath sitting up taller and placing a hand on her midsection. Still offering a reassuring smile, she adds, "My ribs hurt more."

I knew I shouldn't be touching her, holding her at night, wrapping around her as we sleep.

"But your heart is healing you." Willow's statement forces Jane to glance at me before focusing back on her. "Miss Camilla says our hearts know how to heal everything."

Jane gives a quick glance to Ma behind me before a crease forms between her brows and she answers Willow. "Yes. My heart is healing me."

Jane then asks Willow if she can draw her a picture of the new park as a means to change the topic.

I watch them interact another minute, wondering what Jane would have been like as a mother. Inside my chest, the hollowness thumps three times, the rhythm rapid and slightly refreshing.

What would I have been like as a father? Some questions will never have answers.

Still, I can't pull my gaze from Jane smiling at Willow, murmuring encouragement to her, complimenting her coloring skills. The girl leans against Jane's knees while she draws. The image of a mother and child is almost too much, and when I glance at Ma, she has grandchildren-hope in her eyes.

Stepping over to her, I bump her shoulder with my arm. "I'm too old."

Ma levels me with a stare that's compassionate while meaningful. "You're never too old to love a child, my son."

Peering back at Jane, I wonder if it isn't too late to love her.

~

"You never told me what you wanted to talk about the other night?" Jane looks at me across my mother's kitchen table a few nights later. It's late. We'd been working after dinner. Again.

The realization hits me. We work too much.

"What night?" I lift a small canning jar of Ma's scotch, taking a short sip. Ma really needs crystal glasses.

Jane twirls the stem of her wineglass, watching the liquid softly swirl within it. She hasn't been taking her pain medication. My woman is tough. "The night before I fell into the river."

The night I planned to propose Jane and I have sex again. And again. *And again.*

"And you never explained to me why you were kicking a tree? What was Myles thinking letting you work on that tree with him?" Why was my brother even down that slope? With his body's imbalance, why didn't he have his senior tradesman doing the cutting?

Jane shrugs. "The night before, I'd told you about Ripley and the baby. I was . . . angry. The memories." She pauses and cups the bowl of her wineglass. "Kicking that tree felt good."

She mischievously smiles at me, but the lightness is missing from her eyes.

"I hadn't pegged you for aggressive behavior." I lean against the table, crossing my arms on the surface. Does Jane like things a little rough? Could she handle me if I drove deeper, moved faster, took her harder? The thought makes me shiver with the magnetic pull to find out.

"Not aggressive. Just"—she waves a hand before herself—"pent up." Her eyes meet mine before she quickly lifts her wineglass and disappears behind it.

Pent up? God, I hope she's wound as tight as I am, needing the relief I want to give her. Relief only she can give me. I've kept my word to be loyal to Jane. Of course, I'd be faithful to our vows. But what I feel is more than just a commitment to a pledge.

I want Jane.

"Actually, that's what I wanted to talk to you about. Maybe

we could discover more about each other. I know we said only on our wedding night, but we are married, and it isn't uncommon for—"

"Oh." The sharp intake of a masculine voice turns my head. Myles stands just inside the kitchen. "I didn't realize you were both still up."

"Who did you expect to find here?" While my brother lives in the Small House, he's well aware Jane and I are staying in Ma's place. Ma isn't a night owl.

"I was hoping to speak with Jane." Myles hitches his body to lean more prominently on his cane.

I fall back in my seat and wave toward my wife. *My* wife. "Well, speak."

"It can wait." Myles lowers his head like he's been caught doing something he shouldn't. Wanting what he can't have. I have no doubt he's attracted to Jane. She's dynamic and power- ful, organized and creative, and fucking beautiful. And he *can't* have her. Not this time. Not this one.

"Whatever you have to say to Jane, you can say in front of me," I challenge my brother.

"Mach," Jane mutters. Her wineglass is back on the table, and her fingers pinch the stem. She looks ready to pick up the glass and toss her remaining wine at *me*.

"Tomorrow," Myles groans.

"Tonight." Whatever couldn't originally wait until daylight can be said tonight to my wife with me present. Old insecurities return hard and fast, and my attention turns back to Jane, pointing between her and my twin. "Unless there is something I'm not supposed to know about happening here."

Jane's eyes narrow, the glare piercing. "Don't do this."

I narrow my eyes back at her. "Don't do what?" My body hums. Heart hammers. *Is she attracted to him?*

"Don't project onto me something that happened in the past." Jane's attention shifts to Myles before coming back to me.

"Why are you looking at him?" I lean forward again and glare at her, searching her face as if her attraction is written in the fine lines.

"Jesus, not this again," Myles mutters.

"Exactly," I yell, twisting as I stand and knock over the kitchen chair. "This will not happen again." I point from Myles to Jane. "She's my wife, Myles. Mine."

"Cut the Neanderthal act. Jane doesn't belong to you any more than Tracy did. And even at that, the whole town knows this marriage is a sham. She's a means to an end."

Jane's breath hitches.

I level a hard stare at my brother, itching to grab his cane and beat him over the head with it. He has some serious fucking balls to speak about Jane like she doesn't belong to me, like she doesn't matter to me.

"Fuck you, Myles. Don't you dare speak like that about Jane." The hum inside me turns to an uncontrollable vibration. I'd never punched my brother after what happened. I didn't speak to him again, deliberately cutting him out of my life. But right now, in this moment, I'm ready to let him feel my wrath.

Myles looks past me at Jane. "I didn't mean it like that. You're helping us all. I understand that." Myles peers back at me. "Do you? Do you appreciate what she's doing for you? For us? For this town?"

"Of course, I do," I bark.

Jane's given up a lot to stay here, working under a guise with Impact that we have a special client who needs personal attention for an undetermined amount of time. But the project isn't indefinite. *By Christmas.* Only a few more months.

I'll only have Jane as mine for a few more months.

I look back at Jane. Time is slipping away from me.

"Myles, why don't we meet tomorrow?" Jane offers. "On The Curve? Say seven a.m.?"

Her words strike another chord. How often do they meet? Is

she falling for my brother? Is she having sex with him? My thoughts spiral out of control.

I can't take my eyes off my wife, but the light tap of Myles's cane signals his retreat. I hold my breath until he's gone, then I snap, "You will not meet with him."

"*You* will not tell me what to do." Jane's eyes narrow again. The bright blue rivals the first flame on a gas stove. She burns me with every blink of her lids, and slowly, she stands, facing off with me from across the table.

"Do not fall for him," I demand, leaning on the surface.

Jane's brows rise, matching my position. "What are you suggesting?" Her words are short, sharp, and exaggerated.

Swiping a hand over my face, I try to settle my nerves. "Nothing. I didn't mean anything. I just . . . I don't want you to meet with him alone. Okay?"

"Because you think I'd have sex with him?" Her tone is incredulous as if she's read my thoughts. "I'm so easy? Like Ripley suggested. Or maybe you just think I'm desperate? Eager and willing?" Her voice rises with every accusation.

Fuck no. "No, I don't—"

"I wouldn't have sex with Myles." Jane levels me with a glare that could tear down the bridge over the river. "I'm not attracted to Myles, but this isn't about attraction, is it? This is about your history with him . . . and sex." She pauses. "Sex with me."

Her fiery eyes scan my face as if reading my guilt. "You want sex with me. Was that what you were going to propose the other night? No strings attached. Just sex. And for how long? The months while we hide out down here? I can be your secret fuck buddy until the clock runs out."

Jane blows out a breath and her lips tremble. "You might call your position with other women honesty. They knew what they were getting from you. Am I right, Mr. Wright? Sex only for a night. No repeats. Isn't that how you work?" She hastily points between us. "But this will not be friends with benefits."

"No, you're my wife," I remind her. My voice is surprisingly calm while I'm anything but. My heart races. My dick is hard. I want to reach across the table and spread her over it.

"It's just a label, Mr. Wright. *A means to an end.* And right now, we aren't even friends." With that, Jane rounds the table, leaving me stunned.

How did things get so derailed?

Myles. It's always Myles.

32

———————

Playlist: "Meant to Be" – Bebe Rexha ft. Florida Georgia Line

[Jane]

I'm drowning.

The water around me is cold and murky, and I can't breathe. My chest tightens. My heart rate skyrockets. And something comes into my line of sight.

A flathead catfish swims toward me, his ugly mug smiling at me.

I'm going to die. The thought hits me hard, but it doesn't feel like drowning will kill me.

Something is heavy inside my chest, holding me underwater. I kick my legs, but I don't move. I gulp in more of the river, filling my lungs, burning my open eyes.

The fish swims closer.

I gaze upward, sensing the surface above me from the trickle of sunshine streaming over my head. I will myself to fight. My body jolts as my legs tighten in an attempt to propel myself upward.

I fail.

In a last-ditch effort, I open my mouth to scream despite the liquid around me—

"Hey." A sleepy but deeply masculine voice croaks behind me. My lids blink open, eyes assessing my surroundings while the remainder of my body is frozen in place.

I'm in Camilla's home. I'm in bed. Mach is behind me. We had a fight.

"You okay?" His gravelly voice whispers near my ear. His concern has me spinning despite the hammering in my chest and the ache of my ribs. I face Mach and curl my head into his chest.

"Bad dream?" His voice rasps as his hand coasts along my spine.

I nod against his warm skin. I can't clearly see him in the darkness of the room, so I let my fingertips be my eyes. Reaching for his chest, I flatten my palm against the tightness of his pecs. His heart beats in a steady rhythm beneath my touch.

Mach exhales over me, his arms wrapping around my back. Our knees knock. Mach cups the back of my thigh and tugs my leg between his.

I inhale the sleepy scent of man and forest on Mach's skin, breathing deep his nearness and willing away thoughts of a flat-faced fish attacking me underwater. I'm afraid to close my eyes again, so I focus on the darkness and continue to outline his chest. My fingertips stretch toward his collarbone. Touching him here is strangely reassuring.

Our fight was so big.

"Nothing's going to happen to you, baby." He tugs me tighter to him.

I continue to explore him by dragging my left hand over his shoulder while my right flattens over his heart. The beats within his chest resonate through his skin and seep into my palm.

Ba-dum. Ba-dum. Ba-dum.

Acushla, as his mother says. A pulse.

Mach rocks his pelvis forward, the slightest shift, and we touch. My lower belly brushes the stiffening length in his boxer briefs. He's so long, so hard, so ready, but my mind can't release the dream.

What does Mach dream about? Who does he see in his head? Does he believe I'm a means to an end?

I lower my hand and slip it under Mach's arm, reaching around his back to press my palm against the curve of his shoulder blade. My fingers dribble down his spine and rest above the band of his boxers. He's so firm, so strong.

His lips come to my forehead, and he mutters against me. "Go back to sleep, baby."

I'm afraid to sleep but I nod again. Closing my eyes, the fish swimming in my head mocks me with that flat grin of his.

This man will never be yours.

But with Mach's heart beating beneath my hand and our bodies pressing together in dangerous ways, I fall into a restless slumber, dreaming he could be mine one day.

IN THE MORNING, I wake with another start as Mach nearly rips himself from my grasp. He's quick to twist and sit upright, then stand. He disappears into the bathroom like a streak of lightning. The shower turns on, and I close my eyes. I drift back to sleep, dozing as I'd done most of the night.

Our argument from last night lingers. The fish dream still haunts me. My body is wound from Mach's closeness.

I need sexual relief.

Once Mach is finished and leaves the room, I rise from the

bed. I'm desperate for the shower as a place to hide and relieve the tension within me. The tub would be a good place to relax, but the smallness doesn't allow for a full-body soak. The interesting thing about the bathroom is Camilla keeps us stocked with fresh towels every day. Decoratively rolled and set on an open shelf above the toilet, the service and setup remind me of a hotel. But that's not on my mind as I step into the tub and let the warm water pepper my back.

Using a washcloth, I stroke over my skin, my clit pulsing with anticipation, like the sensitive nub knows what's coming. I lightly scrub around my breasts and glide down my belly until curling my hand between my legs. The softness of the terrycloth is the right texture to tease my clit and have me rocking my hips almost instantly. In my head, Mach kneels before me, mouth open and vigorously lapping. I reach for the wall, pressing the curtain that surrounds the tub in a three-sixty fashion against the plaster.

Oh yes. Right there, Mach. Don't stop.

My hips thrust. My fingers rub. My mouth falls open in a silent cry.

And the shower curtain rips open.

The washcloth drops to the tub base with a wet slap. There is no disguising the heaving of my chest. My heart hammers within. I was so close. And I'm shamefully embarrassed.

"What were you doing?" The gruffness of Mach's voice isn't angry or accusatory. His chest rises and lowers almost as rapidly as mine.

I can't answer him. My eyes briefly meet his and glance away. I should scream at him to get out. I should reach for the curtain and tug it between us. I don't do either. Instead, I stand still as Mach's eyes scan my body from the tip of my nose to the hair at the apex of my legs.

"Finish," he demands, snapping his gaze back to my eyes. He releases the curtain and steps back.

"Mach, I—"

He grips the back of his collar and tugs his T-shirt over his head. Before me is the magnificent display of his bright arms and smooth skin with a sprinkle of chest hair over his pecs.

Mach-nificent.

"Let me watch." He pops the button on his jeans and lowers the zipper. All I can do is watch him. His hand disappears into his boxers, and he adjusts himself.

As if my fingers have their own will, I circle the pad of one around my breast, drawing closer and closer to my nipple while Mach's eyes heat. The shower still pours over my side, and my skin pebbles—a combination of exposure to the cool air and the hot desire vibrating off Mach.

"Get out of the tub." His curt voice turns to a growl, like a man at the end of his rope. His hands fist at his sides. His jeans dip on his hips. I don't miss the peep of his cockhead above his boxer waistband.

Mach holds out a hand to help me out of the tub, and I cautiously step over the rounded edge. Once outside the basin, I reach for a towel. My nipples could cut the mirror. My flesh is a ripple of bumps.

"No," Mach snaps, and I blink at his tone. With a hand on my hip, he spins me around, back to his front, and tugs me against him. My wet hair hits his chest while he slides his hand to my lower belly. While he's pressing against me, I lean on him, the dampness of me warmed by his skin.

"Tell me you want me inside you." His rough voice by my ear makes my goosebumps goosebump. I shiver as he places a kiss on my shoulder.

"I want you inside me." The breathless admission falls from my lips, and I close my eyes. The next few minutes are a frenzy of activity. Mach's hand slips between my thighs, and two fingers impale me. I cry out as I pitch forward. Then I groan as he deliciously slides them almost out of me. I clamp my legs together, holding him in place.

He chuckles. His fingers delve deep again, and I moan in relief.

Leaning forward, I reach for the raised lip of the clawfoot tub. Mach works one-handed with his jeans and briefs, shoving them down his hips while never missing a beat to dip deeper inside me before retreating to my entrance, teasing me that he'll leave my body before rushing upward once again.

"You're so wet, baby. And I want you badly." My feet are tapped with one bare foot of his, suggesting I spread my legs, which I do. The warm tip of his cock glides along the seam of my backside before slipping between my legs. "You told me the other day no one has ever had you here."

His fingers release my clit and skitter up my middle. Mach tickles between my breasts which hang heavy in my bent position. "What about here? Anyone fuck you between those gorgeous tits?"

I moan at the thought before shaking my head once more.

"This might be one of my favorite places on you." His fingers continue to stroke between my breasts before lowering back to my hip.

"But this is my most favorite place." Mach tips his pelvis, and his dick surges inward, gloriously filling me in one swift movement. We both grunt. Mach grips both my hips, guiding me forward and back, coasting over his thickness. "Jesus, have I missed you."

The words surprise me as well as spur me on. I arch back, meeting him thrust for thrust, rushing as the lost orgasm rebuilds.

"You touch yourself, thinking of me?" His voice strains as he hammers into me.

"Yes." I huff, the word choppy with our rhythm. The sound

of him sliding into me blends with the stream from the shower. Our bodies clap together, and I'm so close once more.

"Mach," I groan, needing his fingers.

"I got you, baby." He reaches around me, fingertips rubbing my clit while he enters me over and over again. He begins to slow.

"No," I cry out, reaching behind me for his hip, forcing him forward to fill me.

"Like this, baby? Come over me. Burst like that bubbly champagne." Mach holds still while I ride his glorious length. His fingers work my sensitive nub. Then I pop. Like a cork sprung from a bottle, I release, hissing and bubbling, and trickling over him with my own form of wetness.

My orgasm is Mach's cue, and he rocks forward, jostling my body. I push at his wrist, suggesting he remove his fingers and concentrate on what he needs. Our skin slaps. My knees give a little. Mach digs his fingertips into my hip bones, and then he stills. The pulsing of him inside me matches the rhythm of my heartbeat.

Eventually, Mach leans over me, his forehead against one shoulder blade. "Did I hurt you? You shouldn't be out of bed." Immediately, he stands upright, and I follow as he slips out of me. I'm about to protest that I don't need to be in bed any longer. I need to get back to work and a routine. The thought slowly chips away at this moment until I face Mach, and he gently grips my chin.

"Mrs. Wright."

Every argument freezes on my tongue as he looks at me with fire in his dark eyes.

"You're the magnificent one, and I plan to do that again and again to you. You're my wife, baby. I'm not keeping you a secret anymore. You're mine." With those words, his mouth covers mine.

Like a fish uses water to breathe, and humans need oxygen from air, Mach kisses me like I'm essential to his life.

And I inhale him as well, filling my lungs and expanding my heart.

33

———————

Playlist: "Go All The Way" – Raspberries
(from *Guardians of the Galaxy*)

[Mach]

After kissing Jane senseless and fighting the desire to take her again immediately, reason settles in. She's meeting Myles soon, and we don't have time for all I'd like to do with her. I want to carry her to the bed and blow her mind, but I also want more than another quickie with my wife. Tonight can't come soon enough, but there's something else I need to say to her.

"I don't want to fight with you, Jane. Not like we did last night."

She stares back at me, still naked with an orgasm high lingering in her sparkling eyes. When she doesn't answer me, I continue.

"You aren't a means to an end. And please don't say we

aren't friends." I don't have many and when I think about it, Jane is a friend. The best of friends as she's standing by me with all that's happening with Wrightwood.

"We're friends," she whispers, dropping her gaze to my mouth. Still, something in her eyes dims. When she doesn't offer more, I give her a few minutes to finish showering.

I'd come up to bring her a mug of tea the way she likes and apologize for how things went down last night when something propelled me to enter the bathroom. I'd already given myself a good rubbing this morning after I woke stiff and desperate because Jane was plastered against me.

She'd had a bad dream during the night, and I only intended to comfort her. I wanted more from her, but she needed me to hold her, and using willpower I didn't know I had, I did just that. I held my wife in my arms, inhaling the summer rain scent of her skin and slept peacefully. Until this morning, when a raging hard-on woke me, and I needed relief to make it through another day with Jane.

Now, there was no more 'making it through.'

The dam has broken, and Jane is going to feel the rush of me every evening.

When Jane enters the kitchen in skinny jeans and a soft sweater, I want to take her in my arms and spread her out on the table. She greets Ma, reminding me we aren't alone in the house. Maybe I should reconsider us finding a separate place so I can do what I want, when I want, to my wife.

"Camilla, are you considering turning this place into a hotel?" Jane asks Ma.

Glancing at Ma, her face alters a slight shade of pink. *Is Jane correct?*

"Is that why you're selling Trixie's?" I ask. Where did Jane get the idea?

"I've been standing on my feet a long time in that salon," Ma says. "And it's time for something new."

"Something new?" My mother is in her mid-sixties, having had Myles and me when she was seventeen.

"I want to turn this place into a bed and breakfast." Pride fills her voice as she glances around the old kitchen, which needs some serious updates before visitors would want to stay here.

"Why?" She's finally out from under Fischer's finger. The house is all hers. "You just inherited the place. You can live here free and clear."

"That's exactly why I want to change it." She glances around again. "I have a love-hate relationship with this house, but I think I could make peace with it by offering it to others and bringing a little interest to the area."

I turn to Jane. "How did you know?"

Jane shrugs. "I didn't, but the daily fresh towels, and the way Camilla has them displayed in the bathroom reminded me of a hotel." Jane turns to Ma. "You don't need to treat us like guests. We're family."

At the mention of family, Ma beams. Her hands clasp before her and those grandmotherly hearts of hope fill Ma's eyes again.

Inside my chest, a few heavy thumps beat. *Family.* I know what the term means and what it represents. I just hadn't put the word into perspective with Jane. She's my family now.

"This house could be a real attraction for people to visit the area, use the river and simply relax," Jane says.

I don't know how I feel about her encouraging Ma. The river isn't the safest to swim in or boat on. Pollution is doing its damage because of chemical plants dumping waste into the natural resource. Once I learned that information, I became more determined not to add another factory along this riverbank.

"I know someone who might be able to help you," Jane says. "My sister Lindee is a restoration specialist. I don't know exactly what that means other than she's good at renovating buildings to enhance the heritage while updating what needs to be modernized. Her specialty is hotels. She'd love a project like this." Jane waves at the kitchen.

When Ma smiles, there's nothing I can do but consent. If this is what Ma wants, then turning this house into a bed and breakfast is what we'll do.

"Where will you live?" I ask.

"Myles doesn't want to live in the Small House anymore, and I miss my old place. I figure I can fancy it up once I get this place running."

"I still haven't seen the inside of Myles's place. Why don't we take a look, and I'll call Lindee to see what she thinks," Jane offers. "I've been meaning to call her for some suggestions for the businesses downtown anyway."

This is all news to me. I didn't know she planned to call her sister. I also didn't know she hadn't been inside Myles's space. Relief washes through me. I've become a possessive man and a jealous lover with regards to Jane, and I need to start keeping these things in check if I plan to win over my wife. I heard her loud and clear last night when we argued. Jane isn't interested in playing games with me, and I'm too old to play around. I want sex with my wife.

We aren't friends with benefits like she sharply told me last night. It hurt when she said we weren't even friends. Small relief came earlier when she told me we are friends. After what we just did in the bathroom, I'm hoping I've changed her mind about sex with me. Maybe after my apology this morning, her heart is changing a little bit as well.

Then again, I don't deserve her heart as I can't give her mine. I'm not willing to let heartbeats overrule my head.

I won't fall in love again.

~

To my surprise, Jane invites me to attend the breakfast meeting with Myles. I'm certain the invitation is to prove a point, but I give in as I want to spend time with her. I'd promised myself I'd bite my tongue, but I can't keep my hands off Jane, making my own point to my brother.

"Did you hear about The Barber Shop?" Myles begins. We sit on tall stools along the counter at On The Curve.

"What happened?" Jane stiffens. I'd like to think it's her concern for The Barber Shop and not my hand stroking up her spine. We haven't shown much public affection. Initially, I told Jane the action would be easy to dismiss but I'm proving myself wrong today.

"Fire."

My hand stills on Jane. Myles has my attention now. "What? When? How?"

"Last night. Fire inspector doesn't know what exactly happened yet." Myles lowers his voice. "Current report says faulty electrical wiring. But I know the electrician. He would have pulled old wires and replaced them."

Instinct says to snap at Myles. We are trusting him to use reputable, credible workers, but that promise to bite my tongue returns as I glance down at Jane's hand suddenly on my thigh.

"Someone might be sending a message about the renovations."

Hairs on my nape rise, but I still snap at my twin. "Don't be so dramatic. It's probably kids just making a ruckus." A memory fills my head of when we broke into the high school and rigged all the staff toilets. We hadn't meant to break the porcelain, just give a teacher or two a shock when the flush-water backfired out of the bowl instead of draining down it. At forty-eight, I accept the error of vandalism. At eighteen, I was convinced it was harmless fun.

"I'm not so certain," Myles replies, looking over his shoulder.

"Was anyone hurt?" Jane asks. Her hand slides down my thigh, lowering to my knee.

"It happened during the night. We might want to consider some security cameras along the street. Maybe on some lampposts," Myles adds.

"We weren't intending to install lampposts. We'll be stringing lights over the Alley," Jane adds. She's picking up the town lingo and using the nickname for Bridge Alley merchants. "We could attach cameras to the buildings, maybe. That'd be a question for a security company, though."

Myles nods. He's the man with the connections in town, and as much as I hate it, Jane trusts him.

"How much damage was there?" I ask.

"Mainly smoke damage. We can restore the wires. Fix the wall. Air out the place."

"Still, it's another expense." Jane sighs and reaches for her tablet. As the self-appointed overall project manager down here, she knows who has what happening when. She's upset she didn't get to demolish The Barber Shop or Bliss because of her injuries and recovery time, but we have more businesses to resurrect. She'll get her chance to demo walls and rip up floors. But no more tree removal near the river.

The three of us remain quiet a minute as Jane scans something on her tablet and Myles sips his coffee. I continue to rub my thumb in circles on my wife's lower back.

Myles sets his mug down and speaks. "I wanted to mention something about Tanner's Bait and Tackle Shack. Rumor has it the place caught fire from faulty fish smokers, but I'm not buying it. The investigation report claimed the smokers overheated, but the last people to use them wouldn't have left them on. They are more responsible than that."

"Rumors are just that, Myles." My brother doesn't need to be filling Jane's head with suspicious activity based on small town hearsay and a need for gossip.

"The fire happened in June when Fischer knew the end was near. He changed his will around that time," Myles adds, looking at me across Jane. At one time, my brother and I could read one another. I'd know what he's thinking. He didn't have to speak to me.

I can no longer understand what he's trying to say, and a twinge of regret needles me. A strange pinch happens near my sternum, and I sit up straighter, as if to right the sudden, sharp ache with a deep breath and better posture. The sensation does not dissipate, though, as I continue to watch Myles.

"Are you implying Fischer set fire to a building on his property?" Jane asks.

Myles scoffs. "Absolutely not. He couldn't get out of bed and while he *knew people*"—Myles air quotes—"he didn't know anyone who would maliciously burn down old Tanner's place."

"How do you know Fischer changed his will?" I'm stuck on this nugget of information.

Myles only shrugs, turning back to his coffee mug. Did my brother know he wasn't inheriting the town? Did he know he had two million dollars coming to him if we pull this restoration off? What if Fischer hadn't died until November? We never would have completed this project in a month as the end date was specific—Kringle Fest.

What was that old man scheming, and what does my brother know about it?

"It's interesting you mention the bait and tackle shack because I have some ideas," Jane interjects. Her hand returns to my thigh for a brief pat, as if she can feel the tension rising off me.

Of course, Jane has ideas, and I spin on my stool, spreading my legs around hers. My hand remains on her lower back. She pulls up her plan.

"I suggest we tear it down and build a community room there instead."

"What?" I chuckle. "Now we're building new buildings?"

"Not a building, just a low structure. I saw it on HGTV. A community room offers space local residents can rent and draws people to gather for celebrations like wedding showers or engagement parties."

"Sounds kind of romantic." Myles wiggles his brows.

Jane and her romance.

I speak next. "I'm not saying no. I'm just saying—"

"We'd name it the Camilla Wright Community Room. All are welcome here." Jane lifts her tablet, showing me a design logo for the outside of the building. She knows she has me. There's no way I'll say no to naming a place after my mother. "The place would focus on gathering family and friends."

Jane glances at me before peeking over at my brother. "After all, that's what Wrightwood is all about. Fischer wanted to bring his family together and rebuild his town."

I snort. She's full of romantic ideas now, but Myles side-eyes Jane, pursing his lips while his hand cups his coffee mug.

He definitely knows something. I'd bet my million-dollar inheritance that Myles knows exactly what Fischer intended by demanding I return.

"The community building sounds like a nice gesture. Ma would love it and I can build it without it being linked to the inheritance project as it isn't a specification to build something new." Myles's agreeability irks me, and my fingers spread over Jane's lower back. She rounds her back as if to maximize my touch.

"Well, isn't it wonderful to agree on things? Building something new is a good sign." Jane's voice rises like she's a motivational speaker.

Only, I'm not ready to play nice in the sandbox. "As long as it doesn't affect the rest of the projects. By Christmas, we're out of here."

Jane tsks. "As a community center will express family unity,

I'm happy you both agree it's a worthy project." Her hand returns to my thigh, placating me with a pat as she smiles at me before peering over at Myles.

Oh, I see what my sneaky wife is playing at, and it isn't going to work. Myles and I aren't ever going to fully agree on anything.

That's not how this family rolls.

34

———

Playlist: "Come a Little Bit Closer" – Jay and the Americans
(from *Guardians of the Galaxy*)

[Jane]

Mach and Myles each excuse themselves when our meeting comes to an end while I remain in the coffee shop to make some final notes. The tension between the two men would take a chain saw to cut. And I was more confused than ever about their relationship. Myles is so easygoing and agreeable. I don't understand Mach's reticence.

With more knowledge of why Myles limps, I'm curious if Mach's accusations are true. Did Myles sleep with his brother's wife? Did he get her pregnant? Was she going to stay behind to be with one brother while married to another?

I don't know enough about Tracy Wright to make a decision about her. I don't want to judge her, but I also can't wrap my head around loving two men, twins no less. How could she do something like that? Mach is clearly heartbroken by the situation. Brokenhearted enough he hasn't risked loving someone again. It explains his one-and-done dating routine. It also made me sad for him.

Despite what Ripley had put me through, I was willing to love again. His actions hurt. He wasn't fair or kind, but it didn't mean I'd blacklisted love. I deserve to be loved. I wouldn't hold myself back from the possibility of someone else being better than Ripley. He wasn't worth the years I gave him, or the year after our breakup where my heart struggled to move on. But I learned from my sister Lindee, the past is in the rearview mirror. Through the windshield, the road ahead is where your aim should be. My younger sister is a wise woman considering her entire career is based on looking backward into history.

Thinking of Lindee, I had planned to call her and with the addition of Camilla's future bed and breakfast, I have even more to share. The idea makes me giddy, as do most of the projects in town. I should probably update both my sisters on my river accident and my marital status.

Eventually, Willow enters the diner and gives me a timid smile.

"Can I show you the new park?" she asks.

I eagerly agree, and with her little hand in mine, she walks me to the park to show me the improvements. Seeing the natural spaces cleaned up, and the new finish on the deck plus the swings in the trees makes me . . . happy. Also seeing Willow's excitement as she leads me around the newly improved park and then both of us swinging on the sturdy swings warms my insides and wipes away all the Mach-Myles turmoil from my breakfast meeting.

～

AT THE END of the day, I'm sitting in Camilla's front room, reflecting back on the morning with Mach and Myles. I honestly couldn't remember the last time I'd felt as good as I did today. Despite the fire at The Barber Shop, our projects were progressing at a surprising pace. With every new plan for restoration to a business, an unfamiliar bubble of excitement rose within me. And the fact Mach and Myles actually agreed to build a new structure—the community room honoring Camilla—was such a huge win for the day.

Out of the corner of my eye I catch Mach approaching me while spinning his ballcap backward on his head. Then I'm flattened on the couch, and I giggle like a teen.

"Finally." He hovers over me. "I have you all to myself."

Camilla is at her book club and who knew where Myles was.

I press a hand to his chest as he lowers. "I thought you were in a rush for these months to pass." Mentioning his comment from this morning might dampen the moment, and I shouldn't be remembering this slight when I've had such a good day.

"That was for Myles's benefit, but we aren't discussing Myles or the project or the businesses downtown right now. Off the clock, Mrs. Wright. Right now, I want my wife."

His mouth descends to mine, and his kiss curls my toes. I reach for his ballcap and tug it off, giving me access to his hair and the back of his neck. Our mouths move together as Mach balances over me. I hook my leg over his hip and tug him down to blanket me.

Mach chuckles against my mouth. "Greedy for something, baby?"

You. I only want him, but he only wants sex.

How difficult can it be? Having sex with Mach is a dream come true. I've been physically attracted to him since he hired me to work for Impact. On the other hand, my heart knows the truth. I admire Mach. His tenacity, his persistence, his eagerness to get a job done and do it thoroughly. I'm confused by his sudden attention.

He missed me, he said this morning. Or was it that he missed sex? He also couldn't keep his hands off me today, touching me at every turn. Or was that for Myles's benefit as well? Staking his claim like he did with the searing kiss in front of the electrical workers a week ago.

"Stop thinking," Mach mutters against my lips. With his hand under my shirt, his palm creeps upward. When he finally has his fingers between my breasts, he tugs the center gore of my bra together. "I have a date with this spot on you."

"Oh really?" Yeah, having sex with Mach won't be a hardship but it's my heart that I'll need to harden.

"Yep. Need to put my dick right here." His finger strokes between my breasts again. He asked me if I'd been fucked there. My sex life hasn't been particularly adventurous, and I swallow around a nervous giggle. The thought of his hard length between my soft swells sends a ripple of arousal rushing up my center.

"I miss dates." I have no idea why I admit this.

Mach looks me in the eyes. "Like I said, we have one tonight." He presses off the back of the couch, and while that wasn't exactly what I meant, I'm not about to turn him down.

My body is on board to have sex with my husband again.

FOR THE NEXT TEN DAYS, Mach and I work beside one another as we did in the Chicago office. I've turned my Impact clients over to Amelia, but I linger some mornings while Mach talks to Tucker. Then we wander down to town and take up wherever we are needed. Myles has a team of volunteers as well as his crew and some construction help from friends in the industry who traveled to Wrightwood to work on our simultaneous projects.

Today, we finalize The Barber Shop. As I sent my sister pictures of the original place, Lindee helped me make some design decisions. Shadow boxes with Landon's artifacts hang on the exposed brick walls over a new leather couch. We ordered two reproduction barber chairs to be set before individual drawers and large oval mirrors. Black and white tiles in a checkerboard pattern cover the floor. As the final touches are finished, Mach and I inspect the place.

"It's really great," Mach admits about the masculine vibe. To help Mach envision redesigning a store, I suggested he think of the space as a marketing display booth used at trade shows. As Mach is good at working with small spaces, The Barber Shop was ideal for his talent for making an area appealing and comfortable, thus drawing in potential customers.

Mach crosses the room and turns off the lights, then locks the front door. He steps over to the new blinds and runs his hand down the slats to close them.

I laugh. "What are you doing?"

He returns to where I stand behind a barber chair and takes my hand. "Let's have a seat." He circles one side of the barber chair while guiding me around the other side.

I anxiously chuckle again and repeat. "What are you doing?"

He takes a seat and leads me by my hips into the chair with him. He settles me on his lap, spreading my legs so mine fall outside of his. My back is to his front, and he meets my eyes through the reflection in the mirror.

"I don't think this chair can hold both of us." My voice is raspy and quiet.

"If it can hold up to four-hundred and fifty pounds of man, it can hold the two of us." Watching me through the mirror, he kisses my neck.

"Mach," I whisper.

His hands coast up and down the tops of my thighs until one reaches the waistband of my leggings. Mach's hand slips into my pants and dips lower to cup me between my legs.

"Mach!" I shriek a little louder. "People might see us."

Mach ignores my concern and swipes his hot fingers through my damp folds. He continues to pepper my neck with kisses. "No one will see. We're in the shadows here."

The blinds are slanted, protecting us if someone were to walk by on this dark night.

My mouth opens to form his name again, but when his finger slips inside me, I hiss instead. My backside grinds against the firm wedge behind it. His finger slides in and out of me before increasing the delicious torture by adding a second digit.

"Mach, really?" I admonish while my body responds, begging for more. I don't want him to stop.

"I want to christen every place you've touched. You're changing everyone's life here." His eyes find mine in the reflection of the mirror again. The darkness in them appears different, questioning something, puzzled even.

When his finger swipes up and over my clit, I can't concentrate on his eyes any longer. My body rocks, chasing his touch. We've been together every single night since that explosive morning in the bathroom.

"I want to make you feel good." His whispered breath tickles my ear. Wrapping my arm around his head, I twist mine so I can kiss him. As our mouths meet, his fingers work faster, dipping deeper until I can't focus on two things at once. I break free from his mouth, gasping his name again.

"That feels so good," I moan, reacting to his touch.

"I like to watch you come."

I glance down where his hand isn't visible in my pants. His other hand cups my chin and tips my head upward, forcing me to look at myself in the mirror.

"You're so stunning," Mach says, as his fingers drag against my clit. "You bite that damn lip, and you release little puffs of air."

I close my eyes, unable to watch what he describes. I'm no porn star, but my body reacts like I'm one as my hips rock faster, taking his fingers.

"Mach," I gasp. "I want you inside me." He loves to demand I tell him I want him, and he loves when I respond that it's exactly what I want. Tonight, I'm beating him to the phrase.

"Hmmm. Later, baby. Right now is all for you, and I'm selfishly going to watch."

"Selfish?" I choke, fighting to catch my breath as I feel the wave coming, barreling up my legs. "Let's move to the couch."

"Nope." He nips my neck where my shoulder meets it, and I explode. Clutching the armrests of the barber chair, I lean forward, driving Mach's fingers deeper. He wraps his free hand around my hair, fisting it to tug me back to him, and I twist enough our mouths meet once more. Kissing him with everything I have, my orgasm races onward, drawing out the finish. I want to scramble over his lap and straddle his legs. I want to force down his pants and place him inside me. I want to be everything to this man because he is wrecking me for all others.

My heart pounds as I slowly come down from the high.

Sitting in a darkened barber shop, in a new trimming chair, Mach just gave me another powerful orgasm.

I'm the one who feels selfish.

I tug at his wrist and remove his hand from my pants. Scooting off his lap, I stand and spin to face him. When I reach for his jeans, he grinds out my name. Button popped, zipper lowered, I make quick work to find what I seek.

"I heard you'd like the full service, Mr. Wright. A trim and a blow job."

He laughs until I have his dick released from his pants. With my legs on either side of the chair's footrest, I brace myself and lean forward. Swirling my tongue over his tip, I trace the ridge of his head before opening wide and taking him deep.

Mach's hand comes to my hair, and he jolts. "Baby."

I haven't done this to him since our wedding night. While every night is an exploration of one another and an adventure at times, I haven't sucked him since that sacred night.

"Fuck, that feels incredible." He strains through the words as I lick along the length of him, then fill my mouth again. Mach is big, but I do what I can. From the grunts and groans coming over my head, he isn't complaining.

"Baby, I'm gonna . . ."

I take him as deep as I can.

He goes off, coating my throat. Drinking him in, my eyes water from both the effort and emotion. I adore Mach. Like *really* adore him. The danger is more than losing a few months of my life to this marriage charade. Mach could do more damage than any other man because I'm at risk of losing my heart to him.

35

Playlist: "Heartbeat Song" – Kelly Clarkson

[Mach]

My wife is a dream. She's fire in the bedroom and flames outside of it. With one project down, we have so many to go, but I heard what she said the other night about missing dates.

Brushing back her hair, I hold it at her nape while she stands before me. *God bless this trimming chair.*

"We should go out."

"Like on a date?" The spark in those blue eyes matches the color on the flag hanging on the wall, highlighting white stars, and it's the exact reaction I want from her.

"Sure."

"Where?" Jane chews her lip.

I'm learning that habit is not only when she disagrees with me but when she's uncertain of herself. Kind of like my nonblinking thing she calls me out on. I hold still when I want to impart truth as much as avoid conflict.

"Trophy's is really the only local place for dinner, but we could head to Charleston for something fancy. Or we could do a day date, like hiking, biking, or even camping." I haven't gone camping in years. The weather is shifting, but we could probably figure something out.

"A day date?" Jane's brows lift. A hint of excitement lifts her voice.

"Yeah, like going out and doing something during the daylight hours," I explain.

She plays with the collar of my shirt. Her gaze lowering to where her fingers stroke along my throat.

"I haven't really had many of them."

She'd told me about Ripley. They worked. They fucked. They didn't go out much.

"Then it's a date. Thursday, we do something during the day. No work. All play. Just us."

As Jane's smile grows, her face lights up, and my heart beats faster than it did moments ago when she had my dick deep in her throat. The sensation creeping over my body is unfamiliar and almost better than the orgasm she gave me. *Almost.* Still, something warming and kind of nice covers my skin and has my insides shaky. I sound like a teenager. I feel like one again, and then it hits me.

The emotion is the same but different.

Young heartbeats don't match older ones, Ma said.

Was I falling in love with Jane? I couldn't be in love with my wife. We were only having sex. We had an arrangement, an agreement, a mission to complete. But as I stare at Jane before me, my hands in her hair, holding her neck, nothing about us is neatly arranged or agreed upon. We are a chaotic mess, and for once, I don't want to organize or categorize what's before me.

I just want Jane as she is.

Midmorning on Thursday, we head out for the date I have planned. Once inside the old truck, Jane asks a question that's been on my mind.

"Who fixed this up?" Her hand coasts over the restored leather bench seat. The interior has a new car smell overlapping haunting fragrances I can't seem to rid from my nose. River water. Rust. And another girl's perfume which was distinctly different from the passenger presently beside me.

"I don't know." I haven't asked Ma, and she hasn't offered, but I have a suspicion who restored this beast. The bigger question is why? Why would he do this other than to torture me?

Jane watches me. She wants to ask more. Instead, she questions something else. "Where are we going?"

"You'll see." I smile, pleased to surprise her.

When we arrive at Wine Cellar Park, I hesitate. I haven't been to this park in forever, but if memory serves correctly, it has beautiful hiking paths. The fall colors aren't quite in bloom yet, but the place is still spectacular.

"There isn't a wine cellar here anymore, so to speak." I stare through the windshield once I park.

"Oh?" Jane tips her head to look out the window.

"West Virginia isn't exactly the wine capital of the world, but there are ruins of a wine cellar which are kind of cool." I open my door and round the truck to help Jane with hers. She's already exiting her door, so I take her hand and shut the door behind her. With our fingers entwined, I lead her forward. "Before the Civil War, there was a winery here. The ruins are . . . different. I thought you'd like them."

When I turn to face her, her smile is everything.

"Maybe we could hike a bit first?" I don't know why I'm so anxious, questioning every decision.

Looking around us, Jane takes in the lush trees and then nods at me, her smile still bright. We walk a four-mile trail that winds around a lake. As we hike, we share thoughts about our Bridge Alley project.

Jane's newest idea includes painting murals around town. One in particular will be painted on the side of Trophy's, so people see the visual as they cross the bridge into Wrightwood or travel down the river.

You're in the Wrightwood place.

She thinks asking the local high school art teacher for teenage artist recommendations will provide investment in the town's improvements. They'll be less likely to vandalize any property.

"You should have been a city designer," I tell her.

"I just watch a lot of HGTV."

A husband should know these things about his wife.

"When?" I chuckle. I can't imagine Jane sitting still, and I've had no idea what she does outside of working at Impact. She's already mentioned how long it's been since having sex and her lack of actually dating.

"When I can't sleep." Her comment is tossed out there while she walks ahead of me on the trail.

I glance at her ass, checking it out while I ask, "Is that often?"

"It's getting worse as I age. A sign of the *change*." Her voice drops ominously.

My brows pinch. "You're too young for that."

"Maybe." She shrugs as she walks, and I curse Ripley once again for his decision about Jane's pregnancy. Jane wanted that baby, thinking it was her only chance to be a mother, and my chest aches that she might have been robbed of the one opportunity she had. Jane spends a lot of time with Willow in town, taking her to the park and having hot chocolate dates at On

The Curve. It's obvious the child is smitten with Jane, and I worry Jane might feel the same about Willow. What will happen to the little girl when we leave? What will happen to Jane and me?

When Jane and I finish our hike, we visit the cellar ruins, which include three stone archways leading into narrow caves.

"When we were kids, we'd sneak out here in the dark and dare each other to enter these caverns."

Jane laughs. "Camilla has dropped hints that you were quite the rebel as a child. Trouble was your middle name, she said."

I follow Jane as she enters one passage. My gaze drops to her firm ass in tight jeans again. The more casual attire Jane has adopted suits her. She's still a tough businesswoman, but flannel shirts and denim soften her. Being in Wrightwood has changed her, softened her a bit. She's stunning but even more striking when she's naked.

As soon as we're out of sight of the entryway, I gently tug Jane's arm, spinning her and capturing her mouth. Within seconds, she's against the damp stone wall, and I'm thirsting for more of her. My hands coast down her front and quickly find the button on her jeans.

"Mach," Jane mutters against my lips as I pop the button and lower her zipper. "Mach, not here. Someone will see."

The park has been relatively empty as the day is cool. There's a threat of rain.

"No one will see us."

"This is more public than the barber chair." Her voice falters as my fingers slip inside her silky underwear and swipe through her damp folds. I lower my lips to her jaw before moving to her neck.

"You didn't complain about the barber chair." I nip at her ear.

"Neither did you." She gasps as my fingers rush inward. "Mach."

"These are wine cellars. I want a taste of sweet nectar. Vintage 1977." Jane's birth year.

I drop to my knees, taking her jeans down with me.

"Mr. Wright," she whispers harshly. She can't spread her legs far with her jeans at her ankles, but I wedge my face between her thighs and lick. Jane's hips buck forward, and her hands grip the back of my head.

I hum against her wetness. "Definitely 1977. A very good year."

She chuckles while she moans, and I continue my sampling, drinking in her essence.

"I can't believe I'm doing this," she mutters above me, moving her hips to meet my tongue, her body ripe and on the verge of coming. I smile against her, laying my tongue flat to lap across her slit before returning the tip to her clit. Jane is heaven and when she finally orgasms, I'm drunk on her. She's a refreshing summer rain, green grapes exploding on my tongue, and the gentle heat of warm chocolate. She's my favorite blend.

I press a kiss to her inner thigh before standing, bringing her jeans to her waist as I do. My mouth seeks hers once again, and we kiss until voices interrupt us.

"Perfect timing," I mutter against her lips.

"You're a bad man, Mr. Wright." She giggles, sweet and disarming.

"But I feel so good, don't I, Mrs. Wright?" *She* feels good to me.

She chuckles harder, and I block her from the view of additional cellar visitors as she quickly pulls up her zipper and fastens the button on her jeans.

"There wasn't time for you," Jane says, her voice lowering as we exit the dark cavern with my arm around her.

"You'll pay me back later. First, I brought a bottle of wine for us to drink. There's a shelter with a fireplace where we can sit inside and warm up."

"Sounds romantic," Jane teases.

I'm about to protest. There isn't anything romantic about me, but I'm shocked to find I want to offer Jane a little romance. I want her to see we are more than a marriage on paper and sex in bed.

She matters to me.

36

Playlist: "Faster" – Matt Nathanson

[Jane]

As we share wine inside the warming shelter, I talk about my brother Garrett.

"Our granddad always wanted to own land, raise something. He wanted space, and he craved fresh, country air." I sip the crisp Fall wine Mach brought. "When Granddad died, he left Garrett money, which Garrett smartly invested. He's an investor by nature, but he wanted to own something for himself. So, he meets Dolores, falls in love, and sets up a vineyard in Georgia."

"Georgia?" Mach's brows lift. "I thought he lived in California."

I inwardly smile that Mach is finally paying attention to bits and pieces about my family.

"He still has a condo out there. Tucker and Mae have been to it."

Mach shakes his head, and I'm certain both our thoughts shift to his business partner and best friend falling in love with my sister after a whirlwind Route 66 road trip from Chicago to Los Angeles.

"Dolores is from Blue Ridge, Georgia. She owns a diner there, and her grandmother has farmland, a lot of farmland, which includes orchards and fields run amuck. Garrett decided to start a winery on Magnolia's land." Magnolia is Dolores's grandmother, who we all believe will live to be a hundred. "He's doing this for himself. But he's also making that space in memory of Granddad. And, of course, because of setting up a future for him and Dolores."

Garrett giving up his high-profile lifestyle and excessive ways for the lovely mountain woman who stole his heart is one romantic tale.

"Are you close to your brother?" Mach asks before sipping his wine.

"We were as kids. He was all I'm-man-of-the-family, but we had Granddad. I was second in command, playing mother hen and worrying about everyone. Garrett jokes that he was raised by a gaggle of women." Despite being younger than him, my sisters and I had the silent mission of making our brother a decent man regardless of the disappearance of our father and the presence of Granddad.

"We speak often enough. Email and text have brought us closer because we can send short messages or funny memes without long conversations neither of us has time for." The irony in our communication is I find time to chat with my sisters, and his wife Dolores is good about building connections.

Mach is thoughtful for a minute. "I couldn't wait to get out of these mountains," he admits. He's already told me how he wanted to leave, and his wife wanted to stay. He squints at the crackling fire. "I didn't plan to ever come back here, and I hadn't until now."

"I'm sorry you had to return." My voice softens, truly sorry he's had to face some demons being here.

However, diminishing his return means I wouldn't be here. And for me, being here has been life-altering, both because of Mach's attention and the town's restoration. I'm finding purpose I haven't felt in years, even if my marriage and this project aren't long-term. I'm saddened the time won't be longer. I like Wrightwood.

Garrett once said Blue Ridge was the home he never knew he needed. Large spaces, pine trees, and the love of his life. Wrightwood feels similar to me with the river noise, the bustle of a small-town rebuilding, and Mach. Being with him has changed my life. As for love, I don't expect Mach to ever feel about me the way I feel about him, but my heart knows the truth of my emotions.

I'm in love with my fake husband.

"You know, the place might be growing on me again. A little bit." Mach glances back at me. The corner of his lip curls upward, teasing me.

"Just a little bit?" I joke, pinching my forefinger and thumb and then widening the space between them.

"Hey now. At least nine inches worth."

"Nine?" I cough, laughing at the implication. It's not like I've broken out a ruler to measure Mach, and while I'm certain he's the biggest, thickest, lengthiest I've ever had, nine inches sounds extreme.

"At least larger than average. Admit it." His cocky grin grows exponentially bigger.

"Oh, I can admit that."

Mach laughs, hardy and rich before leaning toward me and lowering his voice. "Are you acknowledging that my dick is the best you've ever had?"

"Not that your ego needs the boost, but yes. Yes, you are the best."

Mach hums, pleased with himself. "So are you, Mrs. Wright."

He closes the distance between us for a quick kiss, and while I want to believe him, I don't. Mach has been with tons of women over the years. I don't want to be self-deprecating, but there's no chance I'm his best.

While I give into the kiss, the wrongness of his comment lingers after he pulls back.

And I press at stable topics. "What about *your* brother?"

"What about him?" Mach's eyes narrow. "He doesn't have the best dick, and I don't expect you to ever find out one way or another."

"Not his dick." I dismissively scoff. "I told you about Garrett, but what about you and Myles. Were you close when you were younger? You're twins. Isn't there some dynamic of sameness and reading each other's minds and sharing thoughts?"

"Like sharing a wife?" Mach's voice drops from the playful sound of seconds ago to bitter and rough.

"That isn't what I'm asking, and if you don't want to discuss him, we don't have to. I'm just curious if before . . . if the two of you were close."

Mach stares at the fire again. "When we were young, he was my best friend. For years, we were each other's only friend. But while he got in good with Fischer, I didn't. I was resentful of the years Fischer kept us in the Small House, not letting us into the bigger one. We were his family, but Fischer didn't know the definition of the word."

His comment puzzles me, considering Fischer left the town

to both boys essentially, but I ask something else. "Were you and Myles competitive?"

"Define competitive." He scoffs, lifting his glass for another sip of his wine. "We were always trying to outdo one another, but Myles won in the most important category. He had Fischer's attention. I don't know how exactly Myles did it, but the old man loved him and not me."

"I doubt that's true." How can a grandparent dislike a grandchild? Then again, how can a father abandon his children? It happens.

Mach guffaws like something sour fills his mouth. "It doesn't matter. I'm too old to harbor feelings of resentment anymore, and Fischer is dead."

"Then maybe it's time to make up with your brother." The suggestion tumbles out before I consider how Mach might interpret it.

His previously warm brown eyes turn hard and distant as he glares at me.

Despite his declaration, he is still bitter about his grandfather's lacking attention and his brother's betrayal, whatever that might be. "I'm not defending Myles. I'm just—"

"Are you done with that?" He nods toward the sliver of wine in my plastic glass. Discussion over.

"Sure." I lift the glass and swallow the last of the crisp liquid, which suddenly tastes acidic on my tongue.

Mach is already standing. Date done.

But I'm not certain Myles is the catalyst here. Mach can harbor a grudge.

I can only hope he doesn't regret this afternoon with me now that it's turned to sour grapes.

As we drive in silence back toward Wrightwood, I can't seem to let the agitated bear beside me rest. He didn't have to shut down on me. He could have simply said he didn't want to discuss Myles. As for working things out with his brother, it was only a suggestion, and he'd admitted he's too old to harbor ancient resentments. Mach and Myles don't have to be best friends again, but Mach needs to forgive his brother and let bygones be gone.

So, I poke the grizzly with a different topic.

"Did you sleep with her in here?" I glance around the truck's cab with its new leather seat and updated sound system.

"Jane," Mach growls, fingers tightening on the steering wheel.

"I bet you lost your virginity in here."

"Jesus," he hisses under his breath before adding louder, "Knock it off."

"Where did you propose to her?" The question is one I've been wondering. Was it at the park under the no-longer-there gazebo? Or someplace unique like that wine cellar? Was he romantic then? With her?

My heart races as my thoughts zigzag. My irritation grows, sabotaging this date. But he ruined it by cutting me off, and we've been itching for a fight like the ones we used to have in the office. He'd push my buttons and those nights I'd have extreme orgasms, working myself with a high-powered sex toy to release the tension.

Mach doesn't answer my question but his jaw clenches.

"You asked her to marry you in this truck, didn't you?" It would be all the more reason he doesn't drive this thing. Not only does it hold the memory of her loss, it holds the key to all his firsts. The sexual moments. The romantic ones.

Mach pulls off the main road onto a two-tire strip leading along a field, and we jostle over the terrain until we stop beneath a tree. He cuts the engine. I'm expecting him to turn on me and tell me to get out and walk back to Wrightwood.

He shifts, angling his wrist over the steering wheel and his arm along the back of the seat.

"You're right." His voice is sharp like snapping scissors. "I took her virginity in here and proposed on this bench. Is that what you want to hear? Feel better?"

Why the hell would I feel better hearing this truth?

"Every time I turn around in this goddamn town, there are reminders of her. Of us. Just looking at my brother— " Mach takes a heaving breath. "I can't stand it sometimes."

"The wine cellar park?"

He looks away from me, out the windshield.

I don't know why I asked. I'm a fool for thinking our moment was special. A day date. He lived here half his life. There isn't anywhere he didn't go without her. I shouldn't be jealous but my stomach pitches. There's too much honesty in this truck.

"Let's just get back to Camilla's," I mutter.

"No," Mach barks. "I didn't get my turn in the cellar."

My mouth falls open. "I am not going to suck you off right now." He's de-*Mach*-lussional, if he thinks I'm putting his dick in my mouth.

"No. You're going to get over here and fuck me. I'm trying to make new memories here, Jane. That's why I want to christen every business we restore. I want to touch you every place that's new to you, making it new to me. And if this truck is an issue, then get over here and ride me. Make me a new memory to wipe away all the other ones."

I don't want to wipe his history away. He can have his memories. I just want to understand what I'm up against. Then again, there's no competition. I'm alive. I'm his wife. But I won't ever have his heart. It died in this truck.

"Take me home." I cross my arms.

"Baby, I would never take you by force. I'd never make you do something you don't want to do, but I'm asking you one more time to get on my lap and take what's yours."

There's something about what he said, how he said it, and the way the word *yours* lingers between us that takes my brain a moment to compute and my body another half-second to react.

When my seat belt is unbuckled, Mach slides along the bench seat toward me. We meet in the middle. Suddenly, I'm straddling his lap, and his hands are in my hair. Our mouths come together, kissing hard and fierce like I can erase all the bad memories and maybe even replace a few of the good.

Mach tastes like wine and a hint of me from his mouth on my body earlier. The reminder spurs me on, rocking against the hard-on behind his zipper. His hands lower to my hips, and I reach for his belt, loosening the buckle before unfastening the button and dropping the zipper. I scoot off him to shimmy my jeans down to my ankles and remove one leg, and Mach shifts his jeans to the top of his thighs.

I'm back over him in a heartbeat, and he holds his ready, erect dick at my entrance. Then, I'm falling over him, pulling him inside me, and I gasp at the depth. He's not nine inches, but he's touching me in places I've never been tapped.

"Hold on, baby," he warns, reaching up to flatten his palm on the ceiling. He bucks upward, hard and fast, and I yelp. My hands rest on the back of the seat, keeping me balanced as I ride the wild stallion he's become, fucking me deep in this position.

The windows fog around us, and rain pelts the glass. Our breath is warm. Our bodies hot. The sound of us—heavy breaths, slapping skin—is music in this truck.

"I'm only thinking of you, Jane," he says, staring down at where he's disappearing into me. The force of us coming together coats him with my wetness. His ab muscles work double-time as his pelvis flexes and his hips jolt. He has a hand on my lower back while the other presses on the ceiling as he lifts and lowers himself. "Only. Jane."

I nod, or maybe my head wobbles as I ride him like the bucking bronco he is. Meeting him thrust for thrust, allowing my body to match each surge from him with an eager response to draw him deeper.

He moves his hand from my hip to my lower belly and works his thumb between us to get at my clit. I push him away. In this position, that sensitive nub strikes against his pubic bone, like flint on a rock. I spark and ignite, pausing my urgent rocking. Clenching, clutching, I hold him inside me and milk him with all I have until he cries out when he comes.

"*Fuck!*" The word echoes around us, emphasizing what we've done. There was nothing romantic about our position. This was pure irritation and mad desire and a need to restore balance.

Our chests heave in tandem. Mach's head falls back, and my hands move to the back window to prevent myself from collapsing over him.

Mach's head snaps up after a deep exhale, and he cups my face, tugging me down to him. I expect the kiss to be harsh and quick like how we started, but he's tender, gentle even. Then he pulls back and wraps his arms around me, resting his head on my chest.

"I'm sorry, baby." His voice cracks as he holds me to him. What is he apologizing for? Is it me? Is it her? Is it now? Is it then?

He presses me back by my cheeks but holds my face close to his. Rubbing his nose over mine, he then kisses the tip.

"Jesus, Jane. You drive me mad."

I don't think he means mad as in anger, just . . . crazy. "You're very maddening yourself, Mr. Wright."

He chuckles and glances down where I still straddle him, and he's still inside me.

"This is one of the best sights in the world." He focuses on where we attach. Then he glances up at my face. "Your smile is number one."

The compliment renews my smile, and Mach awkwardly laughs before leaning forward and kissing me soft and slow again.

37

———

Playlist: "Worship You" – Kane Brown

[Mach]

I'd like to say I gave Jane a rest after mad sex in the truck, but I couldn't get enough of her. For the next week, we were sexual in the bedroom and playful outside of it.

My brother notices with envy in his eyes.

Ma comments. "She's been good for you."

I fight smiles. "I don't know what you mean. I'm perfect." *Mach*-nificent as Jane calls me.

Even Tucker makes a comment when I spend a morning on the phone with him. *"You sound pretty happy, Mach."*

The comment sobered me a bit. Am I happy? Is happiness this feeling inside me?

As I wander into town, seeking Jane, she leans outside a building, head pressed back, eyes closed.

Rushing to her, I grip her arms, startling her. "What's wrong?"

Jane shakes her head while chewing at her lower lip.

"Jane?" Panic courses through me. Did someone approach her? Frighten her? Another fire incident hasn't happened, but it hasn't lessened my concerns that someone has it out for the project. For Jane and me.

"I just had an . . . altercation with the owner of Needles & Thread."

The business offers tattoos in the back and yarn and embroidery thread in the front. We've known the owners might be a problem as they are working two businesses in one location. How Fischer let that pass I haven't determined.

"What happened?" I grip her harder, feeling the unsettled vibration in her through my fingertips.

"I explained that they couldn't share the space and we'd need to find an alternative. Knox wasn't happy."

Knox Mathers is the tattoo artist, and I don't give a fuck if he's happy or not. He upset Jane.

"Did he yell at you? Did he touch you?" The hairs on the back of my neck rise. Jane is shaking her head, but my mind is spiraling. "We'll evict them."

"No." Jane places a hand on my chest. "That's not a solution. We're here to help. We'll need to think of something else."

"I know you already have a plan in that sees-the-whole-picture-brain of yours, but this might be a sliver that's more like a thorn."

Slowly, Jane's lips curl. Her gaze meets mine. "I wanted them to separate, one taking the empty space next to Trixie's, but their business name ties them together. Maybe one could move upstairs and the other remain below?"

The storefronts with upper levels are varied in their zoning. Some are residential. Some are for professional services like doctors and dentists.

"Whatever you want. You're the boss," I tease. She's so passionate about this project, and when she smiles, wide and bright, that funny feeling happens inside me again.

Happiness?

Feet slapping the sidewalk turns both our heads. Stella is walking toward us with Willow in her arms.

"Hi." Jane's voice lifts, her demeanor shifting at the sight of Willow. A new smile brightens her face despite the upset from the confrontation with Knox. He and I are still going to have words, but Jane slips her hand around my arm as she turns toward Stella and Willow. "What's going on?"

Shouldn't Willow be in school?

However, the sudden concern in Jane's voice has me looking between all three ladies.

"Another stomachache." Stella jostles Willow in her arms, giving Jane a look.

"Oh, that's too bad. I was hoping we could have some hot chocolate. I could use some cheering up," Jane offers.

Willow lifts her head from Stella's shoulder. "I could drink hot chocolate."

"With a stomachache?" I interject and Jane squeezes my arm.

"Uh-huh." Stella lowers Willow to the sidewalk and reaches for her hand. "That's what I thought." She looks up at Jane. "What I could use is someone to watch her for a bit." She jiggles Willow's hand.

"I could take her," Jane offers. I'm not upset by the suggestion, but I thought we had work to do. "We could take her up to Camilla's until you close the coffee shop at two." Jane pauses a moment while Stella contemplates. "It takes a village, right?"

"Is Camilla around?" Stella asks. I'm offended by the question. As if Jane isn't capable but Jane is quick to answer.

"Of course. I understand you don't exactly know us." Jane

turns to me and back to Stella. "But we'll stay at the house until you're ready for her."

The eagerness in Jane's eyes almost matches Ma's grand-mother-heart eyes and I can't deny that look is doing strange things to me. I also didn't miss how she said *we* would take Willow to the house.

"Okay. I'll let Theo know, just so he's aware, and check in on you later." Stella leans to address Willow. "And you. Be the angel I know you are."

Willow nods and then looks at Jane. When Jane extends a hand, Willow's small smile grows into a fooled-you-all grin. *Stomachache my ass.* But she has Jane won over and we'll be spending the afternoon watching Willow.

"Alright, baby girl. You're going down." I rub my hands together then I lift my collection of cards for Go Fish. Willow turns to Jane who presses a reassuring hand to her back.

"He's just competitive. We got him." Jane winks at me and the time passes with us playing card games. Then Jane and Willow color a coloring sheet Jane printed.

Watching Jane interact with Willow has my insides all twisted up. Jane adores Willow and Willow worships Jane. And both situations have me concerned.

"Today was wonderful," Jane says after we drop Willow off at On The Curve so Stella can watch her the remainder of the day. "You were wonderful."

"Me?" I chuckle, wrapping an arm around her.

"You were so amazing with Willow. She's totally smitten with you." Jane nudges me in the ribs.

"Smitten?" I laugh.

"Hard not to be. You were so attentive, Mach. Seriously, it was like seeing another side to you."

"The not so mean side?" Jane mentioned I could be mean when we shared our original five facts. How long ago that roadside lunch seems and yet it was barely over a month.

"The not so mean side." Her voice fills with something I can't read but she sounds . . . happy. Is this how I sounded to Tucker this morning? Is Jane happy with me?

"So, you wanted to show me Bliss." Jane hired a local camera crew to do before and after shots of each business, making a video montage of our work for a future marketing campaign.

The store hasn't been my focus, allowing Jane to do what she'd like with the place. The renovation has taken the place from borderline thrift store to elegant and chic. The interior colors are muted natural tones. The clothing is the highlight. Inspirational quotes from Leo Tolstoy's *Anna Karenina* decorate the walls as Tanza is of Russian descent. Bliss is written in a crisp, readable font that's feminine and romantic. We're the only ones here, giving it our final inspection before Tanza sees it tomorrow.

"I love this piece." Jane stands before a full-length pedestal mirror in a wooden frame. Standing behind her, I love looking at her in the reflection. Her expression is almost dreamy. *Is she happy?* I picture her as she walked out of the dressing room and saw herself in her unique wedding dress. Did her breath hitch like mine had when I first saw her wearing it?

The thought gives me an idea. "Where's the fitting room?"

"There isn't one exactly. You stand there and pull the curtain around you." Jane points to a larger mirror affixed to the wall with a semi-circular pipe near the ceiling, allowing a floor-length curtain to be dragged around the area for privacy.

I tug Jane toward the other mirror and yank the curtain around us.

She laughs. "What are you doing?"

With my fingers in her hair and my mouth on her lips, Jane

has my answer. We kiss for several minutes before I pull back and stare into her eyes.

Bliss. What an appropriate name for a dress shop. Women dream of weddings, right? Tracy did. What about Jane? Our wedding wasn't fancy. A few hours of engagement. A fifteen-minute ceremony. But that wedding night was . . . fucking out of this world.

I run a hand along her neck and dip between her breasts. She's wearing an open jacket with a thin shirt underneath.

I could make Jane promises. Tell her I'll make up for that rushed wedding. I could tell her how I hadn't ever planned to marry again. Then I could say how I'm happy I did everything with her. But my throat suddenly clogs, and I can't seem to express to Jane how I feel, so unfamiliar with the emotions rambling around inside me.

Curling my fingers into the cotton of her tee, I catch the edge of her bra underneath, and tug her closer to me. My mouth devours her, nudging her back until she presses against the fitting room mirror.

"Mach," she mutters at my mouth. "We can't have sex in this dress shop."

"Yeah, we can. It's called a dressing room. Only I'm going to undress you."

She smiles against my lips. "It's too risky."

"We're protected." And I'm on a mission. The one where I touch her, christen another location with her in a way above and beyond the way she's changing the town, the way she's changing me.

"We have the place all to ourselves." I move my mouth to her jaw and along her neck. Hooking a finger into her belt loop, I twist her to face the mirror.

Her hands catch her on the reflecting glass. "You're so bad, Mr. Wright."

"But I want to make you feel so good." I nip her neck while

keeping my eyes on her through the reflection. She gasps as my teeth scrape her skin, biting the tender flesh in a spot where she'll surrender to me.

Her backside bucks, forcing her fine ass against the firm length in my jeans.

"That's what I thought." I smile against her neck and slip my hand inside the front of her jeans. Her slickness coats my fingers and I watch her reaction to my touch in the mirror.

Pure bliss.

38

Playlist: "Ain't No Mountain High Enough" – Marvin Gaye & Tammi Terrell (from *Guardians of the Galaxy*)

[Jane]

We are in Adventure Dex. The Dexter brothers own the place which offers local adventure, river equipment rentals, and camping and fishing gear. There's a bit of a feud between the Dexter boys and old Tanner's granddaughter who inherited the Bait & Tackle Shack. Namely, she accuses the youngest brother of setting her place on fire as he was the last person to use the fish smokers. This is the fire Myles mentioned a few weeks back during our breakfast meeting. Somehow, I got the four adults to agree to a business merger.

Mach and I are here for a final inspection before their grand reopening. Part of the deal between the Dexters and Katy Tanner included a yoga studio for Katy called Bend and Snap on the second floor. When the lights go off as soon as we enter the studio, I know what's about to happen.

"Let's see how flexible you are," Mach teases, picking up a yoga mat and flicking it outward, causing the rubber material to sharply crack.

I chuckle as anticipation ripples up my center. Sex with this man is never going to get old or lack spontaneity.

"You already know I'm flexible." The positions he's had me in over the last month are some I hadn't imagined my body could manage, but I do. For him, I bend often.

Mach approaches me, and a fiery kiss fuels the constant flame between us. He breaks free and leans down to loosen his boots. I'm wearing knee-high boots, and Mach removes mine next.

"Let's see here . . ." Mach squints at a poster on the wall that offers examples of poses and their name. He spins me so my back is to his front. "Tabletop to cow." He purrs as he guides me to my knees, propping me on all fours.

I'm wearing a flannel shirt which he pushes up to my waist, exposing my backside in leggings. Then he positions himself over me, nudging his heavy length against the seam of my backside.

"I don't think this is how the pose works," I tease, as he rocks back and forth, pressing at me as if he could enter me through my clothing.

He hums. "This position works for me."

It works for me as well. Everything about him works for me.

"Okay, cat to child." With a hand under my belly, he rounds my back upward and then lowers my upper body, forcing my chest to my knees. My arms stretch before me.

Mach hovers over my back. He aligns his thickness with the crease of my spread backside.

"I still want to take you here one day." His voice lowers, and a shiver ripples up my spine.

He springs upward and tugs my hips as he goes. I laugh as my feet falter.

"Downward dog."

With my ass in the air, he smacks me hard, and the spanking stings even through my cotton leggings. "Hey."

His hand cups between my legs, rubbing my pulsing core over the stretchy material. "God, you're so warm here."

Hot yoga has nothing on *Mach*-yoga. I'm sweaty with need and eager for our next movement.

"Lower your head to the mat." As I follow his directive, he gently taps at the inside of my feet. "Spread your legs wide."

I do as he says, feeling ridiculous in this position.

"Wide stance forward fold." His voice suggests he's reading off the poster. His hand coasts over my ass. "I like this one."

Mach remains focused on the poster while I stay in the compromising position. Suddenly, he groans. "Oh God."

"What?" I lift my head which causes my knees to bend because I'm not *that* flexible.

Mach kneels behind me and flips me to my back. "Bend your knees and lift them to your chest."

I do as he says, but he wiggles his lower body between my legs, spreading them wide. He grips my hips and tugs my bottom half upward, lining us up. He taps forward, rocking against my covered center that nearly sizzles with steam and desire.

"This is a bridge. We might have mastered this position a time or two." Mach is so playful in this moment, I laugh.

"And this one might be my favorite." He scoots back, brings my knees together, and then hitches my ankles up in the air. He presses them toward my chest. "It's called plow. Which is exactly what I want to do into you."

Giddy and loud, I laugh again. He's *Mach*-diculous but that nickname is only going to give him more ideas. "I don't know if

I'm that flexible, Mr. Wright." Still, he has my ankles up near his shoulders, and he's balancing over me, tapping against me.

"Can I make you come like this, Mrs. Wright? Clothing on and all?"

"You just might." My clit pulses as if answering for me.

And Mach begins his mission. He rocks forward and rolls his hips.

With my ankles in the air, I'm helpless. The friction is amazing, but it's not enough. I want to be skin to skin. "Mach, I need you inside me."

Mach drops my legs and tugs down my leggings. Within seconds, he has his pants undone and down his hips. He grips my ankles once more, bringing them to his shoulders. Leaning forward, he thrusts into me and holds.

"Plow pose." He pauses, dragging his hips upward before diving back into me. "You have excellent form, Mrs. Wright."

Jesus. He can make everything dirty and sinful and right and pleasing. He works easily in and out of me while I'm nearly jackknifed in half, taking his time to fill me. I'm wet and seeping, and the glide of him into me is very Zen.

Our breaths mingle. The sound of us coming together fills the studio made primarily of wood floors and mirrors. I turn my head and catch a glimpse of our position. Mach tips his head to see what I'm looking at.

"God, you're incredible," he says to my reflection in the mirror. "You fit me in every way, baby. Our drive. Our bodies. Our heart—" He turns his head to look down at me.

Our heartbeats. I hear it in the unfinished word, and I'm overwhelmed by emotion. We aren't making love in any traditional sense, but the mere act of being with him, like this, gives me this strange sense of belonging to someone.

The rattling of a door has us both freezing.

"What the hell was that?" Mach pauses. My legs are still in

the air. He is still inside me, but the unmistakable sound of a door being forcefully jiggled echoes to the second floor.

"Fuck." Mach quickly pulls out of me, and my legs fall to the floor. He fumbles to right his pants and stands. "I'll go check it out."

As the intimacy is severed, I right my leggings and struggle with my boots. I'm shaking from the nearness of an orgasm and the possibility we were almost caught in the act.

"Hey!" Mach's sharp holler filters up to the yoga studio and I'm quick to race down the wooden stairs. As I reach the main floor, Mach passes the large riverside window, running.

I rush for the front door which is on an angle. Standing on the stoop, I twist in the direction Mach ran and see him chasing someone—barefoot.

"Mach!" What is he doing? It's chilly tonight and the pavement is rough.

Without thinking, I follow Mach. The heaviness of my boots clomp down the street.

Mach runs around the old bait and tackle shack property, where the building has been demolished, and he disappears underneath Trophy's back balcony.

My heart hammers. "Mach!" I can't see who he's chasing but everything inside me says Mach is in danger. I should have grabbed my phone. I should have called 911.

A loud splash breaks into my random thoughts.

Horror fills me as I watch Mach plunge into the river next.

"Mach!"

39

———

Playlist: "Easy On Me" – Adele with Chris Stapleton

[Mach]

I fucking hate this river.

The cold hits me instantly, and I struggle to breathe between the shocking water and the exertion of chasing someone.

I gasp as I break the surface, frantically searching for the man who jumped off the bridge.

Whoever he is, I want him alive so we can find out what the fuck was his plan. Why was he present at Adventure Dex, and why did he run off once I called out to him?

My name screeches through the night.

"Jane!" I spin in the direction of my name. *Did something happen to her?*

With limbs that can hardly move, I swim toward the riverbank. Struggling to stand, the heavy sound of boots rushes toward me from underneath the bridge.

"Mach," Jane gasps.

I almost fall over from the force of her throwing her arms around me. Catching myself, I'm slow to return her embrace but eventually lift my arms, hugging her for her heat.

"What were you thinking? What were you doing?" Jane's voice is muffled as she holds onto me, tightening her arms around my neck.

My hand shakily rubs up her spine. "I'm okay." But am I? Who was that man and what did he want?

"You're an idiot." Jane's voice holds no scold, though. "Don't you ever, ever, *ever*, leave me like that again."

A joke is on the tip of my tongue, ready to tease her about losing out on an orgasm but something in Jane's tone warns me not to tease her.

Worry.

Fear.

Concern. For me.

"I'd never leave you, baby." With my teeth chattering, I tighten my hold on Jane, needing her warmth. Too soon, she pulls back but grips my upper arms.

"We need to call the sheriff."

"What am I going to report?" I didn't catch the guy. I didn't even properly see him. And he didn't cause any harm.

Jane glares at me, chewing her lip as she does. "What if Myles was right?"

Fuck Myles. He's the last name I want to hear right now.

"What if that person was at Adventure Dex to break in?" Jane's voice trembles with thick concern. "Or cause a fire?"

"Jane." I exhale, breath misting in the cool evening air. "The fire at The Barber Shop was a fluke. This guy was probably looking to break in, steal some money and run." I pause. "It's not like he could slip a canoe into his pocket."

My attempt to lessen her concern and tease her fails. Jane's hands slip from my arms, and I instantly miss that small touch. I'm freezing.

"We should get you home. You need to warm up."

At least we agree about one thing. There's only one place that can heat me quickly, and I need to finish what I started earlier with my wife.

~

"Jane." Her name is raspy and rough on my tongue once we finally make it to our bedroom. My feet ache from my barefoot run. My legs are still shaky. I'm fucking freezing.

"What do you need, baby?" Her asking me, tacking on the endearment, has me in action. Despite the pain in my feet or damp-cold on my skin, I rush her as we stand in our room, still dressed, wet and shivering.

"Need you," I whisper.

"You should shower to warm up." Jane rubs a hand over my bristled jaw, but my arms are circling her.

"You warm me up." God, she heats me from the inside out and I need her.

"I'm right here, Mach." Her lips meet mine, crackling like a winter flame in a fireplace.

With her words, I'm tugging at her shirt and she's struggling with my pants. We're awkward and desperate as we fight the constraints of soaked clothing and quivering bodies. Once naked, she slams her body against mine, and I groan at the flame from her skin. She melts me in the best of ways. I devour her neck, sucking and sipping at her skin, sinking my teeth into that pressure point that makes her knees weak for me. My dick is raging hard and wedged against her belly. Sliding my fingers to her sweet spot, I dip inside her tight heat.

Jane is always so ready for me, wet and slippery and eager

to take me however I come at her. Visions of her on the yoga room floor return to my head and I groan into the column of her neck. Playfully, I push her to the bed. Jane squeaks as her back hits the mattress and she bounces. I'm quick to drag her to the edge of the bed, grip her knees and lift her legs, bending her, molding her as I did in the yoga studio. With her knees near her armpits, I hold her shins and spread her open to me. Pretty. Pink. Dripping.

Standing over her, I release one of her legs and grip my cock. Jane clutches her shin, keeping herself in this position. One swipe of my tip through her warm folds, and I'm coated enough to slip into her.

We both moan at the fit, the comfort, the way we work so well together.

My Jane. My acushla.

Words I haven't said in a long time rest on the tip of my tongue. I tamp them down, assuming the adrenaline and arousal have my mind spiraling, my heart racing.

Jane slides her hand between us, cupping herself and making a V of her fingers at her entrance. She squeezes my dick as I slip in and out of her, adding extra friction as I drag and drop within her. The sensation is unreal.

"Fuck." *What is she doing to me?* The scent of us coming together fills the room. Jane's back arches. "That's it, baby. Me inside of you."

Tell me you want me inside you.

Tell me I'm already in your heart.

"Going to . . . come . . ." Her ragged breaths cut short as she goes off around me, triggering me. This position takes flexibility, and she's going to feel me long after we are done.

"Hold on, baby." I clasp onto her shins again, stilling my thrusts. Jetting off inside her, I fill her with me.

When Jane is replete, I fall forward over her, then flip us to our sides. Still connected I brush back her hair. "How are you so perfect for me, Jane?"

She shrugs while giving me her famous smile. "Guess I'm just *Jane*-ilicious." Now look who is making jokes.

"Did you just give yourself a *Mach*-ism?" All the tension in me is gone from both the vigorous sex and her only-for-me smile.

"I gave myself a Jane-name." She burrows her face into the bed covers and giggles.

"Hmm. The name I like best for Jane is Mrs. Wright." I brush at her hair and Jane turns back to me. Her sapphire eyes light up.

"Me, too, Mr. Wright." Her tone is quiet yet sincere, and I lean forward to kiss her, long and lazy.

Eventually, pulling back, my voice is just as quiet when I say, "You were worried about me." It isn't a question so much as a statement.

"I don't want anything to happen to you." Jane exhales, focusing on my eyes.

"Nothing's going to happen to me." I lightly scoff, but I like her concern. It means she cares about me, and I care so much for her. "I don't want you to have any doubts."

"Doubts about what?" Jane reaches for my nose, running a fingertip down the bridge.

"About anything." *About us.*

When her brows crease, I press a kiss to that wrinkle, then the scent of sex and river water hits my nose. "I need a shower."

Jane hums to agree.

"Join me." I tip up a brow as I brush back her hair again.

"I'll go wherever you need me, Mach."

Damn. I don't know what I ever did to have this woman in my life, but whatever it was, I'm so grateful. And I never want her to leave me.

40

———

Playlist: "Father And Son" – Cat Stevens
(from *Guardians of the Galaxy*)

[Jane]

I strongly disagreed with Mach not telling the sheriff about the near break-in at Adventure Dex. Whoever that person was, he might have had the answers we needed. At the very least, I wanted to inform the other merchants to be on their guard against potential break-ins. Mach again disagreed, telling me break-ins were the nature of all businesses and they should have a plan with insurance and security services. In general, Mach refused to believe what he called Myles mumbo-jumbo and small-town rumors.

I let it go, but I was still worried.

By mid-October, another mural is painted on the river side of Adventure Dex.

"The rivers flow not past, but through us." John Muir's inspirational words would greet those traveling the river.

Camilla gave me another idea for a mural. "The river flows, making it never the same waters twice. Just like love." She'd paraphrased Heraclitus as I looked up the saying to make certain we weren't plagiarizing someone.

She gave me a pointed look as she spoke, tacking on her extra simile about love. Did she mean we never love the same? We can experience love a second time or a third time but it's never the same each time we fall. A new person. A new stage in our lives. A different experience. Never the same feeling twice.

I'm pondering this, propped up in bed when Mach exits the bathroom. Our marriage will soon be two months old, and we've fallen into routines … like nightly sex. My God, the sex is amazing.

Mach climbs up beside me, falling on the bed in that heavy manner he has. He perches up on an elbow and looks up at me. The fine lines by his eyes endear me to him. His mouth is quirked. He has something on his mind.

"We need costumes for the party at Trophy's," Mach states.

Trophy's is going to have a porch opening celebration on Halloween. The once-balcony off the back of the building was glassed in for year-round use. A giant bar was built the length of the glass enclosure, offering a great view of the natural wonder prominent in this town—the river. Charlese and Beau are hosting an adults-only event called Frank-N-Steins, offering hot dogs, brats, and a variety of beers.

"What are you thinking?" I'm surprised he's the one suggesting costumes.

He lifts a hand and places it on my belly, plucking at the cotton shirt. "Maybe we could go as a couple."

"Like matching costumes?" My voice rises in shock, melting Mach's expression like I've tossed ice water on him.

"We don't have to. I just thought—"

"No, I love this idea," I reassure him, cupping the side of his face. "Who should we be?" *Romeo and Juliet?* Too romantic. *Wonder Woman and Superman?* They weren't a couple.

"How about Gamora and Peter Quill from *Guardians of the Galaxy?*"

Mach likes to mix up my playlists, adding in songs that remind me of the movie. Just like I told him with our five facts, he loves older music while he looks like a country musician.

Mach's head pops up, his gaze leaping to mine. "That's my favorite movie."

"How did I not know this about you?" I teasingly gasp, placing a hand over my heart.

"A wife should know these things about her husband." Mach playfully bites his lower lip and wiggles a brow. He's so *Mach*-nificent when he playfully looks at me like he is right now. Like I puzzle and surprise him in a good way, and he might, just maybe, have feelings for me that are more than great sex and doing him a favor, like a fake marriage.

"Funny," I flirt back. "But I'm certain I don't know all your secrets."

"Pretty much." He tugs a pillow underneath his perched elbow, lifting him higher. He moves the hand on my belly between the valley of my breasts as I'm not wearing a bra. "What's a secret you haven't told anyone?"

I sigh. I swallow. I toy with offering Mach this tiny truth about me.

"My pregnancy was ectopic. That means the baby was developing inside my fallopian tube. They had to remove the entire tube and my ovary. In a routine follow-up, they told me I had something suspicious on my other ovary. It was ovarian cancer."

"Jane." Mach's voice is soft while his body stiffens.

"The cancer was localized, but I had them remove what remained." A hysterectomy.

Mach's eyes don't leave my face, but he blinks as if fighting a glance at my stomach. As if seeing me from the outside will offer him a glimpse of my insides.

"The survival rate is pretty high, and I'm past the five-year mark. I did preventative radiation, and I'm on medication. There are no signs the cancer spread anywhere else in my body." There was no way to detect if cancer would return or if I'd develop it in some other location in my body, but as far as my lady parts were concerned, I was free and clear. The doctor reminded me not to live my life on ifs but to enjoy every second I had before me as some women aren't so fortunate.

"How could I not know this?" Mach's voice is tender. A crease forms between his brows.

I shrug. "I scheduled appointments on Fridays. And worked remotely on occasion." And sometimes worked even when I felt sick. Thank goodness I was in an office that allowed distance-days based on need. Only our Human Resources person knew the truth for insurance reasons. I was too new at Impact to willingly share the information with others.

"I'm sorry that happened to you. And I'm sorry I didn't know." I know enough about Mach to know that he means what he says. He might have even been generous in some capacity like he has been with other employees in the office, but I didn't want those acts of kindness. I battled through the ordeal with only my sisters knowing the truth.

"I don't think there's any secrets left to share with you," I admit. I wasn't someone who had a large past. Ripley. Miscarriage. Ovarian cancer. Those were my three hits in life. My closet was now empty to Mach.

Mach's hand leaves my chest, and he flips to his back. He stares upward before slipping a hand behind his head. "I'm Tucker's brother. *Myles* and I are Tucker's brothers."

I've heard rumors of the sort but have always dismissed it as office gossip, calling them brothers from another mother to dispel the eerie hint of possibility.

"Tucker's father was Jonathon Ashford," Mach explains.

This I know. Tucker is a descendant of the famous Ashford's, a once-thriving department store that had locations throughout the country. Eventually, the company was bought out by a larger conglomerate minus the flagship location in downtown Chicago, making that first, and now only store, a historical landmark.

"My mother went off to Charleston when she was seventeen. She worked at the perfume counter of a new Ashford's there. She wanted to work in fashion, clothing, makeup." Mach waves a hand around his face. "And she met Jonathon. He was much older, and he seduced Ma."

Mach exhales. "She swears he didn't force her into anything. He was just charming, and she was young. He made promises, and she believed his city slick words. She didn't know he was married or had a child."

Mach turns his head to face me. "When she found out she was pregnant, he didn't believe her. He didn't think her babies were his. But I believe Ma. He'd been the only man she'd been with then."

I hate the idea of an older man taking advantage of a young, naive woman from a small town. *What is wrong with men?* Especially a married man with a child at home.

"Tucker is two years older than Myles and me. We didn't know the truth when we were young. Ma guarded that secret like it was the last coveted cookie in a jar. She refused to tell her da, which is one reason Fischer was so angry with her. Her mother showed mercy for the sake of the children." Sarcasm drips from Mach's voice. "Granny didn't live long enough after our birth to know us, or us her."

Mach takes a breath. "When I finally learned the truth, it was right around the time everything happened with Tracy. I was more determined than ever to face off with this man, tell him what I thought of him. I didn't want his money, but Ma deserved something for her heartache and hard work over the years. Years of sacrifice and taking her father's emotional abuse." He shakes his head. "But I was too late. Jonathon was dead. He and his wife died in a plane crash."

The history of the famous Ashford's department store couple was common enough knowledge.

"I was ready to take everything out on Tucker when I met him. Ashe, he went by then. He had everything Myles and I hadn't. Recognition. Privilege. And money." Mach sneers and he stares up at the ceiling again. "Only Tucker wasn't anything like I expected. He'd had a similar dislike for his old man . . . *our* father . . . who had more than just Myles and me as illegitimate children."

Mach rolls his head and then twists his body to lay on his side again. His hand returns to my belly, fingers toying with the sleep shirt covering my skin.

"He abandoned Myles and me, but he hadn't ever really been there for Tucker either. And he had other children he refused to recognize." Mach's focus remains on my stomach. "And it's one reason I hold hard to people when I let them close enough. I'm afraid they won't want me like he didn't. Like Fischer didn't. And they'll leave me behind for something better or someone else. Like Tracy did."

"Oh Mach," I whisper, brushing his hair off his forehead like he's a child instead of a man. But isn't that the way of things? Despite how old we are, the child inside all of us still harbors hurts, regrets, and silent fears.

The final part of his confession doesn't settle well with me. I don't know anything about his first wife or her feelings, but I'm certain of one thing. "She loved you, Mach. Why would she marry you if she didn't?"

Mach's head snaps up, and he stares at me.

I swallow around a sudden lump in my throat. "You and I are different," I try to assure him. Our situation is a consensual arrangement. He dangled the proposition of a partnership over my head like an engagement ring, and my agreement to help him was because . . . *why did I really agree?*

Deep down, the answer is clear, but I'm not about to share that nugget with Mach. Maybe I do still have one secret I'm keeping from him.

He shakes his head, lowering his eyes to my belly again. "But she loved Myles, too." His quiet tone is full of sorrow, and the child inside him has shifted to a hurt twenty-something on the verge of manhood. I don't want to believe Myles slept with Tracy, got her pregnant, or convinced her to stay behind. The romance of Mach and Tracy is almost palpable when Mach speaks of her. They were young and in love with a lifetime ahead of them.

Mach shifts, placing his head on my stomach, and my fingers thread into his hair, gently scrubbing at his scalp. Our secrets float around the room. While the truth isn't always comfortable, our position is. He slips his arm around my waist and tugs me flat to the bed while never lifting his head from my belly. I finger-comb his hair and rub his head until he grows heavier against me, where my insides are empty of lady bits.

My heart makes up the difference because it is full of love for this man.

41

Playlist: "Shake It Off" – Taylor Swift

[Jane]

Pressure washing and or painting the exterior of each business is a daunting task. I hadn't anticipated how long it might take to clean up the outsides while we work to renovate the insides. As the weather begins to cool, we need to finish before the cold settles in. We've asked each business to find their own volunteers to help them paint while we offer assistance for the difficult work like removing awnings or old signs and repairing bricks.

I'm working on the vacant location next to Trixie's Trims. Lost in the rhythm of a paint roller bumpily gliding over stucco, I kneel on the cement and nearly come out of my skin when a small hand touches my shoulder.

"Willow?" I lift a hand to my racing heart. "Where did you come from?" Volunteers and workers are scattered here and there, but Willow should be in school. Does she have another stomachache?

"We don't have school today. The teachers are talking to parents today."

Ah. Parent-teacher conferences. The explanation seems reasonable enough.

"Did Uncle Theo go?" He should speak with her teachers. Her weekly stomachache is a cry for attention. I don't want to criticize Theo, but he needs to give a little more to this child. It might take a village, but he's still responsible for her.

"Where should you be?" Attempting to keep my voice light, I don't like how she wanders off from people or walks the town on her own.

"I'm with Jenny today." Willow points in the direction of a woman watching us, and I stand, offering a wave, then redirect my attention to the sweet girl. I crouch down so I'm at her level. "My wandering Willow. Did you tell Jenny you were coming down to see me?"

Willow nods, but I'm not certain I believe her.

"So parent-teacher conferences. What would your teachers say about you and school?"

Willow shrugs. Her lids shutter over her sad, blue eyes. "I don't like school."

"Why not?" Reaching for her wrist, I gently jostle her arm.

"The other kids call me Weeping Willow. They say I cry too much." Her little eyes fill with tears. She pouts. "But I don't."

"Why would they call you that?" My voice rises, outraged by the behavior of other children and irritated that Willow is being bullied.

"They say I'm sad."

She has every right to be sad. Her parents died in the river. An uncle she hardly knows is her guardian. She's passed from one person to another in this town. She needs stability.

But she's also a survivor.

I could explain to her that her name means life after death. It's a name representing immortality and that life goes on after loss. However, I don't think she'd appreciate the symbolism, nor would other five-year-olds understand the beautiful meaning behind her name.

Willow is a testament to moving forward.

Calling her wandering Willow makes me feel guilty.

"Well, we need a new nickname for you." I pause, tapping my lower lip. "How about Wonder Willow, like Wonder Woman? Do you know who she is?"

Willow nods.

"She's strong and brave and smart. And I think you are all those things." I bop her little nose.

"How would I use that name?"

"When other kids call you Weeping Willow. You tell them you're Wonder Willow. Mighty and tough." I puff out my chest, raising an arm in solidarity for girl power.

To my surprise, Willow's little arms wrap around my neck, and she slams her small body against me. My eyes prickle, and I slowly lower my arm and embrace her. She's sad and alone, but she isn't broken. She has a village gluing her together, but she needs something stronger. She needs someone to love her.

"I have an idea." Gently, I press her away from me. "How do you feel about dancing?"

Her brows lift.

"Give me one second." Holding Willow's hand, I walk us back to this Jenny person, explain who I am, and then tell her my thoughts.

Minutes later, Willow and I are inside the vacant shop, which is nothing more than four walls of exposed two-by-fours and a cement floor. We're temporarily using the space for storage. Willow and I have a clear view of the street, and I flip on the lights. I wish there was a mirror in here, but it's okay that there isn't.

"When I was little, I loved to dance. I'd get lost in the music and the rhythm of a song." I scroll through my phone as I speak. "I wanted to be a ballerina, but I'm too tall."

Willow's bright eyes widen.

"Have you ever done ballet?"

She shakes her head.

"Then today is your first lesson with a little twist." I find the song I want and position Willow before me, facing me. "Just follow my lead."

Then I press play, and Taylor Swift's "Shake It Off" fills the space.

And Willow and I shake off all our worries as we jut and strut and race around the vacant store.

"What's going on here?" Mach's chuckle interrupts the last few lines of the song, and I stop. Willow, however, has the beat in her head, and she finishes strong. When the song ends, I crouch and she rushes to my arms. Lifting her, I spin to face Mach.

"Just a little girl time and a dance-off." I lower Willow back to the floor and pick another song. She starts to dance again.

"Don't let me interrupt." He leans against the wall, but I'm not sharing my moves with him.

"No, this is all for her." I step closer to him, and we both watch Willow twirl and spin.

"She's really smitten with you," he whispers in wonder.

"I'm smitten with her." Willow dances across the space, shaking her hips and kicking her legs. I'm totally enamored with her. "I want nothing more than to make her happy."

I turn back to Mach. "Seems silly, right? I don't live here. I won't stay here." I look back at Willow. "But I'd feel better if she was happy."

Mach slips an arm around my lower back and tugs me to him. Pressing a kiss to my temple, he mutters, "You have a huge heart, Jane Wright."

I have a foolish one, actually. One full of love for a man who won't ever return that love and a little girl I wish could be mine. Shaking off the thought, I smile feebly at Mach.

"Are you gonna kiss her?"

Mach and I both turn in Willow's direction.

"My daddy used to kiss my mommy all the time. They were in love."

I swallow around the sudden thickness in my throat, and Mach's lips tenderly curl, offering Willow a warm smile. "Your mommy and daddy were very lucky, then."

Yes, they were. Being in love. Having Willow. They were very fortunate indeed.

42

Playlist: "Fooled Around and Fell in Love" – Elvin Bishop
(from *Guardians of the Galaxy*)

[Mach]

Jane has a prospective business for the old bank building, and we have the community room to build, but things are coming along. Of course, we still had Trixie's Trims and Ma's plans for the big house. We didn't need to fill the empty locations on Bridge Alley. That would be up to the head of economic development, a position the city council agreed needed to be created and implemented once we were finished renovating what existed. We did promise to improve the exterior of vacant businesses to make the empty spaces more appealing.

Jane decided to put *Your Future Business Here* on the window placards instead of *For Rent.*

"It makes the building more inviting."

She hadn't been wrong about any suggestions or decisions she'd made so far for this town.

And it felt like we were guardians of this little galaxy.

Jane was serious about the Gamora and Peter Quill costumes, and she rocks the intergalactic outfit like I knew she would, right down to the green face makeup and painted on scars.

Jane had a shadow in Willow, who found her or followed her whenever she could. The relationship was fascinating to watch. Jane was so good with her, and my chest aches when I remember she can't have children. Of all the things I could give Jane, I can't give her that one wish.

Because Willow was her sidekick, Jane suggested we add Willow to our costume theme, making her Rocket Raccoon. Children are not included in Trophy's party, though. She additionally hinted Myles could be Drax the Destroyer.

"Myles is not joining our team." My declaration might have been more forceful than necessary, and as always, Jane chewed her lip, signaling her disagreement. She too often mentioned I should talk to my twin, implying more than the minimal conversations we have about the construction projects around town.

I didn't want to talk to my brother.

On that note, I'd had an argument with Tucker earlier in the day about Jane's partnership.

Only tonight wasn't the night to discuss the situation with Jane.

My woman had every man in the bar wanting to chat with her, eyes roaming her subtle curves in that formfitting costume. Many men were going to have fantasies about fucking alien women, only they were not getting the real thing.

Jane would be going home with me. I wanted to take her right here inside Trophy's and let the entire town know how I felt about my wife.

She is mine.

"Let's dance." I slip my hand up her spine and cup her nape. She smiles at me over her shoulder. "I want to see these moves you reserve for your apartment."

The comment is the first hint that Jane lives separately from me in Chicago. When we return, we wouldn't be together.

"Isn't there some scene where Gamora says she doesn't dance? She's an assassin." Jane continues to grin at me, her dark-painted lips teasing.

We did a *Guardians of the Galaxy* marathon in preparation for our costumes. I couldn't remember the last time I watched two movies in a row, cuddled up on a couch with a woman tucked into the curve of my body, spending the evening snacking on popcorn.

The last time had to have been . . . with Tracy.

"Well, you're killing every man's heart in this place if that's what you mean?" I joke.

Jane shifts to face me. With her nose scrunched up, her puzzled expression is adorable. "What do you mean?"

"Every man in here wants to take you home with him and peel off that fake armor." My eyes dip to her breasts highlighted by her costume's metal pushup. "Too bad for them, only I'll get to glimpse of what's underneath."

I lean forward and nip at her neck in a spot that makes Jane weak for me.

She laughs. "Star-Lord is hoping his quill gets lucky tonight?"

I pull back and brush at the hair on the side of Jane's green face. "Peter Quill *is* a lucky man. So is Mr. Wright every night." Every single night I have this woman in my bed, I become more and more grateful for her, for what she's done for me, with me, here in Wrightwood. I need to tell her about the partnership, but I haven't been able to think of a replacement for the promise. I need something else I can offer her.

But not tonight.

"Dance with me." My hand slides down her arm, and I circle my fingers around her wrist, tugging her toward the dance floor. There isn't really a dance floor, though. I've simply pulled her closer to the giant jukebox piping music into the bar.

"Is this where you tempt me with pelvic sorcery?"

My expression must explain I don't know what she means, because Jane's laugh is loud and infectious. "In the movie, Peter's about to kiss Gamora and she pulls a knife on him, telling him she won't fall for his pelvic sorcery."

"What will make you fall, Jane?"

Our eyes lock on one another as the current song ends and another begins. I want her to fall for me. Despite this teeny-tiny thing about the partnership, there isn't a secret between us. She knows everything about me, and while I should feel raw about her knowing all my truths, there's comfort in the honesty. She's a partner of a different sort. She's the other half of me.

The next song begins. I cup Jane's nape while my other hand falls to her hip, moving her pelvis side to side with mine. We both timidly smile as the song is "Fooled Around and Fell in Love" by Elvin Bishop, the same song Peter Quill shares with Gamora before he tries to kiss her.

Only, I get away with kissing her, with all of Trophy's patrons as witnesses.

Yeah, I'm making a statement. This alien woman is mine, and if the stars align, I'm keeping her.

43

Playlist: "Lose It" – Kane Brown

[Jane]

Like some interstellar, cataclysmic shift, something about this night changes Mach and me.

When we return to Camilla's home, both of us are tipsy enough that we feel good, and every sensation is heightened, but we aren't drunk. Mach confirmed our condition several times as we made our way up the hill, often pausing to kiss and press against one another.

"If it weren't so cold tonight, I'd lay you underneath the stars and have my way with you," he'd said.

The evening is cool as the month is only a day away from November, but our bedroom is toasty. Once inside, Mach strips me of my costume, teasing me with the slow drag of the zipper. He takes his time to kiss my back, suck on my shoulders and eventually nip me in that pressure point that weakens my knees. As I stand before him, he lowers to his knees, kissing my backside and spinning me to breathe in the scent of my sex.

"Lay on the bed for me." His voice is low, rough, and needy as he presses a kiss to the mound at the top of my legs before standing upright.

Naked, I do as he asks. I'm apprehensive, a little anxious, or maybe this fluttering feeling inside me is anticipation. Because the way Mach looks at me as he shrugs off his Peter Quill jacket and removes the remainder of his costume, he's hungry . . . for me.

He turns toward the closet, giving me a *Mach*-jestic view of his backside. The firm globes of his ass. The tight muscles of his back. The thickness of his thighs. He's something other-worldly.

When he faces me with something white wrapped around his hand, he pulls at a loose end of the material with his other. "Remember that binding ceremony during our wedding?"

His mother wrapped our hands in the Scottish tradition and spoke words over our joined palms, blessing us. I'm not certain the ritual was anything more than a ceremonial act during the brief wedding, but the moment did feel rather spiritual and a bit unsettling at the time. Mach would never be bound to me.

But he tugs at the material in his hand and steps toward the bed, scattering my thoughts. "I want to tie you up."

My breath hitches. I've never been restrained, and I don't know how I feel about the idea. Giving up control would be difficult. Not being able to touch Mach might be torture, but I'd read this type of bondage can heighten arousal. And I trust Mach.

When he rubs his linen-wrapped hand over my ankle and up my shin, I nearly come out of my skin. He slowly unfurls the long strip of fabric, dragging the loose length over my flesh, tickling me, teasing me. Like a ribbon caressing oversensitive skin, he draws closer to my center. Once there, he purposefully swipes, continuing to taunt me with the soft fabric.

"I'm going to tie you to the frame," he explains as he climbs over me. Then he takes one arm and lifts it over my head. Without resistance, I lift my other arm to meet the first. Leaning forward, Mach kisses me, long and soft, promising me with his lips that nothing will happen to me that I won't enjoy. When he pulls back, he reaches for my wrists, tying them to the wrought-iron headboard like a knot expert. A portion of the material remains loose, and Mach pulls it forward, dragging it over my breasts. My nipples, which were already peaked, pebble to hard points. The ache is sweet. Mach draws over me, holding the linen lightly like a string before a kitten. My hips buck underneath him, my clit seeking friction.

He chuckles lightly. "Somebody's eager."

With him straddling me, I can't spread my legs and his balls kiss the top of my thighs. The heavy length of his deliciousness rests on my lower belly. Mach doesn't press his full weight on me, but I want him to blanket me in all his *Mach*-ness.

Humming, I arch my back, as he draws out the torment by caressing my breasts with the linen. Hunching forward, he leans in for one achy globe, sucking at the swell. His tongue swirls around the ripe nipple before he moves to the other breast.

"Mach," I moan. Not being able to touch him is torture.

He moves to press kisses between my breasts. "One of my favorite places on you." He speaks to the valley, widened as my unbound breasts fall to the sides. Mach drops the linen and massages me. Each hand takes an achy swell, pressing the aroused globes together. Images of him placing his hard cock between them comes to mind as he's done that on occasion.

Tonight, he scoots his lower body downward while stretching an arm forward. His hand slides up my arm and tugs at the wrists tied to the frame.

"Okay?" He leans forward and kisses my neck.

I turn, hoping to capture his mouth. He chuckles, leaning away while his fingers lock with mine on one hand. He uses his other hand to guide the tip of his heavy cock to line up with my entrance, dragging it through my folds.

"So ready for me," he hums. He hasn't touched me. He hasn't tasted me. There is no foreplay, but the buildup is exquisite. "Tell me you want me inside you."

Breathlessly, I answer him. "I want you inside me."

Mach takes his time to slide into me. Slow. Purposeful. Tender. Once fully seated, he leans forward and kisses me again, his tongue dancing with mine. He pulls back sharply from my mouth, but his dick takes its time to leave my body. When he completely exits me, his fingertips play.

"Oh God." My body vibrates. The tips of my nipples scrape his chest, and his fingers are delicate over sensitive folds. My fingers clutch on his hand holding mine.

Mach places his cock at my entrance again and glides inward, prolonging the forward motion, pausing a beat to kiss me. Then he pulls out of me again.

"Mach," I groan as his fingers return to my clit, toying with me. My legs quake and my arms struggle just the slightest. I want to grab his ass and force him into me, hold him in place, and feel the weight of him buried deep inside. But Mach has his own agenda as he repeats the lazy entrance and equally idle exit. Only this time, he clutches his thickness and rubs the seeping tip against my clit.

"Baby," he mutters as he glances down to where he's dragging himself against that nub of pleasure. "I'm about to come unleashed." The strain in his voice doesn't match his languid actions. Once more he enters me, and then he holds, diddling my clit with his length inside me. I squeeze, and I clutch, and then a release so sweet, so pure cascades over me. My legs stiffen while my back arches, and I come in a way I never have before. My arms struggle against the restraints, and his fingers slip free from holding my hand. I'm outside my own skin.

Mach presses up on one arm, his other hand still against my clit, drawing out the delicious orgasm.

"Enough," I whisper as I glide away from the release.

Something shifts in Mach. He bends his knees, lifting my thighs over his. My feet come to the mattress for support, and Mach grips my hips. He pulls back to the edge, teasing me, and then he surges forward. I cry out at the sudden swiftness. Back and forth, he pummels, increasing the tempo, clutching my hips to hold me in place while my lower half is slightly raised. The position allows Mach's dick to drag over my g-spot with each and every thrust.

"Oh God . . . I think I'm . . ." I'm going to come again.

"Fall over me," Mach strains, concentrating on where he enters me, thrusting into me faster, tapping inside me deeper one second while rubbing me right where I need on the outside another. Back and forth, he rushes until my legs shake again.

A second eruption rumbles. The orgasm is hardly detected before it's upon me, and I'm suddenly dripping where we're connected.

"Mach," I cry out. The insides of my thighs are slick, and something seeps between the seam of my backside. *What is happening to me?*

I have no time to ask before Mach demands, "Hold on."

Abruptly, he leaves my body, and I'm flipped to my belly and pushed to my knees. To my surprise, my wrists easily move while still keeping me bound to the bed frame. With my ass in the air, Mach is quick to re-enter me. The pad of his thumb comes to the puckered hole, which is an exit not an entrance on me.

"Mach," I hiss in warning after the cry of his name, but the pressure he places there adds to everything else happening to my body. He has control of one hip while he rocks into me and uses that thumb like a weapon of mass destruction. If he pushes it any further forward, he'll be inside me in a place no one has ever entered, and I can't say I'm opposed. I suddenly want him everywhere.

"Mach." My voice cracks in question. I've lost control of my senses and my body. Whatever poured out of me coats me enough that Mach moves forward with the tip of his thumb.

"That's it, baby. Take me. Make me yours. You belong to me, and I belong to you."

Jesus, the addition of pretty words muddles all my thoughts.

"I think . . . I'm going to . . . ohmygod." A third orgasm nearly rips me apart as Mach's thumb slips deeper and his cock stills inside me, jetting off in a way that every pulse feels more pronounced. My own release ripples over his, and I scream into the pillow underneath me.

I've never felt anything like this.

I'm certain I've seen stars or lost consciousness or something because before I know it, Mach collapses over me. His chest heaves as I struggle to catch my breath beneath him. He owns me everywhere, and I don't know how I'll ever be the same.

Mach quickly reaches for the linen binding my wrists, and I fall to my side once I'm freed. He falls heavily to the bed before me, mirroring my position and a smile fills his face.

"You look a little green."

My hand lifts to my heated face, pausing on the evident stage makeup. "Oh my God."

Mach said earlier every man fantasizes about sleeping with Gamora. And it hits me. While I'd just had a profound, awe-inspiring moment of connectedness with him, he's lived out a fantasy with a comic book character.

My heart shatters into a million pieces. He used his pelvic sorcery after all, and I fell for him.

I'm reminded once more everything between us is only fiction.

44

Playlist: "Too Good to Be True" – Faith Richards

[Mach]

I wake with a start. Before I'm even out of bed, a heaviness weighs around me. I attribute it to the loss of Jane. She isn't beside me. Our bodies are not entangled, which has become the norm between us. The sheets are cold, which means she's been absent a while.

Admittedly, I fell asleep before Jane returned to bed last night. After our amazing experience, she wanted a quick shower to wash off the face paint and clean other areas. Plus, she needed a new pillowcase. I was too tired to move and fell asleep with the scent of sex intoxicating me.

Jane is fucking amazing in bed. I loved everything I did to her, everything she let me do. She shatters me in the best of ways, and we need to talk about the future. I don't want to lose her. The time to come clean about the partnership is soon, and

I hope to convince her to consider a different kind of partnership—the permanence of our marriage.

When I finally shower and head downstairs, Jane is in the kitchen with Myles. A tense silence falls between the two of them as I enter, and I'm quick to assume they were talking about me.

Jane was still silently upset that I hadn't told anyone about the near break-in at Adventure Dex. I informed the owners, telling them to be more vigilant, but I didn't have honest concerns. Jane's worry stemmed from Myles's empty suspicion.

Fuck Myles.

I walk straight to my wife, who leans casually against the old cabinets, and rush in for a long, hard kiss, staking my claim on her.

"Good morning," I mutter to her after releasing her lips. My own mouth stings from the sharpness of our kiss. Something is off.

Fighting everything in me, I refuse to glance over my shoulder at Myles. What has he said? What has he done now?

"You weren't in bed," I say to Jane, keeping my back to my brother.

"I didn't sleep well." Her lids lower, her focus on a mug of tea in her hand that somehow didn't spill when I went in for the killer kiss. Jane cups her other hand around the warm ceramic.

"Did I hurt you last night?" My voice is quiet, but when Jane's gaze shifts over my shoulder, my blood boils. Glancing behind me, Myles busies himself on the other side of the narrow portion of the kitchen.

I turn back to Jane. "I liked tying you up."

"Mach," Jane scolds.

"What?" I brush her hair behind her ear. "I enjoy my wife." My voice rises, hoping the hint is clear to my twin, who stands too close for comfort. I'm certain he's listening.

"You're embarrassing me," Jane mutters, her eyes moving from Myles's back to me.

Embarrassing her? "What am I missing here?" I snap, the sharpness unable to be contained.

"I think we should—"

"Jane, lovey, there is someone here for you," Ma interrupts Jane, and we both shift to find a woman standing at the entrance of Ma's kitchen.

Jane rushes past me, setting her tea mug on the table as she rounds it and then envelops the woman in her arms. They hold tight for a second before the other woman tries to press Jane back, her hands moving to Jane's sides.

"Hey. What's this?" The sound of the woman's voice is similar in cadence to Jane's.

Jane releases her and stares into the newcomer's face. "I'm just happy to see you."

The other woman swipes at Jane's cheeks as if brushing away tears. *What the fuck is happening?* Jane is quick to rub her face as well before turning toward the kitchen.

"Mach, Myles, Camilla, this is my little sister, Lindee."

Lindee has hair the same acorn color as Mae's. She's shorter than Jane, and curvier than her. Instantly, I'm met with the sapphire blue eyes all the Fox sisters share. However, Lindee's are lighter than Jane's. Her smile is as warm as her sister's, though.

Only Jane isn't smiling as her arm remains around her sister. Her eyes avoid me. "Lindee is here to discuss the house."

Ma's mouth falls open. "What?" Her voice is pure excitement.

"She's a hotel restoration expert," Jane reminds us.

With a twist of her neck, Lindee is already scoping out Ma's kitchen. "I don't know about expert, but my specialty is restoring old buildings to their original luster while including modern conveniences."

"She's won awards." Jane's face slowly returns to a soft glow. Pride fills her tone.

Lindee shrugs. "Well, I hear you are doing great things here. I want to see everything." There's a gleam in her blue eyes as she looks up at Jane, and they share a moment of unspoken conversation only sisters can have. I glance at Myles, remembering when we were like that. When we thought similar thoughts, acted in mirror manners, and then fell in love with the same woman.

I press off the counter at the same time Jane speaks to Lindee. "Let me grab a jacket. We can walk into town."

"I'll come with you," I suggest.

"No." Jane's swift rejection is a bit too adamant for my liking. "I'm certain you have things to do for Impact."

Today is Sunday. Why would I work? Then again, past behavior dictates I have worked on weekends, filling in the loneliness. On rare occasions, I'd take entire weekends off to play hard, travel, or seek random hookups. But I don't want to return to old habits. I don't want to work on a Sunday, and I don't want to do things alone. I want to be with my wife.

However, I accept that she wants time with her sister. With Lindee in tow, Jane leaves the room without another glance in my direction.

Staring after her exit, out of the corner of my eye, I see Myles watching me.

"What are you looking at?" I bark at him like we're teenagers instead of grown men.

"Machlan," Ma scolds from the other side of the kitchen.

"A broken heart."

"I'm not broken," I argue.

"Not yours. Hers." Myles tips his head to where my wife had stood.

"Fuck you. You don't know anything about Jane."

"Nope. But I know you," Myles snarks. "And you're about to make a huge mistake. Again."

I don't have time for Myles and his bullshit. He doesn't know me now, and he doesn't know Jane. He can take his broken heart shit and shove it up his ass.

"*Acushla*," Ma murmurs, tapping a fist over her heart. Her brows pinch in concern.

I shake my head and excuse myself from the kitchen. My family is nuts, and I have Impact work to do . . . on a Sunday.

45

Playlist: "Torn" – Natalie Imbruglia

[Jane]

"Okay, care to explain?" Lindee has her arm linked in mine as we cautiously walk down the hill. The grass is slippery this morning, the day still waking up from a night of heavy dew. The air is crisp. Frost will soon cover everything.

"The story is so long." I sigh into the quiet morning.

"Try me." While Mae and I are closer in age, Lindee and I are closer, period. The age difference between us had me playing mother to my younger sister for most of our lives. We've butted heads and hurt hearts, but I love her. She's more like me than our free-spirited sister Mae, which doesn't mean we love her less. Lindee and I are just different. It's difficult to explain.

I lead Lindee to On The Curve for her coffee, my tea, and

some scones. Next, I guide her to the park. We huddle together on one of the new bench seats, staring out at the river, and I tell her everything from start to finish.

The truck. The proposition. The pretend. The will. The wedding.

"And now you're redeveloping Wrightwood."

"I don't know about redeveloping, but it's a labor of love. Honestly, I kind of love it here. The town. The people."

I've made so many friends here. I don't have friends in Chicago; I have business acquaintances. I work too much to nurture friendships, and my focus has been on clients instead of people. I work *for* people, not with them. Being in Wrightwood has been different.

"It's a simple rebranding and upgrade, I guess." I dismiss work that isn't that easy to brush off. Our latest addition is a set of sisters who want to take over the former bank building. They plan to open a replica mercantile store, offering home goods and housewares in a variety of antiques and reproductions. The Riverbank Mercantile Company will open soon and couldn't be a more perfect fit for that old building and a great anchor store for the Bridge Alley district.

"This place kind of reminds me of home." Lindee stares out at the flowing water. River City is hundreds of miles west of here. I haven't been home in years. Neither has Lindee. The nature of her job takes her everywhere. She's a wanderer, much like my Willow.

"So tell me more about Mach. How do you feel about him?"

"Being with Mach is . . ." Mach was just too much for me this morning. "Sometimes he looks at me and the intensity is so strong I think he's going to say those three little words. Then other times, I'm reminded this is all pretend." Like last night. I didn't feel great about Mach and me having sex while I wore face paint and reminded him of a comic book character. My head was a jumble from his fantasy and my reaction to our experience, causing my emotions to ping inside me like a wayward pinball.

"You're sleeping with him, right?"

I turn my head slightly and peer at my sister.

"That's what I thought. And there's no way that tall drink of water man isn't satisfying you there, so what is it?"

I almost hate how Lindee can read me. "You know I've had a love-hate crush on Mach forever. I've always wanted to experience him." I wiggle my brows in suggestion. "And now I have him but . . . it's my heart that's in the way."

Lindee's brows lift. "Do you love him?"

I turn toward the river, unable to answer. I've definitely fallen for my husband, but I don't want to love him knowing he isn't capable of loving me back. "I shouldn't."

"But you do?" Lindee confirms.

I chew on my lower lip. "I don't think I'm a sound judge of men." Have I gotten myself into another Ripley situation?

"I don't think you'd ever let anyone take advantage of you again."

"I won't." But hadn't I? Mach and I are having sex, enjoying the physical aspects of a marriage, but the rest of our commitment is a business arrangement. And I need to speak to Mach because I'm no longer certain a partnership at Impact is my future. At forty-five, with twenty years in marketing, the need for something different is creeping in. A new path wants to be forged in my life.

Lindee nudges my arm with hers. "So, let me see the rest of the town." Excited interest fills her voice and her cheer is what I need. When she entered the kitchen, my eyes clouded with tears I fought like hell to suppress. I don't know what came over me. Maybe Mach's response to me still in character was nothing. But I can't seem to shake the unease. Still, I need the distraction my sister provides, so I stand and lead Lindee through town, chattering away about the improvements done and still to come.

"We're still working on painting the town." I'd already sent images to Lindee, describing how I wanted to give the exteriors more character. Bright colors on the plainer buildings. Fresh canvas on old awnings. Hanging signs that offer continuity. A new Wrightwood. The town's transformation feels strangely metaphoric for me.

"I have some time between projects. I could stay a few days and help. Plus, I want to inspect the big house, as you call that huge home, and come up with some specs for a possible renovation."

"Thank you." I exhale in relief.

Camilla is holding firm to her decision to sell Trixie's and use the money to upgrade the house. One of her technicians is interested in buying the beauty salon. Mach and Myles want to gift their mother the changes needed for the big house.

Lindee's decision to stay a few days is a huge relief because I could use some family of my own here. She's the distraction I need to step back from Mach and give myself a little separation from my emotions.

Tell me you want me inside you. The statement has a double meaning. He's deep, deep within me in my heart and my head, but I need to rein in my body. Orgasms are clouding the issue. We are only supposed to be pretending. Within a few months, though, things have gotten out of hand. If I don't step back, I'll misplace more than my perspective. I'm in danger of losing my heart, having it broken again by another boss-employee relationship. Because Mach is still my boss and I still work for him. Overwhelmed by my melancholy mood, I shake off the reminder. I have buildings to freshen up instead.

~

Camilla invites Lindee to stay in the big house, and Lindee accepts, as it will help her develop a better feel for the place's renovations. So far, she isn't recommending much structural work other than the kitchen area. A total rehab needs to be done there.

With Lindee as an excuse, I'm able to keep my physical distance from Mach for a few days. One night, we go to Trophy's for a girls' night on the town with Stella and Georgia. Midweek, Lindee and I go into Charleston to visit a textile place she is familiar with to look at fabric swatches and wallpaper samples for Camilla's home.

Another night, Lindee and I stay up watching romantic comedies that break my heart. I want a love like that—sappy and rich—but life isn't a ninety-minute journey. We travel ups and downs, hearts full and hearts break, and we measure our worth by how we weather the road. Currently, I'm a steady sedan with a faulty tire. I need to fix it or I'm going to crash soon.

After too much wine, popcorn, and laughs, I crawl into bed with Lindee one night, reminding us of when we were teens and occasionally shared a bed on family trips. Or when I visited her in college. Or she came to see me when I first moved to Chicago and only had a studio apartment to live in. Those times feel forever ago, and I need this night with my sister. Snuggling in next to her, we giggle like we did as kids.

"You know, I think he really does love you," Lindee whispers in the dark.

"Why would you say that?"

"The way he looks at you. The intensity is like he wants to devour you and protect you and keep you as his."

"He does not." I laugh, the sound bitter.

"I think he does, but he also looks scared, like any minute he might lose you. You told me about his first wife. Maybe he's just afraid to love again."

Lindee might be right but she's also wrong. Mach is a strong-willed man and if he wanted to love again, he'd find a way.

Like he did in convincing me to pretend to be his wife.

46

Playlist: "Burning House" – Cam

[Mach]

I wake with a start. Jane stands over me, and for a second, I think she's finally returning to our bed. She's been distant with her sister present, giving me excuse after excuse, coming to our bed later than me, or spending the night in her sister's room, like tonight. But something in Jane's face has me sitting upright and reaching for her arm in concern.

"What is it?"

"The town." A sob cracks. "There's a fire."

"What?" I force back the blankets and grab my pants. Jane is wearing her comfy leggings and my WVU sweatshirt from our first night here.

"I heard sirens. They sounded too close." Her breath shudders. "When I went to the window, I could see red lights swirling down the hill. The sky is darker above Bridge Alley."

Fucking hell. Another fire is the last thing we need. We're six weeks out from finishing in time for Kringle Fest.

"Stay here," I demand, rubbing a hand down her arm and kissing her temple.

"I'm going with you." Jane's tone is the strong one she uses when she disagrees with me. The I'm-about-to-put-you-in-your-place voice which I haven't heard in weeks. She follows me as I tramp down the stairs, solidifying her intentions. "I won't be kept from my town."

Stubborn woman. She slips into a jacket hanging by the front door, and we head down the hill. The smell of smoke is strong. The crackle of fire echoes in the night. Flames leap over the tops of the east side buildings.

Rushing faster than Jane, I slip and slide down the grass. My mind spirals. Was this another case of faulty wiring? Was it a new wiring issue? Or had someone done this on purpose? It was difficult to dismiss the last question, although I'd dismissed all possibilities that night at Adventure Dex. It was only a potential break-in, I told myself. Fire is much worse than any robbery.

As I skid to a halt at the base of the hill and round to Bridge Alley, nothing prepares me for the scene. Fire trucks and a raised ladder. Flames surging out from a storefront.

Is that . . .

I run down the street.

Trixie's Trim is fully ablaze. The flames lick at the newly restored The Barber Shop next door. Fire also engulfs the vacant store beside Ma's beauty salon. We'd been storing the exterior paint in the empty space along with tarps and rollers. And turpentine.

Rushing to the fire chief, my breath is haggard as I explain who I am and why I have a right to be here.

"You need to step back," he orders before addressing a firefighter nearby with the information I shared. I stagger backward until a hand presses at my spine. Spinning quickly, I find Jane standing behind me. Her eyes are wide, reflecting the flames taking out Trixie's and the vacant space.

"We can fix this," I say quickly, determined to wipe away the concern in her eyes. "We can fix it."

"Was anyone in there?" Jane's typically smoky voice is unrecognizable. The fear inside too deep.

"The places were empty." I wrap my arms around her, but she doesn't shift. She doesn't melt into me. Her gaze is focused on the flames. Her body stiff yet trembling in my arms.

"Let's get you back to the house." There isn't anything we can do here, and Jane's stricken face concerns me. For now, we need to let the firefighters do their job and wait on an investigation.

Thoughts wrestle inside me. Could I have prevented this if I'd told someone about the night at Adventure Dex? Should I have pressed for more information when the fire happened at The Barber Shop? Was Myles onto something when he suggested the fire last summer wasn't random?

I ignore those questions, attempting to push Jane back and turn for the house.

"I'm not leaving," Jane grits out, but her shoulders fall. "All this work." Her voice strains. I wait for tears, but none happen. My woman is in shock. This is a huge setback, but it isn't like we haven't rallied before. We can still get this done. We just might miss our deadline of Kringle Fest.

Which means Jane will be my wife for a little longer.

BRICK AND MORTAR can be replaced, but I'm upset for Jane. She's worked so hard. Setback after setback, she's continued to persevere for this place. She has fallen in love with Wrightwood, and the evidence is in everything she's done here. She's left her mark everywhere. Her dedication to the town is remarkable, and she feels responsible for it. It's killing me to see her crushed by this recent incident.

My *acushla*, as Ma calls her, has had her heart ripped apart, but we have time. We hadn't started on Trixie's Trim yet. The vacant space next door will need a total gut job, but I don't want to think of that tonight.

"Don't think the worst." Jane and I finally stand on Ma's porch, taking another look in the direction of town. We both smell of smoke and ash. The sky above Wrightwood hints at dawn but the heavy plume of smoke suggests midnight. The fire is mainly out, but the fire department remains to watch for sizzling embers and potential re-sparks.

"I'm trying not to." She's been detached as we watched the flames subside.

I open my arms. "Baby, come here." Jane slips to my side where she belongs. Where she should have been the past few days and nights. I don't fault her sister being here, but I miss my wife.

"If we don't make the Fest, we still have until the end of August next year." Jane's voice is dull. Her words aren't encouraging. "But Myles won't get his portion of the inheritance."

My brother could have been awarded twice as much as me. He could move out of Ma's house. Hell, he could even sell his business and leave Wrightwood. But I don't want to think about Myles.

"You'll get to stay my wife a little longer." My teasing tone isn't strong enough to hold humor, but I tug Jane tighter in my embrace.

"I'm not going anywhere." She blandly reassures me. "We have an arrangement."

Her words aren't quite what I want to hear. A distancing

silence floats around us. We need to discuss the future, but tonight is not the night for such a conversation. Tonight is about relief. Relief I hadn't known I was holding in.

Jane wasn't in that fire. She wasn't hurt. She's in my arms where I want her to stay.

47

———

Playlist: "The Chain" – Fleetwood Mac
(from *Guardians of the Galaxy*)

[Jane]

"No, I haven't told her yet." Mach's terse tone stops me in my tracks as I enter the front room. I've hardly slept and neither has Mach. The smell of smoke still lingers in my nose, and every time I closed my eyes in the wee hours of the morning all I saw were ugly flames eating up the town.

Mach's back is to me. One hand on the back of his neck, the other holds his phone to his ear. He's wearing jeans that dip on his hips and hug his ass. I miss his body. I miss his hands on my skin. I miss him, and we need to seriously talk, but with the fire disaster, I can't think straight.

"I know she can't be a partner." He huffs, removing the hand from his neck to scrub down his face.

My heart rate speeds up. My stomach plummets. I take a step back, tucking myself just outside the room's entrance.

"Does it help if it was a promise made with my fingers crossed behind my back?" Sarcasm fills Mach's voice. His words are childish, while his tone is one-hundred percent hard man.

"You're right. It's not funny. I shouldn't have offered . . . but I needed her, Ashe. You know the story. And now this. I still need her. This new development is a fucking disaster."

Silence falls, and I assume Tucker speaks his mind to Mach. My mind reels with the words I've heard.

I shouldn't have offered.

I needed her.

Mach exhales. "The marriage contract is for a year, but we were hoping to finish by Christmas. We'll just need to regroup and stay here a little longer. What a shitshow, though. We were almost finished, and life could go back to what it used to be."

Used to be. Before we came here. Before we were married for real. Before we fell into bed with one another.

Another pause follows Mach's statement and I wish I could hear Tucker's argument.

"Fuck," he growls. "I know. *I know.*"

And I know, I've heard enough. He was never going to give me the partnership. I wasn't even certain I still wanted it, but that wasn't the point. Mach lied to me. He promised me something he couldn't follow through on. He used me.

The truth should smack me in the face, but it's been present all along.

Pretend to be his wife.

Partake in the benefits of marriage.

Partner with him on every fucking decision for this town but never be worthy of being *his* equal.

"She's our best account executive, Ashe. She'll get the job done and then—"

Account. Executive. A valued employee. I stay late and arrive early. I work weekends, holidays, and vacations.

I work, and I work, and I work.

I give, and I give.

And he takes.

And now, Machlan Wright has personally used months of my life.

"I don't want to lose her. Impact needs her."

Pressing off the wall, I've heard enough and turn toward the kitchen, exiting through the side door.

It's time to take one for me, not the team. Not the town. And definitely not Mr. Wright.

48

———————

Playlist: "Breaking Hearts" – Sam Smith

[Mach]

When I can't find Jane after my upsetting phone call with Tucker, I search for her, eventually going to the last place I wanted to visit. Myles has a construction office outside of town. Building supplies, work trucks, and miscellaneous items fill the massive yard outside an old warehouse. With Jane and I sharing my truck, no vehicle gives away her presence here, but I still need to check.

With a heavy tug on the front door of Myles's warehouse, it doesn't take me long to find my brother and my wife. A corner of the wide, open space is sectioned off with floor to ceiling glass panels allowing anyone within the warehouse to see within the office.

And what I see is my brother hugging my wife. "What the hell is going on here?"

Myles quickly steps back, taking a seat on the edge of his huge, wooden desk while Jane stands before it. Her arms are folded around her middle in a protective stance. Or maybe she's holding herself together as her fingers clutch the sides of her sweater.

"Just what the fuck?" My body vibrates like I'm strung tighter than a chain saw cutting wood. Jane swipes at her cheek which appears dry.

"What did you do to her?" I point at my brother before swiping a hand up Jane's spine to comfort her. Only, she bristles under my touch and steps to the side. "What the fuck?"

I face Jane, who keeps her side to me. Out of the corner of my eye, Myles shifts. "I think I'll give you two some privacy."

"Right fucking answer." I stare at the side of Jane's face. She doesn't look like she's been crying. My strong girl hardly sheds tears. Even last night, the reality of the fire didn't fully hit her.

"You should stay." Jane focuses on Myles.

"This doesn't concern him." I narrow my eyes at her before craning my neck to peer at my brother. "Or does it?"

Is something going on with them? Am I not seeing what's before me? Is this Tracy all over again?

"What does that mean?" Myles snaps back, his tone as defensive as mine.

I turn back to Jane. "Are you in love with him?" The question rushes out of me, guilt imposed on her. Is she having an affair with my twin?

Jane turns her head and glares at me, flames as intense as last night's fire in her eyes. "You're an idiot."

What the fuck? My head rears back.

"I'll stay now," Myles sneers, settling in by crossing his ankles and resting his hands on the edge of his desk.

"Get the fuck out," I demand, turning on him. Stepping forward, I'm ready to lay out my brother, but Jane's arm flails outward to block me.

"Please stay." Her voice strengthens as she addresses Myles, and the hairs on my neck rise.

What the hell is happening here? A look passes between Myles and Jane before my brother narrows his eyes at me.

"I'm not leaving." The firmness in his voice is for Jane's benefit, although he's glaring at me. He isn't going to leave her alone with me.

"Do you think I'd hurt her?" The question pops out much like the last one I asked. My thoughts are spiraling. Myles knows I love hard, but I'd never lay a hand on a woman.

"He doesn't have to think about it," Jane says, turning her head to me for the first time. Her tone suggests she knows I'd never harm her, but I still feel the need to defend myself.

"I'd never touch you like that."

Jane shifts her body to face me better. Her arms drop, hands fist. "You'll never touch me again."

The words are like a sucker punch to the gut. I lift both hands as if surrendering to her. "Let's just back up here. What are we talking about?"

Jane grits her teeth. "I heard your phone call with Tucker."

My arms lower, brow lifting. "You were eavesdropping?"

"I don't think that's the point." Her gaze holds mine, a thunderstorm of emotion within those normally clear blue eyes. "You aren't making me a partner."

A second slam comes to my stomach. "Jane, I—"

"You made me an offer because you *needed* me . . . no, you needed a wife." She grounds out the word like it's dirty and distasteful. She swipes a hand through her long, loose hair and then holds a clump at her nape. "You lied to me."

"Jane, I can explain." Her eyes close, and she shakes her head, but I continue. "Ashe and I agreed. It's in our bylaws as partners. No additional partners. We never wanted to risk someone taking from us what we built on our own."

Her eyes snap open. "Because you think I'd do that?"

"No. Jane. No. The rules were written before you were ever a part of our company." Before she was ever part of my heart, which feels like it's being sent through a shredder and headed for the trash. "This was about Rochelle, Tucker's wife. He didn't want her to have a piece of his company. He wanted something for himself." His story was long and not necessary to get into now.

"You know about my father," I state and ignore the sharp intake of breath from Myles. *Yeah, I told her our secret.* But Myles isn't consequential yet. "Ashe and I wanted to prove we could do something on our own, for us, without the Ashford name."

I don't actually bear the Ashford name. I'm a Wright, through and through, which might explain the stubbornness I inherited from my grandfather. I have my father's name as my middle name, though, and Myles has Ashford as his. The secret of our patronage was within us all along.

Jane continues to stare at me. "Rules can be changed."

"They can, but Ashe—"

"Do not blame this on him." Jane clenches her teeth.

"Fine. *We* don't want to change." I exhale and swipe a hand over my face. "Jane, it isn't that you aren't worthy. You're important to the company. You're equal to the task. We just don't have the title to offer you."

Her mouth falls open and then her molars clack when she snaps her jaw closed again.

Myles clears his throat, and I turn on him. "You're still here?" Why the hell hasn't he silently excused himself, allowing us the privacy we deserve? "This is a private matter between husband and wife."

"Is it?" Jane has my attention. "This sounds to me like a business concern. Your company has a policy, but you invoked a promise. And I'm your best account executive. You'd hate to lose me . . . from *Impact*."

Her emphasis has me confused. I *would* hate to lose her from Impact, but I'd hate to lose her from my life even more.

"You are our best executive. I just said that. You're a team player. Loyal. Dedicated. I couldn't have done what *we've* done in Wrightwood without you." We work well together. She's smart and creative. She took over this project. We wouldn't have been as far along without her management. We need her even more with this new setback.

But it's more than her handling this town.

She's stood by me in this mess.

"You couldn't have done this without me." Jane slowly repeats what I've just said. She shakes her head, disappointment in every waggle. "I think you can. I'm going back to Chicago."

"What?" I step closer to her, but she steps back.

"Don't worry. Our secret is safe. I'm good at keeping them." Lasers of hate beam from her eyes. The same eyes that once looked at me like I was the moon. She's my sun.

My skin prickles. She can't leave. "Jane, I have never thought of you as a dirty little secret. I'm not Ripley."

"Nope, you're not." Jane huffs. "This might be worse."

"Don't you say that." Chest heaving, my nostrils flare, and I inhale her summer rain scent, which muddles with my anger. I want to kiss her and be done with this argument. I want to toss her in the truck, take her to our bed, and remind her how important she is to me.

I love her.

The thought slams into me.

"As an employee of Impact, I can no longer ignore my responsibilities back in Chicago." She swallows hard, choking back a sob. "Because that's all I'll ever be to you. A top-notch employee. Good old Jane. She gets the job done. But I'm finished here."

"That isn't true." Doesn't she see she's more valuable to me than working for me? She's beside me in Wrightwood, a place I swore I'd never return. She's in my bed. She's in my heart.

But I'm not about to declare myself to Jane before Myles.

"Last night you said you weren't leaving." My typically deep voice cracks. She was adamant she didn't want to leave the town, staring at it from the hill-top house like a guardian angel.

"That was before I knew the truth." Her voice is like venom and the sting hits me in the heart. Jane might actually leave, not only Wrightwood but me.

"But the fire . . .?" It's my last-ditch effort.

"Oh man," Myles mutters and I side-eye him, watching as he covers his face with his hand.

My hackles rise, spine stiffens. "Why are you here with him?" Is she so distraught she sought out Myles for comfort instead of confronting me? Instead of coming to me to discuss what she overheard?

"This is the part that's between you and him." Jane points between Myles and me. Then she pokes herself in the chest. "And does not involve me."

"You were just hugging my brother. It involves me when my wife is holding onto my fucking twin."

Jane shakes her head, hands balling into fists at her side again. "Your wife?" Jane huffs. "You and I have an arrangement, Mr. Wright."

While I've always loved the sound of the title in her smoky tone, now it's like a knife flaying me open.

"And *we* have an agreement with Myles." Jane circles her hand, implying the three of us are connected. Myles stands to lose two million dollars if we don't make Fischer's deadline. But I don't give a fuck about my brother or the money. I'm about to lose my wife.

"You promised a year." The term of our marriage is one year. It's only been a couple of months and I need more time with her. I need to fix this.

Jane looks at me pointedly. "And *you* promised a partnership. There's no need to continue this act. You can finish the town on your own."

"This act?" I whisper, my voice breaking. Maybe I'm the one in the wrong. Maybe while Jane has become more to me, the partnership has always been *more* to her.

There's something else unsettling here, though. Something niggling at me about this shitshow. She mentioned that I'm ignorant. What am I missing? "Why am I an idiot?"

Jane stares at me, long and hard, before stepping to her right without answering me.

I block her retreat. "Jane? Enlighten me."

Her eyes won't meet mine. Truth warbles around me.

Is it Myles?

Or is it me?

"Tell me." Tell me you want me inside you. Tell me I'm already in your heart as you're in mine. I tip up her chin. Her eyes swim with liquid. The shimmering blue is sapphires under water. She's a rare gem in this river town.

"I can't do this." She swallows hard and swipes at the corner of her eye. "Not with you, Mach. I'm going back to Chicago."

"Baby," I whisper, blocking her one more time. But when my hands come to her shoulders, she lifts her arms to push my touch off her.

"That's enough," Myles states, reminding me once more he's present, and when I turn on him, my wife brushes past me, rushing out the door.

49

Playlist: "Memory I Don't Mess With" – Lee Brice

[Mach]

Jane has completely escaped me. I don't know how she got to Myles's office, but she hasn't returned to Ma's or the town as I searched for her there. When I finally circle back to Ma's, she's really gone.

"Her sister took her to Charleston." Ma stares at me. "What happened?" The softening in her question, along with the unspoken censure, suggests Ma thinks I did something.

Old defense mechanisms react. "Why is this my fault?"

Ma chuckles. "Because you love hard, Mach, and you smother."

I stare at my mother as we stand inside the dining room. My hands rest on the back of a dining chair while she watches me from the opposite side of the table.

Ma breaks first and shakes her head. "You act first and think second." The narrowing of Ma's eyes says she knows I've done it again.

Lowering my gaze, I stare at the dining room table, worn and scuffed from years of use. "I offered Jane a partnership stake in Impact in exchange for her to pretend to be my wife."

"Mach," Ma sorrowfully mutters. A long pause passes between us. "And she's upset because you broke a promise."

"I shouldn't have offered it in the first place." A partnership wasn't something I could give her. When I reflect on it, I'm not certain I have anything to offer Jane.

"So, you lied to her."

My head snaps up. "I didn't lie."

"You didn't tell the truth."

"I didn't lie," I repeat defensively, like the teenager I once was, standing in this room facing off with Fischer about something inconsequential now.

I didn't steal your car. I borrowed it.

I wasn't breaking into your fridge. I was looking for food.

"Is the partnership the real issue?" Ma brings me back to the present.

"That's why she left." *Is she coming back?* She said she's returning to Chicago, and maybe it's for the best. Tucker and I are struggling to run a company with each of us taking time away from the office and leaving a newer account executive in charge of the place.

"It's not about a business partnership, Mach. She's your *acushla.*" She stares at me, clutching clasped hands to her chest, like I should understand, but I don't.

"Ma, enough with the heartbeat crap." But just thinking of Jane leaving me behind has my heart racing, missing her already.

This was Tracy all over again.

Everything slams into me at once. The fight we had. Her stating she wasn't going with me. Despite being my wife, she wasn't leaving Wrightwood for Chicago. She wanted me to go to graduate school without her and then return to this town, raise a family here. I'd been pushing off the family idea, hoping to be established and financially set up in a major city first.

Then she died.

Pregnant, which Myles knew, because Myles was in the truck with her.

Tracy was with Myles.

Jane went to Myles as well.

Tracy never wanted to leave Wrightwood.

Jane doesn't want to stay. She doesn't want to see this project to the end. She doesn't want to be married to me. She doesn't want me. "She left, Ma. Even if she was my heartbeat, I'm not hers."

I turn for the front door and exit the big house. There's a place I need to visit, and my presence is long overdue.

"HEY." I stand on the narrow grass strip, staring down at the cold stone. I don't expect a response. Even if she was alive, she might not talk to me. It's been nearly twenty-five years since I've been back here. The day of her funeral, I left and never glanced in the rearview mirror.

At the time, I'd been on a mission to right another wrong in my life—a father I didn't know. I was set on a path of destruction. I wanted to ruin the perfect life I surmised he'd had when I'd lost so much.

Then I learned he was dead as well.

I stare at Tracy's headstone, a small slab, because it's all we could afford. Who budgets for a funeral when you're twenty-two years old? She's buried in the same cemetery as her grandparents. There's no plot beside her.

Wife. Sister. Daughter. Never a mother. We decided against

listing her condition. I didn't want to add to her parents' grief, so the coroner respected my wishes not to mention her pregnancy. I couldn't face the shame that she'd been with my brother. The baby could have been his.

I don't really know what to say to the person I didn't grow old with. She didn't pass twenty-one years of age. She didn't become the mother she wanted to be or live out the rest of her days in this small town.

My thoughts are an ancient photo album, flipping through fuzzy memories and out-of-focus images. I'm not certain I remember anything clearly.

We were in love. I recall saying it but not the sensation of it. We were so young. Life was ahead of us, or so I thought. We had plans. *I* had plans.

"I'm sorry," I whisper into the wind.

The weather is changing. A storm is coming. My thoughts flick back to the town and all Jane's work painting the storefronts and pressure washing the sidewalks. The rain needs to hold off until everything dries.

Shaking my head, I pull myself back to where I stand, finding my heart thumps for a woman who is alive. As for the girl who has passed away, my heart beats for her as well, but the pulse is a melancholy rhythm of regret cradled within memories. Memories are all I have of her now.

"Hi."

I flinch at the awareness I'm not alone and turn in the direction of the female voice greeting me.

"I didn't want to disturb you, but I wanted to drop these off."

I stare at Ainsley, Tracy's younger sister, as she holds a bundle of sunflowers. She hoists the bouquet upward. "Last of the season, I suspect."

"I haven't been here since . . ." *Since the funeral.* A husband should bring flowers to his late wife's grave. "I guess I wasn't a very good husband."

I don't know what flowers Jane likes. A man should know what kind of flowers his wife likes.

"Oh, no one faults you. Life moves on." Ainsley steps forward, and I move aside so she can place the bundle beside the headstone. We both stare down at Tracy's name.

Tracy Jean Wright.

The first Mrs. Wright.

"People were surprised when you just disappeared, though," Ainsley states, and I glance at her. Her head remains bowed toward her sister's marker. "No one expected you to stay in this small town, Mach. You were too big for it, but people had hoped you'd linger a little bit. We needed you to help us grieve."

She isn't casting stones but making a statement.

"I just needed to get out sooner rather than later. Everything was so messed up."

"I get that. That you had to go, and Tracy accepted that about you. She knew you were meant for bigger things. She worried she wasn't enough."

My gaze remains on Ainsley, and she finally looks over at me, offering me a timid smile. "She loved you so much. She just wanted to be your everything."

Anger rolls through my veins. "Apparently, *I* wasn't enough. She wanted to stay with Myles."

"She did not." Surprise laces her voice as Ainsley twists to face me. Her hands slip into her jacket pockets. "Why would you say that?"

"She left that night with Myles. They had been best friends. He always loved her, and she loved him."

"Like a sister loves a brother." Ainsley's eyelids flutter in surprise as she defends her sister.

"She didn't want to leave with me." I jab my chest.

"That doesn't mean she wasn't going. She was scared, Mach. It was a big change for her, but she would have gone to the ends of the earth with you if you asked her to."

Ainsley doesn't know. That isn't the truth. Tracy wasn't leaving with me.

"She went home with Myles." That night, she left Charlese's house with my brother. We'd had a fight earlier in the day where she told me she wouldn't go with me. Or was that just one more fuzzy memory? Did she say she didn't *want* to go? The difference was semantics, or was it?

"He was drunk that night. So were you. She offered to give him a ride. She was coming back to pick you up."

I don't recall that at all. She left with Myles. She was going to stay behind with him. "She was pregnant with his child."

Ainsley's eyes open wide. Her face brightening in anger. "The hell she was."

"She was pregnant when she died."

Ainsley gasps, unsteady for a second before her legs catch her and she restores her balance. "I didn't know."

"Only Myles and I knew she was pregnant. He told me."

Ainsley's eyes narrow. "But that doesn't mean it was Myles's child. He wasn't sleeping with her."

"How do you know?" My voice strains. My blood boils. How does she know anything about her sister and my brother?

"Because I have faith in my sister's loyalty to you. She would never, ever cheat on you. She loved you, Mach. She. Loved. You. She was your wife, and that meant everything to her."

The words strike hard. Deep, deep down, I know she's right. Tracy wouldn't have been unfaithful to me. She was better than that. She would have told me if she was unhappy. She did tell me. And she wouldn't have stepped out on me to prove some point or find comfort in another. She would have faced off with me. It's one of the reasons I was so upset that night. We'd had that fight, but it still didn't make sense that Myles knew before me that my wife was pregnant.

"As for Myles. I know for a fact he wasn't sleeping with Tracy. He wouldn't have done that to you." She waves toward me. "You are his brother. His twin. He would have never crossed that line."

"He loved her like I did."

Ainsley tips her head, searching my face for a moment before looking to the side. "That might have been so, but he wasn't sleeping with her."

"How can you be certain?" I practically yell.

Her head snaps back, and she faces me once more. "Because he was sleeping with me."

All the wind is knocked out of me. I stare at Tracy's younger sister, a mirror image of what my late wife might have looked like as she aged. They didn't look similar as young women, but the blonde hair and green eyes are the same.

"I didn't know." My stunned voice cracks.

"No one did." Her hands cover her face, and she sobs.

I step over to her, wrapping my arms around her, tugging her tight to my chest. Heartbreak vibrates off of her.

Did she love Myles?

Myles might have even been in love with *Ainsley*.

He's my twin, and I didn't know.

How could I have been so wrong about everything?

50

Playlist: "Good as You" – Kane Brown

[Mach]

The truth about Ainsley and Myles is a pile of puzzle pieces without a guiding image to follow. Everything inside me is a jumble, and I need to talk to someone. The first person I think of is Jane. Her absence is a gaping hole in my dark heart. I've sent her text after text and phone call after phone call, needing her to speak with me. Ainsley and Myles are only a sliver of the issue.

I want to know how to fix Jane and me.

When my imagination ran rabid with drastic scenarios, like colliding with a bridge, drowning in a river, or crashing on a plane, Jane finally responded to at least one text.

I made it back to Chicago.

Her silence was destroying me, but her message was clear. *Leave me alone.*

The night after Jane left, I sit outside Ma's house near the firepit. A fire doesn't burn. I haven't been able to tackle a single issue with Trixie's fire or the vacant store. I simply sit among the rustle of leaves with the bridge in the distance glaring at me, and I stew.

"Here." A glass of scotch appears over my shoulder and rests against my upper chest. Myles stands beside me. His eyes don't meet mine.

"Thanks." I take the glass canning jar from him and give the liquor a sniff. Ma's special blend. I could use the bite, and I take a drink as Myles hobbles around me. He limps to a woodpile a short distance away and wobbles back with a few logs under his arm. I stand and remove the stack from him.

"Thanks," he mutters.

I drop the few pieces on the charred pile within the brick ring. Myles leans forward and strikes a match, laying the flame against some unburned twigs. A thin stream of smoke floats upward, and the crackle of wood catching fire stirs the night.

I sit back in my seat.

Myles remains standing, leaning on his cane and watching the flame build. "Ainsley called me."

"How did I never know you were fucking her?"

"Hey!" The blaze in his eyes is brighter than the fire in the pit. The defense in his voice suggests she was more than an easy lay to him.

"Sorry," I mutter, but arch a brow. "Well?"

"You weren't meant to know. Plus, it was a long time ago, and it doesn't matter now." His voice grows distant as he turns back to stare at the slow-growing flame.

"Did you love her?" I watch my twin.

"That doesn't seem to matter either." Regret and loss fill his hollow voice.

Damn. "Myles, I thought that you and Tracy—"

"I know what you thought." His voice turns harder, edgier

than I've ever heard as he faces me. "You didn't stick around for the truth. Maybe it was better that way, though."

"How can you say that?" I shift in my seat, leaning forward to place my elbows on my thighs. My glass dangles from my fingers.

"You wanted to believe what you wanted to believe. Maybe hating me took away the pain of losing Tracy."

"Nothing could take away that pain," I defend my heart. My first love. My first wife.

"Not even Jane?" Myles stares at me, notching the string, and flinging an arrow. *Bull's-eye.* Because Jane was taking away the pain. She wasn't erasing memories, but she was building new ones. As Ma said when I first arrived, Jane was my *acushla.* And my heart's rhythm has been erratic ever since she left.

"Riddle me this first. Why did Jane come to see you the day she left?"

Myles shakes his head, looking back at the firepit. "She wanted to make sure she wasn't screwing me out of my inheritance if she left. She didn't want to disappoint me." He turns to me again. "I hugged her because she looked like she could use a hug."

He takes a deep breath. "I had no idea about the rest until, you know, the two of you had it out in my office."

Fuck. "And you couldn't have given us privacy?"

"Something in her eyes begged me not to go. I think she feels weak around you."

"Jane isn't weak."

Myles sighs. "Maybe weak isn't the correct word. She knew she couldn't be strong with you. She's wrapped around your finger just like Tracy was."

"Jane isn't wrapped around my finger," I sputter, dismissing the idea. "And as for Tracy . . . I thought you fucked my wife."

"Ainsley might have mentioned that." Myles bitterly scoffs.

"No wonder you've hated me all these years. And I thought it was only the fact Tracy died under my watch."

I could ask why she was even with him, but I now have an answer. My thoughts flip through all my brother has suffered. The loss of his friend. Perhaps the loss of the love of his life with Ainsley. The weakness of his leg. Months of rehabilitation for his body. Years enduring Fischer after I left.

"I thought you got her pregnant." I sip my scotch and watch Myles over the rim of my glass.

He fumbles against his cane before catching himself and looking over at me. "How could you think that?"

"Because I thought you were sleeping with my wife." The truth is blanketed in twenty-five years of pent-up hurt and anger. Unwarranted anger that could have been righted had I only asked questions or confronted my twin. Instead, I chose my reality of the situation and misread the rest.

Myles narrows his eyes at me. "Do you really think I'd do that to you? Do you think Tracy would?" His voice rings incredulous. Ainsley reminded me that I didn't actually believe Tracy would sleep with my brother, but perhaps it was easier to think she had than accept her death. Harboring that hatred toward Myles took over the grief of losing my wife and child.

"How did you know she was pregnant?"

"She told me. She was driving me to Ainsley that night. She told me about your fight and how she couldn't stay here. She suspected she was pregnant, and she'd taken a test. She hadn't even been to the doctor yet."

Our argument floats through my head.

"Maybe we should call this what it is, if you don't love me enough to go with me."

"What is it?" Tracy had questioned.

"The end of us."

My eyes close. Yeah, the fight had been brutal. Words had gotten ugly and vindictive because when you're twenty-two with the world before you, you want to start running, and you want your wife by your side in the sprint.

You react before you think, Ma said.

"She told me she couldn't let you go. She didn't want to raise the baby without you. She was committed to you. She was going to tell you the next day."

The day after . . . the accident.

My eyes burn. My nose prickles. I whisper to my glass of amber liquid. "I hadn't told her I loved her."

Myles's glare weighs on me.

"Even if we fought, we never went to bed without I love you said."

That night we didn't go to bed together.

"You tell Jane you love her every night?"

"Jane and I aren't like that." The sour words pour forth, and I lift my glass to choke down more burning alcohol.

"Why not?" Myles's curiosity rankles.

Because we just aren't. But the truth is, why hadn't I told Jane how I felt? Why didn't I say I love you to her yet? The answer was the partnership. I wanted to clear that up before I laid my emotions before her. Part of my fear was Jane's reaction. If the partnership was all that was important to her, she wasn't going to share my emotions. She wasn't going to love me in return.

My heart couldn't take the battering.

"You know Jane and I had a marriage of convenience."

"Convenient for you, maybe, but Jane is in love with you."

My head rears back, and I stare at my brother, still propped on his cane. "How can you say that?"

"Anyone looking at her knew how she felt."

The inside of my chest thumps, like a soft mallet on a bass drum. The sensation repeats. My breathing grows shallow. "Not me."

"Because, like Jane said, you're an idiot." He stares at me, squinting a second. "Your eyes weren't open wide enough because your heart was closed."

Myles's lips curl in the corner before growing to a knowing smile as he watches me. "You really had no idea?"

I shake my head. I had no idea my wife was in love with me.

"I need to go." I abruptly stand.

"Never expected you to stay." Myles's smile curves into a genuine grin, and I stare back at my brother, which is like looking in a mirror.

"I'm sorry, Myles." The apology is weak and overdue, and we have so much more to unpack between us.

"Get outta here." He nods. "And don't come back unless your *acushla* is with you." Myles chuckles, almost mocking me with the term, but he isn't wrong.

Jane is my heartbeat and the only one who can restore this irregular beat to a steady hum.

ONLY I DON'T LEAVE. After a quick phone call to Tucker, I'm stopped in my tracks.

Jane quit.

She left Impact.

She quit us.

She left me.

Punch after punch, blows hit hard as Tucker rails into me with the news that Jane quit on her first day back in Chicago and then took long overdue vacation time during the two weeks which should have been her notice time.

"I am not telling you where the fuck she is," Tucker snarls through the phone.

"Just tell me she's safe." My brother who shares a father, but has another mother, must hear the panic in my voice. He knows accidents can happen. A life can be over in an instant and your life can be thrown off course with the loss.

"She's safe," he huffs, not offering me more. Tucker and I have a lot to discuss but he's giving me grace to get this shitstorm in Wrightwood under control. Right now, I need patience with Jane.

Because of Wrightwood, you bastard. Or should I blame Fischer? He got me here. I'm invested. And none of this would have happened without Jane.

My acushla.

FOR THE NEXT WEEK, everyone gives me a wide berth as I wade through issues surrounding the fire damage. I bury myself in work. Exhausting my brain so I don't think of Jane. Hardening my heart to her absence.

One evening, I find myself standing in the new park, watching the river roll underneath the bridge. My thoughts are random, rising and falling like the miniature crests in the water below.

Hard-soled shoes scraping over gravel turns my head and I watch Landon approach me. Looking at him, his body language suggests he has something unpleasant to tell me.

Is Jane divorcing me?

"Landon." I greet him with a head nod.

"Mach." He exhales and narrows his eyes at the river.

"I'm not going to like this, am I?" I stare at him.

He shakes his head slowly before turning to face me. "Frank is trying to contest the will. He's using your marriage as his springboard, stating it isn't legitimate."

"What?" I twist to face Landon and swipe a hand over my head, resting it on the back of my neck. This can't be happening.

"He's making the claim you weren't married before the will reading, which is technically true, but we have five witnesses that will disagree with Frank." Me, Myles, Ma, Landon, and Jane.

Jane.

"But what about my marriage to Jane?" I drop my hand from my neck and slap at my leg. I don't care about the fucking will.

"Your marriage is locked and loaded. While I might have had to pull some strings to procure the license sooner than the two-day period, you and Jane are legally wed."

Relief rushes through me and my shoulders fall. Then I'm hunching forward, gripping at my knees.

"Mach?" Concern fills Landon's voice.

I shake my head, fighting the nausea burbling in my stomach. For a few seconds there, I thought Landon was going to tell me I wasn't actually married to Jane. That the original farce was null and void. Only I don't want it to be a fake. Or pretend. Or an act.

I want my wife.

I straighten, blow out a breath and meet Landon's gaze. "You know Jane isn't here, right?"

Landon sighs. "I heard. But she needs to come back. Her leaving could look like a marital separation, thus breaking the terms of the will. We need to do anything we can to prevent Frank from thinking he has more fuel to add to these fires. You're so close to finishing this project."

I stare at Landon, holding his eyes. "I need to tell you something. A suspicion that Myles had."

Landon's brows lift.

"And I might have to agree with him."

Landon's eyes might fall out of their socket at that statement.

But it's time to come clean about a few things.

~

"Where is Jane, Big Mac?" Willow's sweet voice gets my attention, along with her tugging on the edge of my jacket as I'm walking back through town. We are standing outside the future Riverbank Mercantile Co.

I bend to her eye level. "She had to go home for a little while." The words are bitter on my tongue. Home seems like a foreign premise. Being with me should be Jane's home. As for *a little while*, I wasn't certain Jane wasn't gone for good. With Landon's news about Uncle Frank, though, we played off the separation to the townspeople by telling them Jane needed to return to Chicago for business. We didn't live here. We worked out of state.

But Jane was no longer a vested employee.

She was also no longer interested in me.

If anything, I'm the one who should have returned to Chicago. Originally, I could have left Jane here to manage everything as she has, but I didn't want to leave her behind. I didn't want her staying without me. Myles has been my excuse, but my heart knows differently. I wanted to be near Jane. She felt like home to me.

"When will she be back?" Willow shivers as she's only wearing a thick sweater, and the weather is colder. I reach for her tiny arms and absentmindedly rub up and down.

"I don't know." There is no sense in lying to Willow. Jane adores this child and Willow is smitten with her. Willow needed someone to love her, Jane said.

My woman has a soft heart.

Willow stares at me, reaching for the collar of my jacket. Her little fingers fist. "She didn't disappear in the river, right? You saved her." Her lower lip trembles.

I'm out of my element. If this cutie begins to sob, I might shatter on the pavement.

"No, sweetheart. She isn't . . . she didn't . . ." I can't say the word. I don't even want to think it.

"Then you have to bring her back. You need to save her again. She needs to come home." Her face turns red, and she huffs, blowing out air to ward off the inevitability of tears.

Please don't cry. She's so adorable even in a state of distress. The dark brown hair. The blue eyes. Once again, I consider how she could be Jane's child, if only . . .

Did I save Jane? I saved her from the river. That must be what Willow means. Because, in reality, Jane saved me. She pulled *me* out of that damn river, out of my memories, and brought me back to the land of the living.

I need my heartbeat.

"I plan to bring her back, baby girl."

I didn't know how yet but looking at Willow gave me an idea.

51

Playlist: "What If I Never Get Over You" – Ryan Hurd

[Jane]

The Fox siblings have reunited.

Blue Ridge is a beautiful small town tucked up in the mountains in Georgia and reminds me so much of Wrightwood minus the river. I'd been numb when I first left West Virginia, but once the waterworks fell, I struggled to stop them.

Lindee had traveled with me to Chicago where I promptly left Impact. My heart knew long before my brain caught up; my time in Chicago was over. When I'd entered Tucker Ashford's office, he took one look at me and surmised what I had to say.

I quit.

I'd tried to explain my decision without painting Mach in a negative picture. After twenty years in the industry, I recognized I needed a change. When Tucker had asked me what I'd do next, I told him I wasn't certain. My heart and my head had ached with every word.

The truth was I needed distance to process all that had happened in a matter of days.

Wrightwood's fire. Mach's betrayal. Leaving Impact.

Mae had suggested a road trip to our brother's place in Georgia.

I'd felt terrible asking Mae to keep the truth of our destination from Tucker for a few days, but I needed time. Time for my once-again broken heart to mend. Time to confirm my next steps. Time to erase the pain inside me.

I loved Mach, and he didn't love me back. This was an old song on repeat.

So, to Georgia we went.

Our brother Garrett lives in a renovated pre-Civil War home with his gorgeous wife, Dolores, and her feisty grandmother, Magnolia. The older woman is a hoot, with her pop-bottle thick glasses and her shotgun tales. She's sharp as a tack and entertains us for days. It's obvious she adores Garrett and has a close relationship with her granddaughter.

The place has multiple bedrooms, two parlors, a large dining room, a breakfast nook bigger than my entire kitchen, and a modernized kitchen made for a gourmet chef, but my favorite spot is a screened-in porch off the side of one of the front rooms. My sisters and I often sit here under blankets with warm, spiced wine, dogs at our feet, and deep conversation. Garrett has a chocolate lab named Wally, and when he proposed he gifted Dolores with Rainbow, which is evidence of the romance Mach does *not* believe exists in a marriage.

"We need to do this more often," Mae says. "We need to reunite in person." The years have passed with phone calls and text messages. Short, holiday visits home to see our mother didn't always include everyone.

"Maybe we should make a reunion an annual thing?" Lindee suggests.

"We could road trip again," Mae adds with excitement.

While Mae might love a road trip, the one I took prior to driving to our brother's resulted in marriage mayhem, and my heart ripped in half. "I think I'll pass on more road trips, but we could do destination vacations."

"Like Cancun?" Lindee asks dreamily. She has expensive tastes for someone who restores antiquated buildings. She also loves a good resort.

Mae wrinkles her nose. "We aren't spring break bound. Let's do something that involves more relaxation."

"Laying in the sun with a cabana man bringing me a margarita sounds relaxing to me." Lindee laughs.

"What if we visit areas we haven't seen in the U.S.? Places we haven't been to but want to visit?" The idea excites me, although I have no idea where the suggestion comes from. I haven't had a vacation in years, and the prospect of wandering somewhere—anywhere—sounds refreshing.

"Sounds like a plan," Mae says, lifting her mug of spiced wine for a sip.

"What's a plan?" Garrett enters the screened-in porch and takes a seat next to Lindee. He wraps an arm around her and knuckles her head like she's four instead of forty-one. We all share brown hair in varying shades. Garrett has dark eyes, though, compared to the blue us Fox sisters inherited from our mother.

"What the heck?" Lindee laughs.

"What's the plan?" Garrett asks again.

"We're going on vacation. A girls' trip unless you want to join us." Mae looks at Garrett, willing to include him when girl time sounds better to me.

"I think I'll pass on cabana boys and margaritas."

"Hey, were you listening?" Lindee punches Garrett's thigh.

"You're still so loud. I think they heard you down in Blue Ridge." Garrett scoffs.

Lindee crosses her arms and pretends to pout. How have I stayed away from these people? This is my family.

Mae offers Lindee a comforting smile, but Garrett is watching me. "I thought you meant you had a plan for what you'll do next."

There is something I've been toying with, but the idea is so foreign, so unique from what I've been doing, I'm not certain if it's a good decision for me. Then again, I wear the crown as the queen of poor choices, especially when it comes to men. Why would this situation be any different?

"I'm still considering my options."

Garrett grows serious and sits forward, balancing his elbows on his thighs. "If it's money, I can help you." My brother has more than he knows what to do with.

"It's not money. It's more . . . what will make me happy."

Mae sits beside me and lifts her mug again, smiling behind the rim like she understands.

"You were happy in Wrightwood," Lindee says. "You told me you were starting to love the town."

My brows pinch. Why would she mention this? "I can't go back there."

"But you have unfinished business there," Garrett adds, always thinking about bottom lines and anything related to finances.

"I'm certain Mach can handle it." I lift my mug of spiced wine and inhale the rich cinnamon fragrance. Then I take a hearty drink as the once-warm wine has cooled and hardly washes Volde-*Mach*'s name off my tongue.

"But Mach wasn't handling it. According to Tucker, you were doing almost everything." Mae lowers her mug to her lap and stares at me.

Ready to retort how I'm the best damn employee, I bite my

lower lip, instead. I was handling most things because I wanted to be in charge. I thrived on taking control of the project, and I fell in love with the client—the entire town.

"I have to say, I've never known you to be a quitter. It's so spontaneous of you." Mae's teasing voice matches her wiggling brows. She doesn't mean to offend me, but I'm on the defensive.

"I didn't quit."

"Well, you did quit Impact," Lindee reminds the room.

"And you left Wrightwood." Garrett narrows in on me.

This is rich coming from him. He left our small hometown and never looked back. Then again, we'd all done the same thing. It didn't mean we were runners. We didn't abandon things—*people*—like our father left us.

But I had left behind people.

Tanza. Stella and Kirk. Knox and Georgia. Dex and his brothers. Landon and Camilla. Myles.

I sit upright in my seat, suddenly questioning what I'd done. I'd gone to Myles because I didn't want to disappoint him. However, we were in a position that he could take over. He had all the contacts, although I'd made plenty of connections within the town.

"What are you not saying, Garrett?" I challenge him.

"I've just never known you to leave anything unfinished." He pauses. "And Wrightwood wasn't done, correct?"

Back in Wrightwood, we still had bits and pieces to complete. The fire was a setback. But Garrett is right. I wasn't one to give up. A setback was a challenge I often welcomed. I refused to be defeated. There was only one person who could bring me to my knees.

"I really don't think I can face Mach." The admission is hard to swallow.

"What about that little girl?" Lindee asks, crisscrossing her legs on her seat.

Willow. How could I forget Willow?

During her days in Wrightwood, Lindee had met my sweet little shadow. Lindee had teased me about my attention to her, mothering her, treating her like I'd once treated Lindee as a child. Lindee even commented how eerie it was Willow had features similar to me.

"What little girl?" Garrett questions, turning his head from Lindee to me.

"Willow," Lindee clarifies.

A vision of my girl comes to mind. She isn't actually mine, but we'd formed such a strong bond. My sidekick of sorts, as Mach called her, but she was stronger than a side character. She was a survivor. She was like me.

"I didn't say goodbye," I whisper, realization settling in. I hadn't told Willow I was leaving. Did she wonder what happened to me? Was she hurt I didn't see her before I left? My head wasn't in the right place when I'd rushed to pack a bag and leave Camilla's home.

With Garrett's eyes still on me, I quickly explain who Willow is.

"And you left her?" He sits up straighter, his voice incredulous with a sprinkle of accusation. The four of us share residual effects of our father disappearing on us as children. Garrett and I had it rougher than our younger siblings when our father left. We were old enough to remember him. We remember the fights between our parents before he went away. We remember the tears from our mother and her heartbreak for years as we held our family together while mere children. Mae chooses to forget. Lindee has no memory of him.

"Why do I feel like you're accusing me of something? I don't have a claim to the child." Still, my heart hammers at the thought of leaving her with unanswered questions.

"Do you want one?" Garrett stares at me.

"I . . ." I didn't know how to answer him. I did want Willow, which felt selfish and sad. She belonged to Theo Clarke. Still . . .

"She's not going into foster care." The idea of Willow with people who aren't from Wrightwood, who don't define what Wrightwood means, which is family, friendship, and love, hits me so hard I flinch back in my chair, and it rocks against the hard wood beneath it.

Mae gasps. Lindee stares at me, but Garrett slyly smiles.

"Do you think I let her down?" I glance from sibling to sibling. "Did I let down the town?"

I'd worried about Myles because he was losing out if we didn't finish by Kringle Fest. Wrightwood as a community brimmed with enthusiasm that the festival would happen, bigger and better than it ever had been. Businesses would be open with new faces and interiors, and the Christmas season was going to be extra special this year.

I'd made that promise to them.

And I wanted to be there to see it happen.

I deserved to see all my work come to fruition.

"Uh oh. She has that look in her eye," Mae teases beside me.

"There's the fighter I know," Garrett adds.

Lindee only smiles, sensing my plan.

I wasn't finished with Wrightwood.

As I RUSH to pack and book a flight as close to Wrightwood as I can get, my phone rings.

Seeing Camilla's name, I answer immediately, concerned that something else has happened to the town. "What's wrong?"

Camilla chuckles through the line. "Hello to you, too, dove."

"I'm sorry." I blurt out as I toss more things into my bag. "I . . ." I'm worried about Wrightwood.

"What do you need?" My tone is harsher than it should be. Mach and my situation is not Camilla's fault, but suddenly I can't get back to town fast enough.

"I just thought you should know that Frank is trying to contest the will."

"What?" I straighten as Camilla explains Frank's intention and what he's using as his basis.

"He's citing your marriage to Mach as the primary breach to the will."

For half a second, I consider Mach could be free of me. If Frank proves that we married later than the will reading and we hadn't followed West Virginia's official protocol for procuring a marriage license, our entire sham could be proven exactly what it's been . . . a farce.

Another thought occurs. Being away from Mach looks like we are separated, which would be another point to contest the will.

I need to get back there.

"What does Mach think?"

"According to Landon, who told Mach about Frank, Mach almost threw up."

"Sick with relief," I bitterly joke.

"Heart-sick, actually. And full of fear you weren't legally his wife." Then Camilla adds, "Which you are, according to Landon, West Virginia law, and vows my son made bind him to you."

"Heart-sick?" I choke on the idea.

"Lovey, I've already told you, you're my son's heartbeat. And his heart is losing tempo without you here. Mach needs you."

"Wrightwood needs me," I correct. *Wrightwood* needs Mach to have a wife, to complete the terms of the will, which involves restoring the town.

"There is no Wrightwood without Mach and you. You two are the soul of this place. You've revived everyone's spirits." Camilla pauses. "You brought my son home to me, honey. Come home to him."

How surprised Camilla was to find I was already packing.

52

Playlist: "Homesick" – Kane Brown

[Jane]

"You're here." Mach's voice expresses his shock as he enters his mother's home.

I couldn't get an immediate flight because of the Thanksgiving holiday. Coming to Camilla's hadn't been the plan, but Wrightwood doesn't offer many hotels and the few in the area were booked for the holiday weekend. "This isn't exactly where I want to be, but I couldn't find a hotel room."

The second Camilla saw me earlier, she'd pulled me into a hug, holding onto me as she'd done that first day. *"Thank you for coming back. His heart cannot beat without yours, and you cannot live without his."*

Tears had threatened to fall, but I was tired of crying over men who had made it clear they didn't want me for anything more than an arrangement—secret or convenient—in their lives.

However, I'm standing in Camilla's dining room where all our notes and papers have been collected and removed from the table to accommodate their meal yesterday.

"You quit," Mach chokes out.

I risk looking up at him, knowing the knife in my heart will only go deeper. He looks incredible with that beard of ink and chrome and fine lines near his eyes. He also looks a little broken, maybe a bit vulnerable, although I'm certain I'm imagining things. I recall Camilla telling me Mach almost vomited when he thought our marriage wasn't legal.

Heart-sick.

Quickly, I dismiss the thought.

"I needed a break." The admission is difficult to say. I've never walked away from a project.

"No, I mean you quit Impact."

I close my eyes. *Of course.* His top account executive. The one he's been over and under and entered. "I couldn't keep working for you."

"But you're here." He steps closer to me.

I take a step back, bumping into the dining table behind me. "I'm here for Wrightwood."

Mach's head turns so quickly, it's as if I slapped him. With his cheek toward me, he stares out the front window while his hands come to his hips. "Right. Wrightwood." His tone is rough and bitter.

"I shouldn't have run away like that, Mr. Wright." I straighten, grip the hem of my shirt and pull it tight, steeling myself to face him. "But it won't happen again. I finish what I start."

"So, our marriage?" Mach turns back to me.

"Camilla told me about Frank."

"I don't care about fucking Frank." His voice rises in frustration, and he scratches under his chin. A fact I've learned he does when he's trying to calm down.

"Our marriage can end as soon as we restore the town. If we push, three weeks will be over in a flash and then you can go back to how life used to be."

Mach narrows his eyes. His beautiful eyes. "Jane."

"We can keep up the ruse a few more weeks. It was only a charade. We both know how to play the game."

"Do we?" He steps closer to me, and I'm trapped by the table at my back. "What I know is I was ready to chase my wife. To apologize to her, maybe even grovel a little bit. And then I found she quit her job and disappeared." His voice rises once more. "She quit me."

"Even the best employees are—"

"Stop talking." The directive reminds me of the thousands of times I've said the same thing to him. The moments I needed him to cool down so the rising flame inside me could be doused. Sometimes that flame was annoyance. Other times arousal. The tension between us could be so thick at times I'd need a moment to ring out my panties. Deep breaths. Cold water on my face. Frantic orgasms alone at night.

I'm alone again.

And Mach is breathing heavy like a bull about to charge the red cape.

"You were not just my employee. You are not some charade. You are—" He swallows hard, not having an explanation for who I really am to him.

You are a convenient arrangement.

He exhales, reaching for the hair at the side of my face. I close my eyes, struggling with his nearness, with the sharp scent of man and mountains on him. He asks, "Was it only about a partnership?"

My eyes open, but I quickly look away from him. "I already told you it wasn't."

"Jane," he whispers, almost pleading. "Talk to me."

"You know, Mr. Wright, the funny thing is I would have come here if you simply asked. Even without tossing in the damn partnership, I would have said yes." Without the partnership. Without a proposal. I would have said yes to him because my heart is weak for him.

Tears prickle my eyes once again. Dammit. I will not cry in front of this man. For all the years of strength I've had to keep my emotions tight and locked inside me, I don't want to break now. But the struggle is real.

"If you had only told me the truth," I whisper as Mach's hand settles on my neck.

Five facts. Number one. I hate liars and cheaters.

In some ways, I was no better than Mach, though. I'd lied to the town. We married, but it wasn't real. It was a means to an end. I did wrong to do right by Wrightwood.

And I did it for Mach, and his mother, his brother, and sweet Willow.

And I'd do it again because I'm foolish like that. I fell in love with a town.

My actions were for a village, but I wouldn't succumb to Mach. Not his tender touch. Not his vulnerable eyes. Not his soft voice.

"Let's fix this town and finish." I restore my earlier resolve. I'm here for Wrightwood. Mach can get his life back, and I can move on.

"If that's all you want, baby."

I close my eyes again at the sweet endearment and lie once more. "That's all I want."

53

———

Playlist: "Burning" – Sam Smith

[Mach]

Jane might be back in the house, but she isn't in our bed. She isn't even in our room, and I start searching the other bedrooms Ma will soon turn into guest rooms for her future inn.

In one of them, I find Jane on a bed, curled on her side, tablet in hand. The low light on the side table is the only glow in the dark space.

We've circled one another throughout the remainder of the day. She thought she had some explaining to do to the businesses on Bridge Alley, and the best way to restore their faith in her was to jump in. I didn't have a doubt she'd win them back over. Most businesses were completed. People in general adored Jane.

Thankfully, Riverbank Mercantile Co. and The Barber

Shop didn't have much damage other than some exterior charring. Trixie's Trim was a complete loss, but Ma had insurance. Both the old salon and the vacant space were being rebuilt. Three weeks wouldn't restore them completely, but the exterior should be finished in time for Kringle Fest.

Despite Jane's distance, I can't seem to stay away from her. I flop onto her bed while she keeps her back to me.

"You quit, but where are you going to go?" Anxiety laces concern in my rugged tone. I can't believe she left Impact.

"Worried about competitors?" Her voice is sharp as she shifts to look over her shoulder at me. She's so beautiful. Sad, but still stunning with those piercing blue eyes. I miss her smile. I've erased it from her face. And this snappy attitude might remind me of office-Jane, but I want Jane-my-wife.

"No, I'm not worried about the competition. But . . ." I swallow around a question I hate to ask. I stare at the ceiling above me when I do. "Are you staying in Chicago?"

Jane flips to her back and rolls her head to face me. "I'm certain our paths won't cross, Mr. Wright."

I swipe a hand down my face. "Would you stop it?" Running into her is the last thing I'm concerned about. Her running away from me is my fear.

Jane exhales. "I made a promise to this town, and I keep my promises."

The censure in her tone isn't missed. I've disappointed her and I roll my head to face her. "Jane."

She huffs. "If you had told me, even the next day. If you had said, I made a mistake, Jane. Or apologized for bribing me but explained that you still needed me to pretend to be your wife; I would have done it."

I don't believe it could have ever been that easy.

And I won't apologize for asking her to be my pretend wife. Not when I want her for real.

I shift entirely, lying on my side and holding up my head

with my hand. "Why?" Why would she still have done whatever I asked? I should know the answer. Myles said my eyes weren't open because my heart was closed, but my heart is open now. What am I still not seeing?

"Because I'm a fool, Mr. Wright." Jane looks up at the ceiling. Blinking rapidly, she whispers. "Romantic to the core."

She blows out another breath. "But you told me there is no romance in marriage. I mean, you were right. Mae didn't have it with her ex-husband, Adam. And my mother didn't have it with my father. I should thank you for the reminder. They were all acts. We can be one more on your list."

My brows lift. "You don't think we had romantic moments?" My mind wanders to all the places we christened in town. All the nights we shared in a different bedroom. How we danced during Trophy's Frank-N-Steins party. Our day dates, especially the Wine Cellar Park. Our wedding night.

I hate how cynical she sounds, and I hate that I'm the one who caused this new opinion.

While Jane swipes at her eye, I ask, "Baby, why are you crying?"

She closes her eyes and shakes her head. Taking a deep breath, she opens her lids and stares up at the ceiling again. "It doesn't matter. I have my own list to write."

"What does that even mean?" I swipe at a tear seeping from the corner of her eye and rolling to her ear.

"I'm making some changes in my life."

I love the determination in her voice, but something tells me I'm missing an undertone.

"I'm going to find a house." She breathes out.

"What?" I brace up on my hand.

"And I'm applying for a job." She still doesn't look directly at me.

"Where?"

"It's time for something new in my life. Something for me."

"What are you saying?"

"I'm staying in Wrightwood." Her eyes meet mine.

Her words are a blow to my sternum. I can't breathe. This is Tracy again. She didn't want to be with me. She didn't want to follow me to Chicago. She wasn't my partner for life.

I know the truth now. That was the past.

Jane *is* my partner. And I don't need her to live out my dreams. I want to be by her side as she lives out hers.

"I've been doing some re-evaluating since I've been down here." Jane continues. "I should thank you. If you hadn't asked me to pretend with you, I never would have been here. And here was where I realized I no longer wanted a partnership at Impact. I'd actually been pretending with myself for too long that I was okay, but I wasn't. And I accused you of lying but I hadn't told the truth either. I should have said something to you weeks ago."

"What changed your mind about the partnership?" My voice shakes. My fingers itch to stroke over her arm. While I don't like our discussion, I miss talking to her. I miss these quiet moments we'd shared in bed each night.

Jane shrugs. "Being here put things in perspective. I've been working my entire life, giving up things I didn't even know I wanted." She glances at me. "But now I know what I deserve. Fool me once, shame on you. Or Ripley, in my case. But fool me twice, shame on me." She shakes her head. "Don't worry, though, Mach. My eyes are wide open now, and I'm focusing on me."

"And you want to be in Wrightwood? Wrightwood holds the answers?"

"Wrightwood holds the answers." She nods once, definitively, swiping at a final tear.

A boulder the size of the mountain we are on fills my throat. I don't know Jane's financial status, but I'm certain she's well-off. She doesn't need to work, but she'd never be able to sit still. And she's too young to retire. "What will you do here?"

"This town needs an executive director of economic development. I'd be good at it with my marketing background. I applied for the new position. Tucker offered to write me a letter of recommendation."

Fuck Tucker. "I'll write it." *What was I saying?* She doesn't need a measly letter of recommendation. I own this town. This is my inheritance, and if she wants the position, she can have it.

She *owns* me.

But I want her heart. I want her to love me.

"Thank you, Mr. Wright. And thank you for asking me to be part of Plan A. If I hadn't bamboozled you into Plan B, I wouldn't feel all this . . ." She waves around her belly. "This hope for a better future for me."

The positivity in her voice grows my irritation. "Plan A? Plan B?"

"You bribed me to pretend to be your wife, but I hooked you into marrying me. We both know you hadn't wanted to delve into an actual marriage. A legitimate wedding was the only way to save the town, but a real marriage . . ." Jane shakes her head, glancing at me and then away.

Was she really so quick to brush off all we'd been through in the past few months? The connection we had? I thought we'd come so far. I thought I could keep her as my wife.

"I know where I stand with you, Mach. I take responsibility for my part in this mess."

Mess? Although, hadn't I used the same term before myself to describe our position? The only thing that feels messy now is how I'm going to keep Jane.

Heavy silence falls between us before she twists, giving me her back again, and picks up her tablet.

Shock overcomes me.

Wrightwood.

Move here. Work here. Live here.

It isn't possible.

This is the last place I want Jane to be without me.

And I need a new plan minus contingencies.

With her back still to me, I curl toward her and wrap my arm around her waist.

Jane stiffens. "You don't need to do this here, Mach. We don't need to pretend anymore."

Squeezing her tighter to me, I mutter into her hair. "Who says I'm pretending?"

54

———————

Playlist: "Landslide" – The Chicks version

[Jane]

A heated body presses to mine. After Mach questioned me last night, he remained in the room. Eventually, he rolled away from me, but sometime during the night, his foot sought my ankle. Then his hand rested against my back. He returned to his original position, his front along my spine and his arm draped over me. I hardly slept a wink.

The ache in my heart was deep.

I couldn't believe I'd pulled it off—that I'd found the strength to brush off our marriage, citing his disbelief in romance as a reason. I refused to believe romance didn't exist. Just that love wasn't something available to me. I'd been duped once again into thinking a working relationship—one with actual business as its beginning—could be anything other than a contract of sorts. One with empty promises and no future.

This time around, I was angry. Angry at how much Mach had hurt me. Angry that I was hurt by him when I promised myself I wouldn't be in this position again. As Lindee said, I wouldn't ever let someone take advantage of me. And I had. Down the rabbit hole I fell because it was Mach.

Unlike Alice in Wonderland, I needed to save myself in Wrightwood.

Mach had been upfront from the start. He'd told me he didn't believe in romantic marriage. He told me he wanted to capitalize on our status with sex. What he didn't profess was committed love and unending devotion.

I'm the fool who wanted those things.

He'd made it clear I wasn't worth the risk to his heart.

The lost partnership was a wake-up call. I hadn't wanted it by way of coercion, anyway. I deserved a promotion based on hard work, dedication, and ethics. I'd momentarily forgotten I could apply those attributes to myself. I could use those skills to better me.

Removing myself from Mach's warmth, I slip from the bed and quickly dress.

Once downstairs, Camilla greets me with a hug. "Good morning, dove."

November seemed to pass with a blink, and I've missed her over the weeks. I treasure the comfort of her embrace. While I love my own mother, I wish she were half as supportive as Camilla. My mother couldn't understand the drive to provide for myself, work in a fast-paced industry, or live in a large city. She blamed me for losing Ripley, yet she also had an extreme distrust of men. The hypocrisy wasn't lost on me.

Eventually, Camilla's embrace is too much, and I gently shrug out of her hold before I break again. *No more tears, Jane Wright.*

"I'm going into town. I'll grab tea at On The Curve. I have so much work to do." The false cheer in my voice is the pep talk I need. I can do this. I can be in Camilla's house, with Mach present, for a few more weeks. Then he'll go back to Chicago, and I can start a new journey in life.

Camilla frowns at me.

"I'd like to push to make Myles's deadline." Maybe Landon Hobbs can give us some grace. The fire wasn't our fault. In fact, I need to speak with the fire inspector or the fire chief. I need to know what happened. I didn't ask Mach because I'm trying to keep our communication minimal.

Camilla tilts her head. "Do you really think this is about money for either of my boys?"

I was no longer certain of anything other than what I wanted for myself. What I believed I deserved. A home. A job that brought me fulfillment. Maybe a marriage one day, based on love.

"What else is it about? They both have an end goal."

Camilla sighs. "My father wanted to reunite my sons. He wanted to bring Mach home to *me*." She jabs a finger at her chest. "And he wanted my child to love again."

"Well, two out of three worked." I feebly smile at Camilla.

Her brows crease. "Mach loves you."

"He doesn't." The sadness I wish to hide from her seeps into my tone. "You've known from the start our marriage was pretend, Camilla." The bitterness of the words burns my throat because I couldn't pretend how I felt. I'd fallen for Mach. I wanted to believe he was into me. But I'd been wrong before about men. It was no surprise I didn't get it right this time either.

I give myself a little shake, ridding the negative thoughts as much as I can. "I need to get going. I have a meeting with Landon, and then I have a town to finish rebuilding."

55

Playlist: "Make Me Miss You" – Sam Hunt

[Mach]

From the hallway, I overhear Jane's conversation with Ma, and I am absolutely stunned. I didn't believe any of that crap she spewed last night about romance not existing in marriage. *She* didn't believe the things she said, either, but I'd put the doubt in her head. Somehow, she'd missed what I thought I'd been showing her all along. I wanted to be with her.

And the pain in her voice when she told Ma I didn't love her

. . .

Fuck. I had my work cut out for me to prove both of us wrong. Romance is alive.

Ma had been right. My first marriage was youthful with a rebellious heart and a penchant to run. This marriage is different. There is a calming comfort in Jane, and I'll be damned if I lose her.

If she wants romance, I'll give her romance. I'll do anything to win over my wife.

~

Dear Jane,

Five facts I know about you.

1. *You still chew your lip but sometimes it's when I enter you, like you're fighting the attraction we both feel to one another. Or are overwhelmed by the power of it, like I am. Give in.*
2. *Flannel or silk, you're beautiful in either.*
3. *You love apple pie with crumble on top and black tea with two heaping spoons of sugar, which means you're sweet behind the walls you keep.*
4. *You smell like summer rain and taste like fresh beginnings.*
5. *You love big and with your whole heart.*

~

Dear Jane,

Five facts about me.

1. *I can hold my eyes still when I look at you because you're all I see. All my attention tunnels into you.*
2. *I'm just as comfortable in worn jeans and a ball cap as three-piece suits.*
3. *I've said my favorite spot on you is the valley between your breasts, but it's actually the heart within your chest.*
4. *You've changed me in ways I didn't expect to change.*

5. *I want you to love me.*

JANE DOESN'T MENTION the notes, but she's received them. I leave them folded on the nightstand by her bed in the guest room and they're always gone the next day.

"What's your favorite flower?" I ask as we pass like ships one morning.

Jane's brows pinch.

"A husband should know these things about his wife," I explain with a timid smile.

Skepticism rests in her eyes as she tips her head. She chews at her bottom lip. "I'm certain my husband will figure it out." Her blue eyes narrow behind yellow-rimmed glasses. She hasn't worn them in a while, and I want to bare her of everything but those frames.

"What if I'm wrong?" The desire to reach for her, tug her to me, and hold her tight is strong. She's so beautiful, it hurts my heart. But I'm here to woo, not smother.

"Then you work to make it right."

Somehow, I don't think we are talking about flowers.

Taking my best guess, knowing what I know about Jane, she wouldn't like something garish like red roses. While considered symbolic of romance, they don't say Jane. She is classic and refined but stable and strong-willed.

I leave her white calla lilies one morning. Jane thanks me, but there isn't any emotion behind her gratitude.

Another day, I offer a bouquet of white tulips which are rare for December. She fights a smile and sticks her nose into the flowers, but something still isn't right.

On the third day, I offer her something different.

"What's this?"

"It's a plant. The florist told me it's called a pothos. It's sturdy, long-lasting, and vibrant. This says Jane to me." I pause, glancing down at the vaguely heart-shaped leaves of the bright green plant. "I'm also told they're really difficult to kill. Not that I want to harm you, but it expresses resilience, persistence, and a desire to thrive. That's my Jane."

Jane glances up at me, her expression blank. Her teeth hold in her tender lower lip.

Swallowing down the sour taste of what I'm about to say, I add, "It's also a common house plant, and I thought you might like it for your new house."

Her brows lift. "I haven't found a house yet." She hugs the plant against her chest, dropping her gaze from me.

I scratch under my chin, the hair bristling. "I know."

"How?" Her head pops up. Those blue eyes are my undoing.

"Small town, remember?" I smile and Jane weakly offers me one in return. It isn't the smile she shares with others. It isn't the smile she once gave me. But it's something.

She nods. "I'm going to watch HGTV." She told me she watches the channel when she can't sleep. She looks tired. Still sad. I haven't been in her bed since the night of her return. But God, I fucking miss her.

Has she been lonely in bed like I am? Has she missed me beside her?

"Can I watch with you?"

She softly laughs. "Don't you feel like you're living HGTV?"

What I feel is I'm living my worst nightmare. I'm co-existing with Jane instead of spending my life with her. *Baby steps, Mach.*

"We could watch a movie, instead. A couch date." We haven't watched one since our *Guardians of the Galaxy* marathon. I want to give Jane all the dates. Day ones. Couch ones. Vacations and holidays. Every date on the fucking calendar.

"*Guardians of the Galaxy,* again?" Her growing smile teases me.

"Or a rom-com," I suggest, recalling her laughter when she watched them with her sister.

Jane purses her lips. "Maybe we can just see what's available."

"I'll make popcorn." I hitch a thumb over my shoulder.

Jane is still hugging her new plant to her chest. Lifting it, she nods to the staircase. "I'll take this upstairs and meet you in ten minutes on the couch."

"It's a date." I wink. Her mouth pops open but I don't allow her to respond. I turn on my heels toward the kitchen feeling like a fucking king.

I have a couch date with my wife.

56

Playlist: "All I Want for Christmas Is You" – Lady A version

[Jane]

The town is a buzz of energy as the holiday season is upon us. Hope fills the air despite the fire a month ago. No culprit has been caught. No motive detected. The paint and turpentine in the vacant shop were to blame this time.

However, Myles doesn't believe it. That storefront was locked up tight, he'd said. Myles also informed me that Mach eventually told Landon and him about the near break-in at Adventure Dex, and attempts were made to better patrol Bridge Alley. After learning about Frank's intentions, Mach has become more diligent in questioning things.

To my surprise, the brothers quietly exist without shared scowls or Mach's bark. I've even noticed them talking without crossed arms or defensive body language. I haven't asked Mach about their relationship, because as much as I'm curious, I can't become involved. I need to keep myself as separate as I can from Mach and emotions.

With his flowers and five-fact notes, and couch dates, each day grows more difficult to ignore him, though. He's sweet when he wants to be. Even—*dare I say*—romantic. But I'm convinced his actions are a result of remorse about the partnership offering. True to our agreement, he continues the façade of marriage. A hand on my lower back as we talk to business owners in town or a kiss to my temple before he leaves me to work on one of our remaining projects. Public displays of affection were not part of our arrangement. Mach said it from the start that we didn't need PDA.

So, it's all very confusing.

Thankfully, the town progresses. We hadn't turned on the string of lights zigzagging over Bridge Alley yet, waiting on a lighting ceremony that coincides with Kringle Fest. The festival is next weekend.

This year, I invited local artisans and food trucks to sell wares and delicacies, hoping to bring more interest to Wrightwood. The idea comes from a festival in downtown Chicago held every year before Christmas. It's ambitious for a first year especially after the fire, but I have faith it's what Wrightwood needs.

The storefronts of Trixie's Trim and the vacant shop have been repaired for aesthetic reasons, but boards cover their window spaces. I have an idea for that as well. I want Wrightwood to have the merriest of Christmases.

Only one part of me remains unsettled in this town. Willow.

Landon gave me more perspective on her uncle. Theo Clarke isn't a bad man. He's just negligent. He works hard. He sleeps on his days off. In many ways, he reminds me of my granddad, and I'm certain the responsibility of a small child is the last thing he wanted as a bachelor in his mid-sixties.

As I'm inside the future Riverbank Mercantile Co., Willow wanders in.

"Hey, baby girl." I rise from where I've been unpacking boxes and step over to her, crouching down to offer her a hug since I've spent more time with her, and the community knows who I am. Willow hugs me back.

Mach is also in the store, surprisingly working beside his brother to hang replicas of tin ceiling tiles to provide an antiquated effect in place of modern drop-ceiling panels. He gazes over at me with Willow and offers a warm smile. The struggle to fight the pull to him is real. He's wearing me down one house plant and pretty note at a time. Not to mention, watching him work beside his brother is a total turn on. His inked arms flexing. His thighs stabilizing him on a ladder. His backside snug in jeans.

Tugging my gaze away from Mach when he catches me checking him out, I shift my focus back to Willow. "So, what are you asking Santa for this Christmas?"

Willow leans against me as I kneel on the floor. Her eyes drop to my collar, and she fiddles with the edge of my shirt.

"Santa isn't coming this year." Her quiet voice rings with sadness.

"Santa isn't coming?" *Will Theo not take on the role?*

"He isn't real anyway," Willow adds.

I gasp. She's too young to be so jaded. She should still believe in magic and the holiday season. Jostling her against me, I tickle her belly. "Why would you say such a thing?"

"Because Mommy and Daddy are gone."

Heart. Break.

She isn't even being a Scrooge or a Grinch; she just knows the truth. Without her parents, she doesn't have anyone to be that mystery all children need. A belief that being good has its rewards and humanity is decent.

"Well, I might have a special connection to Santa. So why don't you tell me what you want?"

Mach suddenly stands behind me. His hand comes to my head, stroking over my hair.

He squats beside us. "What are my girls talking about?"

It's dangerous that he calls us his. Dangerous for my heart. Dangerous to my hopes.

"Santa." I emphasize his name with the excitement it should entail. "Willow was about to give me her Christmas wish list."

"Have you been naughty or nice this year, baby girl?" Mach teasingly pokes Willow in the belly.

I tug Willow into my side. "Of course, she's been an angel."

"Mommy and Daddy are angels now."

Tears immediately prickle at the back of my eyes, and I rapidly blink them away. When did I get so emotional?

Mach's hand moves to my nape, tenderly squeezing me.

"That's right, sweetheart," I say, attempting to keep my voice steady. "They're watching over you. Protecting you."

Willow nods. "That's what Stella and Miss Camilla say."

"They're both wise women." Mach glances at Willow's innocent face before giving me a warm smile. "But Jane here is the wisest of them all. So why don't you tell her what you want for Christmas. I bet she has a special in with the man in red."

I love how Mach is playing along. And my heart grows three sizes inside my chest. Hope, silly hope, fills in behind my ribs.

"Santa isn't—"

I quickly cover Willow's mouth, leaning toward her with a fake scowl.

She giggles into my palm.

Mustering an ominous tone, I warn her, "We can't say it, or he won't visit us. You have to believe."

Mach emphatically nods. *This man.*

Willow continues to toy with the collar of my shirt. Looking at my chin, she speaks. "I'd like a dollhouse."

"I had a dollhouse when I was a kid." An image of something feminine and pink, and full of fun furniture and a family fills my thoughts.

Mach chuckles. "I bet you did."

"And do you need dolls to live in the house?"

Willow nods.

"Who do you need?"

"A mommy and a daddy and a little girl. A family."

I chew my lower lip, fighting the ache in my chest as I hold onto this little girl. Dear Santa, I wish I could give her everything she wants. Her dreams are the same as mine in some ways.

"Sounds wonderful, baby girl," Mach offers. He swipes a hand over her head, brushing back her wayward hair, and she smiles at him. Sweet, shy. She's crushing on Mach. I don't blame her.

He's watching me, and I give him my own timid grin. Turning back to Willow, I say, "Maybe you should write a letter to Santa. We can mail it and see what happens."

Willow shrugs, still disbelieving in the innocence of Christmas.

"Willow?" Stella sticks her head into the future store. She lightly chuckles as she enters. "Man, this child can escape me in a blink."

Stella hikes Willow up to her hip. "Child, you need to stop running."

Willow only nods before wrapping her arms around Stella, holding onto her like the lifeline she has been. *It takes a village.*

Mach and I both stand. I, too, worry about Willow's safety. A five-year-old should not wander the streets. The fire still has me unsettled. We don't have hard facts, but it's difficult to dismiss the randomness of three fires in six months. Especially when I'd learned the town has no history prior to June.

Stella tells Willow to say goodbye, which she does, and a longing fills my chest as they leave. It's a ridiculous sensation. Stella takes good care of Willow.

"We can make the dollhouse happen." Standing beside me, Mach runs a hand up my spine and cups my nape again.

I nod, offering a half smile. "I knew you would, Mr. Wright." Pausing a second, I turn back toward the door where Stella exited with Willow. "I worry so much about her."

"You have a big heart."

"It's more than that. I just . . . I want her to be happy. I want her to feel loved." The idea returns the threat of tears once again. My heart shatters whenever I see her face sadden or hear her mention the loss of her parents.

"She will," Mach says, and I turn back to him. My mouth falls open, preparing to ask what he means but he shifts topics.

"Speaking of dollhouses, I found a house you might like. A realtor in town can show it to us."

"Oh." *Oh.* This is generous. Then again, is he trying to get rid of me? I hadn't intended to stay as long as I have at Camilla's, but she has been insistent. Why go to a hotel when she wants to turn her place into a bed and breakfast? Thankfully, she hasn't pushed for me to return to the room I shared with Mach. Maybe she's finally accepting we aren't a couple. We aren't going to stay married.

A lump the size of coal lodges in my throat. I'm not on the naughty list other than some of the sexual positions I've experienced with this man, but I feel slighted, almost kicked out of Camilla's home. Shaking my head, I dismiss the pain the thought brings. "I'd love to see it."

"Perfect. We can make it another date." Mach leans in and quickly kisses my temple before leaving me with my list of wishes, where I need to scratch off the most ludicrous wish of hope.

The hope that Mach wants our marriage to be real and he'll stay with me in Wrightwood.

Dear man in red, please bring me a house and a miniature one for that innocent child.

Then I add a mental postscript.

And if the house includes that child and this man, I promise to be extra good.

57

———

Playlist: "River" – Joni Mitchell

[Mach]

Kringle Fest is here. Jane and I take the long, gravel drive down to town as the grass on the hill has a dusting of snow on it. The waning time feels ominous, like the ending of something special when I'd been holding out hope for a new beginning.

The center of Bridge Alley is set up with booths as Jane had wanted. Tents and canvas canopies distinguish one vendor from another. The strong aroma of nuts roasting in cinnamon and sugar fills the street. The town is packed with children, teens, and adults. Some are shopping. Some are lingering in the closed-off road. Some are even painting on the plywood covering the windows at what was once Trixie's Trims and the vacant store beside it. The artwork being created adds to the festival theme, like Jane's mural inspirations have added to the overall atmosphere of Wrightwood.

I stare in wonder. Jane stands beside me, a smile so large we don't need the lighting ceremony.

"This is Wrightwood, Mach," Ma says softly, coming up to my other side. "We come together here."

She draws in a deep breath of the cold air and nutty-cinnamon scent. "You know, Machlan, Dr. Seuss had a saying in his story about the Grinch. *'Maybe, Christmas,' he thought, 'doesn't come from a store.'*" Ma pauses. "*'Maybe Christmas, perhaps, means a little bit more!'* This is the little bit more, lovey."

Pulling my gaze from Ma, I stare back at the bustling street. We aren't fucking Whoville, but Wrightwood is showing its community. The place that ostracized Ma, Myles, and me forty-eight years ago slowly grew to acceptance and compassion, especially where Ma and Myles were concerned. Or maybe that was one more thing I had wrong about this place. Maybe I'd always been a part of here as well, I was just too busy trying to escape it.

"We need to turn on the lights," Jane's voice croons with emotion. Her face is so full of peace, contentment, and pride. This is the new Jane. And I want to be a new Mach for her.

"Whenever you're ready, dove. The lights are waiting for you," Ma says, glancing at Jane.

"Me?" Jane blinks back at Ma. "I thought the mayor might want to do it."

"It's your town, too, Jane. You can pick whoever you want to flip that switch. Or you do it yourself." Ma watches Jane, but Jane looks up at me, bewildered by Ma's suggestion.

"Jane!" a child calls out. Willow rushes toward us and Jane bends to embrace her.

"You need to come see my painting," Willow says, her voice full of excitement. Her fingers tuck into Jane's hand.

Jane bops the little girl on the nose. "I will in a minute, but first, I have a very important job. Would you like to help me with it?"

Willow peers at Jane before looking up at me. "Hi, Big Mac."

"Hey, baby girl." I lower to my haunches. "Come with us."

Willow looks from me to Jane and back before stepping into my open arms. I scoop her up, and Jane's breath hitches as we stand. Her eyes flick from Willow to me, and she chews her lower lip like she's fighting a smile. I want her smile again. I want one just for me.

Carrying Willow, we enter a door that leads to an office above The Barber Shop. Jane has made the place an office for the future director of economic development, who happens to be her. Inside the fuse box is the main switch for the lights zigzagging over Bridge Alley.

"Flip the switch," Jane says, placing her hand over Willow's when she touches the fuse. Together, they move the lever until a heavy click occurs.

"Let's see what happened," Jane addresses Willow, and we cross to the opposite side of the sparse office. Looking outside, hundreds of white Edison lightbulbs crisscross over Bridge Alley, highlighting the festive holiday merchants beneath them.

"Let's go downstairs and look," Willow says, wiggling so I will put her down. She races ahead of us, turning the corner through the door frame.

"God, I love that child," Jane whispers before we both hear her pattering steps down the staircase.

"We will be right there," I holler after Willow, placing a hand on Jane's arm when she moves forward to follow Willow. "I need to tell you something."

Jane pauses, her eyes meeting mine in the dim office. Through the uncovered windows, the lights outside pepper the glass with glittering sparkles.

"I wanted to thank you."

Jane's breath hitches. "For—"

I cover her mouth with my hand for a second and shake my head. "For all your hard work. For your devotion to this town. You saved Wrightwood." I swallow, dropping my palm to gaze at her lips. "You saved me."

"Mach," she mumbles but I'm not ready for her to speak.

"I've hated this town and felt like it always hated me. And I despised that godforsaken river. But the night I jumped in it, and you were there on the embankment worried about me, telling me to never, ever do something like that again, I knew I was different." I chuckle to myself. That night felt like a baptism of sorts, which would sound strange to say aloud. I went into the water, cursing it, and its history with me, but I came out a man more determined than ever to live for the future and keep my wife. The woman standing before me, slipping through my fingers.

"I just wanted to say I'm sorry I couldn't make you partner at Impact. But you've been a partner in every other way that's important. Standing by me when I returned here. Holding my hand as you married me. Being my wife in so many ways, it felt real. To me. It *is* real."

I reach for Jane's hand and run my thumb over her fourth finger, the one wearing a small ring that binds us together.

"If I can choose a life partner, I choose you, Mrs. Wright."

Jane sniffles and I glance up. A tear trickles along her nose.

"You did good here, Jane."

"It takes a village." She tries to chuckle but fails as she chokes.

"No, Jane. It only took *you* being here to make all the difference."

We hear the patter of little feet racing back up the staircase, and any second, we'll be interrupted.

"I just thought you should know I'm sorry. But I'm not sorry we got married. And I'm not unhappy with you as my wife."

"Come on, slow pokes." Willow laughs as she stands just inside the office. "Were you two kissing again?"

Jane turns to Willow, her mouth falling open, and I lift her hand to my lips. I want to kiss my wife.

"We're coming right now," Jane says to Willow before turning back to me.

I tip my head toward the door. "Go ahead. I'll be right down."

Jane glances from me to Willow and back. Her expression is puzzled. Eyes bright while her brows pinch. Her teeth dig into her lower lip.

"I just need a minute," I whisper, releasing her hands and turning toward the window.

I couldn't say I loved Wrightwood, or it had come to terms with me, but with Jane at my side, I'd learned to appreciate my hometown. I'd come to an acceptance of it, or maybe I finally accepted that I'd had things wrong for too long.

I'd lost so much time and that needed to change.

"Mr. Wright." Jane's teasing yet stern tone interrupts my thoughts. I'd thought she'd gone down the stairs with Willow. Instead, she stands by the door frame holding out her hand. "Let's go see what we've done."

She beams a smile at me. One bright and luminescent like the bulbs crisscrossing Bridge Alley. In that moment, I'd go wherever she wanted to lead me.

INSTEAD, Willow leads us to the storefront windows covered in wood. She proudly points. "Here's my picture. It's a snow family."

The image includes three snowmen, complete with an adult man and woman and a little girl between them. The dark flowing hair gives away the gender along with a pink scarf around her neck.

"How cute," Jane coos, bending at the waist to take a picture with her phone of the painting. She points at blue squiggle lines behind the family. "What's this?"

"It's the river." Willow traces over the lines with her little fingertip.

Jane scowls and glances up at me. We both know Willow's story. She's very open to telling people about her parents' death. Does this picture mean she hopes to join her parents in the river? The morbid thought has my blood rushing like the river water can.

"Uncle Theo told me I'm going to a new family. One with a mom and a dad." Willow's small voice is difficult to read. Is she happy about leaving her uncle? Is she disappointed? Or is she simply stating a fact?

"Oh." Jane stands and crosses her arms over her middle. She blinks once before peering at me. Then she looks down at Willow, her lips twitching as if she's struggling to form a smile. "This is a good thing."

Jane gazes over my shoulder, and I twist enough to see Theo Clarke down the block. He casually waves at Jane, and she lifts a hand. The smile on her face doesn't reach her eyes as she calls out to him. "Merry Christmas."

He nods.

"Jane, can we go get hot chocolate from Stella?" Willow reaches for Jane's hand and tugs.

"Sure, baby," Jane says to Willow, swallowing hard. "How about if you ask Uncle Theo if he'd like to join us?"

Willow skips off toward her uncle, and Jane's shoulders fall. "Oh my God, does she think new parents will come from the river?" Her voice croaks.

"Maybe she just wants to memorialize her parents. The snow melts away into the river and her parents did too."

Jane swipes a hand through her hair. "She's so young for such thoughts."

However, Jane and I can't know what a five-year-old is thinking. All we can know is she's waiting on Jane to take her to On The Curve for hot chocolate.

"She needs someone like you," I say, rubbing a hand up Jane's back. I need her, too.

"She breaks my heart," Jane whispers.

"Let some hot cocoa and time with her seal it back together for now. This night is about celebration. Not sadness." I tip up her chin and tug her to me, offering what I intended to be a chaste kiss. A soft brush against her lips, like snowflakes dusting the air. But the second our mouths meet, I can't pull back.

I need a better kiss before I lose her for another night. The town is going to eat her up like a peppermint stick—sugary sweet and sharply satisfying. That's my Jane to these people.

Jane responds, opening for me, gifting me with her tongue. I pull her closer to me until my name muttered against my lips reminds me where we stand.

Reluctantly pulling away, I try to explain myself. "There's mistletoe over us."

Jane looks up and giggles. "There is not."

"Okay, fine, I just wanted to see my kiss on you." My eyes latch onto hers as she gazes back at me. "Oh, and there's one last thing I wanted to tell you. Something I can no longer pretend."

Her smile drops. Her eyes grow suspicious.

"I can no longer pretend our marriage is an act, a charade, or a sham. Because I'm wholeheartedly, absolutely, and completely in love with you, Jane."

"Mach," she whispers, brows pinched, confusion on her face. I don't need her to say it back. I don't want to hear she doesn't love me in return.

I lean toward her ear. "I have no more secrets left to share." I press a kiss just below her ear and step back. Pointing upward, I wink. "Mistletoe again."

Jane looks up, although she's already aware there is no mistletoe over us, and I spin away from her. Walking away might be one of the hardest things I've ever done, but Jane deserves her freedom. She'll rule this town and own my heart. And I wanted her to have the truth.

I'm in love with my wife.

58

———

Playlist: "Bring It On Home To Me" – Sam Cooke
(from *Guardians of the Galaxy*)

[Mach]

"**L**andon?" Landon and Ma stand outside The Barber Shop. Ma's arms are around his waist and Landon holds onto Ma in return.

"It's beautiful," Ma states, marveling at the lights overhead. She looks beautiful, at peace almost, in a way I've never seen her. When she jostles Landon in her arms and gazes up at him with a generous smile, she looks incredibly happy.

She's in love with him. And the responding look he's giving Ma says he reciprocates those feelings.

Well, shit.

I clear my throat and Landon looks up at me.

"I've been meaning to find you," Landon says.

If he's about to ask me for Ma's hand or something, I'm

going to lose it. Not that I wouldn't be happy for Ma. She deserves someone to love her, partner with her through the rest of her life, but this is too much for my bruised heart.

I also don't think I can take more news about Frank and the will.

"They found the person who set the fires. He confessed to everything."

"Who?" My eyes widen.

"Turns out it was a man hired by Becca, Frank's wife. She wanted to file for divorce but hung on a bit longer to her wayward, adulterous husband."

Frank's affairs with 'an office piece on the side' as he called his personal assistant was common knowledge in Wrightwood. His affair wasn't his first.

"What happened?"

"Frank thought he'd inherit Wrightwood when Fischer died, and his plan was to sell off the town for a multi-billion-dollar deal to a foreign energy company. Becca stood to gain half of that settlement if she stuck it out with him. She stalled on filing for divorce, holding out for Fischer's impending death. When Frank didn't inherit the property, Becca still thought there could be something done to stave off redevelopment."

My mouth falls open. I'm stunned.

"If she could drive you and Jane away, the will wouldn't be fulfilled. Failure to meet the time frame. Then Frank decided to contest the will, sighting your wedding as illegal. Neither action would have resulted in Frank getting the land. The property would have reverted to the state as the will directed. The state would decide on a private sale or the power plant or whatever it wanted with the land. Frank would have had no stake in anything. And Becca wouldn't have either."

Someone in our family tried to sabotage Fischer's plan. The idea is almost ironic. The Wrights seem to feed on their own.

As Fischer often said, *keep your family the closest, because they'll hurt you the most.*

Disappointment worms its way through my chest. Strangely, it's not for Becca or Frank. Let them rot. "Poor Myles."

Ma's head lifts at my words, her eyes questioning me. But, I'm not being sarcastic. I'm sincere. We didn't complete the project by Fischer's deadline. Trixie's Trim especially held us back. Renovation won't be finished until after the new year. Myles will lose his portion of the inheritance.

"What about him?" Landon tilts his head as he asks and glances down at Ma.

Ma watches me, her mouth slowly curling. "You don't know?"

"What don't I know?" These two are so cryptic and all those eye-glances during the will reading come back to me. What a pair. True partners.

Ma grins bigger at me. "Why don't you go find your brother."

As I stroll to the end of Bridge Alley, a light is on in the new community room. The low building will be dedicated on New Year's Day. A ceremony for Ma will be hosted to celebrate the space. Another contribution from Jane.

"What are you doing working?" I ask after entering the single room.

Myles's head pops up, surprise in his expression. "Just wanted to finish hanging these shelves." Painted boards lay on the floor along with a power drill.

Furniture and finishing touches will happen here soon. The rectangular room has a small kitchen area in one corner, and tons of floor space for seating arrangements. Jane says the community room should feel like someone's living room. Three large French doors open to a yard that isn't visible in the dark. A patio has been built with a stone path leading to a trellis. The river is in the background. The bridge beyond. The setting is perfect for a wedding.

I envision Jane and I renewing our vows out there. She'll wear that fairy tale dress she dreamed of wearing for a wedding. We'll throw a party where we serve cake, dance to our song, and drink champagne. My fantasy concludes with me making love to my wife.

"Need help?" I offer. Hanging shelves is really a two-person job.

Myles gives me a long look before answering. "Sure."

I shrug out of my jacket and reach for a board while Myles limps over to the wall, measuring out the spacing and marking it with a pencil. We work in silence for a few minutes. He drills the anchors into the wall, and then we each stand on a step stool to hang the first shelf. Working together reminds me of when Myles and I worked side-by-side to fix up that old Chevy.

Fischer. What a fucking ass he'd been to give us a hunk of junk that we had to restore on our own.

"Why'd you do it?" I ask as we stand back to admire the position of the first plank.

"Why'd I do what?" Myles steps back toward the wall to double-check the distance from the top shelf to the second one.

"Why'd you fix that truck?" After the accident, it was wrecked and waterlogged. Why did he repair that thing I was prepared to send back to the junkyard where Fischer first got it?

Myles shrugs, keeping his eyes on the wall, taking more time than necessary to check the measurements. "It was therapeutic for me." Then he shrugs dismissing his actions. "I guess I didn't want to see that hunk of junk go to waste."

Therapeutic? Hadn't Myles had enough rehabilitation on his body? Or did his head need help? Maybe his heart?

He'd lost his best friend. He'd lost his twin. My insides rumble and roil with the distance between Myles and me. Distance I placed between us. I don't know how much to push him. I don't really have a right to some answers, I suppose.

"I'm sorry, Myles."

He turns to face me, hands coming to his hips. Maneuvering without his cane, he works within two or three steps from the wall. "For what?"

"For not making the deadline for you. For the town being trashed again. For doubting you and Tracy, and just . . . everything."

Myles glances away from me, pursing his lips. "Probably don't need to mention how much your disappearance hurt."

I shake my head. I've hurt him much more than he'd ever hurt me.

"No, you don't need to mention it."

"Also, it isn't your fault Aunt Becca was a crazy bitch."

I softly chuckle. "Yeah, well . . ." I scratch under my chin at the thickness of my scruff.

"And we didn't miss the deadline."

"What?" Myles lowers his head as I stare at him.

"Landon came to see me. He's the judge and jury, right? He told me none of the fires were my fault, or yours, or Jane's. We were so close before the festival, and that's all that mattered."

"But Trixie's and the vacant store . . ."

Myles holds up a hand. "Are the lights on in town?"

"Did you not see them lit up?"

"I did." He tilts his head.

Then why was he asking me this question?

"It was never about the lights or the festival or even the town, Mach." His gaze doesn't leave my face.

"I don't understand." Whatever Fischer's motive, I'd had my suspicion Myles must have known something. "Explain it to me."

"I just wanted you to come home." My twin catches my eyes, holding mine as his match my own. "Fischer had offered me the town, but I didn't want it. I have my construction company. I'm building and rebuilding all the time. There wasn't an incentive big enough to tempt me to take on this project alone. I told Fischer to leave it to you."

My forehead furrows but then suspicion grows. "Why would you do that?"

"I wanted my brother back. I wanted your forgiveness for Tracy dying on my watch. I wanted this divide between us gone." Myles hobbles forward, but his stumbling has me rushing to him, gripping his upper arms.

"But there was all this business about having a wife?"

"Ma had been singing Jane's praises for years. She made it sound like you trusted this woman I hadn't ever met, and I took a risk. If push came to shove, you'd need someone you trusted at your side. You'd need someone strong who didn't take your shit and maybe . . . I don't know . . . I thought at least she might be your friend. She'd help you through whatever you'd need helping with when you returned."

Myles had been right about so many things. I trusted Jane, and she didn't take my shit. She worked beside me, and while I'd always wanted to consider her a work colleague, we did have a friendship. She was more than an acquaintance.

"That was a huge fucking risk."

Myles shrugs while timidly chuckling. "But worth it."

Staring at my brother, I try to process everything. He'd been the one to coerce Fischer to write the directives into his will. He'd given up the town as his inheritance. He requested I take a wife.

"What about you? Who has been here for you?" It couldn't have been easy to recover after that accident. He was wounded. Tracy was dead. I'd accused him of killing her. He'd watched his best friend die beside him. He'd lost Ainsley, a girl too young for him at the time. And I'd left town with my faulty accusations and misbeliefs about everything.

Myles shakes his head.

Fuck. I am the worst brother in the world.

"I'm sorry, man." Pulling my brother against me, I wrap my arms around him. He doesn't reciprocate the hug, but I don't need him to embrace me. I need him to forgive me. "I'm so sorry, brother."

Myles awkwardly pats my lower back twice before pulling away from me. He's not willing to touch me. He may never forgive me.

"It's been all my fault." I try to catch his eyes, but he keeps his head down. The tension around us is thick but different. It isn't hatred. It isn't sadness. It's the awkwardness of rebuilding our relationship, like rebuilding this town. We needed time and resources. Most of all, we needed each other to get the job done.

"Let's finish hanging some shelves," I offer, accepting that working side-by-side with my brother is the best way to fulfill Fischer's will, which spoke of Myles's desire.

My brother wanted me home.

And I was back.

59

———

Playlist: "Love Story" – Taylor Swift

[Jane]

The festivities fill our weekend, and once it's finished, I'm ready for a long winter's nap. One of the things I'm trying to be better about for myself is time off. I start my new position as economic developer for Wrightwood after the first of the year, so I have some time to find a house and move my things from Chicago. The new year is looking bright for me.

"Can you go somewhere with me?" Mach asks. Since his mistletoe trickery and laying on me that he's in love with me, he's been standoffish, quiet even. Then again, the weekend was hectic, but I have things I want to tell him as well.

"Such a man of mystery, Mr. Wright," I tease as we climb into the truck and cross Wrightwood Road to the other side of town, which has more houses than businesses. We climb deeper up the mountain.

Eventually, we pull up before an adorable, red brick weathered home with a large front porch and columns supporting a second-story balcony. The place looks spacious with a good bit of yard around it.

"What's this?" I ask.

Mach opens his door. "Let's take a look."

As we approach the house, a Christmas tree lights up the front window. Mach opens the front door with a code on a giant lock pad. Once inside, I'm drawn to the front room with the tree. The large space is absent of anything other than the tree and a miniature house before a fireplace.

"What . . ." I cross the hardwood floor. The dollhouse I imagined for Willow—pink and feminine—stands before the fireplace.

"Theo agreed to let Willow come over here on Christmas morning." Mach stands in the center of the room.

I stare back at him, not understanding.

"Jane, I have a proposal for you."

"Uh-oh," I groan. "The last proposition you made required me to marry you."

Mach steps up to me, gripping my upper arms. Watching me, his hands slide down to my hands, taking each of them in his. "I'm proposing you live here. With me."

"Mach." *Is he teasing me?* It's almost too much. I attempt to pull my hands free, but he tightens his hold.

"Baby, I've asked a lot of you. Coming down here. Pretending to be my wife. Actually marrying me. And then taking over the Wrightwood project." He pauses, rubbing his thumb over the simple wedding band I haven't had the heart to remove yet. I know about Myles meeting the deadline and receiving his inheritance. Any day, Mach will do the same, and our marriage can be over.

"I'm no prize. I'm difficult and irritable. I'm quick to assume and hard to love."

I glance away from him, but he squeezes my fingers, wanting my full attention.

"When *I* love, I love hard. I can smother and overreact, and . . ." Mach exhales. "I can be intense."

I bite on my bottom lip, uncertain where he's going with all this.

"I've already told you this comes from fear. Fear that I'm not good enough. Fear I'll never be enough for you."

"Mach, you're more than enough," I whisper. Aggressively chewing my lower lip, Mach reaches for my mouth, tugging the lower curve free from my teeth. Then he rubs his thumb along the puffy swell.

"I miss seeing my kiss on you."

That kiss under the invisible mistletoe was a torturous reminder of what I'd missed.

"Tell me you miss me kissing you."

"I miss you kissing me."

Mach steps closer to me, bringing my hands to his chest. His eyes hold on mine. "You once said we needed to have our story straight. Let me see if I remember correctly. How did we meet? How did I propose? And why did I marry you?"

I softly chuckle and shake my head. I can't believe he remembered my line of questions.

"Here's our story. For eight long years, I've wanted you and denied the attraction. It wasn't just company policy. I was afraid. Afraid I didn't know how to love you because you're a woman a man should love. But I'm not scared anymore, baby."

My lower lip trembles, and my gaze shifts to where he holds my hands tucked into his. He squeezes again drawing my attention to his face.

"I didn't propose properly to you the first time, but I'm hoping for a second chance." He locks both my hands in one of his and reaches into his coat pocket. He lowers to one knee, eyes never leaving mine, and tears seep into the corners of my own.

Mach holds up a gorgeous diamond ring. One with a giant clear-cut gem and a ring of sapphires around it. "As for why I wanted to marry you, the obvious answer is because I love you. I love you, Jane, and I want you to remain my wife. I want to love you for the rest of time. And I hope, one day, you feel the same about me."

He shrugs, vulnerable in his position, but confidence fills his words. "Five facts, Jane. I love sleeping next to you. My body has this strange need to touch you and remind myself you're there for me. I want to be there for you, too. I'm proposing a new partnership."

I softly laugh as tears blind me. He squeezes my hands once more. "A true partnership, Jane. You and me. Mr. and Mrs. Wright."

"That's not five facts, Mr. Wright," I teasingly chastise him, my mouth unable to fight the largest grin.

"I've lost count of all the things I know about you, but the things I want to learn are endless."

"You once said you wanted all my secrets. Here's a secret I still haven't shared with you." I sniffle as a tear glides along my nose. "I've been in love with you for eight long years, too, your *Mach*-esty."

Tears come faster as Mach is first puzzled by the nickname and then slowly smiling wide and bright.

"And all those times you asked me to tell you I wanted you inside me . . ." I puff out a breath. "Mach, you're already there." I tug a hand free and pat my chest. "In here." I sniff again. "You're inside my heart. And I love you." My voice cracks.

Mach quickly stands. "Jane, baby. Say you'll stay married to me."

I vigorously nod. "I'll stay married to you."

Mach stoops to get a better view of my face. "Not just for a year, but for a lifetime."

"For a lifetime." Looking up at him with tear-filled eyes, I don't think I've ever smiled so large.

Mach lifts my left hand and slips the diamond ring down my finger, kissing it against the silver wedding band he gave me.

"We can have a new wedding, if you want," Mach whispers, his eyes fixated on the sparkle of the diamond and the marriage of the two rings on my finger.

"I don't want to erase the ceremony we had." I look up at him, and he meets my eyes. "I wouldn't change a thing. But maybe I could get the feathery dress, and we could throw a party. We could have cake and dancing."

Mach chuckles, nodding as if agreeing with my plan. Then he stills and gazes directly at my eyes, holding his uncannily still. "What about our wedding night?"

I glance at the rings on my finger before tipping my face up to his. "That night was pretty special. I don't think I'd change that."

"Yeah, it was perfect." With that, Mach brings his mouth down to mine. The first kiss we shared Mach became my husband. And every kiss afterward, he'll remain that man beside me. When we finally take a breath, Mach smiles at me.

"I like seeing my kiss on you."

"I like wearing your kisses."

His mouth returns to mine, and we kiss standing in the vacant room before Mach breaks free once more. Without explanation, he steps back, guiding me up the stairs to a bedroom filled with unlit candles and a bed.

"Foregone conclusion, Mr. Wright?" I arch a brow as he begins to light the wicks. Candles stand on the floor and along the windowsill. And a bottle of champagne chills in a stand.

"No conclusions, Mrs. Wright. Only fresh starts." He

finishes lighting a candle and crosses the room to me. "And love. So much love, baby."

60

———————

Playlist: "I'll Be Home for Christmas" – Rascal Flatts version

[Mach]

Later that night, Jane is absent from our bed. Our *new* bed. Our new bedroom. Our future home. Slipping on my pants, I notice a blanket is missing from the bed. No wonder I woke up cold although Jane's body missing from next to mine is more the reason.

I wander downstairs where Jane sits on the hardwood floor before the dollhouse and Christmas tree. The lights are still on, illuminating the dark room. Jane has the missing blanket wrapped around her body.

Lowering myself to the floor, I slip my legs around her body and tug her back to my front. "Whatcha doing down here alone, baby?"

She tips her head to my shoulder. "Wondering if I'm dreaming."

I press a kiss to her neck. "It isn't a dream." Or maybe it is. One finally coming true. "I have one more gift for you."

Jane shifts, glancing over her shoulder. Her eyes tease me. "I've never known you to be so full of surprises."

"I'm trying to be romantic."

Jane presses up and kisses me, sweet and soft but long and loving. *She loves me.* Being with her is nothing I could have dreamed while everything I imagined it would be.

Breaking the kiss, I keep my eyes on her and tilt my head at the dollhouse. "Is that an envelope in the attic of that dollhouse?"

Jane's brows pinch. Cautiously, she follows my gaze and narrows her eyes. I pat her side. "Take a look."

Scrambling forward, Jane reaches for the flat envelope slipped into the top space of the dollhouse, then comes back to rest between my legs. With hesitation, she opens the envelope and pulls out a set of papers.

"What is this?" A tremor fills her voice.

"There's a little girl who needs a snowman family."

"Mach." Jane's voice cracks on my name, and I press a kiss to her shoulder.

"So, I have another proposition for you."

Jane shifts, her side to my chest. "Do not tease me." Her smoky voice reminds me of days back in our office at Impact when Jane was fierce and a force. She's still both those things but softened around the edges.

"I had Landon draw up adoption papers for Willow. It won't be as easy as just taking her in. We need to undergo interviews and visitations, but I think we have a good chance of making Willow ours, if you want her."

"What about Theo?" Jane looks up at me, her eyes a storm of questions.

I swipe my thumb over her lower lip before her teeth get ahold of her kiss-swollen mouth. "I spoke to Theo. Explained what we wanted. What he could still have with Willow. I want them to have a relationship. Maybe more like grandfather to granddaughter, though."

Jane's eyes widen.

"He agreed. It's one reason he's bringing her here on Christmas morning. I thought we could spend the day together."

"We need to ask her if she'd even want us as her parents." Jane's voice hesitates.

"Who wouldn't want you as a mother?"

Her eyes fill again. So many tears lately, but I'm confident the ones from last night's proposal and the ones currently glistening in her eyes are from joy.

"This is more than I'd hoped for," Jane whispers.

"There isn't anything I wouldn't give you, if I could." No more empty promises to Jane. Only the truth. Only what I can give to her. My heart. My love. And hopefully, a little girl.

"Mr. Wright, don't you dare tease me with this." Jane shakes the adoption papers in her hand. Then she narrows her eyes. "You didn't bribe Theo, did you?"

I should be insulted, but instead I laugh. "Ye of little faith." I flatten my palm over her chest. *My acushla.* "I simply promised we'd love her. We can do that, right?"

Tears streak down her cheeks again. "That's a promise I can keep."

"Me too." I smile large, emphasizing the truth in my declaration. I promise to love Jane . . . and Willow.

"What do you think Willow will think of all this?" Jane pauses. "She's gone through so much already."

"She knows she's up for adoption and what that means for her. A new family. I thought we could ask her together. Ask her to be part of our snowman family If Willow agrees, if she wants us, we'll work everything out through Landon with Theo, making it official and legal. Then, we will be her parents."

"She'll be ours," Jane whispers but stiffens before me, shifting even more to face me full on. "What about Chicago? And Impact?"

"I'm not ready to give up Impact."

"I'd never ask you to do that." Jane places a hand on my chest. My heart hammers under her touch.

"And it will be difficult to be separated from you at times."

Jane's hand retracts, but I catch it and place it back on my chest, pressing my hand over hers.

"But I've seen how Tucker and Mae make things work. He's never been happier, and neither have I." I sweep her hair around her ear. "You want to be here. I want to be with you. Tucker and I can work it out."

Jane scoots close to me, shifting the blanket around her as her legs hook over mine. With my hands around her lower back, I tug her even closer.

"I want this partnership more than anything." Jane runs a hand down my cheek and cups my chin.

"So, a snowman family?" I arch one brow.

"I can't believe we're really doing this. That you'd do this for me." Excitement fills her voice while her eyes search mine. "And you're certain? About the occasional distance?"

"Not going to lie." Mach scratches under his bristly chin. "I hate that we'll spend nights apart. I'll miss out on a few things down here once in a while. But I don't want you to give up your dream. And I want to be part of that dream. Here or anywhere."

Jane braces a palm on either side of my face and leans forward, but I have one more thing to say and press a finger to her lips before she kisses me. "I never would have compromised like this when I was younger, but I'm older and wiser, and committed to you, *my acushla*. I can't live without you, so I'll live however we can."

"Thank you for making all this happen. For making my dreams come true," she whisper-sobs. "If you hadn't proposed that I pretend to be your wife, I wouldn't have ever been in Wrightwood. Then we wouldn't have fallen in love and ended up right here."

"And where are we at, Mrs. Wright?" My arms tighten around her, and I look around the room lit by a Christmas tree and containing only a dollhouse.

"We're home, Mr. Wright." Jane closes the distance between us, kissing me soft and long. "Our home."

"Home," I mutter to her lips, wearing my kiss. "You are my home, Jane. Small town. Big city. You are it, baby."

"I love you so much, Mach."

"I love you, too."

And then we christen our new living room as we've done everywhere else.

EPILOGUE

Two months later

Playlist: "Lover" – Taylor Swift

[Jane]

Willow and I have the music cranked up, and our dance moves down as we skid around the kitchen. She isn't officially our child yet, but she's living with us. Landon helped us follow the proper channels for legal guardianship, which Theo willingly signed over to Mach and me. With the pressure off, Theo has turned into an incredible pseudo-granddad, taking Willow on ice cream dates and skating trips. He even took her to get her ears pierced. Willow doesn't spend the night at his place, but he spends time at ours, sharing dinner once a week with us.

Willow sings along with Taylor Swift and lifts her hands in the air as she wiggles her little hips. I join her, lifting my hands as well and sashay around the table. I spin in a circle and screech at the man leaning against the doorjamb.

"Jesus," I hiss.

"I didn't want to interrupt."

"Big Mac," Willow shrieks and rushes to him.

He bends and lifts her into the air, rubbing his nose against hers. "Did you grow again? I swear you get bigger every single time I'm out of town."

Mach was scheduled to be in Chicago for three days, and he wasn't due home until tomorrow night.

With Willow appeased by his greeting, she wiggles in his arms, and he sets her down.

"Mr. Wright," I say, stepping up to him.

He tugs me to his chest. "I swear every time I'm away from you, I miss you more." He breathes into my neck as we hug.

I'd love to rush him and jump into his arms like Willow did, but we try to keep the PDA respectable before the child. We've learned to be creative in our sexual endeavors, adjusting to a little one in the house. We're still newlyweds, but I don't think my desire for Mach will ever wane. We just need to be a little quieter when we're in the bedroom, or the laundry room, or the kitchen late at night.

"I missed you, too," I whisper, squeezing him tighter. "You're back early."

He pulls back without fully releasing me. "I didn't want to stay away a minute longer than I needed to." He scans my face and then glances over at Willow. "I see I've walked in at the right time. Can I join the dance party?"

He sways against me, holding my hips. The music is more upbeat than the pace he's setting, and the way his center drags over my lower belly, the kind of dance he really wants isn't appropriate. Yet.

"Later," I whisper.

"I'm counting the minutes." Mach lifts my wrist and kisses my pulse point.

After we bought the house, he decided he wanted another tattoo. To my surprise, he got a band around his right ring finger with the date of our wedding. Then he had my name inked over his heart within the waves of a heartbeat.

I'm terrified of needles poking me, but I gave in and have a similar tattoo of heartbeat waves with Mach's name inked on my inner left wrist. Mach likes to kiss me there.

"Big Mac, are you going to kiss Jane again?" Willow giggles.

He pulls back and smiles at me. "I can't seem to help it." Lowering his voice, he adds, "I like seeing my kiss on you."

My face heats that we've been caught by Willow. Then again, it's important for her to see a loving couple. She said her mom and dad used to kiss, too. One day I hope she'll call us Mom and Dad, but I don't ever want Willow to think we are replacing her parents. They loved her. We love her. How lucky she is to have so many angels in her life.

If we remain Jane and Big Mac to her, I'll still be happier than I've ever been in my life. At forty-five, I finally have everything I've ever wanted.

"What are you thinking about, Mrs. Wright?" Mach guides my hips side to side.

"How *Mach*-nificent my life is."

Mach slowly nods. "I'm all yours."

"And you have me."

"And I'm never letting go." He leans forward to sneak another kiss.

Then we both glance to the side where Willow dances in circles, singing her heart out.

And everything feels just right.

EPILOGUE 2

[Lindee]

Playlist: "Girl On Fire" – Alicia Keys

There is something about the open road that soothes my soul.

And I'd been on the road often in my forty-two years.

Maybe a bit of my absentee father resides in me. A need for escape lives inside me.

I can never decide if my admiration is the sound of eighteen wheels whirling on a highway or just the swish of another speeding vehicle passing by me when my windows are down, and the wind tosses around my hair. Maybe it's the fresh scent of wide-spread land, the dense fragrance of forests, or the tangy nose-burn of asphalt.

Whatever it is, the road is a balm.

And the newest stretch I drive isn't a straight line, but a twisting, turning ribbon through thick trees with a sharp drop off to my right and boulders to my left as I climb the mountains of Tennessee and cross over to North Carolina.

I'm on two missions.

The first is to master this road, famous for motorcyclists and high-speed enthusiasts. I'm not a cyclist, but my Jeep was made for this kind of terrain. Spring is in the air and the leaves on the surrounding forest are just starting to bud. The street before me is an S-curve, slithering like a snake which makes its name almost appropriate. The Tale of the Dragon. Route 129 is twelve miles long with 318 curls before I hit Deal's Gap, the official start or finish line for travelers on this elusive highway.

As for me, I'm clutching the steering wheel like it's my last gin and tonic on a hot summer day and strongly questioning my sanity.

The second purpose in taking this difficult strip of road is that it was the best route from point A to point B despite all the hairpin curls. A lodge in Robbinsville is my destination. Once owned by an aluminum company and the location is now a traveler's delight near hiking, fishing, and white-water rafting in the Appalachian Mountains. I'm a bit of a hotel restoration expert. I didn't have a degree in interior design, though. I just sort of fell into the path of rehabbing and I love short-term stay locations. Homes into bed-and-breakfasts. Motels from ruin to rejuvenation. Historical landmark hotels returned to their glory. I love a secret hideaway tucked into the landscape or a small-town treasure. Whatever the case may be, the concept of never staying long in one place is who I am.

Only, I'm growing older, wiser, and a little weary of never having a place to call my own. As I travel often, anything of great value is at my mother's home. I don't visit often, and I prefer it that way. My mom can be domineering at times, complacent at others, although she's the only parent I've ever had.

That's a story for another day.

Today, I'm letting the breeze ripple through my open window and holding my breath around another slinky curve. Motorcyclists are slowed by my pace, and I wave my arm out the window signaling them to pass me. I'm not in a hurry. I'm only trying to prove something to myself. I can tackle anything, like bumps in a road, or in this case, the curling of one.

The Iron Dragon is a marker that coordinates with the beginning of the highway headed north. I'll take a picture on my return trip. Tomorrow, I'll be meeting my sisters in a Tennessee valley cabin. This is a new thing for the Fox sisters. In an effort to better reconnect and impose reunions, it's been decided we should meet up once a year in a location none of us have ever visited. As this was Mae's idea, we let her decide on our first location.

For tonight, I'll be staying at the Opatoc Hotel here in North Carolina.

When I pull into the parking lot of the lodge, a deep breath escapes me. My hands still clutch the steering wheel and as I remove them my fingers ache. My arms are tense. My shoulders tight. The perilous drive was both exhilarating and exhausting, and yet a strange hum vibrates within me. I tackled the Tail. The loops and bends of this road deserve mad respect, and pride fills me that I can add this road to the long list of many I've traveled.

On shaky legs, I exit my Jeep and inhale crisp, mountain air ripe with sunshine. I need a Coke, or perhaps something stronger.

Arriving at reception, I learn my room isn't ready which is fine with me. I don't want to be indoors. The day is a comfortable sixty-something degrees and in my sweater, booties and jeans, I'm sweaty from the taxing drive. The receptionist mentions there is a patio located outside the gift shop, and I head in that direction.

Once outside, I descend a set of stairs that dead ends on a stone patio. My legs continue to wobble as I step downward, and I inhale to calm myself, willing the fresh mountain air to settle into my lungs. In the early spring, no flowers are in bloom, but swatches of dirt suggest plants will soon blossom along a brick wall bordering the patio. Before me is a gently rushing river of crystal-clear water running over a picture-perfect display of river rocks in varying tones of brown and gray. Beyond the river, the forest begins in its sleepy position of waking up for spring.

The spot should feel serene but I'm too keyed up to relax.

A set of wrought iron tables are cluttered together near the base of the staircase to my left. A few patio heaters are interspersed among the tables and the people seated in them. However, I veer to the right where a series of plastic Adirondack chairs sit with their backs to a rock wall. Each seat faces the river, and a man sits in the furthest one.

At first glance, he's striking with whiskey-colored eyes that meet mine for the briefest second. His long legs are stretched out before him and casually crossed at the ankle. Thick boots cover his feet. His pants are a Carharrt-brown color along and he wears a thick sweater with the sleeves pushed up to his elbows. His hair is a dusty mix of light brown and gray. His jaw is covered in the same combination.

How I notice all this in a glance is mystery to me.

"Mind if I sit?"

"Suit yourself, sugar." His voice is as thick as his thighs and sends a ripple up my spine rivaling the river before us.

I toss myself into a seat three chairs away from him and tip back my head. The sun is behind me, but the warmth still covers my cheeks. I sigh once. I exhale even deeper. While I will myself to sit still, my body won't settle. Everywhere feels tight, like a rubber band wound and ready to snap.

A waitress nears me.

"Can I get you something to drink?"

"I'd love a soda." I don't know why I drag out the word or even call it such a thing. My sisters are both Midwesterners and call the carbonated drink pop. I typically follow their lead. As the youngest of four, and the last sister of three, I've been in their shadows most of my life. Maybe that's another part of my need to keep moving. Outrunning their successes. Trying to create my own.

The man beside me chuckles and I turn in his direction, taking another glance at his profile. The wave of his hair. The thickness of his beard. The long length of his body, relaxed and slouched in a plastic chair. A chunky gold ring circles his left ring finger.

Married.

Quickly, I turn away, glancing at my own fingers, naked of jewelry. Vacant like the promises once given to me.

"Have you ever done something so out of character?" I blurt, not directing my gaze at the man but staring off at the simple river, tumbling over rocks, with a rushing melody.

"Pardon me?"

I turn toward him, noting how he leans his arm on one rest, elbow bent. He glances at me over his shoulder.

I shift, facing him better. "Out of character? Something extreme. Something no one would expect of you." Staring at him, hopeful he knows what I mean, I surmise almost instantly he's done more than I've ever dreamed. His size. His casual confident position. His heavy boots. At a glance, he's a man who has more experience than me in everything.

His thumb pushes at the hefty ring on his finger. The gold glints in the afternoon sunlight. "Sure," he mutters.

Twisting back in my seat, I face the river again, uncertain why I've asked him. Unclear what I expected in his answer.

He clears his throat. "Have you?"

Want to know if Lindee has ever done anything unexpected: *Rhode Trip.*

Rhode Trip

Thank you for reading *Merging Wright*.
Please consider writing a review where ebooks and paperbooks
are sold and discussed.

Want to read a little bit more about Jane and Mach,
CLICK HERE.

Merging Wright Bonus

You can meet the original gang of sexy silver foxes, especially
Jane's older brother, Garrett, and his love, Dolores in WINE &
DINE.

PLAYLIST

You can enjoy the playlist here: SPOTIFY

1. "Road Less Traveled" – Lauren Alaina
2. "That Ain't My Truck" – Rhett Akins
3. "I'd Do Anything for Love (But I Won't Do That)" – Meatloaf
4. "Marry Me" – Thomas Rhett
5. "Take Back Home Girl" – Chris Lane
6. "Lake Shore Drive" – Aliotta Haynes Jeremiah (from *Guardians of the Galaxy*)
7. "I Don't Know About You" – Chris Lane
8. "Momma's House" – Dustin Lynch
9. "Kinfolks" – Sam Hunt
10. "You Are The Reason" – Calum Scott
11. "Spirit in the Sky" – Norman Greenbaum (from *Guardians of the Galaxy*)
12. "What's Your Country Song" – Thomas Rhett
13. "Red" – Taylor Swift
14. "Hooked On a Feeling" – Blue Swede (from *Guardians of the Galaxy*)

15. "Craving You" – Thomas Rhett, featuring Maren Morris
16. "Run" – Matt Nathanson ft. Sugarland
17. "Heaven" – Kane Brown
18. "I'm Not In Love" – 10CC (from *Guardians of the Galaxy*)
19. "Blue Ain't Your Color" – Keith Urban
20. "Yours" – Russell Dickerson
21. "If I Didn't Love You" – Jason Aldean & Carrie Underwood
22. "Hold Back the River" – James Bay
23. "Chasing After You" – Ryan Hurd ft. Maren Morris
24. "O-o-h Child" – Five Stairsteps (from *Guardians of the Galaxy*)
25. "Hey Brother" – Avicii
26. "Come and Get Your Love" – Redbone (from *Guardians of the Galaxy*)
27. "Starting Over" – Chris Stapleton
28. "I Want You Back" – Jackson 5 (from *Guardians of the Galaxy*)
29. "If I Die Young" – The Band Perry
30. "Best I Ever Had" – Gary Allen
31. "Without A Fight" – Brad Paisley ft. Demi Lovato
32. "Meant to Be" – Beba Rexha ft. Florida Georgia Line
33. "Go All The Way" – Raspberries (from *Guardians of the Galaxy*)
34. "Come a Little Bit Closer" – Jay and the Americans (from *Guardians of the Galaxy*)
35. "Heartbeat Song" – Kelly Clarkson
36. "Faster" – Matt Nathanson
37. "Worship You" – Kane Brown
38. "Ain't No Mountain High Enough" – Marvin Gaye & Tammi Terrell (from *Guardians of the Galaxy*)
39. "Easy On Me" – Adele with Chris Stapleton

40. "Father&Sons" – Cat Stevens (from *Guardians of the Galaxy*)
41. "Shake It Off" – Taylor Swift
42. "Fooled Around and Fell in Love" – Elvin Bishop (from *Guardians of the Galaxy*)
43. "Lose It" – Kane Brown
44. "Too Good To Be True" – Faith Richards
45. "Torn" – Natalie Imburgia
46. "Burning House" – Cam
47. "The Chains" – Fleetwood Mac (from *Guardians of the Galaxy*)
48. "Breaking Hearts" – Sam Smith
49. "Memory" – Lee Bryce
50. "Good As You" – Kane Brown
51. "What If I Never Get Over You" – Ryan Hurd
52. "Homesick" – Kane Brown
53. "Burning" – Sam Smith
54. "The Landslide" – The Chicks version
55. "Make Me Miss You" – Sam Hunt
56. "All I Want For Christmas Is You" – Lady A version
57. "River" – Joni Mitchell
58. "Bring It On Home" – Sam Cooke (from *Guardians of the Galaxy*)
59. "Love Story" – Taylor Swift
60. "I'll Be Home For Christmas" – Rascal Flats version
61. Epilogue: "Lover" – Taylor Swift

MORE BY L.B. DUNBAR

<u>Sterling Falls</u>
Seven small-town siblings muddle their way through love
over 40.
Sterling Heat
Sterling Brick
Sterling Streak
Sterling Clay
Sterling Fight
Sterling Touch
Sterling Stone

<u>Chicago Anchors</u>
When your eyes are on the silver fox coach more than the ball.
Elevator Pitch
Catch the Kiss

Parentmoon
When the mother of the groom goes head-to-head with the
single father of the bride.

Holiday Hotties (Christmas novellas)
Holiday novellas certain to heat the season.
Scrooge-ish
Naughty-ish
Grouch-ish

Road Trips & Romance
Three sisters. Three destinations. All second chances at love over 40.
Hauling Ashe
Merging Wright
Rhode Trip

Lakeside Cottage
Four friends. Four summers. Shenanigans and love happen at the lake.
Living at 40
Loving at 40
Learning at 40
Letting Go at 40

The Silver Foxes of Blue Ridge
Small mountain town, silver fox brothers seeking love over 40.
Silver Brewer
Silver Player
Silver Mayor
Silver Biker

Sexy Silver Foxes
When sexy silver foxes meet the feisty vixens of their dreams.
After Care
Midlife Crisis
Restored Dreams
Second Chance

Wine&Dine

Collision novellas
A spin-off from *After Care* – the younger set/rock stars
Collide
Caught

The Sex Education of M.E.
The original sexy silver fox.
When a widowed professor decides she'd like to date again,
and a local fireman volunteers to give her lessons.

The Heart Collection
Small town, big hearts - stories of family and love.
Speak from the Heart
Read with your Heart
Look with your Heart
Fight from the Heart
View with your Heart

A Heart Collection Spin-off
The Heart Remembers

BOOKS IN OTHER AUTHOR WORLDS

Smartypants Romance (an imprint of Penny Reid)
Tales of the Winters sisters set in Green Valley.
Love in Due Time
Love in Deed
Love in a Pickle

The World of True North (an imprint of Sarina Bowen)
Welcome to Vermont! And the Busy Bean Café.
Cowboy

Studfinder

THE EARLY YEARS

<u>Legendary Rock Stars Series</u>
A classic tale with a modern twist of rockstar romance and suspense.

<u>Paradise Stories</u>
MMA romance. Two brothers. One fight.

<u>The Island Duet</u>
Intrigue and suspense. The island knows what you've done.

<u>Modern Descendants – writing as elda lore</u>
Magical realism. Modern myths of Greek gods.

ABOUT THE AUTHOR

www.lbdunbar.com

L.B. Dunbar loves sexy silver foxes, second chances, and small towns. If you enjoy older characters in your romance reads, including a hero with a little silver in his scruff and a heroine rediscovering her worth, then welcome to romance for those over 40. L.B. Dunbar's signature works include women and men in their prime taking another turn at love and happily ever after. She's a *USA TODAY* Bestseller as well as #1 Bestseller on Amazon in Later in Life Romance with her Sterling Falls, Lakeside Cottage, and Road Trips & Romance series. L.B. lives in Chicago with her own sexy silver fox.

To get all the scoop about the self-proclaimed queen of silver fox romance, join her on Facebook at Loving L.B. (Dunbar) or receive her monthly newsletter, Love Notes.

+ + +

CONNECT WITH L.B. DUNBAR